Pirate's Passage

Pirate's Passage

Written and illustrated by

WILLIAM GILKERSON

TRUMPETER

Boston & London

2006

TRUMPETER BOOKS
An imprint of Shambhala Publications, Inc.
Horticultural Hall
300 Massachusetts Avenue
Boston, Massachusetts 02115
www.shambhala.com

9 8 7 6 5 4 3 2 1

First edition
Printed in the United States of America

♾This edition is printed on acid-free paper that meets the
American National Standards Institute z39.48 Standard.

Distributed in the United States by Random House, Inc.,
and in Canada by Random House of Canada Ltd

Designed by Lora Zorian

LIBRARY OF CONGRESS CATALOGING-IN-PUBLICATION DATA
Gilkerson, William.
Pirate's passage/written and illustrated by William Gilkerson.
p.   cm.
ISBN-13 978-1-59030-247-7 (alk. paper)
ISBN-10 1-59030-247-8
1. Pirates—Fiction. I. Title.
PS3557.I3672P57 2006
813'.54—dc22
2005017077

To the brotherhood of the coast

Contents

Pirate's Passage

1

Unexpected Guests

Note to the reader: Most of these recollections are of events that happened over a half-century ago. All are burned in my memory. Because a few of the people described are still alive, I am changing some place names and almost all other names, except that of the captain himself, as I knew him, and whose ghost attends me in many ways. I cannot say for sure that the story is yet ended, but I have a sense that it is time to tell it, beginning with the day he blew into my life. It was mid-November of 1952, and I was twelve years old.

That Friday started badly, and it got worse as it went along. An early winter gale was thrashing the Nova Scotia coast, and just getting out of bed was a chilling event. Below, Meg ignored me at breakfast, and my mother was fretting over the inn's unpaid bills. For my walk to school, there was freezing rain, with a lot of slips and one hard fall into a deep puddle of muddy slush, much to the delight of some of my classmates. During morning English, I was wrongly accused and convicted of shooting a paper clip at the blackboard, and was made to sit in the cloakroom, where everything was as wet as myself. I got no lunch because my sandwich had perished in the puddle, along with my dignity, such as it was.

In the afternoon, it amused the Moehner sisters to mock me in various snide ways. Outside, the gale backed easterly, bringing flurries, so when school let out, the Moehner brothers could throw snowballs at me. I plodded home with the wind in my face, except for the last few hundred feet, when I had to run flat out from a genuinely dangerous dog that was terrorising my life at that time. Home, the inn, brought safety but little comfort. My mother was on the point of tears over a letter from a creditor, and Meg was talking to the floor she was washing. I found some hard rolls to munch, and went upstairs to my room to change clothes and try to do homework. My room was a wintry universe of its own. It did have a fine, broad view of Grey Rocks Harbour and the bay beyond, but its only warmth leaked up from the kitchen below. We could not afford the fuel to heat the whole place.

Dry clothes helped, and I sat down and tried to think about what to write about pirates, which had been my choice of subject for an important history essay. No doubt I had been inspired by *Treasure Island,* and imagined myself as Stevenson's fictional Jim Hawkins, which is a name I like well enough to use here. Anyway, whatever vision of buried treasure on a lush, tropical beach that had once inspired me, it was now long gone, leaving me stuck with the assignment and my burdensome life in general.

A hard gust rattled the old glass of my windows. I peered out into the gathering twilight, trying to conjure the Caribbean. Between snow flurries, I could see waves breaking even into the inner harbour; beyond, out in the bay, every shoal was clearly marked by white breakers. Then, unbelievably, I saw a small yacht, a simple working sailboat with tan sails and an old gaff rig, plunging in the seas, running for its life before the storm.

It was hard to imagine what folly had caught the little boat out in such weather, or how it had survived thus far, but here it was, and now fast approaching its doom, unless by some miracle it could make in over the bar. That was almost closed by heavy breakers at the moment, and looked impossible even for one of the locals who knew the water. I wasn't the only watcher, because a red distress flare went up from the lighthouse on Grey Rocks Point. In a minute the harbourmaster Tom—who had a radio—hurried down to his boat with a couple of volunteers, all putting on their oilskins. I watched these events unfold through the old binoculars my grandfather had left me. He taught me to sail well enough so that I had come to think of myself as a kind of authority on the subject, and one of his first lessons had been never to get yourself into anything like the situation that the skipper of this boat was now in. Disaster loomed.

Flying under shortened sail, the vessel kept the channel well enough, yawing on the crests but keeping control, not jibing. The bar was a cauldron in front of it. I could see a lone helmsman at the tiller, with nobody else above deck. It appeared to be a yawl, maybe thirty-five feet, with a small mizzenmast carrying only a red ensign. From the mainmast flew a scrap of yellow flag. Everything vanished from my view as the vessel plunged into a deep trough, but then she rose, reappearing on the crest of a comber that picked her up and carried her across the bar in one long, breathless swoosh, past the breakwater, and into the relative safety of the basin. Very, very lucky, I thought.

Here came the rescue boat fighting its way out of the harbour, just in time to exchange shouts with the yacht, as it shot past on its way in. Tom gestured toward our dock; the yachtsman turned toward me, and I glimpsed him in the last light. My startled first impression was of a young pirate, a dark figure right out of the illustrations in my books, wearing a tricorne hat and wrapped in a boat cloak, an apparition from olden times. The lone sailor yelled something to Tom, then put his helm down, and trimmed his sail. Suddenly realising that he was steering for the inn's wharf, I grabbed my coat and took the stairs three at a time, alerting my mother that something was happening as I raced to the back deck; there I took another skid, but made it down the steps to the wharf just as the boat nosed in toward the leeward side, next to my own little sailboat, the only other one on the dock at this season.

The boatman leapt to the halyards and dropped his gaff. With the sail flapping, he took up a coil of line and threw it across my arm, leaving me to hitch it to a piling while he tended to a stern line. Then there was a hurried fussing with a pair of spring lines, and the sail to be furled. "Come aboard, lad, and give me a hand," he yelled at me, his head buried in wet, flogging canvas, and so I scrambled aboard and busied myself helping gather and gasket the sail. I was struggling with a last strop as the skipper finished with his end of the job, and ducked below through the hatch.

"Come down," he called, and I was right behind him into the cabin. It was dark and damp, but out of the wind. A moment later it was lit by the glow of a kerosene lamp, and for the first time I had a clear view of the newcomer, who was nothing like the pirate I thought I'd seen through the binoculars. He wasn't young at all: old in fact, with a short white beard and close-cropped white hair, as I saw when he removed his hat. It was no tricorne, just a plain hat with broad brim that the wind must have cocked when he was sailing in. His old-style boat cloak was real enough, though; under it he wore a navy-surplus pea jacket, and under that an outer sweater, all of which he peeled off down to an under-sweater, hanging things here and there to drip dry. He had a square, creased face with wide-set eyes that looked tired.

"Captain Charles Johnson," he introduced himself, plumping down onto a settee, motioning me to do likewise, "at your service." He immediately pulled a tobacco tin out of a rack. "I'm getting too old for this kind of life," he remarked, putting a gnarly finger into the tin, frowning. "It's too damp to smoke. I'll have to dry it out. Who might you be?" I introduced myself, mentioning that my family owned the Admiral Anson Inn, at whose dock he was now laying. His face brightened, then broke into a smile, missing one tooth. "Well, then, I can tell I'm in luck, because an inn's what I need, and a hot bath, and this snug berth for my little boaty, an' a bit of good company, which I can tell is what's here, to my great good luck." I asked him where he was from and where he was headed.

"The sea," he said with a sweep of his arm, "in answer to both your questions."

Here came a thumping on the deck. "That'll be my mother," I said, and the old man was up, throwing the hatch open. "Come aboard," he said, helping her down, apologising for the poor quarters. He bowed to her, which she wasn't used to, but didn't seem to mind. "All I have to offer for drink is rum," he said, drawing a bottle from under the settee. "No? Then I hope you won't mind my having a nip to take the chill off me." So saying, he poured himself half a cupful, and took a swallow.

My mother picked up the questioning where I'd left off, and with better results. It seemed our guest had sailed from Bermuda, and was headed for Boston, making the long passage late so as to avoid hurricane season in the North Atlantic. Adverse winds had driven him in here, "far off course and in distress, as you can see, and with my engine down." He said he was a retired English sea captain, sailing "here and there," supporting himself and his old yacht as "an historian," as he put it. He had a round, English accent, cultured, but tempered with a regional dialect of some kind.

"A rich man I'm not, but I can pay my lodging, board, and berthing for *Merry Adventure*." This was the name of his yacht, which he said needed some repair before he could be off for Boston, so he hoped the Admiral Anson could accommodate him for a while, starting now. Mother had an automatic sympathy for anyone in distress, and his story sounded all right; there was room for him and welcome. Indeed, there were no winter guests at all.

While Mother and the captain talked their business, I had my first chance to look around at the cabin of his yacht. It was plain as a workboat, with no varnish except to the table, which at the moment was covered with soggy charts. There were the settees, and a wide, rumpled bunk with a puddle in the middle of it, plus a bunch of shelves stuffed with things behind battens: books, boxes, tins, many covered with sailor macramé. Under the hatch was a little galley, with kerosene stove, copper sink, pumps, garbage pail. Forward there was another space of some kind. The thing that took my eye was the only decoration in sight, a flourish of antique weapons—a blunderbuss, a pistol, and a cutlass, racked on the forward coaming in a rope-work frame.

These objects captured my attention, but there was no more time. Mother had hurried along the business and had to get back above, with me, to get ready for whatever Friday guests might show up for supper. There would be our new person for sure, who said he would come up when he had secured his vessel, pumped her bilge, and dried some tobacco in his little oven. As I slid the hatch closed behind us, he was taking another swallow of rum.

"That was different," Mother commented. "He's the most cheerful thing of the day, but I hope he hasn't made himself sick." She fussed that he probably wasn't doing himself much good, sailing around in storms at his age, and resolved to make him a good tea and honey mixture. This was her first line of treatment for the ills of the world, I think, because she made everybody drink so much of it. Motherliness was at her core, although she was a young woman, and I think likely the best mistress and manager the Admiral Anson Inn had ever had, because of that quality in her. She was tall and slender with an explosion of disorderly blond curls, but she had been working too hard for too long, and our current worries were taking a toll on her. Yet she was an optimist: "The snow's stopped, and cars are moving down on the street; maybe we'll get some guests after all."

The inn had fallen on hard days, not for the first time, or even the second or third during its nearly two centuries of operation. But hard days were turning to desperate at this moment in the rich history of the place. Our living, such as it was, depended heavily on the summer people. During the other nine months of the year, business was thin. This year there were no winter bookings at all, and the only locals who came for a drink or dinner were those that had always come, and they seemed to be getting older and dying off, leaving no replacements. The taproom was open from 5:00 P.M. to 11:00 P.M. Tuesday through Saturday, and a set dinner was served Friday and Saturday. There was no menu, just whatever Mother fixed that night. The place that got the most local business was down in town; the Sou'wester Beverage Room, which did have a menu, and a neon sign, and stayed open all hours. It was where most of the fishermen went because they could play pool and be loud. "I won't have any of it in my place," said my mother, and she didn't, and there we were, a crumbling refuge of antiquity for an aging clientele. Much of the work fell on me.

One of my many chores was to lay and tend a fire on the two supper nights, and it was among the few duties I liked. I would have kept the fire going all the time, except we couldn't afford the wood. It was the original kitchen hearth, huge and ancient, but maintained and still there to warm up my favourite room in the place. My family had fully restored the public room to the way it had looked in the beginning, and it had a certain magic, especially by firelight, when the waxed old beams, panels, and shelves glowed. My mother had baked loaves in the original bread oven, just to see how it worked, and it had worked fine, although it was too much trouble to use. We had a functional kitchen around the corner, out of sight. The bar ran across the end of the room, with a framed photograph of my father plus his medals in the place of honour, next to a faded print of Admiral Anson. No bottles were kept in sight. There were three conspicuous brass beer taps, two of which worked, which was one more than we needed, because we only had one kind of beer. The inn was long on charm, but short on choices.

I was building the fire when the gate bell rang, and Tom came stomping in, full of questions about our lone mariner. Mother and Meg were in the kitchen, so he drew his own beer. Tom had special privileges. Besides being harbourmaster, he was a longtime patron and friend. I was spared answering when the captain came in through the deck door. He was full of thanks to Tom for coming out to save him; grateful that it wasn't necessary, and wanting to buy him a beer. "I'll buy you one," said Tom, all admiration for the way he had handled his boat coming in. The old captain repeated the same story that I'd heard earlier. Tom was an experienced skipper of fishing schooners, the knockabout schooners that we still had then, and he knew the sea. He marveled that the old man was doing what he was doing with no crew, "Like Slocum," he said, comparing him to the famous Nova Scotia captain who single-handedly sailed his own small boat around the world.

"Nothing like that," said the captain, protesting there were lots of small-boat sailors since then, and that he had no ambitions for glory, just to get to Boston. He feared that by the time he could effect his repairs to *Merry Adventure,* the season would be too late to attempt it. He might have to winter over, and he had all kinds of questions for Tom as to where his boat could be hauled, who could work on his engine, and suchlike.

Around this point in the conversation, Milton and Merle Eisnor came in. It was Milton's birthday, and I got them seated, and alerted Mother, who came out to say hi, and express her sympathy for the passing of their older brother, Charles, who had done our roof repairs around 1940, and who had been in the Anglican church choir until just a couple of months ago, when his voice failed. Meg took their drink order (beer for both), and I went back to Tom and the captain.

"I called Customs and Immigration and told 'em you're here under the duress of storm," Tom was telling him, "and that's important because Grey Rocks isn't a port of entry, as you prob'ly know. But around here there's a lot of sympathy for anyone in trouble on the sea, such as you, and I expect some official will come over from Baywater on Monday and clear you. The police might come sooner because of your quarantine flag." He was talking about the rules of entry that apply to ships flying the yellow flag, sailing in from foreign waters. "I told 'em I cleared you to dock. Meanwhile, here's to your being here, safe and welcome." They hoisted their glasses, then Tom had to get back to his family. I told the captain I was going to turn the radiator on in his room so it would be warm for him when he wanted it.

"I'll just sit and enjoy the company and this grand room, and have a bit of supper, when your sister can bring it." He gestured toward Meg, who was the waitress but not my sister, as I made clear right away. I should mention here that I had a crush on Meagan O'Leary, who was exactly twice my age, and infinitely out of reach, except as my friend. I was awkward around her, and she was as kind to me as she'd been to her old cat, Cleo, whom she had loved. Cleo was gone now, so I was getting more attention from Meg, off and on, although she'd spent today talking to herself.

The captain tried again to catch her eye, but she had been delayed by Tom flirting with her as he paid his tab. Tom could usually get a laugh even out of grim people when he set his mind to it, and he was giving Meg special attention because she seemed down. The captain turned to me with a touch of impatience: "I've been living on hard cheese and cold corned beef for about the last five days, getting a workout, and I've got an empty glass. Could you find it in your heart to fetch me my supper, Jim, anything your mother recommends, and another beer?" I told him Meg would have to do it because I was too young to serve spirits; I just bussed tables, and those were the rules. "Ah, yes, the rules," he sighed.

I was on my way to fetch Meg for him when there was the bell again, this time the McCurdy family, a party of four with their visiting aunt from Saint John's, and right behind them was Jason Mosher with his new fiancée; suddenly the place was busy in spite of the weather. Captain Johnson waited with good grace while all the seatings were done, and exchanges of pleasantries and hanging of coats. By the time everything got sorted out, the captain finally caught Meg's attention by waving with both arms, which caused her to ignore him while taking orders from the other tables.

"Now you," she said to him when she eventually got there. "I'm guessing all that arm waving was practise for the next time you're out at sea and have to make distress signals."

"Yes, indeed," he agreed, "and with any luck somebody will save me. Right now that'll take another beer, and a tot of rum, and what's available for supper?" Meg took her time looking him over, not seeming particularly impressed or pleased by what she saw. "There's kuduffle soup, lobster and dumplings, buttered peas, bread, blueberry pie for dessert. If you want something greasier you'll have to go into town." Meg was being Meg, and I was afraid she might drive away the inn's only winter guest before he even moved in. But he seemed more amused than offended.

"Bring it on," he said, rubbing his hands, and she went away. "Where are you in school, and what are you working on?" he asked me. I told him I was in grade eight because the year I was in grade three, there were only two children, my friend Jenny and myself, and we both got popped into grade four, so I was a year ahead; at the moment I was working on a history of the pirates. This got a laugh out of him. I noticed he had a paunch, although the rest of him was tough as leather. His dark eyebrows, surrounded by white hair all around, gave his eyes an intensity; when he looked at you, you were engaged.

"How's your pirates project coming?" I told him honestly I

was having a hard time starting. This seemed to amuse him, but before he could say whatever seemed to be on his lips, Robin came in through the door, Corporal MacMaster that evening, second in command of the Grey Rocks Constabulary, and in uniform. Robin was also my uncle-in-law, and therefore family, as well as another of my few friends. For a change, he was here on duty, come to see our new guest. His arrival coincided with the captain's soup.

"You're the gentleman with the small boat that came in with a quarantine flag?" He was talking about the rules of entry that apply to ships flying the yellow flag, sailing from foreign waters.

"Captain Charles Johnson, at your service, please have a seat. Well, dear sir, here's my passport, and the ship's papers." He had them ready. "I'm cleared from Bermuda to Boston, as you'll see, but there's been this weather, and I'm lucky this place is where I got blown on the coast." He repeated his story between slurps of soup while Robin had a look at his documents, making note of the captain's British passport. According to it, he was born in Hartland, Devon, in 1890 (making him sixty-two years old), and his profession was listed as "retired mariner." Robin was sympathetic regarding his age and difficulties, but concerned that he had come ashore without clearance from Customs and Immigration. "The harbourmaster had no authority to land you, but I can appreciate your needing to get ashore and recover. Don't remove anything, though, and don't go anywhere until you're properly cleared, all right?" I heard all of this while taking a long time tending the fire.

On Robin's way out, he stopped through the kitchen to see my mother. "Looks like you've got kind of an interesting old guy to fill a room for a while," he noted. Mother agreed; the income was a godsend. He cautioned her the guest wasn't supposed to go anywhere, or bring anything ashore until he'd been officially cleared, and said to notify him if there was any violation of that. As a cop, Robin was by the book.

He almost didn't leave, because as he was going out the door, Klaus and Todd Moehner came in with Carl Sputz, their side-kick. Not only were Klaus and Todd rough characters who never came around the Admiral Anson, but they were the nephews of Roy Moehner, who had great influence and who wanted to take the inn away from us. I should point out right away that the name Moehner, which looks like it should rhyme with "moaner" because of its spelling, is actually pronounced "meaner," which better describes that whole family.

"Mind your manners, boys," said Klaus as they piled through the door. Robin took his time coating up, watching them to their table. They were exaggeratedly polite as Meg, stony-faced, seated them. "So nice," Klaus simpered, "so genteel." Mother came out and went over to Robin, looking worried. It was as though a lump of lead had come down on what had been shaping into a good evening for a change. "Now they're attacking us in a new way," she said to him. "Do I have to serve them?" Robin nodded. "Under the terms of your licence, you do unless they make trouble." He would like to have stayed around for a bit, but couldn't because he had the duty car, and the whole town to patrol, and it was a Friday night. "But if they don't behave, call in; Jeb will get me on the radio, and I'll come over and sort them out." As soon as he was gone, the Moehners got louder, keeping up a mocking dialogue.

"Who's that lot?" the captain asked, when I could return to him. He'd gotten his main course, and was making appreciative headway with it. I explained the Moehners were a family that was doing everything it could to make our lives miserable, and that these ones were fishermen, and their usual bar was down in town. "Fishermen," he nodded. "Well, there's fishermen and then there's fishermen. Some good, some otherwise. Like kings and lorry drivers."

"I propose a big drink to this . . ." Klaus Moehner was on his feet, loudly toasting the whole room, ". . . to this old, really old . . . and I mean really, really old place, and to you really, really old people in here tonight, I want to drink to the future." He got a nervous response from our guests, with applause from his own table, and the atmosphere dampened. I stoked the hearth, but there was a chill it couldn't dispel. Klaus had started talking loudly to the other guests. "Retirees, are you? Still able to get out and about a bit?" This got my mother out of the kitchen in a fury.

"Oh, I beg your pardon madam," Klaus put his hands together as though in prayer, "and we'll just drink these beers, and enjoy all the antiques. This is a kind of cultural event for us. We'll be sociable, and maybe help entertain your guests." My mother told them to keep their conversation to themselves, or she'd have to ask them to leave, and went back to her kitchen with a worried look at Meg on the way. The Moehners kept on with their game. The captain mopped up the last of his plate with a chunk of bread.

"Your mum's a good cook, and that was a fine meal, and I'll be back for my pie when I've checked out *Merry Adventure.*" So saying, he put on his peacoat and went out the back door to the dock. I hated to see him duck out because he seemed like the one man in the room who might be worth something if it came to a confrontation with the Moehners. That is where things looked like they were headed. Klaus had started describing the garments of the other guests, one by one, as though narrating a fashion show, and it had become too much. Mother was coming out again with her face flushed, but before she could say anything, the dock door banged open and there was the captain, on a gust of wind, looking urgent and authoritative: "My boat's busted her lines. Who's a boat handler? Are you chaps fishermen?" he called to the Moehner gang. "C'mon then!" and back into the gale he went.

Now the one thing that will get a Nova Scotia fisherman out of his chair, or bed, or whatever, is a distress call from another mariner. This has nothing to do with who he is, or his qualities as a human being, it is a pure knee-jerk reaction from longtime training, and the Moehner trio was up and out without putting on their coats, with me right behind them. Down on the wharf, the captain appeared to be straining to hold onto the one stern line that still held *Merry Adventure,* although he had a good turn with it onto a piling. The wind was streaming the vessel from the dock, bows out.

"Help me get her in enough so we can get a bowline back onto her," he yelled. Automatically Klaus, Todd, and Carl tailed onto the warp and hauled her back within reach. "One of you young lads—you," he nudged Klaus, "get onto her stern, so we can pass you a bowline, and we can get her back alongside. Now you others find a dock line to throw, and I'll hold on here." All of this was in the dark, except for the light from the inn's windows, and there was some confusion. "Oops," said the captain, and there was a yell from Klaus, because just as he was stepping onto the boat, the captain let the line slip, and Klaus's feet missed the stern, causing the lower half of him to plunge into the water. Swearing, he hauled himself aboard. "Never mind," the captain urged him on, "get ready to take a bow warp! You other boys found the lines?" They had, and Carl sent a dripping coil of rope sailing through the air to Klaus, who caught most of it in his face. Klaus got the line secured forward, so the bow could be brought in. There were no broken ropes that I could see, and I could not understand how the lines we had secured so well had come undone. I saw something else too, a mostly-sunk safety line, unseen by the Moehner boys, who were too busy to notice anything.

"Mates, you helped me when I needed it," the captain said as they finished resecuring *Merry Adventure*, "and let's get back inside before we all catch a cold. Sorry about your taking a little dip there." This was directed to Klaus, whose shoes were so full of water they made squishing sounds as he went up the steps, and his pants were sodden. "Nothing to be embarrassed about. I've gone into the pond too many times to count. Easy to do, eh?" Klaus agreed. His teeth were starting to chatter as we got back inside.

"These chaps are heroes," the captain announced to the room. "Without them my little floating home would be a goner, and I certainly hope you'll join me in giving them the round of applause they deserve." He clapped vigorously, drawing in everybody, even Mother. The Moehner boys suddenly found themselves with halos, which put them off balance. "Now, what about my taking you downtown and buying you the beer I owe you? Klaus, you're dripping a bit, so you'll want to get some other things on, and then we can meet up." As he talked, he was moving toward the coats, which they all seemed glad to get into. Just as the captain was preceding them out the door, he abruptly stopped, with a look of dismay. "I almost forgot, I'm not meant to leave here until Customs and Immigration clear me. I'll have to owe you that beer until they let me go to town." He was once again effusive in his thanks, admonishing Klaus to get into dry clothes right away, and they were gone.

"Now I'll have that blueberry pie," he told Meg as he went back to his table, "and maybe another rum." To Mother, he apologised for all the fuss.

"How did your boat get loose?" she asked, phrasing the same question I'd been thinking about. He shrugged.

"My carelessness. Still blowing some out there."

Inside, the rest of the evening was quiet. The captain ate his pie and drank his rum, and then another one after that, until all the other guests had gone. He complimented Mother on her cuisine, and announced that he was ready to turn in, so I took him up to the room that had been prepared for him. He told me he appreciated my help down on the dock, and tried to give me a dollar. It was four times my weekly allowance, but my Nova Scotia teaching was that you didn't take money for being helpful, and so I didn't. "How *did* your boat come adrift?" I asked him.

"Hard to say. She seemed good when we tied her up . . . didn't everything seem decent to you?" It did indeed, and I started to say something about it, but he interrupted me. "I think she'll be fine now. Ah, a real bed with sheets and dry covers." He sat down on it and bounced a couple of times with a pleased smile. I showed him where the bathroom was and how to manipulate the hot water tap to make it work, and went back downstairs to help with the washing up.

He was the main topic of conversation between Mother, who had a good impression of our new guest, and Meg, who didn't. Mother was making the case that not only had he paid in advance for a fortnight, but he was a gentlemanly sort of person, and whatever the problem with his boat, it certainly had gotten rid of the Moehner boys. Meg couldn't argue with that, but Meg never let facts get in her way.

I weighed in on his side, telling them about all I had seen down on the dock. "In other words," I explained, "he was never in any real trouble, because he could have pulled in her bow and got her secure again, probably without any help. So it was all a big diversion to get those guys out of here, and it worked." I was very pleased with myself for having figured it all out, and with what Captain Johnson had pulled off, although I was aware he had cried wolf.

"Well, he's just a big actor and a liar, then," said Meg, "and I'll be sure to keep an eye on him. He was a bit of excitement, I'll give him that. We'll see how he feels in the morning, if he isn't too hungover to get himself out of bed."

The Admiral Anson Inn

The old mariner was up early, as it happened, full of cheer, pumping his boat, checking the lines. The storm had eased to a gale with driving rainsqualls. Returning, he seated himself at his same table of the night before, by the hearth, with his back to a corner, and asked that I make a fire. I told him the rule about fires only on weekend evenings. "It's the cost of the wood," I explained.

"Damn the rule, and damn the cost of the bloody wood," he growled. "When the North Atlantic gets into your bones, the best way to drive it out is with a sweet little fire crackling in a dear old room just like this one, and here's where I'm going to be all day, and likely tomorrow, and tell your mum to bill me for the wood." He produced an old wallet. "Here's two pounds sterling; as I told your mum, it's the only kind of notes I've got until I can get to a bank for some paper dollars. Will that do?" He got his fire, and a generous breakfast. While he was dealing with it, I asked if it wasn't true that he had invented that whole incident with his boat. "Why would you say such a thing, Jim?"

I told him about everything I had seen, including his secret safety line, hastening to tell him how grateful we were that he'd disposed of the Moehner boys so neatly. He gazed at me with unreadable eyes, then smiled, beckoning me to sit down with him, which I did.

"Who have you said this to besides me?"

"Nobody, just my mother and Meg, but they won't talk about it."

"Mmmm. Thing is, any kind of rumour like that getting out, true or not, would probably not sweeten the feelings of those chaps from last night toward anybody here, and they might decide to pay us another visit, which would probably go a lot worse for us. Best all around is that nobody," he tapped the table, "and I mean *nobody*, ever gets such a foolish notion as the one you've proposed to me." His dark eyebrows lifted. "Are you with me on that?" I assured him that we all were. He sat back in his chair.

"I have a proposal for you, Jim. You're a bright young lad, as I can plainly see, and a loyal one. Are you a loyal chap? Good. So what I need, with your mother's permission, is some part-time assistance, as it appears I'm to be around for a while. Just little things that come up, from time to time, that you can handle between your school and chores. Being on call. For my end of the bargain, a dollar a day is the pay, whether there's ought for you to do or not. Also, I'll help you with that treatise on pirates that you're trying to write. What do you say?" I must have looked stunned. To me at that time in my life, a dollar a day was wealth undreamed of.

"You'll earn your pay. As to the kind of work, I'll need a hand with *Merry Adventure* off and on, some errands, local information. For instance, you can start right now if you've a moment, by indulging my historical curiosity about this place. What's the story of it?" This first question was easy enough, because the inn's history was in our brochure.

The inn was built in 1755, or maybe 1757, depending upon whom you believe, on top of an older structure's foundations that nobody knew anything about. The building we were in became an inn during the second (unless you consider it the third) English-French war by accident, according to hearsay. There are no written records, but British ships often sailed into the bay to shelter, and the inn was started then. Or so it is thought, because it was named in honour of Anson, First Lord of the Admiralty. His portrait painted on wood still hung on its iron bracket in front of our gate, repainted and re-repainted so many times nobody could guess how the original looked anymore. The last time, he had gotten a pink face and a more lopsided wig.

My listener questioned me more about the original structure's date of building, but all anybody knew was that it was here before the nearby settlement of Grey Rocks. The inn's advantage was in being the only one on our stretch of coast, except for Lunenburg and Chester, but they were at a distance, and Baywater did not yet exist. Grey Rocks Harbour was small, but the bay offered good close anchorage in most winds.

During the American Revolution, Grey Rocks got its share of all the Loyalists, those who stayed loyal to the monarchy. They had to get out of the former colonies, by choice or not. Those

were bad times for many, but good times for the inn, and they lasted through the War of 1812 when Grey Rocks was building and
manning privateer vessels. Then there came the first overland
road, which passed the place by, and the fortunes of the inn took
a dip. In the 1840s it housed the local jail in its cellar; in 1863, the
proprietors were charged with aiding the Confederate States in
some conspiratorial way, but were exonerated; in 1890 it was the
hidey-hole of a royal duke and his girlfriend for a moment, far
from the eyes of the world. By the turn of the century the New
Englanders had started to come beyond Chester with their
wealth, and the whole inn was repaired, top to bottom; the original old gun platform for the small battery guarding the harbour
was made into a broad deck, with iron tables that had big um-
brellas over them. A turn-of-the-century photo printed in the
brochure shows them giving summer shade to elegant people.

Then there were some thin times during the First World War,
which is when Grandfather bought the place for what seemed like
a bargain, and then there were good times again in the 1920s,
(when all of Grey Rocks was a haven for rumrunners during
Prohibition), until the depression. Then a guest committed sui-
cide, and the place started a long decline that had gradually gotten worse to the point of ruin. There were a lot of things the
brochure did not talk about, such as all our family money going
into the renovation, a labour of love. During World War II, my
father was called up to serve, and became a lieutenant in the Royal
Canadian Navy. He died when a U-boat blew his corvette out
from under him. That was in 1943. I was so young I hardly
remembered him. In 1950 my grandfather died of pneumonia,
and my uncle Bill had to move to Halifax with his family in order
to make a decent living, so the Admiral Anson fell to my mother
to look after.

This she had done ever since, with whatever help she could find or afford to hire. That wasn't much. Me, mostly. And Meg. I suppose I must have become glum at that point, because the captain pointed out that we seemed to be running things very well, and the place itself was astonishing (a treasure, he called it), not only for its antiquity, but its rare beauty as well. There it was on the front of the brochure, commanding its own small peninsula, separating harbour and bay. "In truth, it's a place reeking with age and charm. Who could not love it?" he asked.

I found myself telling him about the many reasons so few people came, starting with the plumbing that seemed unfixable, causing spontaneous and drastic changes in water temperatures, as well as pressure that fluctuated wildly. There were eternal troubles with the wiring and fuses. Then there were the ill-fitting doors, windows, and crazy angles because of ancient foundations settling unevenly over generations; the crumbling stonework, wavy floors, and a cellar that flooded periodically. I did not mention that it also had rats. (Mother didn't kill things, even rats; until recently that had been the job of Cleo the cat.)

I did tell him the old stories that somewhere below us there were tunnels, built by smugglers, but walled off long ago. My grandfather had diligently searched the cellars looking for traces of them, but found nothing, which seemed to discredit the old hearsay.

"I'd like to see," said the captain, but I told him no guests were permitted down there, and there were parts of the cellars where nobody at all went. So well had he kept me talking, it occurred to me that I was probably giving too much emphasis to the Admiral Anson's difficulties. He seemed to read my mind. "Jim, I've real sympathy for your hardships, but everything of what you're telling me about this grand old place makes me love it all the more, from up to down. I liked that young policeman chap, by the way," he said, abruptly swerving the subject. "Your uncle-in-law, you said?"

I told him about Robin, who was not only the best cop in the Grey Rocks Constabulary (which wasn't saying much), but also in the region, and a real detective. Everybody agreed his talents in law enforcement were wasted in a place where there wasn't much to detect, except who had stolen somebody's outboard motor. He had been offered a better career in the Royal Canadian Mounted Police, but as a Mountie he would have to relocate, and Aunt Karen couldn't, being now in a wheelchair most of the time. She needed all our care.

So keen was the captain's interest in all of this that I went on, telling him (at his prodding) about the other town cops, whose chief was a Moehner appointee, and whose other three constables were also of that camp. They were good at handling brawls, but Robin was most of the brains of the outfit, I bragged, and most of the virtue, too. I asked the captain why he was so interested in the police.

"Jim, I'm interested in everything, wherever I sail, and I'd be lost without that. Since I'm to be in Grey Rocks for the winter, so it seems, I want to know about the place. Simple as that. And the inn. And this Moehner family. What's the problem you mentioned?"

I told him that the Moehners were one of the oldest families in town, whose German ancestors had been sent over as immigrants by George II. Now they had two and a half pages of listings in the telephone directory and much else: the five-and-dime, the Sou'wester Beverage Room, the fish plant, and lots of other properties, not to mention their considerable political pull and banking influence. But the Moehners wanted more. Especially they wanted the Admiral Anson Inn, in order to develop it.

"Develop it into what?" the captain wanted to know.

Something a lot more modern, I told him, with a new hotel attached to the building, which was to be rebuilt, with a swimming pool and a yacht harbour with gas pumps. "Rebuilt?" he winced. "Is your mum going to sell it to them?" I didn't know. Neither did she. Years ago she had taken a mortgage loan in order to keep up with the repairs, and that was from Roy Moehner. If we missed a quarterly payment, he'd foreclose in a minute, so then there would be an auction, and Moehner Realty would be able to buy it at last. They'd had a long-standing offer for it, but the old inn was our all, even with its grief and work, and Mother loved it, as did I.

Hence, the Moehner clan was as mean as its name, and doing everything it could to make our lives painful to the point where Mother would sell. The visit of the night before was an obvious part of their campaign. So was my harassment at school, and my problem with the dog, Grendel, and the inn's problems with various authorities about various regulations and their supposed violation. The word was out among the Moehners to make our family feel that being somewhere else would be better. The trouble was, we had nowhere else to go, and our enemies were winning.

This dismal dialogue was interrupted by Mother, summoning me to my duties. Very respectfully, the captain asked her permission to hire me for some part-time help. I chimed in that he was also going to help me with my essay.

He nodded. "And I can say for sure that *Merry Adventure*'s going nowhere until spring at the earliest. She needs work over the winter; I'd like to extend my booking until then." He offered to pay in advance for a further three months. With what we had saved, it was a sum large enough to allow the inn to make its quarterly payment, nearly due. My mother sat down. She was glad to accept his offers, but had to caution him that the inn was operating on a shoestring, and beyond March 1 she could not guarantee that any of us would have a roof.

"Madam, allow me to do whatever I can in helping us all through the winter." Out came the old wallet again, and enough banknotes for our three-month reprieve. While Mother made out his receipt, he told me he would later need my help in shifting something aboard his boat, and also that he was looking forward to resuming our conversation.

"And then there are the pirates," I reminded him.

"There are indeed," he smiled.

When I'd finished sweeping enough for Meg to mop, the rain had stopped, and I was sent to town for fresh bread and some lightbulbs, enough to replace all the blown ones for the first time in months. Yesterday's slush had cleared, so I could ride my bicycle, which was not only faster, but far safer from Grendel.

Grendel was my nemesis, a raw muscle of a big mongrel dog with lots of teeth, an active animal intelligence, and a thirst for my blood. Avoiding him had become my first order of business soon after the beginning of the present school year, when his attacks had begun. I had avoided his first ones by luck; soon realising that I was being somehow stalked by Klaus Moehner's dog, I began taking evasive action, and tried to tell people what was happening to me.

My own theory was that my old grey sweater that had gone missing from the school cloakroom had been swiped by one of

Klaus's kids so that its scent could be used to train Grendel to attack me. I thought he was being deliberately put in my way. And he was, but nobody believed me, not even Mother or Robin, who couldn't call the dogcatchers unless I was actually bitten. I pleaded that I was not exaggerating; the beast was known for its viciousness; it was famous for killing other animals, which only amused his owner; worse, last year it had attacked a teenage hitchhiker and put him in the hospital. That had gotten Grendel locked up at last, and Klaus was sued by the lad's parents. The suit dragged through the court, then was dismissed by the magistrate (Klaus's other uncle), so Grendel was again at large, free to terrorise whomever Klaus took a notion to turn him onto, currently me.

The inn was my fortress, and it was built like one, with a thick, ten-foot-high stone wall curtaining it from the outer world, starting with the parking area on the neck of our promontory. The wall was penetrated by a twin gate opened only for truck deliveries; for foot traffic, there was a smaller main gate, with an oak door. I pushed it open and surveyed the terrain beyond like a soldier before leaving a safe bunker for a run through no-man's-land. Grendel generally wasn't to be seen on our side of the road unless he was chasing me, but he was always a caution.

Seeing no sign of the enemy, I went fast out of the gate, mounted my bike at a run, and stood on the pedals for acceleration. I took the most direct route for the centre of town, where Grendel had apparently been trained not to go. His ambushes came from the wooded places or bushes on the way, always when nobody was around.

Rounding onto Dock Street past the fish plant at a good clip, I entered safe territory and could slow down. I went first to George's general store, which had for sale the box of paints and brushes I had long wanted. Their cost had been out of reach until my newfound employment. Now I could give George fifty cents to hold the paint set for me until I got paid by the captain. Then I did my other errands and headed home with a full cargo of bread and lightbulbs.

I had hoped the return trip would also be uneventful, but it was not. As I rounded the route's final curve before coming to the inn, there was Grendel in the road in front of me, poised, not making a sound, but with his mean, eager little eyes riveted on me, and a show of teeth. If I had been on foot, he would have had me, but my bike gave me a speed advantage. I swerved onto Princess Road and pedaled like a Grand Prix champion, not needing to look back to know where Grendel was; I could hear his breath, and his claws tearing at the road. I had to get past his sprint, where he was as fast as I was, but only for a short distance; then he had to slow down for a long run, when I could gain on him if nothing went wrong.

So I led Grendel on a half-mile chase along a roundabout route circling back toward the inn, which I got to just in time to open the gate, get my loaded bike through it, and slam it shut about a second before Grendel caught up and lunged. His body hit the other side of the heavy gate with force.

"You're out of breath," the captain observed when I had delivered my load to the pantry. He had his spectacles on, and had made a desk of his table in the public room, which was now littered with papers and a journal in which he was writing with a pen that had to be dipped in ink, which I thought only schoolchildren did. I told him about Grendel. He capped his inkwell and listened.

"Hmm," he said when I had finished, "so you've got speed on him. But a stern chase is a long chase, eh? You're about spent, and lucky you didn't take a skid, or that your bicycle didn't break." Indeed, those were the hazards, I affirmed, but what else was I to do?

"Attack," he suggested. I told him he didn't understand the power and dedicated fury of Grendel. "Right, but he's still a dog. If he's between you and where you want to go, and you've got speed, try steering to pass him close, then, at the last second, turn right at him. Make him have to jump for it, and you'll be past before he can regroup. You'll still have a stern chase, but you can head directly for home, rather than having to get winded circling the whole neighbourhood."

While I was absorbing the terrifying idea of charging Grendel with my bicycle, the captain rose. "Before you take your coat off," he said, while putting on his own, "come with me." I followed him out the back door, down to *Merry Adventure,* and into her cabin, where he needed my help in extracting a large, locked chest out from under his bunk. He explained that there was a leaky plank behind it that he needed to be able to get to and tend until he could haul the boat and fix it once and for all. So, with much prying and grunting, we wrestled the chest free.

"Now we need an out-of-the-way place to put it," he said. In the cramped confines of the yacht, I could see no such place. "There's no room down here for it," he echoed my thoughts, "so we'll have to get it out the hatch, up onto the dock, and . . . didn't you say something about a cellar where nobody goes? Does that locked door off the wharf go down there?" I nodded. "Well, do you have a key to the cellar door?" I told him I could get it, but asked about the rule not to take anything off the boat yet.

"Ah, the rules," he said, "Right. I appreciate the reminder to be sure. What it means is that we mustn't tell anyone we shifted my old chest, or there'll be a big fuss over nothing." I asked him what was in it. "Why, all the silly treasures of a long life. Little things I want to keep: some old journals, papers, odds and sods." He smiled at me. "I'm not smuggling any rum, or tobacco, or diamonds, Jim, my word on it. I'd open it up for you, but the key's gone missing. I'll have another look for it while you're fetching the key to that cellar door." And before I knew it, I was helping him. I also thought I was helping my mother—protecting her innocence in this minor matter by simply not telling her about it. I avoided her as I picked up the keys and a flashlight.

The captain's old chest was heavy enough, but it had rope beckets, which made it easier to carry once we got it onto the dock. The hasp lock to the cellar took some work with the key, but it eventually yielded; the old door creaked open on its pintles, admitting us into the dank darkness of what used to be a storage chamber for boat gear.

"This will do fine," said the captain, who had brought a flashlight of his own. He wanted the chest against a foundation wall among some old kegs and coils of rope, where he dragged a mildewed sail over part of it. On top of that he placed a couple of empty boxes, until it was perfectly camouflaged. "That'll do," he said, darting his light over the ancient stonework surrounding us. Parts were vaulted, and there were doorways to other chambers.

"Where do those go?" he asked, moving to have a closer look at the nearest one. I explained to him that the cellars were on three levels; we were standing in the middle one, which extended through several similar chambers at the same level, including the powder magazine and the old jail, to where it went so deep under the inn that there was another cellar over it. The upper one was used for storage, and the furnace, and it communicated with the kitchen by stairs. That level was blocked off from this one. Down below us was the lowest level, or sub-cellar, which sometimes flooded, and where nobody was allowed lest a piece of ancient masonry fall out of the ceiling and conk them, or some other accident befall.

An iron grating covered the stone steps that led down to it, and its padlock was thick with rust. The last time it had been opened, to my knowledge, was when my grandfather had yielded to my pleading and taken me down there, which got him in trouble with Mother when she learned about the expedition. I had found it less interesting than I had hoped—a few bare chambers joined by alleyways that dripped, and rodents' eyes glowing red in our flashlight beams. Nothing about it had made me want to go back. The captain, however, took a keen interest in it at once.

"This is the sort of thing that historians such as myself find fascinating," he explained, peering through the grating. "This lock's a goner; what do you say we cut it off, and I'll replace it with a good one after I've had a chance to look around a bit?" I told him we couldn't do that without my mother's permission, and I didn't see a lot of hope for that. "Well, maybe later," he said, and led the way out. As I relocked the door, he had a last caution for me: "Remember, Jim, mum's the word." I nodded, and he returned to his boat to tend its leak. I went back above to sneak the key ring back onto its hook.

No other excitement marked that Saturday. The captain took up station at his table by the fire, and spent the time weaving macramé onto an old rum bottle. Robin made his usual call to check things out and chat with my mother. I heard him ask if our new guest was keeping his quarantine. She said he had not gone anywhere, nor brought anything ashore, which gave me a twinge, but I had nothing to say. Robin had a sociable word with the captain, whose only other interruption of the evening was his supper. As he gathered his things to go above, I asked him if I could get his help with my essay the next day, after church. He nodded, asking when the services began, then retired.

"You're getting almighty cozy with that old sailor," Meg observed as we were cleaning up.

"He's going to teach me things."

"Maybe," she said, "but so far it looks to me like you're the one doing all the teaching."

3

Scoutings

Sunday morning found the captain bringing a roll of clothing from his boat. "It is my poor old black wool suit," he explained, unrolling it, "and it's been stowed a while, all through the tropics. I'm afraid it needs some love—at least an ironing—if I'm to wear it to church."

"Church?" Mother was as surprised as I was, nothing of his habits having indicated any great bent toward piety. "What is your church?"

"The church of the sea. But services there are irregular." He smiled. "Today, my church is your church, and you can vouch for my having gone nowhere else, should the Immigration officer ask. I doubt he will. I've already been allowed ashore, and a visit to the house of the lord shouldn't ruffle anybody's feathers." It seemed a reasonable bend of the rules, and Mother immediately took on the project of getting his suit in good enough condition for him to present himself before the eyes of God and the congregation of the First Anglican Church of Grey Rocks. I shined his shoes.

When the captain came below, he was transformed into a gentleman of a former generation, with a slender-cut tailoring to his old suit and waistcoat. In place of a tie, he wore a neck cloth; instead of an overcoat, he wore his old boat cloak, and he carried a substantial-looking walking stick. He was a tall man, and altogether imposing. His outmoded wardrobe might have looked like a costume on somebody younger, but on him it somehow seemed natural.

"My, aren't you elegant!" Mother exclaimed, and off to church we went, squired by our new guest. Meg had gone ahead to get into her choir robe and warm up her vocal chords. The sun had come out, and all over town the ringing of bells began to summon the faithful, not just Anglican, but the parishioners of the United Church, and the Lutherans (including most of the Moehners), and the Baptists, and the Catholics to Mass at Saint Michael's. In that time and place, everybody who did not want to be seen as morally dissolute went to church whether they felt particularly spiritual or not. Those who didn't go were more noticed than those who did.

As usual, Mother set a brisk walking pace, chatting with the captain, telling him about the town while I kept an eye out for Grendel. I didn't expect him to be set on me when other people were around, but watchfulness seemed prudent. I noticed the captain noticing my preoccupation. We arrived as folks were still standing outside, so Mother introduced him around, until Robin's car pulled up and she went to help with Aunt Karen, unloading the wheelchair, then getting her into it. Turning his back to Robin's line of view, the captain asked me about Grendel and his range of operations. I told him that was anywhere between the inn and the school, another five-minute walk from where we were. My real worry was how I was going to avoid him when the snow came, or freezing rain, when I couldn't ride my bike. On foot, I didn't see how I could get away. I told him I was going to get a heavy stick so that at least I'd have something to protect myself when, inevitably, he nailed me.

By this time everybody had gone inside, and Deacon Sidebarrow started to close the doors, so we scooted into a rear pew just as the opening hymn was starting. While I fumbled with the hymnal, the captain hummed along. "I'm afraid I never learned that one," he commented as we sat down, "but it sounds like they've got a good choir." I told him to just wait until they sang on their own, and he was in for a surprise. With a half-dozen empty pews in front of us, we could comfortably whisper to each other without bothering anybody. Deacon Sidebarrow sat down across from us, waiting to take up the collections in due course, but he was stone deaf.

"I think a stick is a bad idea," the captain opined.

"Sure, a gun would be better," I told him, but my only realistic option for a weapon was a good stick, something that could also be a club like the one he was carrying. I asked him what his objections could be to it.

"Two objections, actually. First, if you start carrying a stick to school, you'll be known as the boy with a stick." Here he paused. The liturgies had ended, all prayed, and the Reverend Burton

Corkum mounted to the lectern to deliver his sermon. This week it was his slant on sin overall, and how little sins all together make big sins, seven to be precise, which he started to inform us about in his best radio announcer's voice.

"What is the other objection?" I whispered.

"It's the more important one. From what you've told me about this dog, you're not going to stop him with any stick, even if you were trained to use it properly. And if you did manage to whack him with it, you'd just make him madder. What to do, then? Evasion's all you've got, sounds like. He's faster, and he's got you outgunned. Show me where your school is on this." He produced the copy of the inn's brochure that I'd given to him, and opened it to its town map. Together we went over it, and Grendel's ambush spots, while Reverend Corkum led the rest of the congregation down the seven paths to perdition. Finishing, he raised his voice and his arms simultaneously, like a big bird. "'Ye who enter here abandon all hope,' reads the inscription on the gate of hell!" he intoned.

"They always bloody well get that backwards," the captain growled. "It's heaven that has that particular inscription on it, not hell."

"Then what's hell got on it?" I asked.

"Embrace hope."

Before I could ponder that, it was the choir's turn to stand and hold forth, which they did very beautifully, considering that Earl Eisnor's loss of voice had deprived them of their baritone. Then came Meg's two solos—two because she sang so sweetly that one hymn from her wasn't enough. Her hosannas rang to the heavens in a soprano that the angels must have envied, not to mention her looks. Meg was an Irish redhead, with big green eyes and a spray of freckles, and she had turned more heads than my own.

"She has a voice like a burst of butterflies," the captain commented as everybody rose for the doxology. This he knew well, and he sang it in a vibrant baritone that found its way to the front of the church: "Praise God from Whom all blessings flow . . ." The choir glanced in our direction, finished their lyrics, and let the organist take over while Deacon Sidebarrow passed his plate, first to us two, since we were sitting at the back. I put in the weekly quarter I was issued for the purpose; the captain put in a dollar, and the deacon moved on.

"Tell me about Meg," the captain said. I didn't know how well I could do that question justice in any short form. Meagan O'Leary was the child of an unmarried Irish immigrant mother who had abandoned her in Halifax in order to sneak into "the Boston states" and vanish. In fact, nobody local knew much about Meg's history until she was placed with a Grey Rocks couple when she was about ten, still a ward of the state. John and Betty Langille were paid to take her in, though by no means enough to make them want to keep her for a second year, so she'd gone to another family, then another one after that. She had been known as a handful, bright, eccentric, always rebellious, musically gifted not only as a singer, but just about the best fiddler in Lunenburg County. The late Reverend Trelawny had taken her on as a violin student, and she'd so melted the heart of her teacher that he'd given her his second instrument. With it, she made magic. "Witchy Meg" was one of the names she'd gotten, but her most usual nickname was just "Mad Meg."

"Why mad?" asked the captain, just as the service came to the closing prayer, and we had to put our knees onto the prayer rail. Then came some long announcements from Becky Eisnor, speaking about the activities of the Women's Auxiliary.

"One summer night with a full moon," I told him, "Meg went

out on our wharf and played her fiddle in the nude." This private sacrament had unfortunately coincided with the arrival of several Grey Rocks fishing boats; they passed her close and put spotlights on her. I said that was only one of the odd things she'd done that had gotten her a dubious reputation. She'd had a few boyfriends that she hadn't kept long, who had retaliated for being dropped by saying bad things about her.

Meg had first come to work part-time at the inn. After Father's death, she'd moved in to stay. When she turned eighteen, there was no more money for her from the government, but she was earning her keep, and had become part of the family. She wanted to go to music school somewhere, anywhere, but there was no money, and her help at the inn had become indispensable. "I'm doomed to spend my whole life in this boring town, mopping floors, folding laundry, and pouring beer," she told me once, when I found her playing her fiddle to herself, crying. Nevertheless, with us she had found a family and a home for the first time in her life, for herself and her trusty cat Cleo, who'd been with her through thick and thin. Five years had passed, with pressures building up in her as we found out last July, when Meg had a bad week, with grouty customers, no tips, another boyfriend gone sour, problems in the choir, and finally a blowup at my mother over some trivial thing.

So Meg quit. She stayed until Mother could hire replacement help, then left on the bus to Halifax with two suitcases, a huge bag with a shoulder strap, her fiddle case, and Cleo. By then she and Mother had made up, of course, and there were a lot of hugs and moist eyes, but it was plainly time for Meg to follow her destiny into the universe beyond Grey Rocks. She had the phone number and address of a man in the music business who had told her he would help her start a career.

Here Reverend Corkum concluded the service with a resonant reminder to ponder well the transience of mortality, and the
consequences of accumulating small sins. Again the bells tolled,
and the captain and I emerged from the church before anybody
else. The day was clouding up, turning smurry and chill.

"If we clear out before your policeman uncle sees me, it will
save him the trouble of having to take any official notice of my
leaving the inn," he said, suggesting that I show him my school on
the way home. "Obviously Meg came back," he prompted me as
we strolled. Indeed she had, just last month, and in a desperate
condition. Whatever happened to Meg during her three months
away was nothing she wanted to talk about to anybody except
Mother, who tended her bruises and kept what she'd been told to
herself. Cleo was gone. So was Meg's violin, and some other
things, and we were all treating her very tenderly.

"Hmmm," said the captain, swerving the focus, "is that your
school over there?" It was. "Let's examine the terrain." This we
did, walking around it while he correlated our surroundings with
the little map. "You have here three basic routes between the inn
and the school," he observed, tracing them with his finger.
"Here's one, two, and three. Now, every day take a different one.
Never let the enemy know where you're going to be. That's for
starters. Next, let's have a look and find the safety spots."

These turned out to be various familiar places that he led me
to view in a tactical way—sheds and garages with unlocked doors,
even houses, and more than a few fences, which were good
because I could jump them, get on the other side, and when
Grendel ran around to my side, I could jump back, gaining
ground. Also there were various climbable trees, and some
parked vehicles I could maybe enter if they were there, and blow
the horn. "If he trees you, or runs you into somebody's house,

then you'll probably get a witness, which will force the cops to deal with the animal. Meanwhile, chart your course from one safe anchorage to another. That's how the pirates had to evade the frigates of the Royal Navy, and how merchant ships evaded pirates, with a bit of luck. So there's a small start to your understanding about the subject."

We were approaching the gate to the Admiral Anson Inn, with his painted portrait overhead. "Now there was a pirate if ever there was one," said the captain, stopping under the sign to have a look at it. I reminded him that Anson was First Lord of the Admiralty. He nodded. "And the biggest pirate of his time, some who knew him would say." He was amused by the portrait's crooked wig. "And he's a bit pink, but the funny thing is, he did look just like that after about his eighth glass of sherry." He said this as casually as if he had recently dined with the man. I pointed this out. "Quite. And so I did, although not so very recently." It was an odd thing for him to say, and odd in the way he said it. He turned his gaze from the sign to me. "I speak as a student of naval history. I've spent many an evening studying Anson's career, looking at copperplate engravings of him and such."

Here, we were interrupted by Robin driving up, with Aunt Karen, for our family's weekly Sunday dinner. Again there was the process of her wheelchair, and an introduction to Captain Johnson. Aunt Karen had been catastrophically afflicted (soon after her marriage to Robin) with a crippling kind of arthritis that had ravaged her body, making her too fragile to even shake hands with people.

"You're the sailor I've heard about," she said to him.

"Very likely," he bowed.

"And how did you like Reverend Corkum's sermon?" she wanted to know, as Robin rolled her through the gate.

"Madam, I took it to heart, because in order to go hear it, I was committing a transgression, a little sin which I trust our Lord will forgive on the grounds that I was visiting His house on the Sabbath."

"I reckon He'll forgive you," she said, "and I think you'll also be forgiven by the local authorities." Robin had nothing to say about the captain's delinquency from quarantine, although obviously it had been well noted. Robin didn't miss much, and Aunt Karen missed nothing at all. She had an eye like a scalpel, as Tom once put it, and dissecting the world around her was just about the only thing she could do for entertainment, other than reading. Inside, Mother invited the captain to join the family table for Sunday dinner, our traditional noontime meal. Here, he came under Aunt Karen's further scrutiny, which was stringent.

"Where were you coming from before Bermuda?"

"Carriacou, an island . . ."

"In the Grenadines, south part of the Lesser Antilles, in the Windward Islands," Aunt Karen finished his sentence for him. She had been a schoolteacher, and knew many things. "Vacationing?" This got a nod.

"Just that. A vacation from a vacation. I'm retired from the sea professionally, but sailing remains my lot. The reward is getting to come to a place like this, and to meet good folk such as yourselves." He was very gracious, but Aunt Karen was by no means done with him.

"And before Carriacou?"

"The Cape Verdes; Las Palmas before that; Spain before that; from England at Bristol, which is where my motor was last working." He turned to Robin, asking his recommendation for a good marine mechanic. Robin told him to ask Tom.

"What kind of a historian are you?" Aunt Karen wanted to know. "What have you written?"

"Oh, odds and sods. This and that. Bits and pieces here and there."

Here I piped in: "He's going to teach me about pirates for my essay."

"You've studied piracy?" Aunt Karen pursued him.

"A bit," the captain responded. "It's so much a part of everything. And it's particularly part of this coast, which is where the pirates came to recruit, and to careen their ships and repair, in an out-of-the-way corner with a lot of out-of-the-way places where the Royal Navy didn't go, if they could avoid it." Here, he'd turned the tables on Aunt Karen.

"For instance, take Mahone Bay, which was named *Mahon* by the French, because that was their word for pirate at the time, and because it was a choice place for pirates to come. They could work the Caribbean in the winter, New England in the summer, and come here to tuck in behind an island and work on their ships, scrape the barnacles off their bottoms, pick up some local lads to fill in their crew, and then be off again. That was all along the coast between here and Newfoundland, which was their favourite recruiting ground of all, primarily because there were a lot of poor people there who couldn't escape, having been painted a rosy picture by their governments, seducing them to emigrate to a stony wilderness. There they were enslaved, stuck cleaning fish. To many of them, a pirate ship was their only gateway to freedom. Many a religious man chose that door."

"That's something not much taught in school," Aunt Karen observed. "Are you an apologist for piracy?"

"Madam, if I'm guilty of being an apologist for anything at all, I would deserve a slap from the teacher."

"Who were your teachers?"

"I wouldn't know where to start. And yourself?" He turned the conversation to her. "You've taught history? What's your own area of study?"

"My own study? Primarily, living with the pain of my disease." Aunt Karen was no whiner, but she was very straightforward. "Trying to make friends with it. Beyond that, all I'm able to do in my little life—what's left of it—is to observe the things that Providence puts in my path. I, too, am retired. You're an interesting man. I apologise if I've been too direct. It's my way. At least tell me who has been your main teacher."

"I would have to say the sea," said the captain, standing. The meal was over. He expressed his thanks for it, and the company, and excused himself on the grounds that his own small ship needed some tending and pumping, and he had to change clothes and go do it. On his way out, he promised to meet with me at four o'clock in order to get me started on my paper.

"Now there is a gentleman who's hard to read," Aunt Karen remarked when he had left. "He's cultured, but with a rough edge; his English wanders around between Oxonian and West Country dialect, with some Americanisms thrown in. He has no interest in telling us what he has written, which could mean he hasn't written anything. The thing that I can do through the library services is to find out anything that's been published under the name of Charles Johnson, or perhaps Captain Charles Johnson. He's got me curious."

I was waiting for Granddad's ship clock to ring four o'clock, and when it did, I presented myself at the captain's table, notebook and sharpened pencil in hand. The fire I had been tending was crackling. Outside, a light fall of snow had begun. He wasn't there, however, although he had been only a few minutes ago, scribbling away. "Where did he go?" I asked Meg.

"Don't know; don't care," said Meg, "but with the number of rums he's had, I reckon it's the loo."

I sat down to wait, listening for the distant sound of a flushing toilet, which would tell me whether he had gone to the downstairs gents, or one of the upstairs facilities, but there was nothing. When the clock went to twenty minutes past our appointed hour, I went up to his room, listened at his door, and heard music on the other side.

"It's me," I announced with a rap.

"Go to my table and wait for me," came his voice, and as I left, the music started again, some kind of flute, or whistle. So back down I went, reflecting on all of the teachings I'd ever had to be prompt. "Punctuality is Virtue," read an inscription (in Latin) over the doors of my school, and it was part of me, and still is. As the minutes ticked past, my image of Captain Charles Johnson began to fade. Click, I distinctly heard the big minute hand engage its next station. Either he had totally forgotten the time he had given me for our appointment, or he was purposely keeping me cooling my heels while he practised his instrument. If it was the former, it was forgivable; if it was the latter, it was beyond my experience. When the clock rang another bell (marking the half-hour), I was just gathering up my notebook to leave when he came down the stairs, very businesslike, and a bit rumpled.

"Now," he said, standing in front of the fire to warm his backside. "It's pirates. Well, before I go into it, I have one thing to say to you that is more important than anything else about the whole subject. It's the thing you must remember always." Here he paused. "In fact, it's much too important to address without a refill of this empty glass; can you find Meg? Tell her to make it a double ration."

So off I went; not finding Meg or Mother (the inn being closed for the Sabbath), I took it upon myself to pour him his rum—damn the rules—double ration, and deliver it.

"Now," it was my turn to say, leading him to where he'd left off.

"Here's to now," he toasted. I prompted him that there was something he wanted me to remember. "About pirates, you were saying . . ."

"It's a big subject, pirates. Piracy. My side of our bargain, as I take it, is that I'm to teach you about it, but let's start smaller. How many words are you given in your essay?"

"Five or six written pages."

"You'll need more," he said. "When is it due?"

"Before the Christmas holiday."

"You'll have to extend it."

I said, "I doubt pirates would be considered an important enough topic to break the rules for."

"Rules are a given," he said. "What could be more important than seeing who makes 'em, and who breaks 'em, and who makes their own, and how it's worked throughout time?" He paused to take a sip of his rum. "The rules. I reckon the first act of piracy happened when a caveman on a raft from one side of a river met another chap from the other side, attacked him, took everything he had, and made the rule that the river belonged to him, and his family, of course. So there came government, and anybody from the other side of the river who did the same thing was a criminal committing an act of piracy." He groped for his tobacco and pipe.

"Minoan texts are full of pirates. Much later Julius Caesar was captured by pirates. They held him for ransom, and released him when it was paid; he went back with warships, captured his captors, and hanged them. Pirates were throughout time, and they're here still. History would remember Julius Caesar as a pirate if he had done the things he did in ships. He broke all the rules. So that's important in seeing how the political world works, but it's not nearly as important as women."

"Women?" He seemed to be losing the thread of the conversation.

"Women. They're a very important thing to understand, lad, and it's hard to do that without understanding pirates and horses."

"Horses?"

"Aye, but we barely have time to deal with pirates, who have a special place in the hearts of most women, and in their dreams. A very special pirate, no slave to any rule of man, who will always sweep her from the bonds of her life in a ship with sails spreading free, and a loyal crew that is very respectful of her gentility. He will fight to the finish for her, her own Captain Blood, or the chap from *Frenchman's Creek,* or any of those movies and books." Here he lit his pipe. "I could have made a lot more in royalties if I'd written fiction."

I reminded him that my essay was required to be a factual history, probably starting with the Vikings.

"And it's not just women who love pirates," he continued, "it's everybody, children on up, back to the olden times. It's always been that way. Why does everybody always like pirates? Why do you suppose that is?" I shook my head.

"Well," he sighed, "We'll get to that in due course. As to the Vikings, what have you been told about them?"

"That they were pillagers, murderers, and thugs."

This got a solemn nod from him. "That is essentially correct. Doing exactly what they'd been trained to do."

"With what possible justification?" I asked. He ruminated.

"Go back a thousand years. Instead of this cozy room, you've got a northern winter ahead of you cooped in a very smoky hut somewhere in Norway or Sweden or Denmark, with nothing to do but listen to tales of battle, learning that the best thing in the world is to be a good warrior. Your uncles practise fighting with wooden swords. You do too. It's your school. You learn to throw a spear, swing an axe, get good at it, get ready to put your life on the line; if you're killed, you'll go to Valhalla, Viking heaven, where you can sit around drinking mead with all of the other fallen heroes for all eternity. You'll be favoured by the gods."

Here he blew a big puff of smoke in my face, causing me to try to wave it away. "So, imagine after a winter of breathing an atmosphere like that with every breath, spring comes, and you're out. The boats are launched, and you've got the fresh air, on an open deck, and you're headed south, most likely. A fair wind carries your ship across the North Sea, and a beautiful ship she is—double ended and graceful, a marvelously crafted thing that can ride easily over stormy seas, or be rowed through calms. Mostly she sails. She has only one square sail, but the grander sailing ships of later centuries will work the same way, just with more sails and more decks. Your ship has only one deck, and it's open to the rain and the stinging salt spray. For protection, you can pull your skins around you. You are trained to be as tough as your shipmates, and if you can be tougher, that's all to the good.

"Other ships like yours have carried settlers to Iceland, Greenland, and even the great western continent beyond. Columbus won't get there for another five hundred years. In the hands of good sailors, this little vessel can take you anywhere you want to go, and you're among the finest sailors of all time. You can land where you want, pay a surprise visit, and be off again before any force can march to challenge you. Or you can stay and claim the place, which is how big areas of Europe's seaboard got resettled by Norse people. And you'll keep your old teachings for centuries to come." A pop from the fireplace punctuated his point.

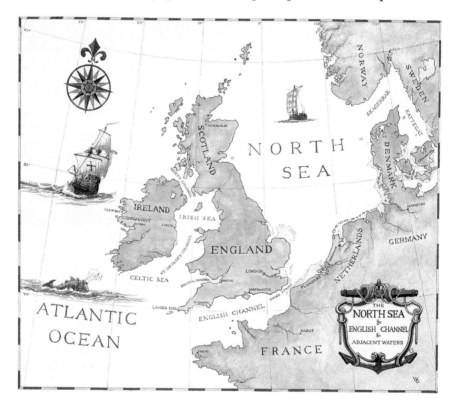

"You're carrying some cargo to swap, furs, maybe slaves, but you're hoping for plunder along the way. That would be any ship weaker than yours. Looking for one, your captain goes probing down the English coast—let's say he's chosen the Eastern Channel—sailing by day, anchoring at night. He has a sea chart that's pretty rough, and short on a lot of important details, so he relies more on his nose than anything."

"Nose?" I questioned. I had learned coastal navigation from my grandfather, with compass, protractor, and dividers.

"Nose." He was very definite about that. "Today it's nearly a forgotten instrument because there's radar, and motors, and sonar, and all the other gadgets." A sniff. "Technology has cost us our nose," he added, having a swallow of rum.

"Now you've got a brisk northwester, sailing broad between the Flemish Banks to port, and the Goodwin Sands to starboard, heading fair into the Dover Strait, one of the richest hunting grounds in the Northern Seas, as they were called. You sight a ship far ahead. There's a bit of sail trimming to be done, and then you're foaming along at eight or nine knots, maybe ten, with a fair wind and following sea. Your prey tries to run. It's bigger than your ship, and looks much the same, but it's a lot slower. You gain on it. There aren't many people to be seen, just tempting bundles of cargo on deck. As you approach, you take up your shield and weapons. It's the moment for which you've been praying to Odin: Battle. Your helmsman nudges the ship's stem into your opponent's quarter, and all of you swarm over his rail on the lift of a wave."

The captain paused, glancing behind me. So spellbound had I become, I hadn't noticed Meg entering the taproom, which was dark tonight, except for our table. It was six o'clock, suppertime.

"Chowder, cheese, bread, and brussels sprouts," she

announced, setting down her tray and summarily laying out his supper.

"Ahhh," he said, rubbing his hands, asking for a beer and another rum.

"Another? Where'd you get your first one?"

I said I'd poured it because nobody else was around, which got me a stern look, and the reminder that I was due in the kitchen for our own supper. I went there and ate with Mother, Meg, and the distraction of having been left sword in hand, ready for some action.

"Where are you tonight?" asked Mother.

"With pirates," Meg answered for me.

"Vikings," I corrected her, and it was a half an hour before I could get back to hear the rest of the story. The captain was writing again, this time a list of things he needed to do as soon as he'd cleared customs the next day. "Do you have a good family dentist?" he asked, and noted down Doc Wentzel's name. I was impatient to hear about the rest of the battle.

"Right. Well, where did I leave off?" Memory refreshed, he plunged me again into the fray. "Just as your feet hit the deck, the bundles of cargo shed their coverings and turn out to be a troop of armed men; others rise up from behind the bulwarks where they've been hiding; too late, you realise you're facing another crew of Vikings, just as fierce as you are, and twice as numerous. They've dragged ropes in the water to slow down their ship, and now they've got you. You've fallen for a trick that's been the undoing of many a pirate. Before you have a chance to recover from your surprise, you're under a shower of spears, and you don't have a chance.

"The ending of the story is, if you fight, you'll be chopped up. If you don't, you'll be sold as a slave to somebody who cares less about you than your mother does. Here endeth the lesson for today." He smiled. "Would you run up to my room and fetch me my pennywhistle? It's on the bed."

This turned out to be the tin flute I'd heard earlier. It was a flageolet, the simplest of instruments, but when he put it to his lips and played an air with great precision, it brought Meg out from the kitchen.

"That's 'Black Donald's March,'" he said, finishing.

"And it's not how it goes," said Meg.

"How does it, then?"

"Like this," she said, humming it.

"Like this?" he played it her way, which wasn't much different to my ear.

"Better," she commented, collecting his dishes.

"You have a lovely voice," he told her.

"I do," she said, returning to the kitchen with her tray.

When I went to bed, he was still playing to himself by his fire.

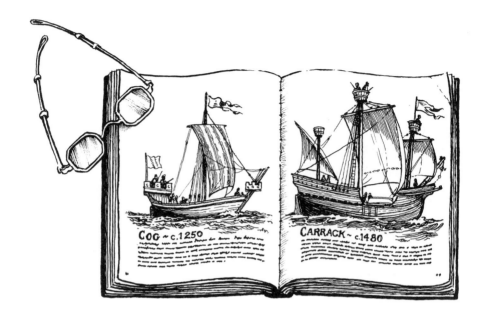

4

Books and Lessons

Monday marked a return to my workaday world of school, where I arrived without incident. The weather had cleared, and I did not expect an encounter with Grendel, because Klaus's boat (a red cape islander), was out—gone from its berth near the end of the government wharf, which I could see with binoculars from my room. (I had soon learned to keep track of its movements. When it was gone, that meant Grendel was either out running traps with his owner, or penned up somewhere.) It was math in the morning. For a change, I had a hard time getting into it. A piece of my mind was still at sea, captured by the Vikings.

"You seem far away today," said Jenny when we got together during lunchtime. Jenny MacGregor was my best chum. We had started kindergarten together, then we had been bumped ahead a grade, setting us apart from everyone else, and together we were the best students in our class (although we were a year younger), which did not endear us to anyone except sometimes our teacher, Miss Titherington. Jenny and I were each other's only friends in school.

I told Jenny the story of my weekend, leaving out the little secrets that had come up, describing my new friend Captain Johnson, and bragging about his talents as both a sailor and as a storyteller. Lunchtime wasn't long enough for the full account, so I picked up where I'd left off at afternoon recess, trying without success to recreate something of the power of his peculiarly vivid narrative. I tried to imitate it with feeble results.

"Anyway," I left off, "for a second he made me *feel* what he was saying as though it was really happening, and I keep thinking about it."

"Maybe he's a hypnotist," she cautioned me. I thought not. He hadn't dangled any watches, or told me my eyelids were growing heavy. "Well then, maybe he is an avatar, one of the wise ones who are immortal and have secret errands. They move among us in disguise." I should mention right off that Jenny lived in a world inhabited by all the invisible beings she'd ever read about, and she read everything she could find about ghosts, avatars, spirits, vampires, hypnotists, levitation, Madame Blavatsky, and anything else occult. She had a round face on top of a thin neck, and had to wear glasses. Jenny spent even more time by herself than I did. I told her I doubted avatars needed dentists or drank rum, and I thought he was just a particularly talented storyteller.

"I would have to hear him before I could say anything more," she pronounced as the bell rang. I said I would ask him if she could listen in. The last hour of the day we spent on art projects, with Jenny painting big, yellow sunflowers. I drew Viking ships with spears whizzing through the air between them.

The bike ride home was uneventful, but I was surprised back at the inn; as I came through the gate, there was the captain in his cloak with a naked cutlass in his hand, poking with it at the ground under the pantry windows.

"Hah!" he said. "Foundations. Look here. Feel along this line with the blade tip." He handed me the cutlass, and I did as instructed, finding the edge of a buried wall a few inches under the soil. "It comes to a corner here, where I've put a rock to mark it, and another one there," he pointed, "and rejoins the inn over there. I think it has to be what's left of the original structure that the inn was built over. Let's pace it off and get a rough measurement." This activity was interrupted by a car pulling up outside the wall. "I've been entertaining myself while waiting for the officials to show up and clear me. This may be them. You'd better run down to *Merry Adventure* and hang that sword back where it belongs; that will save us from having to explain what we're doing with it."

So off I ran, just in time to avoid the two government officers who came through the gate, representatives of Customs and Immigration. As the captain led them down to the wharf, I saw him telling again the story of his distressed entry. He was finishing as they arrived at the boat. He introduced me as his new assistant. They clambered aboard, looking around, then went below to look around some more. I noticed that the vacant spot we'd left under the bunk (with the removal of the chest) had been filled with some boxes and bits of gear that looked very natural there.

"Are you carrying any bonded stores?" the Customs man wanted to know. "Spirits, tobacco, or firearms?"

"Spirits?" The captain seemed confused.

"Whisky, brandy, spiritous liquors," the Customs man patiently explained.

"Of course. Yes, I do understand. Forgive me if I'm a bit slow today. I've taken quite a battering for an old chap, and not quite recovered. Your pardon. I do have a bit of rum, just a bottle or two. Maybe three." He groped under the settee. "Here's one, half-full, offer you chaps a drink? No? Now, what else? Tobacco. Just this bit here," he reached for his tin, "which needs a refill. Firearms? I have this." He produced an old brass flare pistol, which the officer looked at and handed back. I saw his eye touch the decorative antique weapons and move on.

"Have you carried anything at all ashore?"

"Uh," the captain pondered. "Toothbrush, that kind of thing, clothes, just personal gear. You can have a look at my room if you like. Frightfully good of you to let me come ashore. A lifesaver, that." Here the Immigration man demanded papers, which the captain had to rummage for. He seemed disorganised and bumbly, smaller and older somehow. "Ah, forgot, had them in my pocket!" He produced the papers, and they were examined. "Since your entry here was accidental, how come you asked the harbourmaster to point you to the Admiral Anson's dock?" (This was news to me. I had assumed he was there at Tom's suggestion, when they had exchanged shouts.) The captain said he'd heard about the place at one time or another, had an antiquarian's interest since it was where he'd been blown, and started on a ramble about some of the other old places he'd seen in his life.

"How long do you plan to stay?" the Immigration man interrupted him. The captain scratched his head. He had a small bald spot right on top of it.

"I have to have the old girl out of the water for some work to her planks before I can safely put to sea again, and there's my old Ailsa Craig diesel to repair, and here's winter. I'll be off for Boston come spring. Have you ever been in the Boston Athenaeum? Marvelous collections; some quite valuable source material." The Immigration man glanced at his watch and started stamping the captain's papers without further examination.

"Who told you about the Admiral Anson Inn?" I asked when they had gone. He scratched his head again, still in bumbly mode, unable to remember because it had been so long ago.

In the week following, I saw little of him, although we heard through the Grey Rocks grapevine of his activities. He had gone to the bank to exchange his money into Canadian dollars, and he opened an account. On Tuesday he made arrangements with Tom for *Merry Adventure* to be hauled into a boat shed where she could undergo whatever needed surgery and repair to its blown engine. Getting the parts was the main concern, the engine being very old.

On Wednesday, the captain spent all afternoon in Dr. Wentzel's dentist's chair, with the consequence that he could eat only soup for supper. Mother made him a chicken broth, and he went to bed right after. On Thursday, somewhat recovered, he went for a long chat with choirmaster Campbell, who invited him to sit in with the church choir's practise, where he filled in the missing baritone so well as to be asked to join the group for Sunday services, much to the annoyance of Meg.

"He's worming his way into our lives," she said.

On Friday, he paid me six dollars, per the terms of my employment, allowing me to get my paint set and colour my drawings of Viking ships. I'd had to do so little to earn my pay; I began to haunt his table in the hope of something to put my conscience to rest, and also for another of his stories. This he promised for Sunday afternoon at four o'clock sharp; and he agreed that Jenny could sit in, if her parents allowed her to come. Jenny's parents were protective of her—too much so in her view—but they agreed to bring her to the inn for the special lesson.

All during the week I kept track of Klaus Moehner's boat, taking full precautions whenever it was in its dock. Soon, I knew, it would lay up for the winter, and there would be no safe moment for me. On my Saturday errand-run to town, I thought I saw Grendel, but it was another dog. On Saturday evening the captain got Meg out again by playing his tin flute for the last of our customers, who bought another drink and stayed to listen. Meg had some criticism regarding the way he was playing a tune, and in learning her version he got her into singing while he played, which made a music so sweet that the room was transfixed. Much as Meg had gotten a distaste for the captain, she could not resist singing a few more airs to the sound of his pennywhistle. At the end of the impromptu concert, she gathered the best tips she had seen in some time, gave him a curt nod, and retired to the kitchen, where I followed her. I was amazed at what they had accomplished with no practise.

"He doesn't embarrass himself with his instrument," Meg conceded. This sounded thin, and I told her so, but she had nothing more to say to me. There had come a distance between us, but then, Meg had put a space between herself and the world, so I didn't take it personally. I went back to the captain's table, to watch for an appropriate moment for a question or two, but he was gathering up his papers.

"I'll need you Wednesday after school to help me shift *Merry Adventure* over to Tom's yard. The tide's right then. And I'll see you and your friend at four o'clock for class," whereupon he retired.

There was no more whispering in church the following Sunday morning. I sat with the family, and the captain was at the front with the choir, wearing a robe. His voice made a resonant foundation for the others, mostly women, except for Ernie Fischback, whose high tenor was pleasing but soft. The captain's baritone descended into basso during one of Meg's solos, and it became a duet, with sounds that competed and made a perfect balance. The hymn was much remarked on after the service, where the captain came in for a lot of compliments out on the lawn.

There were more comments at Sunday dinner, to which the captain was again invited. Aunt Karen couldn't resist having another go at him, this time more subtly, starting with his music.

He had learned to sing in Devonshire. Further probing, however, only got her a very teacherly lecture in the geophysical character-istics of Devon and Cornwall, with notes on its indigenous flora and fauna, sociological history, and more. When he excused him-self, there was some relief.

"He does have a talent for not talking about himself," Aunt Karen commented when he had left the table, "and I think he's given me a warning of what to expect when he's questioned."

Meg agreed. "I just learned more about Cornwall than I want-ed to know."

As four o'clock approached, the captain was not at his table. Remembering his tardiness of the week before, I reckoned he would be at least fifteen minutes late, maybe more. There was still some warmth in the late afternoon sun, so I went to meet Jenny at the gate when her parents dropped her off. We lingered outside for a few minutes as I tried to prepare her for the vivid storytelling she was about to hear, then we went in to wait. But to my surprise, the captain was there, pacing in front of an old National Geographic map of the world that he had mounted and propped up. He had changed into a baggy tweed suit and vest that was unironed; he wore what looked like a school tie of some kind, and his spectacles were perched on his nose in a way that made him the perfect image of a professor. He was as sober as a judge.

"By that," he said, indicating the clock with his walking stick (now a pointer), "you are exactly nine and a half minutes late, which is very disrespectful not only to your teacher, but also to your own education." This was gently spoken, but he put a hard eye behind it. I started to take the blame, but he didn't want to hear it. "Get seated and get your notebooks and pencils out." He regarded Jenny. "Your name? Right. And you're here because you want to learn about piracy? Very well, Mistress MacGregor, your reasons are your own, but it is an important subject. You are welcome to audit the class, which today deals with the transitional period between the end of the Viking era and the adaptation of their methods during the medieval period and into the early Renaissance. We are discussing the evolution of piracy only in Northern Europe, not the Mediterranean or Asia." He tapped the map with his stick. "Have you got that?" We scribbled away. "I presume, Mistress MacGregor, that you have read your colleague's notes about Vikings by way of preparation?"

"No, but he's told me about it."

I found myself putting my hand up, as in school.

"Question?"

"If the Vikings were really so powerful, why did they die out? What defeated them?"

"A new religion. In this case Christianity, with the basic virtues that the major religions hold in common. Different teaching, rather, where chopping people up came to be more frowned on. The Vikings lost their Valhalla, and turned to farming, fishing, and trade. Also, the kingdoms were getting better sorted out, and things were a bit less of a free-for-all than during the Dark Ages. Europe got a middle class—people who were better off than the serfs, but not aristocrats, although they came to support the aristocrats. There were a lot of shipowners among them, and trade flourished, and taxes were collected." He paused to let us write it down, nodding to Mother, who had come to listen, wheeling in Aunt Karen. Even Meg had ducked in.

"So there were a good many ships about. The graceful ships of the Vikings spawned other forms, grew bigger with more decks, more masts and sails, like this." He opened a book he had brought to a picture of a thirteenth-century cog. "Those ships evolved into these," he indicated a fifteenth-century carrack, "which made a rich prize for any pirate. Who *were* the pirates? Just about everybody at sea, or at least that was a prudent rule to go by if you were the skipper of this carrack. Ashore, there had come boundaries and the laws of nations, but these held no sway at sea. As in Viking times, the big fish ate the little fish. Because every ship and cargo you pirated fattened everybody of your home port, from the merchants to the local baron to the monarchy itself, it was thought to be a very good thing for you to do, and you taught your children how to do it, and life went on. Or not. If the chaps whose ships you were taking got hold of you, they would hang you. If you were lucky. Sometimes some rather more unpleasant things were done. Those were barbarous days," he added, darkly.

"Ughh," said Jenny, who wanted to know when we were going to get to Captain Kidd. "He buried his treasure on Oak Island in Mahone Bay," she added, "and they're still looking for it." The captain scowled.

"Please do not interrupt, Mistress. I will discuss the infamous Kidd when you have the foundation of how he came to be. Without understanding who he was, how could anybody expect to find any alleged treasure he might have left? We won't get to him for several classes yet. We'll move along faster if you make shorter notes.

"About halfway through the medieval period, there came efforts to bring some law to the sea, at first by the seaports, and then nations, issuing licences to their own pirates, written letters under seal saying the captain carrying it was not a pirate, and therefore should not be hanged if taken, nor his crew. If you wanted this licence, your authority charged you for it, then told you whose ships you were not supposed to take, and got a share of the prizes that you did take. Your authorities were also the adjudicators of what you brought in. Your judges. This worked out very well for the authorities, who could never be accused of piracy because they were, after all, the authorities, and also because they didn't go out and chase ships.

"The sailors who did, and who had a licence to do it, came to be called privateers, and often enough their papers saved their necks when they were captured, because the other chaps were doing the same thing. To your victims, whether you were a legal pirate or an illegal one was a technical point of little immediate concern.

"During the later 1300s, the first cannon were mounted on ships; over some generations they became bigger and efficient enough to sink a ship, which happened for the first time in 1513. Did you get that date?" This was directed at Jenny, who rolled her eyes, but wrote it down. "Good. Not that the pirates wanted to sink anybody, for obvious reasons, but cannons were useful for slowing down a chase by crippling the rigging, and necessary for self-defence. For the capture, however, the pirate still used spears and swords, along with pistols, muskets, swivel guns, and grenades. By the middle of the 1500s, warships were being built that looked like this." He turned to another picture in the book as Jenny tried to stifle a yawn. Mother and Meg left, taking Aunt Karen. He had passed the teacher test. The clock rang one bell. "With ships such as these, you could sail anywhere in the world you wanted to go, looking for places you didn't know were there, if you didn't mind a long painful voyage through uncharted waters. In those days, sailors still had their nose."

"Nose?" Jenny inquired. I whispered that I would explain it

later; the captain ignored her and pressed ahead, indicating points on the map.

"Opening a trade in slaves, ivory, and gold, the Portuguese navigators explored the African coasts well before the time of Columbus." Jenny made a wriggle.

"Question?" It wasn't a question, just Jenny's squeamishness on the whole subject of slavery, although she said she realised it was a long time ago, and now people had learned that they couldn't own one another. "Who ain't a slave?" growled the captain. "Do you think slavery's a thing of the past? I urge you to examine the world more closely. Back to our subject, the explorers. Columbus got credit for discovering a continent that had been found by the Norsemen, and revisited by Basque fishermen, and some Scots with a Venetian navigator, as well as others who kept mum about their fishing grounds. Chinese junks landed on America's West Coast. Indeed, by the time Columbus came along, he wasn't even the first Italian to discover America, though he certainly did come onto an interesting enough new part of it.

"Fleets followed him, exploring and claiming for Spain the lands and islands of the Americas, starting here," his pointer went to the Antilles, then swept through the Caribbean to the Spanish Main and beyond. "All of this," he made a sweeping circle encompassing Florida, the Gulf of Mexico, and most of South America, "with this bit, Brazil, going to the Portuguese, all by decree of the pope in Rome. There was a certain cost to the pope's sanction, of course, but the profits to Spain were beyond the dreams of men. The Spaniards had only to explore, loot, settle, and defend, in that order.

"Noting their success, English and French explorers did the same thing for their own sovereigns by following along in the northern wake of the Vikings, carving up North America, which was big, but nowhere near as rich as what Spain had got. Dutch ships went out, too, from here," his stick tapped Holland, "around Africa, all the way across the Indian Ocean, through the Straits of Sunda, to here," his stick encircled Indonesia. "They claimed much of it, and it yielded good booty in gold—and spices that were worth as much as gold back in Europe. A lot of poor sailors died getting it there.

"In other words, the European powers now had the ships and weapons to do to the whole world exactly what the Vikings had done to Europe centuries earlier, and the same thing that the caveman on his raft did to the chap from the other side of the river. So nothing had really changed much, except—in what history books call the Great Age of Exploration—the great pirates sailed out with the blessings of their governments and of course God." Jenny's hand shot up.

"Question?"

"God would never condone piracy," she declared.

"It is a moot point, Mistress, because they all sailed 'by the grace of God,' all of them, and it was their great gift to the many peoples who had not yet made the acquaintance of that god, in exchange for all the worldly goods they had. All through history, pirates have been some of the most religious people. Your Captain Kidd chap had a pew for his family in New York's Trinity Church; Bartholomew Roberts took over four hundred ships, but he always conducted church services on the Sabbath, with prayers during the week; and there were plenty of other God-bothering pirates, too." I could see that Jenny was having a hard time absorbing this, but she was not to be put off her point.

"Whatever you say, pirates are bad. Everyone agrees on that. Every book."

"Hmm," the captain pondered. Then he neatly tore a piece of paper into quarters, wrote the word *bad* on two of them, and *good* on the other two, and handed each of us a pair. "Regard those as labels," he said, "and put them on whatever you think appropriate." Neither one of us was quite sure what he meant. "Here, let me start," he said, taking Jenny's good label and holding it over me. "Would you agree that this chap is a good thing?" She nodded, as I did when he put my good label over Jenny. He smiled. "So far, we all agree. Now, what about this?" He turned to a picture of a cannon in the book. I liked cannons and put my good label on it at once, but to Jenny it was bad.

"There, you see?" the captain said. "There's no good and bad when it comes to taste; the words lose meaning, which you can call the first point of awareness, leaving you with no good and bad to fall back on. When you can accept that, you can come back to good and bad again, because they're not yours anymore. But we have digressed. Now we've got the British and French in North America, the Dutch in the East Indies, and the Spaniards just about everywhere else; and, arguably, they were the biggest pirates of their age, which made them tempting targets for other pirates, opening the world to what we have come to call the Golden Age of Piracy. I confess I've never thought of it quite in those terms. In any case, it certainly started a golden age of pirates against pirates, known to your history books here as the Elizabethan era, from 1558 to 1603." He regarded Jenny.

"How would you label Sir Francis Drake?" he asked her.

"Good." The answer was unhesitating. "He was a hero."

"Well, then, you've just labeled a pirate good."

"Have not!" said Jenny.

"Queen Elizabeth called him 'my pirate' and nobody disagreed; I will deal with him in the next lesson."

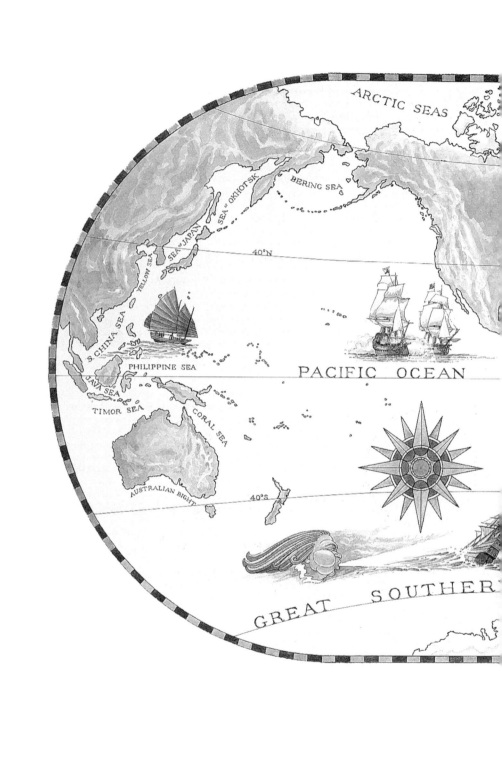

& ICE
BARENTS SEA
BAFFIN BAY

NORTH SEA
BALTIC S
BLACK S
CASPIAN S

ATLANTIC OCEAN

MEDITERRANEAN SEA

RED SEA
PERSIAN GULF
GULF of ADEN
ARABIAN SEA
BAY of BENGAL

INDIAN
OCEAN

OCEAN

~ the ~
SEAS & OCEANS
of the WORLD
COMMONWEALTH of PIRATES

MMV

Jenny, bored, became irritated by the captain's professorial posture. "Why should we believe any of this?"

"You mustn't. I urge you not to believe anything I've told you, or anything else, either. You've talked about your books; go check them. Check facts, and live your life, and look around." The clock struck. "That will do for today. Thank you very much for your attention. You are dismissed." With that, he gathered up his map, book, and stick and went above.

"I hated that," said Jenny when he was gone.

"Well, he does know his history," I defended him. "You have to give him that."

"Fill your boots. I don't care!"

5

Schemings

T he weather held fair during the first half of the week, so Klaus's boat was out working, which meant freedom from Grendel for my trips back and forth to school and for errands for Mother. I was with her when she brought Roy Moehner's development company (of which Moehner Realty was a part) the payment on the loan that would keep the inn out of his hands for three months more. She was delivering the cheque personally to make sure there was no question about its having gotten there. The last payment had been mysteriously delayed, supposedly in the post, making no end of trouble for her. Roy Moehner emerged from his private office with a gentle and welcoming smile. "What a nice surprise to see you, and you, Jim."

He seemed like a loving uncle. I didn't want to shake hands with him, but I had to, or else be rude to a man who had a power that was not to be trifled with. He was once mayor, and had picked his successor in that office, so that he himself could concentrate on making more money. He was grey-haired, looked like an aging movie star, gave generously to all the local charities (as well as the volunteer fire department and the police retirement fund). He headed the Lion's Club, was chairman of the board of this and that, and was the undisputed chief of the Moehners.

"How can I help you?" he asked, with a gesture that seemed to offer the world at his fingertips.

"I came to make sure there's no confusion this time about our payment reaching you," said Mother. As he accepted it, his face took on a kind sadness.

"I'm of course glad to have this, but I can't help but be aware of the difficulties you're having with the old place; I know this can't be an easy obligation for you to meet."

"It would be easier if you would refinance my note, as I've asked you before. Any bank would do it for me."

"Now, you're aware this company's rules about mortgage loans won't let me do that, much as I would personally like to."

"Mr. Moehner, I believe you make the rules."

"My concern," here he took on a look of genuine concern, "is that you now, at this time, have the opportunity to sell the inn, getting a good enough sum for it to start an easier and, I think, happier life. The alternative, foreclosure, means a tedious process that will leave you with next to nothing by the time it's all finished. I'm speaking to you as a friend. Why ruin yourself with a hopeless effort when you don't have to let everything go to the dogs?"

"Mr. Moehner, I'll consider what you've said." She gave him a polite "Good day" and out we went, with his reference to dogs hitting home. Grendel. Grendel was his nephew's dog. He had to know about Grendel. I told my mother.

"Jim, that man is bad enough without you stretching your imagination to make him worse. I'm more worried about your dwelling on this dog all the time, when our main worry right now is where we'll ever get the money by March 1 for the next payment." With this, she sent me off on other errands. As I was pedaling home, I was surprised to see the captain in his peacoat going into the Sou'wester Beverage Room. That establishment wasn't exactly our competition, but it was certainly the place where our enemies congregated. It hadn't occurred to me that he would ever go there.

The following day, after school, I went down to his boat on schedule to help him sail it to Tom's boatyard. He was waiting for me. "Now, *Merry,* I want to properly introduce you to Master Jim," he said. "He's a good young chap, and he's going to respect you, and you'll like him." He nudged me. "Say hello. You're crew now."

"Hello, *Merry,*" I said.

"That's good. Now let's get the lines off her." This we did, and her sails up, and away from the dock in a gentle twelve-knot breeze. It was perfect for a short downwind sail up the harbour to the place where Tom had a cradle waiting, but the captain trimmed the sails to a windward tack in the other direction.

"*Merry* wants to have a short, last sail before I start carving on her. Also," he added, "there's an hour yet to high tide, and if you're comfortable I'd like to behold the inn from the sea, as I mostly missed when sailing in, in the circumstances. Ready about," he commanded me, giving me the jib sheet to handle as he put the helm down. "*Merry* is a Falmouth boat, and she's handy in stays." The little vessel did have a quick response, and then we were bubbling along on the other tack, passing the inn's promontory from seaward.

"Is that a cave?" the captain asked, directing my eye to the base of the low cliff below the inn, where the sea had carved spaces in the rock. He pointed to a particularly deep one. I had sailed past it many times, but I didn't know. There was no access to it from any direction; a dangerous surge permanently seethed in and out of it. "Let's have a look then. What's the depth of water off your point?" I told him the rock was steep-to, so toward it we sailed. The fissure was indeed like a cave, although there was no way to approach its boiling surf in order to find out what was in its darkness.

He examined it closely. "I wouldn't be surprised if that's the way the water's getting to your cellar at spring tide." This caught me. If I had mentioned the flooding to him at all, certainly I had not told him anything about its tidal schedule, although he was right about it.

"There is a buoy missing," he said, pointing to our position on a coastal chart folded to a detailed inset of Grey Rocks Harbour and approaches. I told him that the buoy had been washed out in a southeaster two or three winters ago, and never replaced. He penciled in a correction on his chart. It was another peculiarity, that he had such a fully detailed chart of a small fragment of the Nova Scotia coast, where he wasn't even planning to be. A yacht had no room for such an inventory. I commented he'd been lucky to have such a good chart for the exact place he got blown into on our coast, a very long way off his course.

"Aye, lucky. Just so," he agreed, gazing around, correlating what he was looking at with the chart. "Old Landing," he read from it, taking a sight line on Lighthouse Point. "What's that?"

"It's where the first Grey Rocks settlers are supposed to have stepped ashore. And it's where our cannon is," I impulsively added. At the time, I had no idea of where this simple remark was going to lead.

"What cannon?"

"The one the Moehners stole from us. There were two to begin with, but there's only one left now, and that's where it is." The captain made a minor course change to take us in that direction, wanting to hear more, starting with what kind of cannon it was. I told him it was a brass gun, beautifully ornate, one of a pair that an old admiral named Holbourne had put ashore to augment the Grey Rocks battery, which was on the point adjoining the inn, where the sun patio was now. When the old battery fell into disuse, the ancient guns had simply been rolled into storage, and their oak carriages had rotted away down in the cellar—where his sea chest was now—until the Grey Rocks bicentennial celebration. For that, the town council got federal and provincial grants to make a little park area at Old Landing, with a lot of expensive stonework laid by a Moehner contractor. The whole thing became a major event, with everybody in town participating in one way or another. I sighed. It was still painful to talk about. He urged me on.

During preparations for the festivities, Mother was approached by Phyllis Moehner, who was Roy's wife and the chairwoman of the local chapter of the Imperial Order of the Daughters of the Empire, which was pretty much running everything. Phyllis requested the cannons for the event, and Mother willingly loaned them as a civic contribution, asking only their return after the festivities. This was promised. Moehner Woodworkers Inc. built new carriages for display. The cannons were never fired off, being stuffed with popcorn boxes, but it was all very successful, with tents, fireworks, local musicians, and food and drink concessions that did well because of all the visitors. The trouble was, we had never gotten our cannons back. Nor did it look like we were going to, and one of them was now gone.

"Gone where?"

I shrugged. Supposedly, in the version of events reported to Chief Moehner, one had been stolen. The scuttlebutt around town had it that the cannon had been sold to a wealthy American collector who had paid a lot of money for it, and had it crated up and shipped off. The word was he tried to buy them both, but Roy wanted to keep one for himself, and it was still decorating the Old Landing, which was a part of his property. "Is that it?" he pointed. It was. The captain reached for his binoculars. "How do they justify not bringing it back to you?"

"Now, they say that our cannons were really town property all along, being abandoned government artefacts," I explained. We had no papers on the cannons; they had been there forever. Uncle Bill, who was a lawyer in Halifax, had filed a civil action on our behalf. He had told us that we had a good case, but that we didn't have much chance of recovering our cannon in the courts, because it would be claim and counterclaim, and the whole thing would take a lifetime to drag through the system, where possession was 90 percent of the law in cases like this. The captain put down his binoculars, glanced at his watch, and prepared to jibe around to run back for the harbour.

"Why don't you just get a pickup truck and go get it?" he wanted to know. I explained that it was a gated private road, through the Moehner estate, with all their dogs, and was closed off to the public. No private vehicles allowed. "You mean he got public tax money to fix his own property in the name of a public event? Plus the profits from contract kickbacks and such? Plus your cannons?" That was about it, I agreed. He had another look through his binoculars.

"As best I can make out, it looks to be a light four-pounder gun, is that about right?" I didn't know. I had once put an apple into its bore, and it was a pretty good fit. "D'you know its weight?" I didn't. It had taken three men to get just the barrel onto a pickup truck. "That's useful to know," he said.

"For what?"

"Getting it back." This was different.

"You mean . . ."

"Getting it back is what I mean."

"Stealing it?"

"Retrieving it, I would say. If you ask it of me, I'll help."

"Mother wouldn't . . ."

"This is not about your mum, or anybody else. It's you and me. But it's your choice. If you want my help getting the inn's cannon back, you've got it. Think it over while you fetch me a tot of rum from that bottle under the settee." Doing that, I was torn between my want for our cannon back, and my fear of what could happen. I pulled out his rum bottle, poured him a tot in a mug, and was about to carry it above, when I took the notion to have a taste of it. It burnt my tongue and throat, but I got some down without gagging.

"From the sour look on you, I reckon you don't like my idea," he said.

"No," I gasped. "I mean, I do. Let's do it. What's the plan?" He regarded me thoughtfully.

"That," he said, "is up to you. I'm just your help." I told him

I wouldn't know where to start. "Well, do it as Sir Francis Drake would have done it." I said I still didn't know. "In that case, you'd better pay rather close attention when I tell you about him. Stand by your jib sheets, and be ready to jibe again." We were rerounding the breakwater and I felt a bit light-headed. The run up the harbour took little time. The next thing I knew we were handling her sails again, then coasting into the cradle at the top of the tide.

"Welcome," said Tom, coming out to help adjust *Merry* between the uprights, so that she could be hauled for the winter work. Then the little boat was winched up and out, hosed down, ready to start drying enough to work on. Tom and the captain examined the hull, agreeing on the places where planking was to be replaced. "We're going to take good care of you, dear girl." He patted her hull with affection.

Our return trip to the inn was on foot, in the last twilight. "He was about your age when he went to sea," said the captain as we walked. "Maybe a year or two younger." I must have looked confused. "I'm speaking of Francis Drake. He was a little chap, considerably smaller than you, I should think, because fully grown, he was quite short. Fierce, though. He had red hair. He was born in Devonshire around 1540, got educated mostly by his father, who taught him the sailor's arts, and navigation. Then he went aboard a trading bark, where he found the life he wanted.

"He learned ship-handling, the movements of wind and currents, forecasting the weather by the look of the clouds, the behaviour of seabirds, the direction of waves set moving by distant winds, the smell of land on a dark night. He learned to pilot his ship by reading from nature's book. By measuring the angle of the sun or a star to the horizon with a cross-staff, he learned to find his latitude on the broad plane of the ocean. And from all his various shipmates and teachers, he learned about sailors, who are quite different from persons who are not sailors, in a number of ways that don't change."

"I don't have my notebook," I reminded him.

"During his first voyage to the West Indies—by now he was a young man—he was given a small vessel under Hawkins, who was an elder among the Queen's Sea Dogs, as she called them. Hawkins, Raleigh, Frobisher, Grenville, Cavendish, Drake, that lot. In any case, your Hawkins chap had been making a tidy profit running African slaves to the Caribbean, where the Spaniards bought them because they needed slaves for their plantations. So that's what Drake was doing there, and peaceably, except the rule came down from His Catholic Majesty King Philip II of Spain, that there would be no more colonial traffic of any kind with the English. Philip wanted all of the profits from his vast empire, y'see, every bit. Think of him as Roy Moehner with a pointy beard, and picture Klaus and his other nephews as conquistadores, his thugs. Did you know, by the way, that they had war dogs to unleash on their enemies?"

"War dogs?"

"Lots of them. They were a standard weapon. In any case, the Spaniards seduced the English into a trap. Having promised safety, they pounced, and in a surprise bit of treachery they decimated the Brits, took most of their ships, killed a lot of Drake's mates, and captured most of the rest. But not Drake. He barely escaped with his ship, and in a desperate condition. Being the master sailor that he was, he got what was left of his crew back from the Mexican Gulf to England. There he learned the fate of his comrades who hadn't made it, and it wasn't a pretty story. The Spaniards tortured some of them, and others they burned alive.

Not one of your more preferable ways of having to depart this earth, I should think, eh?"

"Because they were pirates?"

"No, because they were Protestants, who were regarded by the Holy Inquisition as heretics who therefore could be burned in the name of God. The Protestants, who had a somewhat different version of God, never matched them for studied cruelty, but got in their licks by chopping up a lot of Catholics. Drake was very upset by what the Spaniards had done, and from that time on he devoted his career to making them wish they had been nicer to his shipmates. When he paid his next visit to Spanish America, he had his blood up."

We walked in silence for a while as I dangled, anticipating Drake's revenge. "What did he do?" I asked after what seemed a long time. By now we were approaching the inn under a starry sky.

"That's for after supper, and after the ladies have turned in. It should be your special interest, regarding our project."

"Were you serious about stealing the cannon?" I'd had several misgivings since impulsively going along with the notion.

"If it's as you've told me, the cannon is your property. Your lawyer uncle chap says it is, and if possession is as much of the law as he's told you, it would seem to me to be more a repossession. But it's up to you. I'm just the help."

"Why would you do that?" I couldn't help asking. He shrugged.

"Call it a whim. Also . . ." he paused, "perhaps there will be some odd thing you can do for me some day."

"What if that was something I didn't want to do?"

"Then you wouldn't do it." This seemed all right, but it didn't ease my fears about getting the cannon back.

"Mother . . ." I started to say, but he cut me off.

"You. Not your mother. Or me. Just you. You're on your own about that. Your choice." We arrived at the inn, and our conversation was curtailed.

The captain had started to play his pennywhistle at his table at about the time when Meg finished her evening duties. Tonight, he had a surprise for her, starting with a question as she was clearing his table. "Do you play the violin?"

"I do," she said, wiping down, not looking at him.

"Then, my dear girl, you should have this." He reached under his chair and produced a battered fiddle case, which he opened to reveal a violin. Meg glanced at it, and her eye was captured longer than I think she wanted it to be, before she recovered and went back to the business of wiping down. The captain continued: "It's no use to me, and it's taking up space on *Merry*."

"What price?" she asked him.

"The price? Why the pleasure of your playing it with me this winter, whenever you're inclined. That's all. You mustn't deny our music, whatever you think of me." Meg wiped.

"I'll tell you this, Captain Johnson," she said, engaging him squarely. "I think you're a pack of trouble. You've done some helpful things, and there's nothing I can put my finger on to back up my instinct about you, but friends we are not, and you won't buy me with a fiddle."

"Not you, dear girl, your music. You'll note the instrument comes with no strings." Indeed, it was unstrung. "But there's loops of wire there, waiting to be strung by your good hand, and a pretty good bow."

Meg gazed at him. "The trouble is, who in the name of holy old twist are you?"

"Regard the music," he told her.

"Yes, and you're a clever piper. There's that, too." Her eye was drawn back to the violin. It was a well-used, and much-repaired thing, but it glowed a lustrous orange in the candlelight. "Bargain," she said abruptly, closing the case and taking it away with no backward glance.

"Now Drake," he said, turning to me. "You're him. It's 1571. You've got two ships, a few dozen men, and you've decided to take on the whole Spanish empire, even though your country, England, is not at war with Spain. There's friction, but no war, meaning you're on your own account. You've got no little document from your queen authorising you to do all the things you've got your teeth set to do."

"Meaning," I interjected, "you're a pirate for sure."

"Not me, you. You're Drake. I'm just the chap who's telling you about him. Yes, you are, or are about to become, a pirate. But you are encouraged to do that by your government, which can't officially authorise it, but can and does give you a big wink. Elizabeth does not subscribe to the notion that Spain owns everything it claims, but she can't afford a war. The thing she can do is show Philip the vulnerabilities of his colonial sources of wealth, where the laws of Europe do not apply. In the great imperial chess game, you are a knight."

"But you . . . I, I mean, can also be hanged for piracy."

"Head chopped off, more likely, if it's by your own side, which is preferable to what the other side might do."

"Why would the English punish me for doing what they want me to do?"

"Politics. Knights are sacrificial. Your best chance of getting away with it is in bringing home so much Spanish gold that you're a hero instead of a criminal. If there's enough cash to interest the Queen in taking a big cut, and she does, you're off the hook. If you're empty-handed after making a lot of fuss, your position might be more tenuous. The game has its risks."

"But the law . . ."

"The law has ever been a very fluid thing, seldom immune to injections of money in various, indirect ways. As to money, Spain's galleons brought back emeralds and gold from Peru, silver from Bolivia by the ton, pearls, wealth beyond imagination. They sailed in well-protected convoys, and were difficult to intercept. If you did find one of their flotas at sea, you were going to have a lot of powerful warships shooting quite a lot of cannonballs at you." He paused, seeming reflective. "Jim, can you have any idea of the authority in a ten- or twelve-pound iron ball traveling toward you at several hundred miles per hour? It's quite astonishing. Anything in its way more or less vanishes; if one erupts through a bulwark near you, if it doesn't get you directly, you'll likely catch one or more of the tremendous splinters and fragments it's set flying. Now imagine cannonballs coming at you in truckloads, and you'll find great incentive to avoid the situation. Drake's first rule was: avoid confrontation with a superior force, which I should think you might take into consideration in forming your own plans."

"If you mean the cannon . . ." He cut me off, putting a finger to his lips, glancing toward the kitchen, where Mother was fussing.

"Your mum's better off not knowing, nor anybody at all. No-body. Drake's second rule was secrecy: Never let the enemy know where or when you're going to pounce. The only way to be sure about that is not to tell anybody. Also, in the case of your family, you'll do them all a favour by not involving them. If things go wrong and there's a flap, they're innocent." I told him that some-thing going wrong was my exact worry.

He nodded. "There's always risk. Your Drake chap, however, is quite skillful at minimising that risk, and has a number of important advantages that can be maximised. First, he has the handiest little ships in the world, manned by the best sailors—islanders descended from Norse mariners. The target area is huge and indefensible, with a number of key ports where the Spaniards have to accumulate their treasure, warehousing it until the next flota can take it to Spain. These are the points where you plan to strike. In order to do that, however, you need intelligence. Drake's third rule: You want to know as much about the enemy as you can, being careful not to let him know you're around."

"How?"

"You and the Spaniards aren't the only people in the neigh-bourhood. There are a lot of slaves called Cimarrones, who've escaped their Spanish masters, and have fled to the forests; also there are quite a number of indigenous chaps, native Indians, although not nearly so many as there once were, before they were decimated by the smallpox and other diseases the Europeans brought. Most of those who have survived are no more fond of the Spaniards than the slaves are. Both know the territory, and are glad to help you by telling you everything you want to know about where the enemy's soldiers and ships are deployed, where he's gathering his wealth, how much, and suchlike. Besides being your spies, your local friends supply you with fresh water, victuals, and local pilots who know all about these coasts and their special hazards. You treat these people with great respect.

"Your Drake chap was very good about not being arrogant with native chaps. He was very respectful of them and their ways, trading fairly with them, never threatening them with his powerful weapons, or bullying. Thereby he made friends. His second voyage to the Spanish Main was spent doing that along the Isthmus of Panama, where pack trains of treasure were brought from the Pacific. Look here . . ." My heart sank as he produced from among his papers another map. He had been holding my interest so far with Drake, but I feared another lapse into lecture, and I told him so. I begged him to go back to the way of his Vikings story.

"No time for that right now. Pay attention. Drake shows up on his third voyage and strikes here, working the shallows and taking ships; on his next voyage, he captures Nombre de Dios, a treasure town, with thirty-two men, and raids the trail to Panama, where it's only sixty miles from ocean to ocean."

For the next half hour, I was led through a detailed analysis of Drake's strategies, tactics, and further rules. These included the rule of surprise and flexibility (whatever your plan, don't get married to it); the rule of extracting yourself quickly after the fact, and finally the rule of justification (that is, how much money you brought home).

"How much did he bring home?"

"Enough, and he was only getting started. And now you know enough about him to tell me how he would go about getting your cannon if he wanted to take it."

I had been thinking of little else. Quite unexpectedly I was Drake, and my blood was up, too. I said it would have to be done by water, because the base of the peninsula was inhabited by hostile forces—not just Klaus and Grendel, but other Moehners and more dogs, all hunters. The nearest of their houses was only a five-minute walk from the park, where the cannon was in plain view over open ground. It would have to be done at night without arousing anybody, especially the dogs. We could use my own fifteen-foot boat, *Annabelle,* a legacy from my grandfather, now floating at our dock until Tom found time to haul her out for the winter. She was an open boat with a full build, and would carry the cannon barrel. The thing I didn't know was how just the two of us could hope to get the cannon over its parapet and down into the boat, considering that we couldn't even lift it.

"I noticed there's a flagpole right behind it, just a few feet away. How many feet?" We worked out this calculation to his satisfaction, and he reckoned a simple cargo boom could be rigged to it with blocks and tackles. The cellar was piled with old tackle blocks, spars, coils of line—everything needed. He had other questions as we both pored over his chart showing the Moehners' peninsula and, before I knew it, we had a complete plan.

Here I became nervous again. "When do you want to do it?" I half hoped the season was too late for the adventure.

"Not me, you; when do *you* want to do it? I'm just assisting here, and you keep forgetting that. If we get caught, I'm going to tell everybody that you asked me to help you retrieve your cannon, and that I was doing it as a favour. So go ahead and ask me."

I hesitated, and he read my mind.

"You're worried that if something goes wrong, there'll be a big fuss, with your getting into all kinds of trouble, embarrassing your family, getting me nicked too, maybe deported, leaving my poor *Merry* high and dry." He sighed. "Those are reasonable fears, especially with a police chief who'll wring us any way he can, and a magistrate who'll back him up, and no way your Corporal MacMaster chap can help. You've come up with a pretty good plan here, but plans do go wrong. In fact, they almost always do. So maybe you'd like to have a little think about that while I go to the loo, and you fetch me another rum."

This I did, again having a nip of it on my own. It seemed a manly thing to do.

"Will you help get our cannon back?"

"I'd be delighted," he smiled. "Thought you'd never ask." His tone became abrupt. "Now the work starts. There's a number of rusty blocks I've got to get greased so they don't squeak in the night, then rig 'em up with a boom. I'll need simple tools and that key to the cellar. You'll need to make *Annabelle* ready to sail, and not be conspicuous about it. Grease her rowlocks. We'll need a dim torch, meaning a red bulb for it from the marine supplies place. You'll do that?"

"Good night," said Mother, emerging from her kitchen, looking pleased that I was so engaged in my history lesson.

"Good night," I said, fearing for a moment she was going to come over and kiss me; I turned to stir the fire, and she did not. The fire crackled.

"Now that we're on our plan," the captain said when Mother had left, "we'll see what the weather has in mind for us. We'll hope for a calm night, preferably overcast with mist. That would be the best, but maybe we'll get back-to-back storms, snow, who knows? Anyway, it'll take us a day to prepare; after that, we should be ready. Are we together? Good. Then let's shake hands on it, and vow our loyalty to one another, as shipmates on our own account. Together." We did so, and my hand felt very small inside his.

"Welcome to the Brotherhood," he said.

6

The Night Raid

It was a calm night, overcast and misty from sea rime that blanketed the water with a haze. We were ready to go, and this space between winter gales was our moment. "The gods have smiled upon us," said the captain softly as I tended the fire. It was Saturday supper, with enough customers to keep Meg and Mother from noticing my nervousness as I went about my duties. The captain had his meal, then submerged himself in the intricacy of his macramé work. Robin paid his usual visit, stopping by his table for a cordial word, and afterward Tom visited for the duration of a beer. I tended the fire constantly, in order to be near the captain's table.

"Stop hovering," he told me when nobody was looking our way. "Take a deep breath, let it out, and do it again. It's just an ordinary night. We won't speak anymore. I'll meet you aboard *Annabelle* at midnight. Dress warmly."

Around 10:00 P.M. there was another impromptu concert with Meg and her new fiddle, to which the captain played an accompaniment, again to warm applause. Cleanup was finished soon after the departure of the last customer, and all turned in, including the captain with a conspicuous yawn.

Half an hour later we met, two dark figures on a darkened dock, me with my teeth chattering, not entirely because of the cold. Few words were spoken as we cast off and set sail in a light breeze. We had rehearsed in detail everything we were going to do, all under the cover of history lessons, and now we were doing it, ever so silently. The loom of the darkened inn vanished as *Annabelle* ghosted into the night and mist. Our touchstone to the universe was our little compass, dimly illuminated by the shaded, red flashlight. Above all, our objective was to be seen by nobody. I held the tiller while the captain navigated, which was just as well. I had sailed around our point in and out of the bay innumerable times, but never when I could not see around me. This was different.

"Come starboard a point," said the captain, "and set up to come about." There were rocks to both sides, invisible, but close, which was a scarier way of navigating this familiar place than Grandfather had shown me. "Now, put your helm alee."

I pushed the tiller to leeward, and *Annabelle* pivoted in her referenceless universe, a dancer through dangers known but unseen. "There's no light at all—none," I said.

"It's perfect," said he. "Now set up to come about again, and make us a rhumb line for the landing." I plotted our compass course, with allowances for current. My mentor checked my calculations, approved them, took the tiller, and sent me forward to keep a lookout ahead. It was a lonely position. I would have been more comfortable next to him. I reckoned that in this breeze we would have no more than a half-hour's sail to where we were going, creeping through the darkness; I peered into it and thought my thoughts, and it was a long half-hour.

"What's our depth of water?" asked the captain, clicking on the flashlight to look at the chart. I unhitched the lead line, and heaved it as I had been taught, swinging its lead weight to fall in the path of the boat, letting the line uncoil through my fingers, feeling for the markers and the spot where it hit the bottom under us.

"Only two fathoms," I said, hauling the dripping line back aboard.

"We're there." As he said it, the shore loomed in front of us, a close presence, enemy territory. But which way from where we wanted to be? On which side of our target had we landed?

"I would say either to the right or to the left. What do you think?" I could not guess. "What's your nose for it?"

"Uh . . ."

"Never mind thinking; what was your first impulse?"

"Right. Starboard."

He put the helm up. "Starboard it is. Out oars." And so we rowed, skirting a shore we could better hear than see, by the lapping of the surf. Just as I was becoming sure we were going the wrong way, a short promontory loomed in front of us, and we were there. I jumped ashore with a line, took another from the stern, and together we positioned our craft under the cannon's parapet.

The next business was to unlash the twenty-foot spar that the captain had picked up from the cellar and fashioned into a boom. It was five feet longer than *Annabelle,* sticking out in front like a bowsprit, and was heavy enough to make a clatter as we hoisted it off the boat and over the parapet. A lone dog barked in the distance, barked a second time, and then all was silence again. Every movement we made seemed to be several times louder than necessary.

Here in the darkness was the cannon, and the flagpole near it, about where we had calculated. We lifted the boom parallel to the pole, and put on a lashing to hold it in place while I climbed onto the captain's shoulders with the double tackle he had prepared to lift the boom. I attached it with rolling hitches, just as I had rehearsed. Then its foot had to be secured to the base. Without so much as a creak, we positioned it over the cannon, grasping its barrel with a sling. Its trunnion caps, securing it to the wood carriage, were detachable, freeing the barrel to be lifted with a second tackle. It all seemed to take forever.

"Handsomely now," said the captain, starting to haul on the lift tackle as I tailed on. Anybody who is aware of the power of a two-part tackle will understand how an elderly man and a boy could lift a cannon weighing more than three hundred pounds. As we did so, however, the old spar we were using for a boom let out a sharp cracking noise as it took the strain. The wood held, but again the dog barked, this time not stopping.

"Steady," said the captain, adjusting the position of the dangling gun over the boat. Another dog picked up the barking, and then another. "Now we'll lower it," he pronounced after what seemed an eternity. I did this rather too precipitously. The gun fell heavily onto *Annabelle*'s thwarts, with a noise that got even more dogs barking, until their din was alarming. Somewhere in the distance a door slammed.

"Steady, steady," said the captain, making a last adjustment, then going down into the boat to lash the gun into place. The barking intensified. "Look smart," he said, returning, "and hold the light while I get this boom gear unrigged and back aboard." As we both worked by the dim ray of our hooded flashlight to unrig the boom, the barking of the dogs became louder.

"They've been loosed," I said, "and they're coming for us fast."

"Quite. I'm afraid you're right. Leave this. Get in the boat, and smartly." I didn't need any further encouragement. Casting off the bowline, I jumped on board *Annabelle;* the captain, freeing her stern, was right behind me. "This is what's known as your fast extraction," he said, taking up his pair of oars. The first dog on the scene looked like it was going to try to jump aboard, but the beast hesitated for just the moment we needed to push off and pull into the night.

"We're free!" I exclaimed, my heart pounding.

"Not quite. We've left our gear, and we're not yet out of range of a strong light if somebody comes out here to look around." On the beach, an unknown number of dogs barked and barked. A light appeared, distant at first, coming closer. Noiselessly, we eased *Annabelle* farther into the mist. There were voices. No . . . one voice, somebody talking to the dogs, calling them home. The barking petered out, and the light receded without probing.

"What would Drake do now?" the captain inquired, resting on his oars.

"Wait until the enemy goes back to sleep, then sneak in and get the stuff we left?"

"Quite. I reckon we should give it a half hour out here, lay-

90

ing off, staying warm as best we can, perhaps by thinking about California."

"California?"

"Spanish California, and points south. Here resumeth the lesson. The Pacific is where your Drake chap wants to strike next." He had done this to me earlier, this kind of sudden swerve into a story from where we were at the moment. Listening to the captain reminded me of the time Burt Amos had let me ride his mare. After a lesson or two, I was able to stay in the saddle, and even let her gallop, which was happening when she took a sudden—very sudden—turn toward her barn, although I had meant to keep going straight down the road. In fact, I did keep going in that direction, but only briefly before fetching up in some thorny bushes. Keeping my seat with the captain's rides had that quality.

"Are you with me?" he asked, in the darkness.

"Where Drake strikes next." I was.

"Good. What was bad was Spain's defence of her American west coast, although that was where most of the treasure was coming from. The problem was getting there. The cold we're in here would be a warm day off Cape Horn, which you had to go around if you wanted to sail from the Atlantic to the Pacific."

Before I knew it I was bucking horrendous seas into the teeth of unrelenting westerly storms, with ships that were playthings of the wind and waves, proceeding with wrong charts through an area my mentor called the rocky cauldron of the angry gods.

"With three ships, you make it around into the Pacific, only to be blown back again by a storm, a great-grandfather of storms. In the words of Drake's nephew . . ." He quoted:

*"The winds were such as if the bowels of the earth had
set all at liberty, or as if all the clouds under heaven had*

been called together to lay their force upon that one place. The seas, which by nature and of themselves are heavy, and of a weightie substance, were rowled up from the depths, even from the roots of the rockes . . . exceeding the tops of high and loftie mountains."

He delivered this as though the archaic language was his native tongue, and instead of drifting on flat water, I found myself manning a pump aboard *Golden Hind,* as my ship lurched and plunged in a howling tempest.

"You sail through the Strait of Magellan with three ships. You watch one swallowed up by the storm, and another turn tail for home. Surviving, *Golden Hind* at last breaks through into the Pacific. Now you have a yachting holiday, sailing north with ever-warming, favourable breezes that are perfect for surprise visits to Spanish ports and shipping. No enemy has ever been seen on these shores, and you keep moving, never staying long enough to let word get ahead of your arrival. Your ship is faster than anything in the neighbourhood, because the Spanish vessels here are locally built, not for speed, but for carrying cargo. You are having a marvelous time. In one place, you see a whole pack train loaded with gold and silver, go ashore and get it, and move on. Farther along, you catch up with an undefended ship loaded with twenty-six tons of Peruvian silver ingots, among other things.

"With all of this loaded into *Golden Hind*'s belly, plus the plate, bags of gold and gems, and jewelery you've looted, at last your ship will hold no more; there's only the job of getting it all home. You can't go back the way you came. You've left quite a lot of very angry Spanish chaps in your wake who are now fully alert and waiting for you. If you make it through that lot, there's Cape Horn again. Now what do you do?"

"Uh ..."

"Well, think about it later." He checked his watch again, listening. "Let's think about getting our own cargo home, as soon as we've got our gear back." We took up our oars and again pulled for the enemy shore.

Ever so quietly we landed, unrigged the boom, loading it and its tackle back aboard *Annabelle,* leaving the Moehners their gun carriage. Like wraiths in the night, we were then gone, back into the mist, where I raised sail for the reach home.

"Your decision?" He picked up his story as though there had been no interruption. I had to make room in my brain—which was boiling with what we were still going through—for Drake's predicament. I had no idea.

"Well, you go north, as far as you can, hoping there is a north-west passage around America, but when you get past Northern California, the prevailing winds are still in your teeth, and that's out. Your ship needs work and provisions, so you find a place to beach her near what is now San Francisco, and immediately make friends with the native locals. Again, you are very good about this. Also, you take people of all races into your crew, making no distinction, and you require officers to work shoulder-to-shoulder with common sailors. You are a great egalitarian, a true liberal. Also, you make a point of never killing any enemy who surrenders, and treating prisoners with courtesy. These things are very unusual, and much remarked on. You have in your crew a full chamber orchestra. They play courtly music for dinners and ceremonies, with a lot of krummhorns."

During the next quarter-hour, *Golden Hind* reached across the whole, broad Pacific, felt her way through treacherous and uncharted waters to the Indian Ocean, rounded Africa and sailed back to England after a three-year, fifty-thousand-mile circumnavigation, with the greatest haul of loot in anybody's experience.

"How much?"

"Nobody rightly knows. It's hard to measure in today's terms, but historians reckon it about equivalent to the annual income of the British government at the time. Be still." This last remark was in a low tone. "Do you hear that?" I heard only the lapping of wavelets as *Annabelle* loafed through the night. "Let's get down her sails," said the captain, "and stand by oars." When I had furled the sails, my ear picked up what he had heard, the low, rhythmic growl of a vessel's engine, somewhere in the mist ahead.

I had no idea what boat might be out in the cold, moonless wee hours of a Sunday morning, or which way it was going, or why. I hurriedly started to ship my oars. "Do nothing until it passes," the captain stopped me. "Just wait." Everything, our entire plan, hinged on not being seen by anybody. We waited. The engine noise receded, and we began to row. "Things by night never seem to go out of fashion," he commented.

There was nothing wrong with the captain's navigation, because the first shoreline we came to was the breakwater. Ten minutes later, *Annabelle* was alongside our dock, and we were again rigging the boom, this time to her own mast. Here was less distance to hoist the gun—onto a sturdy wooden sled that the captain had made to receive it. It had drag ropes by which we were able to skid it down the dock, then attach a tackle to drag it up the steps without making too much noise, and to the end of the service drive, in plain sight where delivery trucks dropped things off.

"There's that," muttered the captain, when we had levered

the gun off the skid. Then there was the boom and its tackle to put back into storage, and *Annabelle* to secure as though she had never been out, and the sled to dispose of, until 4:00 A.M. had come and gone, by the captain's watch.

"Now we'll turn in," he said, cautioning me to be up on time and ready for church. "And try to look bright-eyed, not like somebody who's been up most of the night."

L ust is not limited to the flesh," Reverend Corkum enunciated. The Reverend was still embedded in the seven sins, devoting a full sermon to each of them, week after week, and I went almost immediately to sleep. I had gone to sit next to Jenny, who was with her parents, and I told her to help me stay awake. This she was unable to accomplish, but she did keep me propped up, and nudged me for prayers and hymns. The captain sang with the choir with good aplomb, and after the services joined us again for the family's Sunday dinner.

The immediate topic of conversation was the discovery of our cannon, first noticed by Robin while wheeling in Aunt Karen. "Who brought it?" he asked. Mother's surprise was real, and Meg's. Nobody knew. It was a big mystery. Everybody in the family was very aware of the entire cannon incident; all had largely given it up for lost, and here it was, returned anonymously, raising many questions. Why had the Moehners brought it back without telling us? Why had they brought it back at all? After some speculation, there was a consensus as to the most likely explanation, which was that one of the Moehners who didn't like Roy brought it back to us just to tweak his tail. When the Moehners didn't have a feud going outside the family, they were famous for feuding with each other. Robin questioned when a truck could have come in through the inn's gates, opening and closing them without anybody hearing it. Nobody could say, not knowing how long the old barrel could have been lying there unnoticed. It was not all that conspicuous, with its grey-green colour.

"We are assuming it came by truck . . ." Robin started a thought, but was interrupted by the captain, who had listened politely to the conversation without comment. "Is it permitted for me to know what the situation is with this cannon? Or is it family business?" Robin, hastening to mind his manners, briefed our guest as to what everybody had been talking about. The captain listened attentively, with a bare glance at me, hearing again the story I had told him.

"It sounds like it's your cannon," he said to Mother, "and whatever providence is at work here, it would seem possession puts the law back on your side, eh?" This put a cap on the subject of the cannon, pending further revelations, but the conversation had another twist in it.

"Captain Johnson," said Aunt Karen, as he was just finishing his dessert.

"Madam?"

"Captain Charles Johnson?"

"Yes, Madam?"

"In checking for your writings through the library, I have come up with a curiosity." She produced a book, opened it to the title page, and displayed it to him: *"A General History Of The Robberies And Murders Of The Most Notorious Pirates,"* it read; "by Captain Charles Johnson." Aunt Karen cocked an eye at him. "We see this is a 1926 reprint, by Dodd, Mead and Company, New York, of a very much older work, 1724 to be exact."

"Yes. Quite," said the captain, engaged with his apple crisp. Aunt Karen pressed on.

"This edition opens with an editor's note. May I quote?"

"Please," said the captain, munching.

"'Nothing is known of Captain Charles Johnson: the name may even be an assumed one. All that can be stated with any certainty is that in 1724 a small octavo volume appeared, entitled *A General History Of The Robberies And Murders Of The Most Notorious Pirates* . . . by Captain Charles Johnson. Nor, beyond a general remark in the Preface, is there any hint of the sources whence the author got his information; that he was accurate, even to the smallest particular, is attested by every English or American historian who has had occasion to corroborate his stories from other sources . . .' and it goes on." Aunt Karen regarded him with a quizzical smile.

"Yes," he nodded, dabbing his lips with his napkin. "Johnson. He is the cornerstone source for any study of English pirates of the early eighteenth century. He was not totally accurate. It's ready for a corrected edition. But he knew more about the pirates of his time than anybody; that's something all the historians have agreed about, and will agree about all the more in future years, as more evidence comes to light."

"What is your relationship?"

"He is my teacher. One of them. Also Anson, Dampier,

Esquemeling, plus others. How do I come to have the same name and occupation? I would have to ask, why anything?" A smile. "Madam, I have no officially known record of a relationship to this two-hundred-year-old author."

"I've read it," said Aunt Karen, leafing through the pages, "and given it some thought, and my own view is that this Captain Johnson could not possibly have known as much about the pirates of his time as he did, and in such intimate detail, unless he was one of their brotherhood."

"Hmmm," said the captain, pondering the thought.

Aunt Karen continued: "He was a sailor. No doubt about that. I used to sail, once, and I've read the logs and journals of Johnson's time, and he writes in a seaman's language. He is genuine. Nor was he a pseudonym for Daniel Defoe, as some have suggested. I have read all of Defoe, and he is not this Captain Johnson." The captain nodded. " So, who do you think he was?"

"I would not presume to guess. I would say a knowledgeable chap in his field who wished to be anonymous." He excused himself, and went upstairs where he slept until suppertime.

The following week was a nervous one for me. In town, Christmas lights began to sprout around the stores, and I was set to making wreaths. Day-by-day, I expected a visit from Chief Moehner and his big nephews. Or something. Robin told us he had officially logged the anonymous delivery of the cannon, as discovered by himself, and his report got no comment that he knew about.

"Why is there no rumpus about it?" I asked the captain, when we had a moment to ourselves around midweek. On his advice, we had been avoiding each other.

"Nobody knows what happened, not even the Moehners. They think no one except themselves had access to it. They're probably trying to figure out which one of them drove out there and got it, and why, and family politics, and it's likely occupying a lot of dinner conversation. But what can they do about it?" He ruminated. "I think it would be good to make a proper carriage for the gun, using its original ironwork, and mount it on the inn's deck."

On Thursday, Uncle Bill notified the court that the disputed cannon had been returned, presumably by the borrower, arguing that the point was now moot. "They can drag this thing out," he advised Mother, "but now the shoe is on the other foot, and I would say you have your cannon back. Who do you suppose delivered it?"

On Friday night, the captain and Meg made music again, this time with customers clearing aside chairs and a table so that they could dance, and we didn't close until midnight.

On Saturday, while running errands, I saw the captain in conversation with Noel Nauss. This was disturbing. For the past two weeks, I had seen my new mentor talking to all kinds of people. He had spent considerable time chatting up Becky Bushnell, the head lady at the post office, and he had gotten two haircuts from George D'Autrement, hanging out to converse with the usual group that frequented George's barbershop. I had even seen him telling jokes to Klaus Moehner in the Sou'wester Beverage Room, but none of his diversions had been as surprising as his apparent interest in Noel Nauss.

Nobody talked to Noel Nauss. Noel was a logger with the physical qualities of a Sherman tank, and a similar temperament. It is not that he was a bad person as such. Indeed, he had his own notions of morality, which were usually correct, and he went to church; but he lived alone, and was given to great rages if his sense of balance was upset. The one thing that nobody in town wanted to do was trigger this delicate mechanism in Noel, and the best way not to do that, all had learned, was to avoid him.

Not even the police, or anybody in their right mind, wanted to take on Noel when he was upset. Recreationally, Noel lifted small automobiles by their rear ends as you or I would lift a book. Notoriously, he had once demolished Jeff Moehner's garage because there was a dogfight there, with betting. Noel liked animals better than people, judging by the number of men he sent to the county hospital that night. He would have gotten into a lot of trouble, except the cops had an excuse to leave him alone because it was an illegal event to start with. "He would have been a handful to bring in," was Robin's remark about the incident. I thought it prudent to warn the captain about Noel, but he showed no sign of having heard me.

"What do you think of having a Christmas concert?" he asked, first to me and then the family at Sunday dinner. It turned out to be an idea to which he had given some thought.

"You mean," said Meg, "music by just you and me?"

"And the choir, if they care to come, and perhaps another fiddler or two you might know. I'll bet we can pack the place." Everybody liked the idea, even Meg, and especially Mother. Mother was never happier than when putting together a special event, and there hadn't been one since the funereal reception for Floyd Watson's family the previous spring, a very subdued occasion.

"We'll need to give the place a good cleaning," she fussed, "and get all the old chairs out. How many people do you think might come?" And so the planning began. Later that Sunday I heard the end of Drake, by the fire.

"Elizabeth knighted him for what he had done, even though it helped to destroy what was left of her relationship with Philip of Spain, leading eventually to war. Drake sailed for the West Indies again, now with twenty-five ships, ravaging the Caribbean with great success. Philip had had enough, and started gathering a great armada of ships intended to carry the soldiers it would take to invade England, capture it, and reinstate Catholicism—making the whole annoying island a reasonable place again in his view. The port where the expedition was being put together was Cadiz, and the process took long enough to be well known to Elizabeth. She unleashed Drake on the operation.

"Again, his tactic was total surprise. There he was all of a sudden, with a fleet sailing right into Cadiz Harbour, under its very guns, with a whole night in which to burn everything he could get at. That was a lot. Besides ships and supplies, he torched all the cured barrel staves that had been accumulated to build the kegs to hold the water and salt meat that the armada would need for its thousands of sailors, soldiers, and officers. Then he sailed out again and went home. The raid delayed the Spanish invasion of England by a year, and when it did come, it faced an enemy that was fully prepared.

"The rest is history. Into the English Channel sailed the proud Spanish armada under Medina Sidonia in overwhelming force, with Drake and his colleagues nibbling at their edges. The Spanish—we called them the Dons—headed for Flanders to pick up an army under the Duke of Alba, but the English kept at them, nibbling, then sending blazing hulks drifting into their anchorage at Gravelines—Drake's idea—so that they had to make sail again in confusion and were dispersed. After that, the English could take them one by one. Also, all the Spaniards by this time had the squitters because their provisions were casked in uncured barrels since Drake had burned Cadiz. On top of that, the wind was southwest, so they couldn't get back to Spain without sailing first around the northern tip of Scotland, and then south around Ireland. There they were battered by storms and many were driven ashore. And that's where we'll leave off with Drake. He made another, last voyage to the Caribbean, where he died of a fever in 1598. But the Spanish ships of the armada that went down off Ireland are where we should pause, until your friend Jenny can come back. When does she plan to come back?" he asked.

I fumbled, trying to tell him her visit was more or less a one-time thing, and that she would not be back.

"Hmmm," he said, groping in his pocket, bringing out an envelope, folded a number of times. He opened it fold by fold, extracting another fold of cotton, which he laid gently open to reveal a single gold link, clipped open, apparently one piece of a golden chain. "Give this to Mistress MacGregor, and tell her that it is a fragment of the treasure of Grace O'Malley, who was the pirate queen of Ireland, as she's known to history. Tell her if she wants to know any more about this trinket, she should be on hand Sunday, eight bells sharp. That's 4:00 P.M. to her. Now let us rest."

7

Of Queens and Princes

ew of us got much rest over the next week, or for a while to come. True winter descended with a southeaster that clung for days, and the last of the boats were hauled out before the annual freeze, including Klaus's boat. I was again on Grendel alert, taking my different routes to and from school, and to town. I had more errands than usual because of the preparations for the inn's Christmas concert now in the works, scheduled for Boxing Day, less than three weeks hence.

"We've got a lot of things to do before then," said Mother, issuing orders right and left, pressing everyone in sight into service. Besides multiple errands, I got the assignment of making posters.

Meg's job was rounding up the musicians, which she did right away. She got hold of Jason McGridley, who was the oldest and best fiddler around, who said he would come with his guitarist and flutist and niece (who was a good step dancer), if Meg would sing with them. She would. She also recruited the First Anglican Church choir, some of whom had worked up a couple of numbers on their own time that they couldn't present in church. She even got a promise from Tapping Tim MacCurdy to come and play a set, and he was passing famous.

"That sounds like enough to make a draw," the captain commented, finishing a draft of the story he had composed for the *Baywater Beacon*. "Admiral Anson Inn Christmas Concert," he read the title to us. "In a musical celebration of the season, the oldest continuing establishment in the province will host an afternoon and evening of music and dance by a rare gathering of talent. This includes . . ."—here everybody on the program was named—an impressive list. The event would begin at three o'clock and proceed through suppertime, when there would be a ticket charge at the door; food and beverages would be served; no reservations. The notice had an added emphasis that this was a chance to hear good music live and sit close to the performers, which was even better than television.

"The way I see it," said Mother, "if just one person comes to hear every person who's performing, we'll have a full house. And there'll be more, meaning we'll have to open the whole room." This had not been done in years; with a diminishing clientele, the inn's public rooms had been closed down, except for the dining room around the bar. Tables and chairs were there, but everything needed a cleaning blitz, and there were boxes of long disused tableware and glasses to be found and cleaned.

Whether or not the event could make enough money to make

up our next payment was questionable, but it did give us a fighting chance. Meg had put the word out to the performers that this was going to be a benefit gig on their part, because the inn was struggling. All of the musicians were easy with that, and glad to help. So were Bertha Hirtle, Becky Eisnor, and several other ladies from the Women's Auxiliary who volunteered to come over and wait tables or do whatever else was needed. Folks around Grey Rocks knew about the inn's struggle and the Moehner plan to modernise the place, and nobody much wanted it to change. The captain chuckled. "You're Drake," he said to me aside, "and you've got the native chaps on your side." This threw me.

"We *are* the native chaps," I prompted him.

"Exactly. Drake sails in and meets the locals the same way your family did when they bought this place. You're from away, but made friends, and here you are to everybody's benefit, under Philip II, his regime. However, being polite people, nobody wants to voice it just like that."

"You mean Roy Moehner?"

"Quite. He's city hall here."

"Which is what you can't fight," I reflected.

"I'd say you've made a rather good start, Sir Francis. What about Klaus's dog, have you seen anything of him?" I had not. "Don't let your guard down," he advised me, "about that or any other little thing. Now, fetch me my pennywhistle. I must say," he grouched, "Meg has some new twists on some very old tunes, and she makes me learn 'em her way, y'see. Ah well, it keeps me young, I suppose, except I've got a lot of practicing to do for this bloody concert." I started to remind him that the concert was his own idea, but he seemed a bit grouty, so I got him his tin flute and went to work on the posters. Later, Meg and the captain played for two hours, the same tunes over and over, so that I learned them too from afar.

Sunday services were given largely to Avarice, and Sunday dinner to endless discussion of the concert. The *Baywater Beacon* had printed the captain's story much as he had written it, and there had been a number of encouraging responses. When the subject of the cannon came up, Robin could report nothing at all, except that Chief Moehner had remarked that he would personally look into it. A week after the cannon's remarkable return, nobody had come forward with any knowledge about it. I avoided looking at the captain. Aunt Karen did not.

"Captain," she said, "I thought it might amuse you to know that I have come up with another Charles Johnson, a playwright who wrote a drama called, let's see . . . I've made a note . . ."

"Called *The Successful Pirate*," the captain snorted, "which ran on Drury Lane in 1713, a piece of claptrap. The man knew nothing about pirates. He was a hack plagiarist who was contemptuously fat, and spent a good deal of his life at Buttons' Coffee House, drinking cheap wine with a lot of honey in it, and eating mounds of pastry. If he had ever styled himself 'captain' they would have laughed him out of the place."

Aunt Karen blinked. "I do not understand, then, how this Captain Johnson could have written what he did and just vanished without any trace."

"You're not the first," the captain said.

hen Sunday lesson time arrived, I again went to the gate to meet Jenny, whose reluctance had been overcome by her curiosity about the golden link to a pirate queen. Her entrance was stormy. She fairly leapt from the car when her mother pulled up to drop her off, slamming the door with tears in her eyes. Jenny was in an embattled period with her parents, particularly her mother, over what she considered her overprotectiveness.

"I can't even go to the library alone!" she fumed. "Nowhere. They're so afraid something will happen to me. So nothing ever happens to me."

Inside, the captain was by his fire, this time with no pointer, tweed, book, or map in sight, just his macramé, and a warm greeting for Jenny.

"I'm so pleased you've come back," he beamed.

"What is this?" Jenny asked, producing the link. She had found a little jewellery box for it. The captain insisted she hold it in her hand, close her eyes, and just feel it.

"I've already done that," she said.

"And did you feel the presence of Granuaile in it?" He pronounced it "Gran-you-ale." Jenny looked uncertain. "You should have done, because it's from a chain she wore, a Spanish chain, brought to her by a nobleman. He was a survivor from one of the galleons that went onto the rocks of her coast in the great gale that wrecked much of the armada there, after Drake and his friends had done with it. Jim here is Drake, by the way, so let's let you be her, Grace O'Malley, daughter of Dubhdara, who was chieftain of Murrisk, and descended from the old kings. He was a very good sailor. All of the O'Malleys were, along with their friends the Burkes and the O'Flahertys, and they ruled the coasts in much the same way that modern nations do. That is, they patrolled their inshore waters and regulated the coastal shipping according to their laws. They provided local pilots for a price, taxed vessels, or took them if they were deemed enemies."

Jenny commented that that sounded reasonable enough. He nodded.

"They thought so, too, but it was all very informal. You captured a ship, decided how much of what they were carrying was yours, and took it. Simple as that. You were in your own waters. The only difference these days is, when a government confiscates a ship, or a cargo, there's a lot of paperwork, eh?" Jenny asked where the piracy was in that.

"The English had a different view about who should control Ireland. I don't have a map with me today, but if you look at one, you'll see how the western approaches of England—its connections with all oceans—are dominated by Ireland. In Drake's time, Queen Elizabeth was pressing to take Catholic Ireland in very much the same way Philip of Spain wanted Protestant England: to get rid of it as a nuisance, and absorb it into the empire.

"Elizabeth was crafty. Noticing that the Irish clans were constantly fighting each other over this or that, she picked a side and sent forces to help her new Irish ally defeat his enemy. This she did again and again, until the English began to get control, but not over the coasts and unmapped mountains of Mayo and Connaught, where Granuaile grew up. When she was about your age, her father took her to sea with him. Do you like to sail?"

"I want to," sighed Jenny, "but my mother won't let me go out in boats. My mother won't let me do anything," she added.

"Well, here's your chance, because you've got a father who dotes on you, and is pleased and proud that his daughter shows such an aptitude as a sailor. As chieftain, he controls many ships, from deep-sea vessels to small, oared sailing boats that are directly descended from Viking craft, with little change and the same sweet double-ended form. You learn how to handle them all. He takes you to Spain and other places; you experience the freedom of the sea, its demands, and how to handle a crew. You learn everything that Drake learned, except you are a girl." A smile. "And Irish.

"And you grow into a very handsome girl indeed, by all accounts: 'with a most feminine appearance,' according to an English governor who is one of the many who are taken with you. You have dark eyes, and black hair, after your father. *Dubhdara* means "black oak." Portraits of your descendants will show beautiful women with these features. You are taught to read and write in Latin, and trained in the arts of politics and war. You do have a brother, but he becomes a piper, and you're the one who takes on your father's role when he dies."

"I never marry," pronounced Jenny.

"On the contrary, when you're sixteen you marry an O'Flaherty chieftain's son, Donal, called 'Donal of the battles' after his main interest. But he's no sailor. While he's off to war, which is usually, you are in charge of thousands of people, various fortresses, and a lot of ships. You get to know him well enough to bear him two sons and a daughter. When he is killed in one of his fights with some neighbours, you muster your forces and save the day. Now you're on your own, and your legend begins."

"I will never remarry," pronounced Jenny.

"Mistress MacGregor," the captain cranked her back into the present, "if you want to be Granuaile, leave your mind open for surprises. I'm not making this up. Now I'm ready for another rum," this to me. I got it for him, and had a nip, out of sight behind the bar, a bit more than previously. The captain cocked an eye at me as I returned. Jenny was impatient to get on with it.

"What do I do?"

"You fall in love," said the captain, with a look of great softness. "With . . . ?"

"A shipwrecked and half-drowned young mariner you find in the surf and nurse back to health. Your love is brief. He is murdered by the neighbouring clansmen from the Isle of Doona. You attack, rout their stronghold, put your lover's murderers to the sword, and add the place to your own holdings. Hereafter you are called the Dark Lady of Doona. You are also called Grace of the Gamblers, because you gamble with your men. All the O'Malleys are great gamblers, none more than you, in your castle at Clare Isle. It is well placed as a raider's lair, commanding the coastal sea-lane, and the entrance to Clew Bay. Below your walls is an anchorage well sheltered from the westerly gales, with a beach where your Norse galleys, like their Viking forebears, can be dragged up in case of an easterly, or for work." He lit his pipe, sighing.

"The place looks much the same today, except your little castle is roofless now. The O'Malleys still gather in the pub, which is the one commercial establishment on Clare Isle, where your tomb is. Today, they like to play poker. But I digress."

"How old am I now?" Jenny asked.

"Around thirty, and you do get married again, this time to a war chieftain of the Burke clan known as Iron Richard after the armour he wears around much of the time. Another soldier. There's something about him that niggles you, because you lock him out of your castle when he straggles home after a campaign. Standing high above him on the battlements, you pronounce the words of divorce according to ancient Irish law: 'I dismiss you.' You say it three times, and there you are, divorced."

"I shall never again permit him in my presence," said Jenny.

"Well, you do, because you afterward bear him a son, Theobold of the Ships as he'll be known, who you deliver at sea in primitive circumstances while on a trading voyage to Spain. The next day, while you're nursing your infant, your vessel is attacked by Turkish pirates. The ships close and clash, hulls grinding together. It soon appears the enemy is getting the upper hand over your people, so you gently place Theobold in his berth, snatch up a loaded firearm, and plunge above, yelling in a fury at your men: 'Can't you do without me for even a day?' It shames them as Irishmen. They rally, slaying their enemies, capturing their ship.

"England is not so easy to deal with. Elizabeth is outflanking you on land, encroaching on your own territory, making chieftain after Irish chieftain take the vow of loyalty that she wants from everybody in exchange for her authorised title to their own lands. Your response is to step up raids on English shipping in and out of Galway. This is when the English brand you a pirate."

"But . . ." said Jenny.

"Never mind the whys of it. There you are. A pirate, a wanted woman. You are captured, taken by surprise, imprisoned, no freedom, bad food, disrespectful treatment. A new and unwelcome experience, eh? Over the months, you see three other rebel prisoners led to their executions for smaller offences than yours, and you're waiting for your turn. So you bargain. There are times for that, and this is one. You've been behind bars for a year and a half, and your prospects are not good. You make a formal submission to the English so that they will release you, letting you regroup against this new force that is threatening everything you have ever come to love. What do you do next?"

"Fight on," said Jenny.

"And so you do, humouring your enemy while building your clan's strength; also building a network of beacons around Clew Bay. They alert you in your new castle at Carrickahowley to the traffic on your coast. Again, you're a threat. And you're really on your own, because your second husband has died. Now the English march in force into your domain. You fight back, but your people suffer terribly. Women and children are murdered, cattle driven off, homes burnt. Hundreds of your clansmen are hanged, and you are again captured. A gallows is built just for you."

"I die for my people, and for my beliefs," said Jenny.

"In point of fact, you pay a thousand head of cattle and get off, but before you can recover, the English come for you again, again pillaging your kingdom. You fight on. Your people—those who have survived—are still behind you, and nobody can challenge you at sea. This is the time, 1588, when you meet the Spanish chap who gives you the gold chain with the link you are holding. The Spaniards are your best allies against Elizabeth, but Drake and his friends have decisively disposed of them. You strike the English again and again, by land and sea, but you realise at last that your way of life is no more. In your future are only old age, poverty, and ever more blood. Your best kinsmen are in English jails, including your sons. You are now sixty-three years old."

"Now I die for my beliefs?"

"You're past beliefs. There's nothing left for you but submission, but you're still a bargainer and a gambler, so you decide to submit to Elizabeth in your own way. In July of 1593, you set sail, in command of one of your ships. You round Ireland and Land's End, avoiding the famous Killigrew pirates that control those waters, then head up the Western Channel, pass Dover, thread the treacherous sands and currents off the Thames, and steer to London. There you land, requesting to see your old adversary Queen Elizabeth. Perhaps she will decapitate you, quite likely without even giving you an audience. But your nose says she will see you, and maybe something can be worked out."

"And she does?"

"She does. The English pirate queen getting a chance to chat with the Irish pirate queen. How could she resist?"

"What do I wear to court?"

"Your Gaelic chieftain's cloak, a plain thing, fur-lined. You are in striking contrast to the richly ornamented, bejeweled and powdered Elizabeth I and her court. In any case, you meet and talk at length, two powerful women, alone. You get on very well, speaking in Latin. You don't speak English, but besides the common language of scholars, you do have a lot in common. At the end of your conversation, Elizabeth gives you everything you could hope for: freedom for your imprisoned sons, a full pardon for you, even an assured income from your family estates for the rest of your life. Rare treatment for a pirate."

"She dies peacefully?"

"They all do, Granuaile and Elizabeth in 1603, soon after Drake and Philip II of Spain. And which of them was the greatest pirate, would you say? Was it Philip, whose conquistadores looted all the Americas and more? Or Elizabeth, who sent out fleets to loot the looters? Or Drake, the greatest looter of them all? Or was it Granuaile, who looted England's shipping after Elizabeth looted her homeland? What do you think?"

"Where did you get this?" Jenny asked, fingering the gold link.

"That's another story for another time."

"Why should I believe it's really from a chain that she wore?"

"You shouldn't, even though it is. But if you hold it and feel it in your hand, you won't have to believe it because you will know." The clock bell rang two bells, the lesson was over, and Jenny's mother was at the door to pick her up.

"That was good," she whispered to me on her way out.

My concern was that my pirates essay was due in a few days,

and we hadn't even gotten near the pirates that I had meant to write about. He advised that I title what I learned so far: "Western Piracy through the Elizabethan Period," and tell Miss Titherington I wished to stay with the subject for my next semester's essay. I thought she would probably allow that, but I was feeling confused. If everybody so far was a pirate, then who wasn't one? This got him up and pacing by the hearth.

"That's the very question that had *everybody* confused. At the beginning of the seventeenth century, nobody had any more idea than ever. Not just the Caribbean, but Europe's home waters were swarming with pirates. There were all kinds of aristocratic types, like Granuaile, who claimed their ancestral coasts. For instance, Cornwall was the territory of the Earl of Killigrew, called the Pirate Baron of Land's End. Under James I, Killigrew prospered, paying off whoever needed paying off in courtly society in order to get away with taking a lot of passing ships. Of course, one didn't do that oneself; one got a professional captain to do it. In Killigrew's case, that was a young aristocrat named Peter Easton, and he handled his fleet so well he nearly stopped shipping traffic in the Bristol Channel in 1610. Very inconvenient."

"Why didn't the king send the navy after him?"

"Dear boy, aside from the fact that, one way or another, the king was getting a share of the take, he didn't have a navy. Navies hadn't happened. If you were a reigning monarch who needed ships, you borrowed them. That's what barons, earls, dukes, and such were for. Everything was about to change, however, thanks in good measure to Easton. Mr. Easton finally niggled so many rich shipowners, other aristocrats and whatnot, that they put together a squadron of warships to go clean the pirates out of Cornwall."

"But if Easton was working for Killigrew, and Killigrew was in with King James, how could they . . ."

"Everybody paid off the king, who then let 'em all have their little squabbles between themselves. Same situation in Europe, and the seas were still up for grabs, with no laws pertaining. In any case, the coalition of niggled shipowners who went after Easton put their battle fleet in the hands of another young aristocrat named Henry Mainwaring. Good sailor, and well connected at court." He pronounced it "Mannering" and told me to remember it well, because the name loomed large in the subject he was teaching me.

"When Killigrew and Easton learn what's coming for 'em, Easton takes his ships and clears out."

"To where?"

The captain told how Easton, with ten ships, sailed for Newfoundland and more or less took it over (to the delight of the Newfoundlanders, though not their governor), using it as a base for raids on the Grand Banks and the Caribbean. He was very successful, sacking Puerto Rico, taking ships, finally sailing for the Mediterranean Sea. Tunis was a longtime haven for pirates, where loot could be traded and sold. Then, with great wealth, he sailed to the French Riviera, where he bought a villa at Villefranche, and a title, making him Marquis of Savoy. "He had a patio done by the best stonecutters, with a mosaic deck and a marvelous view of the bay. Also the best wine cellar you can imagine."

"What happened to Mainwaring?"

"So here comes Mainwaring to Cornwall to find Easton, and there's him, gone. Well, what do you do? You've got a bloody expensive fleet, and a great responsibility to get your sponsors some kind of payoff. The only thing for it is to go after Spaniards, which is always an option. And you do, and then you, too, sail for Newfoundland, and do the same bloody thing that Easton did. He's long gone, o'course. So you take over, raid the Grand Banks, then the Caribbean, do rather well. Then you, also, head into the Med, go to Tunis, flog your loot, and go to Villefranche. By this time, you're listed as a pirate in the British *Book of Public Records.*"

"I'm still chasing Easton?"

"Not for years, but you do catch up with him at last, and instead of shooting a bunch of cannonballs, you drink a very pleasant vintage to one another's health and continuing success. Just close your eyes and imagine it, with palm trees, wine, moonlight . . ."

I closed my eyes, and by some trick of mind, I heard the whisper of breeze through palm fronds, felt a brush of it on my cheek, and it was like velvet. I distinctly heard a clink of crystal, laughter, a toast, and an image began to form of moonlit water below a terrace, the silhouettes of anchored galleons . . . all astonishingly vivid, and getting more so by the moment, until the captain brought me back.

"No time for that right now. We're about done here, finished with Easton, who's happy where he is, but not quite yet with Mainwaring, who wants to go home, back to merry old England. That means he has to buy a pardon, which is how aristocrats who have been naughty with their ships get away with it. Mainwaring pays the price that King James bills him for, and agrees to a very important condition attached to his pardon. That is that he returns right away, and helps stamp out piracy around the British Isles. Set a thief out to catch a thief, eh? So home he sails, carrying what's recorded as 'a large sum of money,' to take up his new career as the king's chief authority against pirates. He's not yet thirty years old.

"His first advice to the king is to stop pardoning pirates. His own pardon is of course secure at that time. He tells the King . . ."

(here he closed his eyes and quoted) "'. . . to take away their hopes and encouragements, your Highness must put on a constant immutable resolution never to grant any pardon, and for those that are or may be taken, to put them all to death, or make slaves of them.'

"In other words, as long as the government winked at piracy, there would be pirates. Mainwaring also advised closing up shop on all the baronial pirates around the British Isles, and licencing privateers to chase them down. Thieves against thieves again. Last, and most important, Mainwaring recommended a standing navy, answerable only to the Crown, in order to regulate the privateers, y'see. Some call him the father of the Royal Navy. Be that as it may, Mainwaring, ex-pirate, was knighted and elected to Parliament, and rose to vice admiral in the new navy that he wanted. With it he made good on his promise to squeeze piracy out of home waters forever. Rather ironic, eh?" A yawn. "Now, dear lad, I confess a certain exhaustion with the subject at this moment. Now let us return to now. We both have much to do, and much to be careful about."

8

The Concert

As to staying alert, I didn't need the captain's caution where Grendel was concerned, as will be very well understood by anybody who has had the occasion to flee from a deadly beast, then to be stalked by it. I varied my routes to school and town, not encountering my nemesis, but with no way of knowing whether that was because my evasion was working or if Klaus Moehner had simply lost interest in tormenting me with his evilly trained dog. In class, I had semester final exams, and all work fell due, including my essay, entitled "Western Piracy, Part One."

"Saints alive!" said Miss Titherington when I handed it to her, all fourteen pages of it, neatly penned. "Part one?" Pleased with my commitment to my topic, she readily agreed to let me pursue it during the second semester.

I was to have no more piracy lessons for a while, however. At the inn, everything was given to preparations for the concert, an event that had become problematic, not for lack of interest, but for too much of it. As word of it got around, more musicians wanted to come, and Meg found herself having to program things so those she deemed worthy would have some chance to play, yet trying not to hurt the feelings of those she felt were unready to perform for a paying audience. The promise of success also meant a crush of preparatory expenses. All the food, a gross of candles, twenty pounds of coffee and such could be bought on credit, but not the liquor and beer needed to stock the bar for an overflow crowd. The liquor commission wanted cash, and Mother had to empty our bank account in order to get it.

"This thing had better work," she fretted. "If there's a blizzard, or if anything else happens to keep people from coming, we're all going to be eating the same food until March, when we'll be evicted anyway." In fact, Mother's vigor had increased as she fussed over every detail, recruiting more help, rehearsing people in their jobs, all with an efficiency that swept everybody before it like cobwebs in front of a broom. My life had no more time for piracy lessons, or anything else.

The captain remained more or less aloof from all of the activity that his suggestion had generated, spending his days in Tom's boat shed, starting the serious work that *Merry* needed, returning to the inn for supper, then tying little knots by the fire until Meg appeared with her fiddle for their evening practise. Her only communication with him, however, was the signaling that musicians make to one another. When she spoke, it was generally an instruction as to how she would prefer to hear him play the tune.

"Like this?" he would ask.

"More like this," she would say, and off they would go again. In the community where I grew up, such deference to a woman (never mind a girl) was at least unusual. I couldn't resist asking why he let her boss him around so.

"Any *why* I gave you would be a lie. But it's no lie that she's got a music that vibrates in my bones. And she doesn't bruise your eye, eh?" He squinted at me with a look that probed my most secret thoughts, and I blushed.

The last working day before Christmas brought a snow that was heavy enough to blanket the landscape, making everything look like a postcard, especially the inn, with its ancient presence. It also brought the first indication of a threat to the concert other than the weather, and that was the discovery that many of the posters that I had made and put up around town had been torn down. Then around midafternoon an officer from the Department of Public Health showed up, demanding to inspect the kitchen, which he did with surprising zeal. Finding no bug, no contaminant, not even a loose noodle to reward his efforts (not in my mother's kitchen), he went away mumbling that he had been sent as a result of a private complaint.

"Well, they can't close you down for a sanitary violation, or stop everybody from knowing about the concert by attacking Jim's posters," Aunt Karen observed. "But it is certainly a reminder that not everybody wants to see the inn have a successful event. What else might they have up their sleeve?" It was supper on Christmas Eve, and everybody except the captain seemed torn between apprehension and excitement over the gamble on which our fates now seemed to hang.

"I'll keep an eye on things," said Robin. He had been assigned the Boxing Day duty by Chief Moehner, who knew well that the assignment meant his subordinate would miss much of his family's big event. "But the weather's cleared, and I don't know what else they can pull off to stop you."

There were several things, as it turned out, starting with a midmorning visit from Fire Chief Wirtz, who was married to the Moehners and had come to prohibit the inn's occupancy to no more than forty-two people, under new regulations. By a stroke of luck, his visit coincided with Robin delivering Aunt Karen to spend the day, and our Corporal MacMaster had the authority to talk to him nose to nose. Chief Wirtz had some bluster, but he was essentially a shy kind of person, and Robin let him retreat with his dignity. "What next?" said Mother.

Next was Clem Clancy's not showing up as promised to snowplough the inn's parking area outside the gate. His plough (serviced by Moehner Equipment & Repair) was broken-down. This made for a frantic moment, but a parking disaster was averted by Roderick Hirtle, who came over with his plough two hours before the event and cleared an area big enough for lots of cars.

"Let's hope for that," said Mother, who was strung taut and had to be commanded by her sister to sit down and take some deep breaths.

"You're just fussing now," Aunt Karen told her. "You're going to need your energy." So she sat, just as the captain came down the stairs, resplendent in his black suit, as though for church, and wearing a broad smile. But there was something unfamiliar about him, something remarkably youthful . . .

"You've got a new tooth!" I blurted.

"Actually, three, thanks to Dr. Wentzel."

"You look very handsome," said Mother.

He bowed. "That's as befits the beauty of this place and all here." His gaze swept the room, now expanded to a space with twenty-three tables, each perfectly arranged, each with its own candle to "make the old place glow in all its charm," as he phrased it. His reference to the candles caused Mother to spring up and straighten several that were crooked to her eye. Then she was off to speak again with her new crew, who were hovering, waiting for things to happen, and the captain got his customary rum with uncustomary speed from a waitress other than Meg. Grandpa's clock rang five bells. Nervous anticipation charged the air, but the captain was like an oasis of calm. Aunt Karen gave him one of her rare small smiles.

"Captain Johnson," she addressed him, "since we have a moment to fill, there's something I've been meaning to ask you."

"Yes, madam?"

"Do you like old cannons?" On the surface, it was an innocent enough thing to ask, but Aunt Karen seldom operated on the surface. The question set the captain to scraping out his pipe bowl.

"Madam, you pose a very broad question. I confess a certain indifference to most of the many varieties of land ordnance, or the populous mortar family. However, if you mean ships' cannon—the singular is properly the plural—do you refer to long guns, or their shorter cousins, the *canons obusier*, carronades, howitzers, or pivot pieces? In the truck gun family are your cannon royal, cannon, demi-cannon, bombards, licornes, falcons, sakers, serpentines, curtows, and culverins, not to mention your bastard culverins, and demi-culverins, and semi-demi-culverins, on down to the minions. And falconets." Here he took a drink. "Then, of course, there's the swivel family, with the perriers, lantakas, rabonets, cohorns, espingoles, hailshot pieces, sling pieces, murderers, pedreros, and portingall bases, or port pieces, for short. There's also the whole *bouche de feu* family. On the whole, making allowance for your lack of specificity, and my own particular prejudices among the categories of naval artillery in general, yes, I would have to confess to a certain affinity for old cannon."

"Good," said Aunt Karen without blinking. "Because I want to know what you think of our cannon—the one that so mysteriously found its way back, like Lassie come home."

"It is a light four-pounder, Queen Anne vintage, circa 1710, with decorative relief and dolphins. Very lovely. Perhaps I can fashion a proper carriage for it, using its original iron hardware, which Jim here says is still in the cellar. I'm looking forward to getting down there to have a closer look."

"And what is your theory as to how the cannon came home?"

"Any guess would have to be a lie. Do you have a theory of your own?"

"No," Aunt Karen shook her head. "Just questions and thoughts so far. For instance, Robin and I noticed that the ground under the cannon barrel was not dented, as it should have been if dumped from a truck bed. Why not, do you suppose?" Before the captain could be further tested, here came Tom, our volunteer bartender for the evening, and right behind him much of the Anglican Church choir, who would be first to perform, and on their heels was Tapping Tim with somebody to adjust the sound system. When Tim learned there was no sound system he almost went away, but Meg emerged and got him back.

Then the early customers started showing up, friends and family of the choir, wanting choice tables. They got them, along with the tea that most ordered. According to Meg's carefully considered program, the afternoon people (or "cookie-eaters" as she called them) would leave early, opening the tables to an evening crowd, with a door charge. When the first medley of madrigals commenced, it was to the better part of a full room, which included quite a few people who had never been to the inn. During the program's mandatory set of carols Ernie Fischback creatively mimed all twelve presents described in the lyrics of "The Twelve Days of Christmas," and easily got the room amused and singing along. Meg's solo set, driven by the captain's accompaniment on his little tin flute, brought heavy applause that didn't stop until they had performed an encore.

Then came Tapping Tim, by which time we had nearly a full house, and his gravelly ballads needed no sound system. At supper time, a half-hour break in the program was announced, with the reminder there was a door charge for the evening part of the concert, and most of the previous customers went away, as planned, while others drifted in.

"Seems like you've got a success on your hands," Robin remarked, sticking his head into the kitchen where Mother was toiling. "People are parked all the way out to the road." Although on duty and in full uniform, he was immediately drafted to carry a box-load of trash out to the bin. "Anyway," he said, picking it up, "I'll be around to keep an eye on things, unless there's trouble somewhere else around town." But there was that, as it happened. Just as the supper crowd had filled the room, Robin got a call that the fire department was scrambling to a blaze, meaning he had to go too. "But you've got a pretty easygoing crowd, and it doesn't look like you need a cop."

He was wrong about that. Five minutes after his departure, just as a trio from the Fiddlers' Association was getting warmed up and everything seemed to be going perfectly, Klaus Moehner and his cronies came in, this time seven of them, making a beeline for the last empty tables left in the room. They wore work clothes, and conspicuously upstaged the performance while getting themselves situated. Then they amused themselves by flustering their inexperienced waitress. The fiddlers struggled to keep their tempo under the distraction, making brave work of it, until the Moehner gang started to clap to the music without much regard for the beat. I parked my tray and made my way to where I'd last seen the captain, hoping he could somehow dispose of them as neatly as before, but he was gone. Nor was he at the bar.

"Where's Robin?" asked Tom, with a scowl at the invaders. I explained he'd had to go to a fire, and I couldn't find the captain. Nor did I know what he could do. This new attack was obviously a lot more determined than before. Tom looked grim. "They're killing this act, and it won't take much more to kill the evening." The other customers, trying to ignore what was happening, started to chat among themselves, and the concert atmosphere was evaporating by the moment.

The fiddlers simply stopped playing in the middle of their set. Tom went over and spoke with the Moehners' table. Whatever he said did less than no good, because Klaus stood up and announced to the room that he and his friends would fill the break with something they'd been practicing for the occasion. So saying, they all started up an old Nova Scotia sailor's song that made every religious person in the room blanche.

"Away, away, with fife and drum,
Here we come, full of rum,
Looking for girls who peddle their bum
To the North Atlantic squadron . . ."

As everybody knows, the first verse of "The North Atlantic

Squadron" is the most polite one, and a couple of people were rising to leave, but the second verse petered out after two or three words. Moving rapidly toward the Moehner table was the awesome figure of Noel Nauss, all six foot six inches, 350 pounds of him. Yet he moved in a curiously graceful, almost feminine way, like a dancer, which was somehow quite sinister. Klaus sat back down. Noel loomed over their party and regarded them with an expression that was without anger or malice, more what I would call eagerness. He had no message to them other than his unswerving attention. Noel did dart a glance toward the bar, where I saw the captain shaking his head, as though signaling "not yet." Noel moved quietly to a position behind the Moehners, and took up station there, arms folded, gazing down at them with patient appetite.

The show started up again where it had left off and, with no further interruption, quickly recaptured everybody's attention. By the time Jason McGridley and his group performed with Meg, they were playing to a packed place and the room took on its own authority. Lots of toes got tapping in time, and Jimmy Eisnor danced with his fiancée among the crowd around the bar. There, Tom was working flat out.

"It is truthfully said," came the captain's surprise voice from behind me, "that it is the ability to make music and dance that makes men like gods. Don't you think? Look." He pointed out the Moehner boys leaving, closely attended by Noel. Their tables were instantly taken. I turned to ask him about what had just happened, but he was gone again, and when I next saw him, he was back on stage with Meg, haunting a hushed house with "The Dismal King of the Ghosts," then bringing the place to its feet with jigs and reels. At some point the captain addressed the room, raising a toast to the Admiral Anson Inn, then to many more evenings like this one in the future, which got a strong ovation.

After that, Jeremy and Stewie Gallant did their banjo and guitar "Orange Blossom Special" with Meg on fiddle, starting some serious dancing, crowded though the place was. Tom alerted us to the next crisis.

"At the rate we're going, we'll be out of beer in a half-hour, maybe less, and rum." It meant early closure to the best event the inn had seen in living memory, one that was still going strong.

"What do you need?" the captain asked.

"I guess about four kegs of draft, and maybe a half-case of rum would do it, but there's no place where we can get it." But there was. Off into the night went the captain with Noel Nauss in Noel's pickup, returning a half-hour later with the required supplies.

"How did you get this?" asked Robin, who'd come back from his fire.

"I've gotten to know the manager down at the Sou'wester Beverage Room," the captain explained, "and he was glad to sell it to us. Right, Noel?" The captain smiled at him, and Noel nodded, looking pleased to have a friend. He and many other guests, some of them pretty flashed up drunk, stuck around for the midnight "lunch," after which Meg and the captain played a last set of slow waltzes and Robin got Mother out of the kitchen in order to have a dance with her. After that, she closed the bar, turned out the hangers-on, paid off the crew, and collapsed in a chair.

"That was good," she said.

Everybody learned just how good it was at the noon meal the next day, where we gathered after the morning cleanup, and Mother announced the tally of combined revenues from food, bar, and door charges. "Holy old dynamiting Jesus," Meg said, whistling. After expenses, the inn had made enough to cover the dreaded March loan payment, plus a bit more, which would deal with some overdue bills. Another profit from the concert would be renewed local interest in the place, no doubt. "A triumph," Aunt Karen called it, and she was not given to hyperbole. We were aglow with self-congratulations all around, and abuzz about everything that had happened.

The whole multipronged attack by the Moehners was discussed in detail, starting with Robin's call from Chief Wirtz that took him away during the invasion by Klaus and his thugs. The fire was in a derelict farmhouse (on Moehner property), and Robin had to stay around because the chief said somebody might have been in the place. Nobody had, but the ploy had worked.

"Of course, it's all quite unprovable," Robin observed. "I'd love to investigate it, starting with how much insurance they carry on the place, but when Wirtz said there was no arson, he took it out of police jurisdiction."

"Isn't there some kind of harassment charge that we can lay?" Mother asked him, not for the first time.

"Not until they directly break the law in some way that I can prove. The minute they do, I'll file charges that even Chief Moehner can't block, because if he tried to do that, I'd take it to the RCMP, and he doesn't want that kind of scrutiny."

Robin was indomitable. He was not just our family's protector; he was everybody's, except crooks'. But, as second-in-command in a force of five, with all the others being of the Moehner faction, he had no friend on the job. All his pay and his off-duty hours were given to Aunt Karen: driving her to the hospital in Halifax, wheeling her around, being her hands on the bad days when her own hands didn't work, and endlessly playing cribbage with her on the good days, when she could handle the cards if he shuffled and pegged for her. At this moment, his interest was in how well the Moehner's onslaught had been dealt with in his absence.

"Was that your doing?" he asked the captain, who credited Noel Nauss for it.

"We've come to be friends," he explained. "I thought it safe to invite him to come by and listen to the music, and he appeared to take exception when it was interrupted. In all, I'd say he was very well behaved. And he had a very good time, by the by."

"He's rightly thought of as a dangerous man."

The captain nodded. "Quite, but not to anybody who's not bothering the universe."

"I owe you both," said Mother. "Robin, as always, and Captain Johnson for hatching the idea for the concert, bringing your music to it, keeping the bar from running dry and, let's hope, getting rid of the Moehner boys once and for all. How can we repay you?"

The captain smiled his new and lustrous smile. "With a key, ma'am. The key to your cellar so that I can make the measurements I need from the old iron bits of the cannon's original carriage. I want to work down there on a duplicate of it. Jim's going to help, and so is Tom. For wood, we'll use black locust. I want to see the old piece mounted properly out on the gun deck, again commanding the harbour, so it can fire a salute to *Merry* when we sail away."

"What a lovely idea," said Mother, and all agreed.

"But there's a problem I must mention," he said with a frown, producing a satchel he had brought. From it, he drew a dazed-looking kitten, a furry orange ball made up mostly of eyes, ears, and four paws, held on high by the scruff of its neck. "I found this small animal wandering about the place, apparently orphaned, and feel obliged to call it to your attention."

Meg went to it like an iron filing to a magnet. "You don't hold her like that," she said, taking the little creature from him. And so Cleo was replaced, as all could see.

9

On Dealing with Dogs

T he full dark of winter settled over the community of Grey Rocks, Nova Scotia, population 1,337—and 1,338 as of some time in the wee hours of New Year's morn, when Margaret Maclean gave birth to a daughter at County Hospital. The inner harbour got a glaze of ice, and the Christmas lights all vanished, leaving the little town to darkness without gaiety by night; by day, the sky was darkened by wind-torn clouds.

New Year's Eve brought an ice storm and no customers, so the family celebrated alone, without even the captain, because he was bedridden with an attack of gout. I tried to look after him, but he didn't want any looking after. When I brought him a glass of rum with everybody's compliments, he regarded it longingly, but said he now had to lay off the rum for a week or two. "It's been too much of that, and too much of your mother's good food that's done me in," he growled, sending me away.

When, the day before school, he hobbled down to sit by his fire, I was more than ready for another pirate story. With his peculiar talent for putting me into his narrative, he had left me relaxing on a Riviera patio, looking out over treasure-laden galleons silhouetted by silvery moonlight. I had been starting to enjoy the gentlemanliness of piracy, what with a ship's orchestra, fine wines, Spanish gold, etcetera, and I pleaded for more.

The captain grimaced, shifting his left foot, which wore only a sock, and had to be rested on a chair in order to stay elevated. He stirred the honeyed tea that Mother had given him, sipped it, and grimaced again.

"Quite," he rasped. "Very genteel, all those aristocratic pirates. Fame and fortune, eh?" I nodded, all anticipation. He smiled at me with narrowed eyes, and his smile was not altogether pleasant. "Where would you like to go?" he asked. I thought the Caribbean might be nice. "Oh, aye, to be sure. Quite nice. Coconuts. It's certainly the place where most of the European pirates chose to go when Mainwaring and his lot chased them out of home waters. In the Sea of the Caribs there were no rules. For that reason, merchant ships sailing there needed all the protection they could get, and the new Royal Navy got the job of giving it to them. So let's say a navy ship on convoy duty is how we get you to the West Indies, eh?"

This was not at all what I had in mind. "Why would I want to go that way?"

"You don't. But you're out on a London street one day, going about your business, and by a bloody bad piece of luck you get scooped up by a bunch of toughs off a Royal Navy ship that's there to conscript a crew for it, and they take you away. No goodbyes."

"But," I protested, "as a free man, I'm protected . . ."

"Not from the conscription," he interrupted me, "then or now. Although today they give a chap a bit more notice. And as to being a free man, you weren't. Aren't. You were pinned down by your poverty and without the education you needed to get out of a life where you were going to be worked to death, or turn to crime and wind up hanged."

"Sailing off with the navy sounds a lot better."

"In point of fact, it was worse. Far worse. Whatever squalor, privation, and degradation you've ever suffered as a working lout ashore, it looks like a garden party compared to your new circumstances. They give you a hammock—actually, they're selling it to you—and about twenty-four inches of space to swing it in, so when your neighbour farts, it's right in your face." This got a giggle out of me. "Ah, you see the humour in that? Good, because you're going to need every bit of humour you've got. You're living in a packed crowd of unwashed men, and any contagious disease among your mates will get you, as well as their lice, fleas, and scabies mites. But you have more immediate concerns.

"Your squadron makes a fall departure, gets around Ushant, then gets smacked by an early winter gale that lasts all across the Bay of Biscay. On your second day out, in a driving sleet, you're made to climb the rigging for the first time in your life while you're still puking your guts out, and you nearly get blown off the foreyard. Somehow you make it back safely to the deck, where you get a hard whack from a rattan for having been useless. By this time, you're soaked and shivering, with no way to get warm or dry. The ship is unheated, and the deck over you leaks. You get the shakes, hypothermia, one of the sailor's great enemies in the high latitudes.

"You're young, and you weather it, but the poor bloke in the hammock next to you shivers uncontrollably, until at last his teeth stop chattering, because he has died. As I recollect, the North

American squadron lost a lot of men to the cold during the winter of 1759, right off this coast here, and there've been many more before and since. And may the gods help sailors on a night like this," he added. The wind gusted against the inn's east-facing windows with pane-rattling force. The captain reached for his rum, and realised it was tea. "Bloody hell," he said.

"But at least I'm going south," I put him back on course.

"South, aye, giving Cape Finisterre a good offing, and Portugal, then the African coast, to somewhere south of the Canaries, more likely the Cape Verdes, until you find the easterly trade winds. By then you're warm, but you've had several weeks in which to come to a riper appreciation of your new life's great charms, starting with a level of discipline you cannot imagine."

"I've read that it was severe," I put in. His eyebrows lifted.

"Severe? No, I think not. Severe is much too dainty. Brutal would be a better choice of words, but even that fails to convey. There's a list of rules so thorough that it's hard not to break one, and when you do . . . well, for minor infractions, such as being a moment too late out of your hammock, or into the rigging, you'll simply be beaten with a rope's end, or the rattan. For more serious crimes, such as spitting on the deck, stealing food, or talking back, you'll be tied to a grating and whipped with a cat-o'-nine-tails until your back is sufficiently torn up to scar you for life. And for the really serious crimes, such as refusing a direct order, or trying to desert the ship, you can be flogged to death—given so many lashes they literally strip all the flesh off your back, to the bones. This is thought to be a very good way to deter your shipmates (who are required to watch) from repeating your mistake.

"Or there's keelhauling, where you are bound hand and foot and dragged on two lines along the whole length of the keel, from fore to aft. Chances are, you drown along the way. If not, you might wish you had, because you've been horribly cut up by encrustations of sharp barnacles making very painful wounds that quickly fester. And there are no dressings to prevent blood poisoning. Ironically, if you commit the worst crime of all, mutiny, you'll merely be hanged, which is a peaceful way to go, by comparison. Witnessing punishment is a fairly regular entertainment. The only other ones are drinking your daily grog ration, and music."

"Music?"

"They let you sing while you're working the capstan or hauling on halyards. Your whole life is work: working the sails, the lines, tarring the rigging, tallowing the tackle blocks, oiling the spars, chipping chain, holystoning decks. Your clothes quickly become filthy, and you've got only one change—which you've bought from the ship for a scalper's price to be deducted from your pay at the end of the voyage. If you survive it. Hernias, ruptures, and fractures are frequent, along with a lot of other nuisances for which there's small treatment, if any. Then, on top of all that, there's the danger of a sea battle, which could happen at any time. In your case, it comes as your convoy is approaching the Leeward Islands, after a long passage. You're attacked by two frigates, full of men and guns and showing no colours. You're the only thing between them and your fat, slow convoy, and it's a hot action.

"Remember our discussion about what cannonballs do, and the splinters they set flying? Well, besides that you see men smashed by spars and heavy gear falling from aloft; a careless gun captain's foot is crushed to a pulp by the recoil of his own piece; there are powder burns, and wounds from grenade fragments and musket balls. If those don't hit something vital and kill you quick, they have a way of cluttering up a simple flesh wound with bits of the clothing they clipped off on their way in, causing infection, then gangrene, then death. Which is why the surgeons amputate so many arms and legs straightaway, before that can happen. They have a regular production line going. There's blood everywhere, above and below. It runs into the scuppers, and streaks the side of the ship. Do you think I might trouble you to fetch me . . . oh, another tea I suppose. Heavy on the honey."

When I returned to the table, I was startled to find him baring his teeth at me, until seeing that was because he was easing his foot into a different position.

"Who wins?" I asked.

"Nobody. You send them away licking their own wounds, but your hull has been badly shot up. You're leaking from some holes at the waterline, and your decks are a charnel ground littered with wreckage. Aloft, you've had your fore topmast and bowsprit shot away, so your ship hardly handles, and you drift. If there are winners, it's the ships you've protected. They all fled like a covey of quail while you were fending off the attack so that their owners can make a nice profit.

"What's been demanded from you previously is a picnic compared with what you get in the aftermath of the action. You are of course exhausted, but there's a diminished crew, and the entire ship to be put back in order: jury spars and rigging to set up, debris to clear, shot holes to plug, and all the pumps going constantly. There is no rest. For a musical accompaniment, you have the sobs and screams of the wounded, punctuated by splashes from corpses thrown over the side. No time for prayer services. You collapse from exhaustion, but are whipped back to your feet.

"During the couple of days it takes to get the ship sailing again, you drift north, so far that your captain can no longer lay a course for Nevis, or even the Anegada Passage, so he heads west again, misses the Mona Passage in a gale, and winds up off the north-facing coast of Hispaniola. After the hard, long passage, your water supply is green in the cask, and it's almost gone. What's left is clouded with living, wriggling organisms, and it stinks. The ship's biscuits are full of white weevils with black heads; the salt pork has soured; the cheese is desiccated, and there's been no fresh food for so long that most of the crew has scurvy, including you. It further weakens you, loosens your teeth, and does other unpleasant things.

In the circumstances, your captain has no choice but to anchor off the Island of Tortuga in order to get water, even though the place is French. Of course, France and England have been quarreling for centuries, but out here, everybody's biggest and ongoing quarrel is with the Spaniards, who are such an enemy that they often lead enemies to make friends against them.

"In any case, your ship is soon welcomed by some dugout canoes manned by Tortuga's pig hunters, who bring out fresh stores for sale, including their famous *boucan*. There are a couple of Englishmen among them who offer to guide a watering party from the ship. You are ordered to go out with it, and out you go with a boatload of empty water casks, a few sailors, two marines with muskets to guard you, and a couple of the pig hunters for guides. And so you meet the *boucaniers,* the originals."

"This is going from bad to worse to horrible," I groaned. There was a ring of truth to everything, and it had put me in a very dismal frame of mind, which I told him.

"Welcome to the West Indies," he beamed. "In any case, cheer up, it's a nice climate, very lush, and you're ashore, bare feet in the sand and about to get a drink of cool, fresh water. One of the English buccaneers (as they pronounce the word) gives you an orange, and it is without question the most delicious thing you have ever eaten. You tell him some of your woes, and he tells you he'll help you if you want to desert. So what's it to be? Back to the king's ship, and more of what you've just been through? Or casting your lot to the winds in a place where there are oranges and sweet water and friendly buccaneer chaps?"

I had no wish to revisit the ship he had described.

"The other English buccaneer sells the Marines some palm wine, and while they're distracted, you slip away into the bushes, and follow your new mate up the forest trails and away from that ship forever. By the time your escape is noticed, you're too far gone to chase. As you watch them raise anchor and sail off toward the Windward Passage, you eat another orange, and try a bit of your mate's palm wine. I suppose I'd better have a last mug of your mother's tea and honey. Maybe I'll get a taste for it."

"Why would the buccaneers help me?" I asked.

"Why?" His dark eyebrows shot up. "How should I know why? There aren't any whys. Anyway, why wouldn't they? Like you, many of them have deserted from ships, or jumped their indentures, fled the plantations, or religious wars, or are runaway slaves. At the very least, they've all deserted the world and its rules, and they're free of them. They're refugees, and now you are, too. Without whys."

"Why aren't there any whys?" I wanted to know. I felt it was a reasonable question, but as I asked it, he made a careless movement of his foot, winced, and became testy.

"Because any why answer is a lie, including this one. Now, mark what I'm saying, Jim lad, and let's not have any distractions, because this is the beginning that I'm telling you about, the conception, the root of the whole Brotherhood of the Coast. Here's where it started, on Tortuga, and Hispaniola, and on other islands where other bands of Europeans are making a living in little refugee communities with their own rules.

"Making a living?"

"Quite. And in a very sporting way: hunting, living in forest camps, surrounded by all kinds of first-rate free food. Like your oranges. There are other wild fruits, vegetables, gourds, fish, crabs, land turtles, sea turtles (both delicious), eggs, pigeons, and of course thousands of the wild pigs you're about to start hunting. Back in the previous century, the Spaniards left some pigs and cattle here, where they got on very well, bred prolifically, and their descendants make not just another food source for you, but an independent income as well. When properly prepared."

"Prepared how?"

"First, you have to get a pig, meaning you have to learn to shoot the long-barreled musket you're loaned. The pigs are quick and elusive in the underbrush; you have to be a good shot. Your mates teach you marksmanship, and they're the best teachers you could hope to find anywhere. You're taught to wrap your legs so you can run through the undergrowth without getting them torn up. There are no poisonous snakes or insects on Tortuga, but you have to mind the flora. You shoot your first pig, then butcher it, cutting its flesh into thin strips that are smoked and dried in a dome-shaped hut called the *boucan,* until they are jerky. That word is an English corruption of the Spanish-American *charqui,* by the by. It makes an invaluable kind of provision, very useful not only to ships, but just about everybody before refrigerators came along, because it keeps indefinitely.

"So, after you've brought home the bacon, and processed it, you can sell a bundle of a hundred strips for six silver cobs, or pieces of eight. That's good enough money to sustain you in your new life. It pays for your necessaries, and for a jolly old romp in town every few months. There you have women, rum, music, life, like cowboys in from the range, or sailors from a voyage. You spend your money in the little French port, contribute to its economic flow, and peaceably provide a valuable commodity. In fact, you are an exemplary person, except in the eyes of the Royal Navy, which you do not plan to revisit, and which holds no vote in your new community.

"*You,* however, *do* have a vote, for the first time in your life, as a citizen of the brotherhood. It's the first democratic society in all the Americas, and maybe the first true democracy in the history of the world, when you consider that in Greece, with the alleged democracy inventors, you had to be a person of means in order to have a vote. The rules of the brotherhood have nothing to do with money and pedigree, what religion you are, or colour, or anything else. You're all refugees. You have a fresh start; you're truly on your own, altogether."

"Sounds all right," I commented.

"Quite. And your whole new world would be all right, except for the Spaniards. Remember, Spain claims everything in and around the Caribbean. She can't begin to protect it all, but she can and does harass everybody she considers an interloper, which is anybody who is not Spanish. Spain gets her knickers in a twist over you and your mates, just your being, and from time to time she sends out parties of soldiers to find and kill you. Your band is wary, but after a night of drinking palm wine, you're surprised by a war party of Spaniards who've landed on your island and been led to you by somebody or other. Before you know it, they're among you. In the confusion, you escape into the forest, where you hear the screams of many of your new friends, your family, who are being put to death in various obnoxious ways.

"Now, like Drake, you conceive a visceral hatred for Spaniards. It is widely shared in your community. You escape the massacre to join another band, which welcomes you. All the brotherhood, English, French, Dutch, Flemings, blacks, Indians, the lot, is united against the Dons.

"Your chance comes when a Spanish brigantine drops anchor, and sends out a party of soldiers. You watch from behind the foliage. Off they march to somewhere where you are not and, in the dark of the night, you swarm aboard the brigantine from your canoes and overpower the crew. Now you and your mates are the new owners of a small, armed ship, and there are plenty among you who know how to handle it. And its guns. And out you go, raiding the Windward Passage, which is where much of the north-south traffic passes into or out of the Caribbean. It is the happiest of all hunting grounds, ever so much more lucrative than shooting pigs. Now you're back at sea, but with far, far different circumstances than before, eh?

"Here you have a real charter of rights, to which the rules are cut. Here, the biggest crime is to steal from a shipmate, either directly or by concealing loot that rightfully should be divided according to due process. That's conducted by the officers, who are elected. Here, your officers are made or unmade according to the vote of the crew, so those who endure are those who have commanded your confidence, and kept it. A vote can happen at any time except in action, and you get natural hierarchy."

"And now we're pirates?"

"*Filibustiers* is the word in French, and as soon as you lay hands on your ship, you sail her to Cayona, which is the one indifferently good port on Tortuga. It has a fort, and a French governor. He is an authority who can write you a letter of marque, or of reprisal, or at least some document to say you are working for his government, which you are, in a manner of speaking."

"But Spain claims the island and can land soldiers on it?"

"Again, Spain claims *everything,* but the islands belong to whoever can take and hold them. Most of the islands change hands again and again. Tortuga has been repeatedly raided by the Spaniards, but the French have held onto it with the help of her *filibustiers.* That's the quid pro quo. You get your piracy authorisation from the governor, plus a home port where you're safe, and you help the place stay safe. In case it's attacked, you and the rest of your brethren and their ships are its defence. The governor has no real force of regular troops. You're it. He's been given a post where he's expected to make profits for the government that appointed him, and after that for himself, but he's given precious little to work with, except the authority to collect taxes from the plantation owners, and write authorisations to his buccaneer chaps. He has to make sure there are enough of you at all times to do the job. Aside from that, you're on your own. Have you ever been on your own?" he inquired, with a pleasantness that had a hard edge to it. I shook my head.

"No. Neither have most folks. It's a very groundless place to be. Very demanding, having to think for yourself instead of what people tell you to think. And out here, everybody gets a chance—you, your friends, the colonial governors, the lot. Even the Spaniards. Maybe especially the Spaniards. Just about everybody except for all the slaves and indentured Europeans who can't escape the system."

"But the English governors . . ."

"Were in exactly the same position as the French ones, or Dutch ones. With little or no support from home, they all had their own *filibustiers,* privateers, sea beggars, letters of marque, corsairs, what have you. The Dutch got hold of Curaçao, Aruba, some of the other islands in the Lesser Antilles; the Brits got two or three of the Leeward Islands, but primarily Jamaica. Everywhere it was the same: you overwhelmed some badly defended Spanish island, ran up your country's colours, settled in, got comfortable, and . . . ten or twenty years later, suddenly here's a powerful force of Spaniards out of nowhere to take over again. It was such a big free-for-all."

"When was this?"

"The whole system lasted into the 1700s. The first of the *bou-caniers* formed up around 1630 or so. But let's put you in their next generation, say 1670, when you might have met Mr. Esquemeling. He was a Fleming who wrote a book about it. I'll lend you a copy. In brief, he came to the colonies under indenture, a mistreated refugee like yourself, who joined the buccaneers. Arrrr." He had again shifted his foot.

"Es, Esqu . . ."

"Alexander Olivier Esquemeling. He was an artist. That is to say, in his case, a barber, and dentist, and physician of sorts, for jobs that weren't too complicated. Your Miss Titherington is going to ask you for a bibliography of the source material you've consulted, and Esquemeling should be at the top of your list. He arrived in Tortuga and was the first of the pirates to give an account of it. Your dentist is an angel, by comparison to Esquemeling. He used to spit on his hands before starting in on you. But he could do a workmanlike job of taking off your leg, if it came to that." So saying, he tossed off the last of his tea, and started to gather up his pipe and tobacco.

I told him I was still confused about who was a pirate and who wasn't. "By what you say, even the authorities were still pirates."

"Quite."

"Which makes the very word *pirate* meaningless." I challenged him with his own logic.

"On the contrary. Look at it like this: Johnson's book was called *A General History of the Robberies and Murders of the Most Notorious Pirates,* and it sold rather well with that title. But how popular would it be if it was *The Robberies and Murders of the Most Notorious Authorities?* Or *Most Notorious Politicians?*

Nobody would bother to buy it, because everybody's tired of hearing it. But pirates . . . uh." He grunted, hoisting himself to his feet and hobbling off to bed. "Stay alert," he said. I was left with unsettling dreams and dark images, as the storm rattled the windows of my room all night.

Nor was the weather any better in the morning, so I had to make it to school on foot, which I did with no sign of Grendel. My biggest challenge was dodging some iceballs thrown at me by the Moehner boys. Life was back to usual. Miss Titherington returned my essay with an A-minus. Her written comment read, "Very comprehensive, but you have failed to make the criminal case against pirates (presume this will follow in your Part 2), and I want to see some more source material. Where are you getting all of this history? Give your bibliography!"

Later, at recess, Jenny echoed the question. Over the holidays she had fruitlessly combed our rural library for references to Grace O'Malley, or Granuaile. However, Jenny was wearing the gold link she had been given, tied to a cord she wore around her neck. She had done a complete turnaround on the captain, who was now back on her list of possible avatars. As a direct result of pondering Granuaile's story, Jenny had gone to her mother, as though to Queen Elizabeth, respectfully requesting an audience, "woman to woman," even dressing for the occasion.

Perhaps caught off guard by this novel approach, her mother

had heard Jenny's case for more freedom, and at last granted it, so that Jenny was permitted to walk or bicycle to town and back "without armed guards," as she put it. "Now I can come visit on my own, and I will, too, when your captain has any more women pirates to talk about." I promised to keep her informed. She asked me if I had experienced any more dog trouble lately, and I said no, and about an hour later I found myself again running for my life from Grendel.

I was mostly home, right to the road behind the inn, and saw Grendel as I was crossing. I couldn't have been in a worse place. In front of me was the whole length of the driveway to the inn, a hundred-yard dash where he'd catch me; behind me was no better. I ran for our gate, slowed by galoshes that felt suddenly huge. I knew I was going to hear him behind me any moment, and when I didn't, I peered back over my shoulder. A truck had stopped at our entrance to have a conversation with somebody in a car, and Grendel had been slowed; he was slinking past them, still coming for me, but sneakily, not charging.

The truck started up and pulled away, its wheels churning slush; I was almost to the gate; I heard Grendel's panting just as I hit the latch, spun through the door and slammed it in his face, safe by a couple of seconds.

"You seem distressed," the captain observed, looking up from his macramé. I told him about what had just happened to me. "Quite." He glanced at the clock. "And this is the time when you ordinarily arrive from school?" Grateful for his interest, I told him it was, and that it was my most dangerous moment, because whichever way I traveled home, here's where the dog could ambush me. My only salvation had been that there were people around, and Grendel was too well trained to attack me under the eyes of witnesses.

"I meant," he said, "I need to know when I can rely on your being here to build a fire. The universe has a mortal chill on it, and I'm consigned to tea and honey, and I'd be obliged if you'd tend the hearth." He picked up his pennywhistle, played a quick, angry little tune, and put it down again. "I should be working on my poor little *Merry*," he fretted, "but I can't even get to her, through this weather." He regarded me and sighed.

"I've decided I've had enough of this getting-older business, Jim lad. It's been entertaining enough but, as of now, I'm going to get younger again. Since I'm blessed with that choice. And I'd drink a toast to that with ye, mate, but I don't even have a cup of tea unless you bring it." I did, then left him to his mumbles and his macramé. I felt no hurry to pursue the darknesses of his latest teachings, and he seemed in no hurry to resume. He did loan me the Esquemeling book.

Grendel was there again on the day following, except this time, by luck, I had gotten a ride down from school with Roderick Hirtle, who brought me right up to our gate. Just on the other side of it I was surprised to find the captain stumping around, enshrouded by his cloak, looking like a big black tent. "One needs to get out of doors for a bit," he explained, asking me where I was in my reading of Esquemeling. I told him I was with the buccaneer Pierre Le Grande, who was ambushing Spanish ships in the Windward Passage.

"Aye, ambushing," was his comment. "The trick's to ambush the ambusher." A gust of sleet hurried us both inside. On Friday, I found out what he meant, and in full measure.

Homeward bound, at the bottom of Princess Street, I reconnoitered the road from the shelter of a fence, and there was Grendel, again awaiting me. My own best tactic was to crouch unseen, also waiting, for anything that would distract him. Cars and trucks went past, but none stopped. Grendel just sat, poised, panting steam in the wintry air, sniffing from time to time, but not detecting me. Just as I was considering returning to school and telephoning somebody for help, down the road came the highway department's snowplough, and I darted right in front of it. If Grendel charged, I could jump up on the rig, which had to slow down for me. But Grendel did not, and I sprinted for home as the plough went on past.

Nearing the gate, I realised I was not going to make it this time. I would have been just clear if I didn't have to open the catch, then go through and close the gate again, but I knew Grendel was too close for that. The tearing of his claws put him right on my heels. There was nothing to do but plunge for the gate anyway; it opened as though by a magic hand; I went through it at speed, noticing the captain as I flashed past him, which is when the whole scene was obscured by a boil of smoke accompanied by a powerful explosion. I kept running until realising I wasn't being chased anymore. I turned and trotted back to where the captain was standing with his ancient blunderbuss smoking at his hip. Right inside the gate was what was left of Grendel, after catching a terrific blast. Around the corner of the inn, a window slid open.

"What was that?" came Mother's voice.

"Backfire," called the captain, "Must have been a truck." He handed me a sack. "Dispose of the remains, put a rock with it, and sink it off the cliffs. Get this blood and gore sloshed away with some buckets of water; put the bits in the bag with the main corpse. Best look lively." Regarding the odious job, I protested there was no reason for secrecy, because the dog had been shot while attacking me on our own property. I thought Klaus should have to come and clear the mess.

"Quite," he nodded, "but then you've got an incident on your hands, and Klaus's revenge as soon as he can think one up, and prob'ly the cops taking my dear old musketoon away from me. Now that Grendel's served his purpose, best thing all around is for him to just vanish. So you tidy up while I dispose of this weapon." Off he went with it under his cloak, trickling smoke like some infernal figure.

I stood, stunned, trying to take in everything that had just happened, and the revolting task suddenly before me. "Get to it, then," he said, going inside. And so I was left with bagging Grendel's remains, sloshing down the area, dragging my late enemy to the cliff, and pushing him over into the sea. Afterward, I obscured the drag marks I'd left, and, by the time the inn opened, there was no trace of him, except as another item on my list of secrets, which was getting bigger.

"That was some backfire we heard this afternoon," Mother commented later. I agreed.

10

In the Cellars

The captain continued in his gnarly mood. I approached him after closing time to thank him for erasing the most dangerous enemy I'd ever known, and he took a contrary view. "He was your best friend. He showed you what it means to really stay alert. Say a prayer for him; be grateful for his teaching, and try to remember it without him around. Be glad you met him at an age when you're fleet of foot." He shifted his own foot back onto its chair. I told him I'd save my prayers for worthier things than Grendel.

"What worthier?" he asked with a lift of one eyebrow. "By your own account he was a magnificent animal, intelligent, beautifully trained to do exactly what he had been taught to do . . ."

"Which was attack and kill things, like me!"

"You were just a target he'd been pointed to; he was as loyal a soldier as any conscript, and better trained than most. And with a different teacher, he would have been the cuddliest, best parlor pet you can imagine, bringing in the paper, guarding the children. Never chasing the cats. Poor Grendel." What he was saying seemed so absurd, and his look so dolorous, it occurred to me that he was making a spoof of the whole thing, and I laughed. It felt good to laugh, with Grendel gone, and my nerves starting to steady. But my listener just became more grim and my laugh trickled off. He fixed me with a melancholy eye. "It's a dark and terrible thing to snuff the life of another sentient being; you're taking away everything they have, and . . . well, then that's what you've done. Or what I've done, in this instance."

"Have you ever killed a man?" I asked him. He loaded his pipe, not answering, until I became self-conscious for having put the question. "I mean," I explained, "you must have been through both the world wars, weren't you?"

"It feels to me," he sighed, "I've been through every bloody war in the whole *verdomde* universe."

"*Verdomde*?"

"It's Dutch. That's the language in which Esquemeling first published his book in Amsterdam in 1678. The copy I've loaned you is a later English edition, from 1699. Are you enjoying it?" I had to confess I was finding it difficult to read, first because of the antique printing with S's that looked like F's; second because the content was just a little more horrible than I was ready for.

"As to your first point, sorry I don't have a newer edition. It's never been out of print, actually; very popular indeed. As to your second point, I presume you must have met the Dutchman Rock Brasiliano, and read about his roasting Spaniards on spits, and the Frenchman Nau, called L'Ollonais, who tore open some unfortunate chap and cut out his heart and took bites from it in order to elicit information from his other captives. Is that what's got you feeling squeamish?" It was indeed, particularly right at this moment, fresh after my close, personal disposal of Grendel. He seemed to read my thoughts.

"Well, you get animals in any profession. Brasiliano and L'Ollonais are types who are always around."

"Around where?"

"Everywhere. In every society since prehistoric times. I daresay if you could line up a hundred caveman chaps, and a hundred modern chaps—lorry drivers, dentists, accountants, and whatnot—and could wire up their heads to have a look at their hopes and fears and loves and hates—and problems—you'd get about the same readings. In each group, you can bet there'll be some chap who's a saint, soaked in loving-kindness, and another who's an absolutely awful sod, ready to soak his beard in blood."

"But, the world's come a long way . . ."

"Toward much of the same," he finished my sentence for me with a wave of his arm. "We're on our way to conquering the planet with our machinery, maybe even space, but our minds have stayed the same size." He brooded. "And I reckon we'll always have our L'Ollonais one way or another. The irony is, when Alexander of Macedon, known to history as 'the Great,' let his army commit atrocities that I'll spare you in your fragile frame of mind, it barely tarnished his reputation. Or when Caesar had the hands of thirty thousand prisoners chopped off or . . . on and on. L'Ollonais was a small-timer. And when it came to cutting out hearts, the Aztecs did them by the thousands, which the Spanish put a stop to. Read the journal of Bernal Diaz. Dear boy, you're looking a bit sallow. Let's pass on to a brighter subject."

"If the world's hopeless, where does that leave us?"

"Hispaniola, in your case. It seems to me I left you cruising around there with some rather agreeable new friends who are French buccaneer chaps, but not L'Ollonais. Your mates may be a bit rough 'round the edges, and short on etiquette, but they are not wantonly cruel. Like many other buccaneers, they'll have nothing to do with sods like L'Ollonais. He's a renegade among renegades."

"What happened to him?"

"He got chopped into pieces by a bunch of Darien Indians, and nobody mourned. It was the likes of him that gave a bad name to an honest profession."

"Honest?"

"Well, you've got your letter of marque from your authority, and you're out doing what he wants you to do, which is the same thing all the governments are doing, and there are quite a few ships like yours, large and small. Scores of them. Sometimes you get together with some other buccaneer ships, until you've got a squadron together with enough men to raid a Spanish port."

"Like Drake?" I missed being Drake.

The captain nodded. "Or the Vikings. A surprise amphibious strike in force gets the place just long enough for you to go in, take what you like, and get out before anybody can come against you. It worked again and again. Esquemeling is full of examples, which I daresay you've read."

I said I preferred listening to him, rather than struggling through Esquemeling, and reminded him he'd said something about my meeting that author.

"Did I?" He scowled. "Very well, meet him. He's in your own crew. Decent enough bloke. Came out under indenture, got treated brutally for three years, and is now doing the same thing you are." He became preoccupied with trying to light his pipe with a box of damp matches. I found him some dry ones. "Ahh," he said, puffing.

"And Esquemeling tells me . . . what?"

"Not a bloody thing. He doesn't speak English, and you don't speak Dutch, or much French, for that matter. You are therefore grateful when your ship sails to rendezvous with a squadron of buccaneer vessels under Morgan. There are a lot of English ships, and you join one."

"You mean I jump ship again?"

"No need. Your mates vote to let you go with your countrymen. Remember, it's a free society, where the rules are about the same on all the ships."

"What rules?"

"The rules of the brotherhood, which is quite a huge family, some thousands of free sailors, always on the move, no ground to call their own. But there are plenty of welcoming ports in which to spend your take and fix your ships. As to the rules, it's time you learn them, but not until tomorrow, when I want to get down into the cellar and start designing a proper carriage for the gun." This had been carried back to the cellar by Noel Nauss. "We'll need all the original iron bits so I can measure 'em, and they'll all have to get their rust knocked off. You can do that part. First we'll require an electrical cord down to the cellar." He handed me a list. "And here are some other things we'll want."

Police Chief Moehner showed up on Saturday morning. The Chief had a flat pair of eyes stuck into a face that was also flat, with a squashed look to it. He was investigating a reported gunshot in the neighbourhood the previous afternoon. Mother said she'd heard something she thought was a backfire, and I nodded.

"Do you have any firearms on the premises?" he wanted to know, learning there was my father's old twelve-gauge shotgun. This he asked to see and, while Mother was off rummaging for it, the captain came down and was also questioned.

"Eh?" he asked, cupping his hand to his ear.

"Gunshot? Did you hear anything like a gunshot?"

The captain reflected. "Didn't somebody say a truck back-fired?" He was again in bumbly mode. Yes, he did have a firearm, a flare pistol, which was on his yacht at Tom's, but the chief's interest was diverted by Mother reappearing with the shotgun. It was obvious from its dust that it hadn't been fired in years.

"Mmmm," he said, handing it back to her. "Have any of you by chance seen my nephew's dog, Grendel? I ask because he's missing, and was last seen near here." Mother shook her head, looking at me; I shook my head, too.

"Problem about a pissing dog?" the captain asked, his voice louder than normal.

"Missing," said the Chief, raising his own voice automatically; "a missing dog."

"Oh," said the captain. "No, I'm not missing any dog. Don't have one. Frightfully good of you to come 'round with your concern, however. I do hope you locate the owner."

"Mmmm," said Chief Moehner, flatly, and went away. Mother was amused by the captain's treatment of him.

"Are you having a little hearing trouble, today?" she asked.

"No, Madam," he answered with a straight face. "Never wore a little earring, or any other kind, although I've had a number of shipmates who did."

I spent the rest of the morning rigging lightbulbs and gathering all the tools he wanted so that work could begin after noon dinner. He had made a drawing of the carriage we were to build, and began marking it with measurements of everything while teaching me more nomenclature than I really wanted to know: trunnions, cascabel, astragals, fillets, ogees, chase, vent, muzzle swell and molding, grips—and these things had only to do with the barrel. The carriage and all of its axle fittings, checks, caps, clamps, beds (and other things too numerous to list) made a universe of their own.

"Rather sophisticated for such a plain old thing, eh?"

It was indeed, and I was grateful not to have to memorise the names of all the pieces that I was put to rust-chip and wire-brush, tediously, according to what he called "the rule of procedure." I reminded him of his own teaching that the only rule was that there weren't any rules.

"That, too, is true."

"How can they both be true?"

"A splendid example of the parallel existence of contradictory truths; it's also true that you're holding your chisel at too sharp an angle, and you're nicking through into the iron, which is very disrespectful of the rather rare artefact we're here to restore." I adjusted my chisel. "As to the rules, each ship's crew made their own. Those were the articles, signed by everybody aboard."

"So I have to sign them?" I asked this question simply to prompt him into the present tense, and to spinning his story in the second person. Of all his methods, this was my favourite. There was something in its immediacy that bred my astonishing instants of being in the action, or at least having that very vivid illusion.

"Everybody had to sign the ship's articles," he answered.

"Rule one: no stealing, which meant no concealing of any loot. Every man could take whatever clothing he wanted, but nothing else over the value of one piece of eight—*peso* in modern lingo— on pain of marooning. Maybe death. It was the worst offense. As to the others, nobody could leave the ship without the permission of his mates . . ."

"Which I get in order to join my new ship, right?"

"Please keep your eye on your work, or we'll never finish. Then there was the rule against women sailing with the ship, although in port their presence was vigorously welcomed. No gambling was allowed: too many problems came from it. No fighting was permitted aboard the ship. If a couple of blokes got across each other and wanted to square off, they had to wait until they could take it ashore. Every man was required to be armed, to his taste, with weapons that he was responsible for maintaining and using with skill. It was a martial community, and the chaps all took pride in their knives and swords, pistols and muskets, sometimes pikes, whatever combination they felt best with. Last, everybody did have to obey the officers, first the captain, then the first and second mates, but especially the quartermaster, who was elected like the captain. The quartermaster was the civil authority, led attacks, got command of any significant prizes. Under those chaps came the bosun, and his mates. I make it about four and three-quarters inches."

"Beg pardon?"

"Width of the axles," he said, making another note. "The rest of the rules had to do with shares. Everybody was on shares, like fishermen. The captain traditionally got two shares; the main officers got a share and a half; the petty officers and artists got a share and a quarter." He explained that the word "artist" was applied to all who had a special skill, such as the surgeon, cooper, sailmaker, any navigator, and musicians. "The musicians always got Sundays off, but there was many a Sabbath when we played anyway."

"We?"

"Musicians. We've always been around, and here we are still. Among the brethren of the coast, musicians were held in high regard. A good fiddler or piper could choose his ship. The buccaneer Montbars, also known as the Exterminator, had a wheel-fiddler aboard who got two full shares, same as the captain. Why? Because he could bring that whole rowdy lot to their knees with his music. Even drummers were honoured, and buglers—although as lesser artists, they usually got less share."

"What share do I get?" Trying again to insinuate myself into the scene, I got an irritated look.

"For what? Where've you earned it?" he growled.

I told him that was entirely up to him, expressing my confidence in his ability to make up a story where I could see some action and earn a share.

"Make up, you say." He looked at me in a way that I will never forget. It was a flat gaze that regarded me, looked directly into me, then seemed to drink me (there is no other way of describing this). His eyes became like black holes, pulling me into them, into a bottomless depth of nothingness. I had never seen the like.

"Common hands got a share," he said, continuing as though what had just happened between us had not happened. "Boys might get a half-share, if not worse. But nobody got any share until the social insurance money got paid out . . ." He paused, making another notation, which gave me a chance to recover from whatever it was that I had just experienced, and catch up.

"Social insurance?"

"Oh aye, and the first in the Americas, I would say. Here you had all these refugee chaps, all escaped from some navy, lord, army, indenturer, or owner who never looked after them except to use them, so the first thing they did with their new freedom, after founding their democracy, was to take care of each other in ways no government had ever done for them. And that's how the rules were shaped, starting with payment for on-the-job injuries. For instance, on Esquemeling's ship, the articles paid six hundred pieces of eight to anybody losing his right arm; the left one was worth five hundred, which was also the value of the right leg. Getting the left one shot away or lopped off you got four hundred.

"Funnily enough, the Frenchies only paid one hundred pieces of eight for an eye. The Brits paid more for one of those. Details varied from ship to ship, but the convention was the same on all of them. And if you were killed, your share would be sent along to whomever you had designated. Perhaps your mother. All these moneys were paid off the top of the take."

"What was a piece of eight worth?" I asked. I was no longer so eager for one of his stories as I had been. He gave me no more alarm, however, just an answer to my question. I learned a piece of eight was a silver coin of about the size of an American silver dollar. It was easily clipped into halves, or quarters, or eighths, for making change. Two bits were a quarter. One eight-real piece of eight was worth about five English shillings, which was about one month's wages for a common sailor aboard a merchant ship. It bought bed and board at a decent inn for a couple of days. A hundred of them bought a slave.

Other silver coinage was in wide circulation—crowns, ecus, thalers, ducatons, and various kinds of dollars, but pieces of eight were the standard unit of currency throughout the Caribbean for some three hundred years. That was simply because there were so many of them, made in the millions from the silver mined by the Spaniards in Bolivia and Peru. The Spanish mines also yielded gold, which was minted into doubloons. These were about the same size as a silver piece of eight, but one doubloon was worth a heavy bag of silver. Gold coins were the most desirable of all booty: louis d'or, sovereigns, guineas, and such. According to the captain, the value of gold had remained more or less constant throughout all history, an ounce of it always being worth a full suit of clothes, head to foot, in any time, any civilisation.

Following gold, he discussed the value of gemstones, silks, brocades, religious artefacts, and lesser, more usual, cargo down to logwood, hides, sugar, and rum. Here he paused wistfully, concluding the lesson with remarks on other desirable spirits that were sometimes found: "Brandy, aquavit, wine, gin . . . so many," he sighed, promising to give me another story when he could tell it with a mug of punch in front of him, and at a time with nobody around to interrupt. Then he sent me above to clean up for my evening duties, leaving him alone in the cellar to finish his cannon notes.

The Reverend Corkum had a cold. "Abstinence is the fundamental virtue," he pronounced, pausing for what might have been dramatic effect, except it was a sneeze coming on. "Because," he said, recovering with the aid of a handkerchief, "abstinence is the basic discipline that enables all of the other virtues." The Reverend was making slow but determined progress through the cardinal virtues, giving me a lot of time to examine other things.

There sat the captain with the choir, wearing the robe, looking contemplative under his dark eyebrows, saintly even, with white hair surrounding his face like a biblical prophet. I saw him as a kind of saviour, to the inn, to me, and all of us, even Meg. Thanks to the concert, she had become something of a local celebrity, written up in the *Baywater Beacon*. The first weekly Saturday Music Night at the inn, with her and the captain, had brought in new customers, which was all right.

I felt more estranged from Meg than ever. She was there for her work, and for Chloe, as she'd named her new kitten, but then she was gone, playing with this group or that one. She did not invite the captain. Despite there being something about him that repelled Meg, I was magnetised, and it had come between Meg and me. At the same time, her cautions had lodged in me. He was indeed an actor, enough of one to leave questions. I had been seduced by his stories, but yesterday's unsettling view of his eyes as black pits in his face was fresh in my mind. It had not felt directly threatening, but I was left with a sense of having experienced something outside of my ken, and a danger.

Danger attended him, from his entry in a winter storm, to the secret cannon seizure, to bringing in the dangerous Noel Nauss to deal with the Moehner boys, to the shooting of Grendel. He seemed to take nourishment from danger, creating bits of it quite casually, in an ongoing way that I was helplessly drawn to. If my family had gotten any notion of what had been happening I'd have had a lot of explaining, but he had handled everything so well, there had been no fuss. Just secrets.

"Truth is liberation," proclaimed Reverend Corkum, concluding a sermon that I had mostly missed, and the captain rose with the choir for the concluding hymn. Nor was I the only one who was drawn to him. He had made a very favourable impression on lots of people, including Jenny, after he had given her the golden link from the chain of Granuaile. Jenny wanted to see him again, with some questions she had about it, and told me after the services that she planned to visit. "On my own," as she put it, exercising her new freedom that afternoon.

Sunday dinner was a cheerful gathering, following the success of the music evening and its promise of more to come. Chief Moehner's visit was discussed, but only briefly, because there was little to make of it, except Uncle Robin noted the missing dog was the one I'd complained about. Aunt Karen got in her customary probe.

"Captain Johnson," she addressed him. "I've a question to you, as an historian, and because you are Jim's teacher on a subject. What, in your opinion, is history's value to us, and how is that lesson best taught?"

"Madam, in response to the first part of your question, there are two answers. The first is to the individual historian, who learns to read through mountains of ancient documents, putting it all together, with the ultimate realisation that he, or she, is reading about people who were the same people that we are, our own biggest advantage being that we are not yet dead. The second part is that this lesson is never learned. It appears to be our situation. How is it best taught? I would think, ideally, by bringing the student to the earliest possible experience of it."

Jenny showed up a couple of hours later, but we could not locate the captain. We had no appointment. He was not at his table, nor in his room. The only other place I could think of was the cellar, where we had spent the previous afternoon with the cannon, so there we went. Sure enough, the latch was off the cellar door, and the light within was burning. There was no sign of the captain, however. Investigating beyond the glare of the electric bulb, I found the iron grill over the deepest basement open. Its rusted lock had been cut off with a hacksaw, likely the one I had found for him.

"What's down there?" Jenny asked, peering into the darkness below. I told her the little I knew about the deepest cellars, and she was immediately fascinated, wanting to follow him with our flashlight. I thought it best just to call, which I did, with no response from the blackness.

"Let's go," said Jenny, starting down the stone steps. I tried to protest, but had no choice except to follow her, holding the flashlight so she could see where her feet were leading us.

"Which way?" she asked. I had no idea where he was. The corridor at the bottom of the steps went in two directions; each led to interconnected chambers, but the left-hand fork was the longest one, and the most complex. I called out again. The dank darkness was like a sponge, absorbing my cries. Off to the left went Jenny. "Come on," she said. I warned her there were big rats, which didn't seem to bother her. She went right ahead anyway, and I had to follow along, so that she didn't slip on the slick spots, or take a stumble. When I decided we had gone far enough, I stopped, so she had to also. "C'mon," she beckoned, but she couldn't budge me.

"I don't like it down here," I told her, "and I don't know my way around in it, either. Hullooo . . ." I called out again. Again my voice was swallowed by the darkness.

"Well then, let me have the light," she said, coming back to me and reaching. I pulled my arm away to keep her from grabbing it, hit my elbow, and dropped it. The tin flashlight fell on stone and went out. "Now you've done it," she said. "You'd better get it going again." But no shaking or clicking worked, and the darkness was absolute. Even when our eyes had fully adjusted to it, we could see nothing. Holding hands to keep track of one another, we started back the way we had come, clinging to the right-hand wall of the corridor for reference. There were side chambers, however, and other passages, which were immediately confusing.

"I think I can find our way out," said Jenny, but I didn't trust her with that, insisting that we stick to the wall, and find the other side of its gaps one by one, until we came back to the steps leading above. "Shhhhh," she hushed me. I listened into the silence, hearing nothing except drips from the ceiling splashing into puddles. No, there was something else, the sound of water lapping. On top of our other difficulties, the tide was flooding in—how rapidly I did not know, or to what depth. I told Jenny I thought we had better keep moving. Underfoot, further impeding us, were fallen stones and fragments of ancient mortar.

"This way," Jenny said, trying to tug me in a direction other than the one I was following. I told her she was going into a side-alley, and we argued about it, whispering. There was something about the place that suppressed loud conversation. In the midst of this, at the same time, I heard a gurgling noise, then felt my shoes filling with icy water. I stooped to feel the floor; dipped my hand into a fast-flowing stream, and experienced a moment of terror. Which way to turn? We were soon going to be wading, and then swimming,

"I *know* it's this way," I insisted, and we were arguing some more, when we both were transfixed by an explosion of light out of a side passage.

"Master Hawkins? Mistress MacGregor?" came the captain's

voice, as he played the beam of his flashlight on us. I was standing in water; Jenny had taken refuge on a fallen stone, and still had dry feet. He waded to her and picked her up.

"What are you two doing down here?" he asked, starting to carry her in the direction I had wanted to go. I waded along behind, following his light, nursing the same question about him that he had just asked us. In short order, we found the steps leading above, beyond danger.

"What were *you* doing down here?" Jenny put my question for me. "Because we were just trying to follow you."

"Exploring the foundations, with the natural interest of an elderly historian, and also with an electric torch. I would recommend one of those to yourselves next time you take a notion to go down there, which I would not recommend at all. Particularly without consulting a tide table, or getting proper footwear." He was wearing fisherman's boots, I noticed as I emptied streams of water from my shoes.

"What were you looking for down there?" asked Jenny. "Treasure?"

This got a laugh out of him. "Treasure to be sure, Mistress, the pearl of knowledge. Let's get young Jim here up into the warmth before he gets frostbite in his feet." He started ushering us out of the cellar.

"What did you find down there?" asked Jenny.

"Nothing so precious as yourselves," he answered, slamming down the grating over the stairs, and securing it with a brand-new padlock. Above, I was trying to think of how to explain to Mother my wet shoes, assuming that everything that had just happened was to be kept secret, as usual. I was getting used to secrecy, even developing a taste for it. "Don't tell anybody about this," I cautioned Jenny on our way above.

Jenny had a last question for him. "Do you think there could be pirate treasure buried down there?"

The captain made a helpless gesture. "Dear Mistress Mac-Gregor. Jennifer. Jenny. May I call you Jenny? The pirates hardly ever buried treasure. They simply didn't go around doing that. On the whole, the legends of pirate treasure are myths." Jenny asked again about the buried treasure of Captain Kidd. The captain made a face. "Quite. Well, he's one of the exceptions, but his treasure didn't stay buried for very long; same story with Calico Jack. It's your Robert Louis Stevenson chap who's given everybody the notion of pirates burying treasure, shooting the poor sods who buried it, making secret maps, with X's and skulls and whatnot. Rubbish." Jenny was not satisfied with his answer, I could tell, but she had to leave. After she was gone, I told him that she could be trusted not to say anything to anybody. Both of his eyebrows lifted.

"Not say anything about what?" he asked. "You mean about going into the cellar?" Here he flagged Mother, who was passing by. "Madam, please take this," he said, handing her a key, explaining it was to the new lock he had put on the grating over the deep cellar. She wanted to know why he had removed the older lock. "Historical curiosity," was his response.

"You went down there?" she asked with an alarmed look, and a glance at me. "Did you take Jim?"

"No, Madam, I did not," he truthfully answered. Mother launched into the various reasons why nobody was allowed in the cellars, starting with the dangers. There were also all the vague, old, dark tales: even if they were discounted, there was nothing good or redeeming in those lower regions. Last, there was a specific clause in our insurance policy that called for the lowest cellar to be sealed at all times.

He nodded. "And so it is, but now you have a working lock again."

"I'd prefer it not working," she fussed. He assured her that he was educated to the dangers of archaeological investigation, and had the experience to pursue it without risk.

"What do you hope to find?"

He shrugged. "You never know. Possibly a bit more information about whatever the present structure was built over. By my reckoning, it was indeed here long before the town. It's of no great importance, I suppose. But don't you think it would be enlightening to know more about this ancient treasure of a place that you're caretaking for history?" He was persuasive, but Mother shook her head, not thinking it an important enough reason to risk our insurance. The captain took a new tack. "There's also the possibility that something with some antique value might be found." This got her attention, but she pointed out that Grandfather had explored the place, finding nothing, and no doubt it had been well picked through by others, earlier. "Quite," he nodded, "and perhaps there's nothing to be found, but did you know there's a side corridor that's been planked closed? Nobody's touched that in the last century, I'd say, and who's to know what's behind it?"

"What could be?" she asked.

"That's my point. Who's to know until we pull away some old planks and go in?" He allowed a moment for this question to be absorbed while fussing with his pipe. "My proposal is, I'll supervise the investigation, and if I find anything in that chamber, behind its barrier, I'll take a share of its value. Then the inn should have a share, and yourself, and Jim here. So there's a quarter to me, and the rest of it to you. What do you say?"

The upshot of it was that he got not only Mother's agreement to probe the secrets of the labyrinth below the inn, but my services as well. "I insist," he said, "that anything I might find be witnessed *in situ* by a loyal representative of the establishment. Also, I'll need somebody to hold a light while I break through and then do my work." Whatever questions or doubts that I'd had, they were dispelled by his openness. I agreed, resolving to take two flashlights down there next time.

"Why are you wearing your Sunday shoes?" asked Mother, noticing my footwear. I told her I'd gotten my regular ones wet.

11

My First Toast

Having gotten permission to explore the inn's deep cellar, the captain appeared to lose interest in it. He spent long days working on *Merry Adventure* in Tom's shop, returning for supper. Then he would write, or weave his macramé, always bringing out his pennywhistle around the time Meg finished her duties. Often enough she ignored him. "You know he wants to play music with you," I told her in passing one evening. Alone by his fire, he was piping a sad Gaelic air with long tremolos. She listened with a critical ear.

"Very seductive, but he gets enough of my time as it is, and he's not getting me tonight." So saying, she went off to her room to play her fiddle to her cat, and it was the same tune, minus tremolo.

With Grendel out of the way, the trip to and from school was like floating, though school itself remained unimproved. I told Jenny about my startling experience of seeing the captain's eyes as black holes, then regretted it right away, because it got her into her occult theories. She wanted to see for herself. I assured her whatever I had experienced had to have been some kind of hallucination. Also, she was eager to get back into the cellars. As to that, he hadn't mentioned it again. Nor had he been inclined toward any more stories, and nothing was happening at all. It was like a moment of dead air at sea, soon to change.

He had left me preparing to sail with Morgan's buccaneers, and I reminded him about it several times, finally getting a commitment. He would deal with Morgan on Sunday, after supper, when everybody had cleared out. The two of us were about to be left alone. Robin was driving Aunt Karen and Mother up to Halifax for errands and a doctor's appointment. Meg was going off to play her fiddle at the Longliner Café in Baywater with a guitar player named Lenny. Nobody would be back before suppertime Monday. Mother would leave us a pot of her leek and potato soup, plus plenty of sausages, sauerkraut, solomongundy, and such. We both assured her we would be very well off, and would take good care of the inn. The family left around midafternoon, in a last-minute flurry of instructions from Mother, as though she were going away for a year.

"Yes, Mother," I said, and she finally did leave, again reminding me not to forget to water her plants. At last I was able to present myself at the captain's table, ready to be with him. He was warming up his pennywhistle by the fire.

"Don't you have homework other than your pirates paper?" he asked. I confessed that I did have math and English. "Well, let's get the decks cleared," he said, starting to play his instrument. I brought my books to a next-door table, working my way through some plane geometry while he played amazing variations on little themes that he seemed to make up as he went along. Meg was still around somewhere, waiting for Lenny the guitar player to come with his car. Her bag was packed and by the door, with her violin case. She was going to stay over with friends.

The captain's improvisations must have gotten to her, because she came downstairs, took her fiddle out of its case, tuned it, and began playing with him, picking up the music. This time, she was forced to follow his wanderings because they were no known tune. The music began to really get going, with Meg improvising to the captain's improvisations, when the bell rang over the door as it opened, and Lenny came in, very lanky, with a grin and a friendly slouch. "Should I get my guitar?" he asked.

"We're going," said Meg, putting her fiddle back in its case. "I'll take my instrument and Chloe," she said. "You take my bag." Lenny picked it up, gave us a parting grin, and ambled along after her. The captain's gaze followed them out; then he caught me watching him.

"I don't know why Meg's so rude to you," I tried to apologise for her. "I mean, I don't know why she doesn't like you, what with all you have done for her . . ." He stopped me with a wave of his hand.

"My problem with Meg's not that she doesn't like me, but that she likes me too well." He followed this improbable-sounding pronouncement with a big wink, before picking up his music where he had left off. He used the loud ticking of the old clock as a metronome, weaving it with syncopations. After a while he stopped playing and laughed.

"I think I've got it," he chuckled.

"What?"

"The tune I've been looking for," he said, looking mightily pleased, "and I think I'll celebrate that tonight."

I reminded him he'd promised me Morgan's story.

"And I'll give it to you." The clock chimed. "First, suppertime," said he, rising, and the next hour was given to meal preparation, which he directed as though our kitchen were his own. With the potatoes baking, the soup and sauerkraut simmering, and Lunenburg sausages just starting to sizzle, he commanded the solomongundy to be brought out. "We'll start with that, and you'll find a bottle of aquavit in the freezer," he told me, turning the sausages. I found it there, almighty cold, a kind of liquor that he must have brought from *Merry*, because it wasn't known locally. He wanted a beer to go with it. I said that I guessed his gout must be gone.

"Gone, yes. I've been livin' pure for a month, and also I'm gettin' younger now. Ahhh," he said, tasting the aquavit; it was closely followed by a slug of beer and a mouthful of Mother's solomongundy. Praising her recipe (pickled herring, onions, and herbs) he had another immediate drink of aquavit, before commanding the bottle back into the freezer. "Here's to refrigerators," he toasted. Out of his sight, I tried a nip of the strange liquor, and it was like frozen fire. Copying the captain, I washed it down with some beer. When I returned, he was singing.

"O solomongundy, solomongundy
Good all week long, Mondy through Sundy
Sailing from Lundy to foggy old Fundy,
How I loves my sweet solomongundy."

We had our supper at his table by the fire, and the captain spoke at length of the virtues of solomongundy, a favoured delicacy among sailors for hundreds of years, according to him, with many variations in recipe, but the common virtue of keeping well without refrigeration.

"And the pirates ate a lot of solomongundy?" I put to him. He seemed in a mellow mood, but my simple question made him grimace.

"Oh aye, they et it, I et it, we all et it, except there is no *they*. You can't say 'the pirates, 'because there wasn't any 'the pirates.' Are you sneaking drinks?" he asked conversationally, regarding me with a level eye. After some squirming, I admitted that I had done that once or twice. "Please don't tell my mother," I remember asking him, and he grimaced again.

"We're mates. If you're going to drink, I'm not your judge. Mates don't do that, which is not to say they don't see, however, and what I see is you not being straightforward with your mate, which is me. No blame. I'd just say if you're minded to drink, that's something you can do with a mate. I wouldn't recommend your getting legless, nor anybody, except . . ." he interrupted himself, finishing with the scouring of his pipe bowl, then its loading.

"Except?" I reminded him.

"You're on your own," he shrugged. I went to the bar, drew myself a beer, and returned, asking for some of his aquavit. He pushed the bottle toward me, and for the first time in my life, I openly poured myself a shot of liquor. Feeling initiated, I raised my first toast.

"To the pirates!" I said.

"As I was saying earlier, there aren't any 'the pirates,' but I'll drink to old shipmates and new ones, and to your good education, young Jim."

"If there weren't any pirates, who are we talking about?" I asked, tossing off my drink in the same way he had done. I was pleased I'd accomplished it without getting tears in my eyes. I started to pour myself another, but the captain stopped me.

"Easy," he cautioned, "Saying 'the pirates' is like saying 'the politicians,' or 'lorry drivers,' or 'printers.' If you land on any one of them, particularly pirates—who are even more independent than printers—you get too much of a collection of individuals to lump them together into a *they*. I think you'd better put that bottle back into the freezer, lest it get warm or too soon gone. Neh?"

When I returned, he handed me an old coin, actually a slug of silver, very heavy, highly irregular, and much thicker than a silver dollar. He identified it as a piece of eight, minted in Mexico in 1655, pointing out the old coat of arms and cross of Catholic Spain. "That's a little piece of Morgan's treasure. Look at its highlights, where it's polished from lots of hands, maybe Morgan's. See the darkness of its age in the stamped indentations. Heft it, feel it, and you'll feel its story." I did as I was told. I cannot say I got any kind of "reading," (Jenny's word) from the ancient object, much as I tried. I clutched it and closed my eyes, but its story came from the captain, who said it was one of thousands taken in the sack of Panama, where he proceeded to steer me.

"It is the year of our Lord 1670, by the Gregorian calendar, and it is December, which is quite a nice month in the Sea of the Caribs—balmy and with no hurricanes. As I remember, we had you in the Caymans, aboard . . . what ship did we have you aboard?" I couldn't recollect his mentioning it. "Make it *Satisfaction.* You're aboard the old *Satisfaction,* twenty-two guns (plus swivels), Morgan's flagship, on your way toward the Isthmus of Panama with the greatest buccaneer fleet ever assembled, and satisfaction's what everybody's feeling. You and your mates have suppered on solomongundy, turtle soup, and pork pepperpot; plantains and rum for dessert. You've dined as well as any sailor alive, and now you're having a belch and a smoke and a jar of punch with your mates, watching the sails drawing circles among the first stars.

"It's last twilight. The sun has just sunk into the clouds of the western horizon, and there's a sweet evening breeze, an' all the vessels loafing along on a gentle sea with lanterns lit—sloops, barks, ketches, hagboats, pinks, busses . . . and one of them has a fiddler whose music comes down to you on the wind. Over half the ships are English; a third or so are French, plus two or three Dutchmen, and a few whose nationality doesn't leap out at you. You've got Europeans, colonials, free blacks, West Indians, Orientals, two thousand renegade refugees altogether, with every mixture of race and religion. I wish you'd stop squeezing your eyes closed and let go your death grip on that coin. In fact," he said, taking it back, "let's clear our dinner mess."

Just as he was pulling me into his picture, he tore me out of it, directing kitchen cleanup, making me do every familiar thing differently from the way I'd been trained. During the washing, rinsing, and drying, he summarised Morgan, characterising him as a dark, burly Welshman who came to the Caribbean with the English expedition that had captured Jamaica in 1655. He had been privateering ever since, sailing under Sir Christopher Myngs, who was a student of Drake's tactics. The captain had a high regard for Morgan, not just as a sailor and commander, but as a shrewd tactician with the skills to hold together and actually command squadrons of buccaneer ships, manned by what he called "the least tamable of all beings."

Among his several triumphs, Morgan had looted the principal Spanish ports of Maracaibo and Portobelo, to the great benefit of all who sailed with him; and to Jamaica, whose governor had provided him and his ships their letters of marque. "So Morgan was perfectly legal," I summarised, getting a chuckle out of him.

"Legal? Oh, aye. Very legal, except for the fact that the governor at Port Royal, a chap named Modyford, has been issuing privateering licences even during a time of declared peace between England and Spain, which is a bit dicey. He's gambling on Morgan bringing in so much money, he'll be able to buy his way out of whatever dustup comes from London. But it's his neck on the line, not yours, because your ship has his authorisation. They all do. Some have documents not just from the English governor, but French and Dutch ones too, so whatever country's ship one captures, the correct licence is on hand to justify it. All quite legal, wherever you go."

"And I am going to . . . ?" I prompted him.

"Panama. It is the crown jewel of Spain's American empire on the Pacific, the conduit for untold wealth, and a virginal port, never taken by any enemy. Panama tempted Drake, though not even he had plucked that plum. Now it's your target, and it's why Morgan's been able to recruit thirty-eight ships, packed with the brethren, for the most ambitious raid ever undertaken by buccaneers, then or ever after, and that's where you are."

I noted I had been there for weeks, and I wasn't getting anywhere. "Right," he nodded, promising a change of scene after I'd mopped the pantry. With that done, and the fire tended, I drew the beer he requested, plus another for myself, and sat down, ready to pick up where we had left off. I asked to see the piece of eight again; he handed it to me, sketching on a paper place mat the Isthmus of Panama, describing Morgan's strategy. Panama was a dot on the Pacific side, fortified against attack from the sea, but its only landward defence was a hard jungle trail between it and the Caribbean. Morgan planned to cross this, first taking the fort guarding the mouth of the Chagres River. That was a navigable waterway for the large canoes that he had brought to cover most of the seventy-mile neck.

By the captain's account, Morgan had sent four of his toughest ships ahead of the fleet to storm the fort at Chagres, and they had done it with a great slaughter on both sides. "You get there a few days later, to the stink of two hundred corpses, sunning, awaiting burial. From the fort above you come the sounds made by the injured, who are dying all the time as their flyblown wounds fester in the heat." I smelled the stench of death and disease more vividly than I wanted to, with a rotten sweetness, but I was diverted by having to launch a dugout canoe.

"Nobody in your own canoe takes more than the clothes on his back, his weapons, ammunition, a straw hat, a pouch of personals, a water-skin, and food for a day or two. There'll be plenty of game upriver. You're going to be moving fast. About fifteen hundred of you start out; the rest stay behind to man the fleet and the fort. At first, the river is broad and sluggish; you are fresh, and make good progress."

I felt the wooden bilge of the canoe with my bare feet, the paddle making swirls in yellow-brown water. Suddenly I was alarmed by my experience of these sensations. I'd felt only moments of such reality before; this was prolonged, with no end to its depth. That thought brought me instantly back to the table, and my fire, and the winter wind outside.

"Oh!" I said, looking at him with round eyes.

"It's just thoughts interrupted by other thoughts. Don't think. Let go your thoughts . . . whoosh," he said, with a sudden wave, as though blowing them away.

As the stream narrowed, the current against us increased, forcing rests. The river, lower than usual, shallowed rapidly, and was studded with snags. Rests became more frequent. Even slower than the canoes were the men chopping their way along both banks, the flanking parties whose job was to break up any ambush. The mosquitoes loved my sweat, and there was no swatting while paddling, or no paddling would have gotten done. We were covered in bites that got infected when scratched.

Four days of hard paddling got us to the first of the Spanish stockades guarding the river. Everybody was out of food, nearly out of water, and ready for a good fight, but it wasn't there. The Spaniards had burnt and abandoned the place, leaving no enemy, no food, nothing. The river was too low to navigate any farther, leaving two-thirds of the distance to be covered on a trail where every bridge had been destroyed. The enemy had plenty of warning and plenty of troops, but where were they? More important, where was all the wild game? Itchy and sweaty, I was now hungry as well, really hungry, and it jerked me back to reality, salivating for the sausage that had been leftover from dinner. The captain laughed.

"It's all in your mind," he said, assuring me that I hadn't even begun to get hungry yet. "You're all good hunters, but a whole army of you, fifteen hundred irritable, swearing, bug-bitten buccaneers, has frightened away every edible creature for miles. Also, you don't know which plants are safe to eat here—and some aren't." For the next ten minutes or so, I trekked for three days while eating grass, chewing on my empty leather provision pouch, getting weaker, finally staggering out of the jungle onto hilly grasslands full of cattle. The captain quoted from Esquemeling:

> *"At once they brooke ranks and shot down every beast within range. All got busy: while some hunted, others lit fires to roast the meat. One gang of men dragged in a bull, another a cow, a third a horse or a mule. The animals were hacked up and thrown, dripping with blood, on to the fire to cook. The meat scarsely had time to get*

hot before they grabbed it and began gnawing, gore running down their cheeks."

No longer at all hungry, I found myself walking again, over a rolling savannah where the wind riffled the tall grass like waves running across the ocean. Floating on the captain's story, I marched over a last hill, and there beheld the city of Panama with its roofs and spires all in great detail, although I heard from him no description of architecture. What was I seeing so vividly? As the question popped into my head, the vision vanished.

"It's gone!" I said.

"Don't think about it. At last you see your enemy. The Spanish army awaits you on the plain below, making a wall of soldiers; a long line of infantry several ranks deep, with flanking squadrons of cavalry. Your admiral, who's now your general, a sailor turned soldier, has no cavalry at all, just you lot of outnumbered buccaneers. You camp for the night on your hill, rest, eat again, and clean your weapons while Morgan explains his strategy to his captains and issues his orders.

"You attack at dawn. The rising sun is at your back, and in the eyes of your enemy. Morgan sends you not directly at the Dons but toward a lightly defended hill on the right. With it, he'll command the enemy flank from a position not easily charged by the Spanish horsemen. He hasn't much regard for their foot soldiers, many of whom are militia, but the cavalry is a powerful threat. As you move, you can see the horsemen mounting up in the distance." And there they were, with the morning light winking on their breastplates and lances.

"The next time you see them, you're coming around the hill, and they're charging right at you. Leading the buccaneer attack, however, are three hundred of the best marksmen among you, and their fire is deadly accurate. The front line of horsemen goes down, and then the next, and the charge dissolves. You cheer, but the Dons make an unexpected attack by stampeding a huge herd of wild cattle in your direction. It takes only another volley or two to divert this, and then you turn your long muskets onto the infantry. They are so close-packed, every ball hits somebody; their lines are as hard to miss as a house, but you and your brethren move freely, fanning out, making hard targets.

"The Spanish line breaks, then disintegrates; its remnants run for the city, with cutlass-swinging buccaneers right on their heels, and Panama is yours. That coin you're squeezing came from there." I realised I did have a very hard grip on it. Also, I was breathing hard. He wanted another taste of his aquavit, and more beer. I joined him, pouring our drinks measure for measure.

"To victory," I toasted. It was fun to toast.

"Oh, aye. To victory, whatever form it takes."

Whatever thrill I'd felt began to unravel with the captain's descriptions of Panama during the hours, days, and then weeks after Morgan's buccaneers swept into the city. "At the outset, the place is put to the torch by the Spaniards themselves. In case of military disaster, they've placed barrels of powder and combustibles around to spoil any idea you might have as to getting comfortable in Panama. Also, they have ships waiting, so as you're coming into the landward side of town, the Spaniards light their fuses and escape by water. There are no ships to chase them, and the town's burning."

He described a hellish street scene of flames, smoke, and surprise explosions; in the chaos, every buccaneer made his own plan of action. Some stayed grouped, ferreting out any remaining defenders; some fought fires; others sought taverns, for whatever grog might be rescued; the most businesslike went after survivors carrying valuables. Anybody caught empty-handed was urged to tell of hidden wealth by skilled persuaders. There were instances of rape and murder. Torture. "All the usual," he remarked with a languid gesture.

"Usual?" He had invoked horrors.

"Usual, aye, quite predictable. When a city fell, the survivors could rather expect to be raped and looted. The buccaneers were no different from any other invading army of their time in that way. Everybody got spoils. It's how governments kept the chaps in the soldiering life on bad pay. The Spaniards loot the Americas; you loot the Spaniards; everybody loots."

"But the screams . . ." They still rang in my head.

"Aye, the screams, the inevitable screams. How they echo." He brooded, eyeing me. "What do you do about them?"

"Do?" It was a confusing question. The captain pressed ahead with the aftermath of the battle. The city was charred ruin, making the buccaneers pick for their loot, with sparse findings. Many Spaniards had evacuated well before the action, either by sea, or into forest villages, carrying what treasure they could, or hiding it. Jewellery was thrown into wells, so that all the wells had to be dredged, and the ashes raked through. Armed companies were sent out to comb the countryside for the citizens who had fled there; vessels were found to raid the surrounding islands, where more refugees were hiding. A month was given to the search before Morgan deemed it imprudent to remain longer. Everything that had been gathered, mostly silver plate, was loaded onto 175 mules, which seemed impressive to me. "What's my share?" I wanted to know.

"Fewer than twenty coins like the one that's in your hand. That was the count when it was divided among the whole fleet back at Chagres, and there was a lot of grumbling. The sack of

Portobello was much easier, and paid ten times that much. Some, including Esquemeling, accused Morgan of cheating everyone, but the fact is that the Spaniards simply had enough warning to disperse their treasure. Morgan's buccaneer navy was just too big to keep the element of surprise, y'see. The Panama campaign marked the last big fling by the brotherhood, and Morgan was the last of its great admirals."

I asked what happened to him after that, and what happened to me, for that matter. "You both sail back to Port Royal for a bit of entertainment." He refilled his glass, but not mine, so I did. I was for sure feeling the effects of what I'd drunk before, but I didn't let that stand in my way. Next thing, I was landing with my shipmates behind Morgan, parading through the streets of Port Royal to the cheers and toasts of all the locals who would have our money soon enough. We made a grand procession before dispersing to taverns and bordellos. I wanted to know about bordellos, and he told me a few things of interest, but without more magical illusions. Instead, moving the bottle beyond my reach, he made me concentrate on the ending of his story.

"Morgan and Governor Modyford were both arrested by their own government for the Panama caper and shipped to London. There, they were detained in comfortable conditions until Spanish tempers had cooled. Morgan's little legal difficulties didn't prevent him from being knighted and sent back out as deputy governor of Jamaica. He became a wealthy plantation owner and an authority, who didn't recruit any more buccaneers, but did hang some. He died in 1687 of 'drinking and sitting up late,' according to the physician's report. Five years later, in 1692, most of Port Royal was swallowed by the sea in a massive earthquake and tidal wave. The Spaniards viewed it as divine punishment. How are you feeling?"

I told him I had never felt better, and wanted to drink another toast. "If you have any more to drink, you're going to be feeling some divine punishment of your own," he cautioned, but did not stop me. My toast was to him. My memory of exactly what I said is fuzzy: it seemed important to try to convey my appreciation for him, fumbling for words, finally calling him the best shipmate I'd ever had. Not that I had ever had any shipmates, other than Grandfather, but it was from the heart. Also, I blurted an idea I'd been nursing, which was nothing less than sailing away with him aboard *Merry* when he left. I yearned to make a voyage with him. If he left after June, I could graduate from grade school, then go. High school could wait a year. I would work without pay. "Please?" I begged. He considered.

"I have to sail to Boston in June, and I'll take you along on two conditions: first, you get your mother's permission, and second, that you now go to bed. Tomorrow's a school day," he reminded me.

"Damn school." I felt the recklessness of a warrior who had survived a battle, telling him I'd go to bed when I'd finished my beer. He relit his pipe. I don't remember our conversation after that, but I did drink up the pint in front of me, and when I eventually tried to stand, the floor hove and rocked underfoot like the deck of a ship weathering a gale. Getting up the stairs to my room was an adventure that required some assistance from him; then I was on my back, in my bed, trying to stop the ceiling from spinning so.

Alas, that was not the end of my evening, although I have no recollection of the subsequent events, until their painful aftermath. I later learned the captain had placed a large basin by my bed, but I missed it when I vomited, so he cleaned it up and left me. At some time after that, I tried to find my way out to the bathroom, losing my bearings in the hall, where I threw up again. Then I mistook the cleaning closet for the loo, and peed there, aiming for where I thought the toilet was. Unable to find my bedroom again, I lay down on a hall rug, which is where the captain found me when he came to check on my condition. I was not awakened by his carrying me back to bed. There he left me to sleep past school. He was just looking in on me again at midmorning, around the time I should have been reciting my assigned three stanzas of *The Rime of the Ancient Mariner,* when Mother came in, way ahead of schedule, closely followed by Robin and Aunt Karen. Her doctor's appointment had been canceled, so they'd gotten on the road early. I awakened to my mother's face, a mask of shock and horror, and her voice: "What's happened?" a shrill reverberation on top of the other poundings in my head. "I'm afraid he got a bit legless," the captain answered for me.

"And you let him?" she turned on him.

"Ooohh," I groaned, and promptly threw up again. After that, she found the mess the captain hadn't discovered—the one I'd made in the hall, and the cleaning closet. To this day, I don't like to think about it, though the memory of the incident remains vivid, and I have never regained a taste for aquavit.

12

A Load of Lead

It was a dismal beginning of the memorably bad February that followed. According to the astronomy chapter in my science book, the days had been getting longer and lighter by nearly a minute a day ever since the winter solstice, but in my life, any light was left over from darkness and shadow. First, there was my mother's anger, which was like a thermal force that didn't often erupt, but was fierce when it did. She attacked the stains on the rug I'd left in the upper hall (wearing her good dress), while I got cleaned up and Robin took Aunt Karen home, and the captain situated himself at his table, with pipe. I joined him there, and we both waited by the cold fireplace for whatever was to come. Mother put her buckets back where they belonged with an angry clatter, then came to us.

"Let's hear it."

I was rather hoping the captain would take on the issue, but he did not. "I got drunk," I finally said.

"I'd say. And where were you?" she asked him.

"I was here. I regret your distress. I'd planned to get things sorted out before you got back."

"You gave my twelve-year-old son liquor?" Her jaw muscles clenched, and I jumped in, explaining that it was my doing; I'd snuck drinks and he caught me at it, and he'd said not to, so I didn't, but got drunk anyway, and he'd tried to stop me. Her gaze remained fixed on the captain.

"And you didn't stop him." Here she read him the riot act: aiding and abetting the delinquency of a minor, breach of trust as the responsible adult, allowing a minor to drink on a public premises that could lose its licence for the offense. And there were other items of indictment. He nodded, puffing on his pipe, offering neither rebuttal nor apology.

"It's my own fault," I said again, sounding thin. She ignored me.

"Captain Johnson, I'd tell you to find some other place to stay, but I've spent the money you've paid me, and don't have it to give back to you. Also, you've been a friend up until now, and I'll honour that. But you've used up your honours now, and then some, and I'll thank you to sever your association with my son. You're done with each other." She regarded us both. "Are we clear on that?" We were.

Everything was gone. The voyage I'd dreamed of was gone, and the rest of my dream, which was that I would go away with him, and then come back so that he could marry my mother, and I could paint pictures of the places he had taken me. Gone. Gone also was the precious six dollars a week he had been paying me to

do mostly nothing; gone with his addictive stories and the cellar expedition—gone with everything. I was allowed to bus his table, but not to sit down with him, or to speak with him in any way that was not functional.

"Functional, aye. Well then, functional it is, if that's the rules," he said to me later.

"I hope . . ." I started to say.

"As ye hope, so shall ye fear," he interrupted me in a perfect imitation of Reverend Corkum's voice. "Which is quite true, as it works out," he added. "Let's play by the rules. Functional it is."

A nd functional it was. At school, it was the usual curriculum, and I recited my assigned lines from the *Ancient Mariner:*

"The ice was here, the ice was there,
the ice was all around;
it cracked and growled, and roared and howled . . ."

As though on cue, the old steam radiators in the classroom started to growl and clank. Part of the playground was glazed with ice and swept with snow, so everybody who was of any use played hockey, except I did not, because I was tired of taking thwacks from the Moehner boys' sticks, or being tripped by them, or cross-checked. It wasn't worth the bruises. So I abided with the girls and other supernumeraries such as Job Wirth, called Worthless Job, who was no good at sports, and also mechanically untalented.

There was Jenny to talk to, and I told her what had happened. First, she wanted to know what it felt like to be drunk, then she prodded my effort to describe the sense of reality to his

stories. She had experienced a taste of the same, and concluded that he was definitely a hypnotist, and probably an avatar as well. She judged him to be a very dangerous being, and she wanted to know when she could come over and see him again. I told her that looked like never.

That melancholy thought was uppermost in my mind as I slouched home from school at the end of the week. Without Grendel, I had no need for mindfulness, and I was able to devote my full attention to my embarrassment and general misery. With my eyes on the ground, I went through the gate, left it to click closed behind me, and was nourishing a particularly dark thought when it was blown out of my head in a sudden flash of real pain—a surprise crack from the captain's walking stick on my backside.

"Ow! Wow!" I said, rubbing the afflicted area, backing away from him. "Why did you do that?" I was not amused, but he was having a hearty old laugh at my expense.

"You looked like you were looking for worms, but they don't often come out this time of year," he commented, wiping away laugh tears. "One must stay alert," he said, twirling his stick and strolling inside.

Feeling betrayed, I did not look at him when I built his fire. If he noticed I was ignoring him, he gave no sign of it, being preoccupied with his macramé. It was the same the following evening, when he and Meg were the entertainment for the inn's Saturday Music Night, as it was listed in the paper. There were only eight customers (including Noel Nauss, who had taken to coming around), but that was eight more than usual at this time of year, when most of Nova Scotia stayed at home. He played the theme he had invented, and Meg played to his variations.

That night I had a dream I still remember vividly to this day.

It was a nightmare. I was returning from school in new snow, and came upon Klaus Moehner. He now had three dogs. He smiled at me as he gave them my old sweater to sniff, then they all charged me at once. I tried to run, but my feet were clogged in ice; I looked back as the nearest dog lunged for me with bared teeth, and behind him, behind Klaus, stood the captain, laughing and laughing. I woke up with the blankets twisted around me.

I squired Mother to church next day; the captain following at a respectful distance. Reverend Corkum had finished with the sins and virtues, and passed on to the godlessness of communism. Then the choir held forth; the captain now with a solo, with the female voices taking flight over his baritone. Back at the inn, there was Sunday supper, as usual, but without our guest. He was no longer invited. Mother had commanded his table to be set separately, so there he sat himself down, at a distance. He greeted the family in passing with friendliness, getting courtesy with frost in return. Few words were spoken during the meal. The captain finished in short order, and went out, with a polite nod in passing.

To Aunt Karen, his not having apologised was worse than the original offense, which was the focus of my mother's indignation. I was questioned by Robin, who cautioned me that he might have to file a report, and that I should be sure to tell him the truth. I did, including the fact that I had been sneaking drinks, and he had tried to get me to stop. I lifted the blame from him as much as I could, even though my own feelings in his direction were a lot shakier since he had attacked me with his stick. I did not mention that. In the end, Robin decided no misdemeanor had been committed.

"But I will check him out," he added. "I'll run his name through the system and see what we get."

"That would be interesting," said Aunt Karen.

Surprisingly, it was Meg who rescued him and got the topic dropped. She turned to me. "What I'm hearing is that you just wanted to get flashed up, right?" I allowed that was an essentially correct assessment of the situation. "Right. Well, is it something you want to do again?" Most emphatically not. My sincerity was manifest. "Well, then, there's that out of the way," she said. This settled the issue but not my own mind. Everybody seemed agreed the blame was on him more than me, and I began to see the logic of it. I was ready to ignore him at breakfast on Monday, but he was not at his table to ignore, so out I went, resolving to ignore him at suppertime.

Thwack! There it was again, stinging pain in the same place; I danced away from the surprise figure of the captain, who had ambushed me a second time, to his amusement. I told him I didn't appreciate the joke. When I came home that afternoon, I proceeded carefully through the gate and down the walk. He was nowhere around, however.

In fact, we were to see little of Captain Johnson for the rest of that month. He would breakfast, and go off to Tom's, to work on *Merry,* returning with stops along the way back to chat, at the barbershop or the Sou'wester Beverage Room, where he was very chatty with various of the Moehners, even Klaus, who obviously had not learned much about who he was talking to. The captain had become a popular figure around Grey Rocks. He was a particular favourite with Barbara Boswell, who was postmistress, and knew more about the town than anybody else in it. The captain often stopped in to the post office to see her, although he never got any mail. Nor did he ever send any, as far as I could tell. He played his pennywhistle before turning in. Sometimes Meg played with him. It seemed to me their music was his last connection with any of us ... except I kept a wary eye open when crossing the grounds.

Toward the end of the month, we got other things to think about. The health department people showed up again, three of them this time, armed with clipboards and the thick code of rules governing public eateries. Again, no sanitation flaw could be found, but there were infractions having to do with ventilation, drainage, and other technicalities. They wrote a lot of notes, then went away, promising that we would learn in due course from them what alterations would be necessary to keep the inn compliant with the current regulations.

"It means work that we don't have the money for," sighed Mother, telling Aunt Karen about it. Aunt Karen had taken a turn for the worse, and was staying with us on Robin's duty days, for Mother's care and companionship. "I smell Roy Moehner in this," she said. "He knows who to talk to who can read the rules to cost us." Aunt Karen could think of no advice, except to make the March 1 payment, giving us another three months before the next one to sort something out. We were actually making money in the winter for the first time, with a developing new clientele and prospects for a rosier future.

"That's what Moehner sees, too," Aunt Karen cautioned, "so he's stepping up the pressure. Calling a favour or two in city hall. Let's hope this is all there is to it."

It was not. Two days later the clipboard people from the provincial bureau governing hostelries showed up and spent the better part of the day. Before going off to write up our infractions, their boss tipped off Mother that she should start planning extensive rewiring, modifications to all of the lavatories, and other things.

It was defeat. Mother wept. Aunt Karen pointed out that they hadn't ticketed us yet, and we would have some period of time for compliance; it was likely that Uncle Bill, the family legal champion, would be able to get extensions, maybe modifications. "Make the March payment," Aunt Karen advised, "and we'll worry about what comes after that when it comes."

March brought a series of southeasters that were back to back. The payment was made, with no dread official letter yet. Meg tired of Lenny the guitar player, and took up with a drummer who had a Buick. Aunt Karen's condition deteriorated further, and I got the flu, along with the rest of the school.

"You say the pirates made the first democracy?" Miss Titherington challenged me. She had read the beginning of my second-semester essay, and was clear about wanting a source for that claim. "That's not been mentioned in any history I've ever read," she noted, looking at me sharply over the top rims of her reading spectacles. She demanded a complete outline. "I want to know where you're going with this, and if you have any other unusual notions. And I'm still waiting for your bibliography."

"Yes ma'am," I said, with no idea about any of it, or when I would have any, if ever. I had stopped ignoring the captain, though he showed no discernible sign of noticing, as I cleared his table or tended his fire. He got me again with his stick one evening when I stepped outside to fetch him some more logs, enraging me all over again. Why was he stalking me? My first instinct was to let his fire go out, and never build him another. But he had paid for the wood, and had overpaid me in the past, so I swallowed my pride, and steamed, and tended his fire as he sat and sipped beer. I resolved to do to him what he had been doing to me. I would never have considered such a thing a month earlier, but his ongoing abuse had finally put my hackles up. Under my hands were the newspapers I was crumpling to go under the kindling, and I rolled one up for an attack weapon. I would ambush him on his way to bed. I would dart out when he'd climbed the stairs, whack him on his backside, and see how he liked it, and escape laughing, before he realised what had happened.

I hovered, keeping an eye on him while he played his tin flute, and finished his nightcap; then I went above and positioned myself. I heard him go to the downstairs lavatory. As I re-rolled my newspaper, I had a spate of misgivings about what I was doing, but kept my determination. Any moment he would come up the stairs, and I would strike.

"If you're planning to read that newspaper," came his surprise voice behind me, "you'll find it's several weeks old. Good night." He had somehow come up the back steps, which he never used, and approached from behind me while my attention was riveted in the opposite direction.

Following that, I postponed asking him the questions that I was going to have to answer to Miss Titherington. I tried the local library again, combing the Dewey decimal system under *pirates* for something that would let me go it alone, but, aside from a lot on Peter Pan, and Robert Louis Stevenson, and pictures by Howard Pyle and N. C. Wyeth, there wasn't much. After another prod from Miss Titherington, I had no choice but to seek out my former mentor. Although it would be only a functional exchange about schoolwork, I thought it best to talk to him somewhere Mother wasn't, so after school on the day of the vernal equinox, I peddled down through town to Tom's boatworks.

I found the captain clamping a plank to *Merry,* one of several new ones neatly fitted where the old ones had been removed. "Aha," he said, glancing up from his work. "Ahoy." He was very cheerful. I had rehearsed what I planned to say to him, but I was at once put to work helping support and push on the plank as he fixed the clamps, and by the time it was in place, I'd forgotten my speech. "What brings you here?" he asked. I told him about my essay concerns, starting with my teacher's doubts about the buccaneers having the first democracy. What was his source on that?

"Source?" he picked up an auger and started drilling holes with it. "Why, all the accounts they left. What's your teacher's source to the contrary? Ask her to name you any earlier pure democracy, with a vote for every person, never mind their wealth, or race, or religion, or sexual preferences, or sometimes even gender, for that matter. Anne Bonny and Mary Read were women pirates on equal shares under Calico Jack. Ask your Miss Titherington where anything like that happened earlier, and give her a good, primary source bibliography and you're laughing. She'll have her own question on her own plate."

"What bibliography? What books?"

"The old standard ones will do: Esquemeling, Bartholomew Sharp, Raveneau de Lussan, the Sieur de Montaubon, Ringrose, Dampier, Rogers, Shelvock. And Johnson, of course. I may be leaving out one or two, but those are the chaps who were out there buccaneering, privateering, pirating, call it what you like." He said he would rummage for copies of their books, most of which he thought he had somewhere. "Just a question of finding 'em, what?" He sighed. "One accumulates so many books, I fear, all now damp stained, and dear little *Merry* has to carry them all, don't you darling?" He patted her hull. "You've another question?" he asked me, continuing to drill his line of holes.

I had a confusion of questions: where should my essay end, and how was I going to get there? I didn't have time to read all of those books, even if I could read them. It took forever to decipher a page of Esquemeling. Also, nothing seemed ever to change, with governments sponsoring pirates century after century. Where were the real pirates? He finished drilling his holes, opened a box of bronze screws, and turned the first one home, using a screwdriver head in the auger. The whole place was perfumed with newly worked pine, and the wood smoke from its scraps. Tom's stove glowed red-hot with them. The captain put another screw in place. Had he even been listening?

"As to your questions, there's been no end to piracy, so where you end your paper is up to you. But after Morgan, things did change. There came a new generation of the brotherhood, which I reckon is what you're calling the real pirates. Long John Silver, eh? Johnson's pirates, whom Stevenson cribbed from. Quite. Well, now you've got all the background you need, except for Kidd, who marked a generational change, which is an honour he could have done without."

Before I knew it, there in Tom's shop, with Tom band-sawing frames for a cape dory in the background, I found myself auditioning as Captain Kidd. After my experiences as a deckhand, I wanted to be a captain again, and a gentleman, although Kidd was no Drake, not by the captain's account of his background. "He was a big Scot, son of a Presbyterian minister, who didn't follow his father's calling. He did work his way into command of a buccaneer ship, and helped capture Saint Martin from France for the English governor at Saint Kitts. That was in 1689 as I recollect, just one of the times England and France were at war. After Morgan, the rules started to tighten in the Caribbean. There was still a licenced living to be made, buccaneering, in times of declared war, maybe capturing the enemy's buccaneers, who might well be your former shipmates. It was the luck of the draw, and times were thinner.

"So Kidd chap, who is forty-four, distinguishes himself in some hard fighting—too hard for the liking of his crew, because while he's ashore being honoured by the governor, they sail away with the ship. Very embarrassing." He cinched home another screw. "You're Kidd. No ship, no money, just the clothes on your back. What do you do now?"

According to the captain, the thing I did then was talk the governor into giving me another ship and crew and a warrant to find and recapture my former ship, but before we could get into it, Tom called for our help with something he was cutting, and I didn't get feeling much like Kidd, just then. Nor later, as we went home together, me wheeling my bike, getting a background for wherever he was leading me. With harder treaties, the heyday of the buccaneers in the Caribbean had passed, sending them off to more profitable, less troublesome places, such as the North American ports and the Pacific coast (where some of Morgan's buccaneers had remained after his raid on Panama), and the Indian Ocean.

Relentlessly, Kidd tracked his former ship to New York, an economically troubled colony that needed all the hard cash it could get. Buccaneers were a good source. Kidd's ex-crew got there, sold their loot and their ship, bought another, and sailed for the Indian Ocean moments before Kidd got there to catch them.

"What do you do now?" he asked.

"Chase them down wherever they are," was my notion—mistaken, as I learned.

"Kidd got to New York at a moment when two competing would-be governors were at war. The upheaval stemmed from England's Glorious Revolution, after James II. I'll spare you the politics. You can look it up in your books. Kidd sailed into a shooting war, picked the winning side, running arms, soldiers, and munitions. He missed his quarry, but came out well ahead in New York, honoured for his service, again with friends in high places, plus profits. Swallows the anchor and moves ashore. Marries a well-off widow in 1691, and settles into a pleasing house at 119 Pearl Street, if I remember correctly. Very cozy. New respectability, two daughters, a family pew in Trinity Church . . . , the good life. There was only one thing wrong." Here we approached the inn, and I felt obliged to peddle ahead of him, so that we arrived separately. Mother had noted and approved our real standoffishness to one another and I thought it prudent to keep the impression.

In point of fact, the family had lots more than me to think about. The inn's infractions had come by registered mail, and the news was worse than bad. That Sunday dinner was short on cheer.

"There's no point in getting quotes, because it's going to cost so much more than we can ever pay for," Mother said with a hopelessness that was shared around the table. There seemed no antidote. Meg said she would put together another concert—a brave offer, but futile. Some thousands of dollars were needed. "Maybe there's something in the lower cellar," I reminded Mother of the boarded-up passage the captain had found. This was news to the others. Everybody looked over to where he was sitting, in genteel exile, sipping coffee, reading a three-day-old Boston newspaper.

There was some discussion about the cellar, but without much hope. "People who want to hide something of any value usually make more of an effort to really hide it," Robin pointed out, noting that planked-up doors were not a favoured camouflage. He did promise Mother that he would go down there and have a look around himself sometime during the week. A week would be allowed anyway, before any decisions, while the family got rough estimates for the probable costs involved, and Mother got together with Uncle Bill about any possibilities for legal challenges or delays. "But unless we get divine intervention," she capped the subject, "I don't know what choice we've got but to sell the place for what Roy Moehner's offering. If we let him foreclose, we'll get nothing." Shortly after the meal, they packed up for another Halifax trip, Mother to see Uncle Bill, Aunt Karen to the doctor, and Robin to drive them. It was an emergency.

"*You* are in charge," she told me, "and you're to have no truck with Captain Johnson, am I clear? Functional talking only." I promised, and off they went, leaving Meg and me to clear up. When I returned to the captain's table, he was gone. I looked again around the old room, with its glow of ancient wood, thinking about living in some affordable place inland, with plasterboard walls, and felt very low. What would we do? Here came Meg, on her way out to the trash box, adding to it some letters that she had not opened. Especially since the concert, she had gotten mail, but she never answered a letter in her life, as far as I ever knew, or read one.

Feeling groundless, I asked her what she would do if we lost the place, as seemed most likely. She regarded me with sad eyes. "This old inn's been my salvation, and if there's no more inn, then there's fate shoveling me back out into the world again." Something about the look on my face made her hug me. As she did, her drummer arrived to pick her up. "Bye," she said, leaving with him.

I went up to knock at the captain's door, reckoning he would take my mind off my lonely miseries, but he was not there. He was probably working on his boat, and I had no idea when he would return. Needing company, I called up Jenny and told her everybody was gone, and how would she like to come and check out the inn for ghosts again? She had found six or seven during previous visits. "Maybe you missed some," I suggested.

Jenny did come, although ghosts weren't her current interest. She wanted to go back to the cellar and find the treasure she thought must be there, based on what I'd told her. She had her rubber boots, her own flashlight, and a notepad for making maps. "Either we go down there, or I'm going back. Get your boots." So I did, and the kitchen flashlight, plus a spare from behind the bar.

The padlock was off the outer door, as was the lock on the deep cellar's entrance. The grating stood open, just as the last time we'd come down here weeks before. "He's here!" I said. It hadn't occurred to me that the captain would return on his own. What was he doing?

"Maybe he's getting the treasure while the getting's good," said Jenny, leading the way below. Working our way along the same dank passage we'd followed previously, we were trying to figure which one he had come out of before, when he came out of it a second time, preceded by the beam of his flashlight.

"You two again?"

"I thought you were supposed to wait for me to open the sealed passage," I reproached him.

"I haven't opened anything. We can, though, if you'd like."

My immediate worries about how I would explain to my mother were overwhelmed by Jenny. The direction in which he led us was away from where he'd just come from, I noticed. Picking our way around the puddles, we followed him along the main passage, farther than we had explored, to a bend where he stopped and held his light on a row of vertical planks, nailed to the heavy framework around what had once been a rough portal of some kind.

"Hold your torches on it, and let's have a look." Working his fingers into an open seam, he gave a pull, and an entire plank came away with little fuss. The saltwater floodings of the cellar had kept the wood from rotting, but had completely rusted away the spikes. Our flashlight beams darted into the gap, finding only darkness.

"There *is* treasure down here," pronounced Jenny. "I can feel it."

"That would be a very great surprise, Mistress MacGregor, and I wouldn't get your hopes up," he cautioned her, wrenching away another plank, and then another, opening a doorway into the passage beyond. Entering, we found ourselves surrounded by the natural rock of a tidal cave, carved by nature, and paved with a worn footpath. Piled at its beginning was a jumble of rickety crates, spilling moldy old junk when kicked. Beyond, the tunnel took a bend.

"D'ye hear that?" the captain put his finger to his lips. Coming from somewhere not too distant was the sound of surf. He had to restrain Jenny from running ahead, which was just as well, because when the cave finished its bend, it made another sharp one, then the path ended abruptly in a sheer drop, a fatal trap to anybody walking too quickly. Beneath was a churn of waves surging in and out. I realised this was the depth of the crevasse I had only seen from the sea. Daylight came through from its other end.

"This is where pirates could have landed," Jenny opined, "and rumrunners."

"I'm afraid neither," said the captain. "Nor anybody else, not in any boat. Just look." Close below, the surge rumbled and hissed, churning through sharp fingers of striated rock.

"What's the use of a tunnel to nowhere?" I wanted to know.

"Your question's its own answer," he said, which did not help me. Nor did I much care at that moment. I had never liked it down here, and with the disappointment of no treasure trove, I was ready to go back, but he pursued the point. "Who would build a path to a somewhere that is nowhere, and then board over it later? Why," he answered his own question, "cooks, minions, varlets, and legions of scullery maids bearing bags and boxes of all the trash that this old inn produced over its generations. It was the trash and garbage dump. In the summer, they could just take it out and heave it over the cliff, but this was the way to go under the snow. The kitchen communicated directly with this part of the cellar in the last century. Later on in history, you had trash men coming around to take away junk, and you sealed up the old tunnel because it's dangerous. Look," he said. We had returned to where we'd started, and he stooped to examine the contents of the crates we'd found there. "Kitchen trash." He was right. On top of the nearest box was a pile of battered old tin plates, encrusted with whitish mold, plus empty cans and broken bottles. Rummaging, the captain pulled out a teapot, old-fashioned and very slimy.

"Silver?" Jenny held out a moment of hope.

"If it were, it would be treasure indeed, Mistress, but nobody would have thrown out silver. What we have here is just about the cheapest stuff in the world, pewter. Lots of it. Not just pewter, but lead-based pewter. Over time, it gave everybody who ate or drank from it lead poisoning. When people discovered that around the middle of the last century, everybody who had old pewter got rid of it. Most of it was melted down, but this lot got thrown out. Nearly thrown out . . . brought down here and just left."

For Jenny, there was no treasure, not even a smuggler's corridor with bones. My own hopes for a magical solution to our problems were left in the cave, which the captain reclosed as we left, propping the planks back in place.

"Some treasure," was my gloomy comment to Jenny when she went home.

"There's treasure. Somewhere. I can feel it. It's what he's looking for down there. It's why he came here in the first place." She got me to agree to collaborate in keeping secret eyes on what else he might be up to down below.

13

Kiddings

S o . . ." The captain stoked his pipe. "Kidd had it all." He
was back on point in his story. We had dined, separately. I
had cleared his table, built up his fire, and brought him his
rum, wanting none of it myself. "Successful career as a privateer,
the right patrons, everything a chap could want—loving, wealthy
wife, beautiful children, nice house, family pew in the church that
the right people went to. Everything rainbows except . . ."

"A ship?" I was ahead of him. He nodded.

"Aye. As he sat in that church pew, listening to hymns and
holy scripture, what he heard was the music of the East, and it

was seductive music, played on strange instruments, and he yearned for the feel of a deck under his feet again. The Indian Ocean was where the best buccaneering action had shifted in the waning years of the seventeenth century. The Caribbean was no longer the happy hunting ground, nor was the west coast of Africa. On the other side of Africa, however, you had Madagascar, where slaves were an abundant commodity, and the Arabian Sea, and the Malabar and Coromandel coasts, full of rich wogs. The wogs had ships with fat cargoes—silks, brocades, ivory, pearls, jewels, slaves, silver, gold, the lot—and they were helpless against the warships of the West."

"Wogs?"

"Non-Christian, non-English peoples. 'Them' as opposed to 'Us,' what? With that simple separation, all the 'heathen' of the world became fair game, and you had better ships and cannons, and some kind of document, from your favourite New England governor, in a far ocean where few documents got examined. It was a long trip to get there, but worth it when you did.

"Needing bases, the buccaneers turned their attention to Madagascar: it was strategically placed, and full of warring tribes that could be exploited in the same way the warring tribes of Ireland had been dealt with, for instance, by Queen Elizabeth. That is, you came in with a powerful military force, took sides in the local war, demolished the enemy, became strong enough to dominate your ally, turned on him, then took over. It was a time-honoured technique that the buccaneers learned from their own governments, and put to use on Madagascar."

"Poor wogs," I commented.

"Poor wogs indeed," he agreed, "but nothing new. The Africans had their own slave trade going among themselves for centuries. The Westerners simply opened a new outlet to the market. In any case, by Kidd's time, factors had come out from New York and established fortified trading posts where booty could be liquidated without having to sail it home. Goods and slaves could be exchanged for spirits, sailcloth, nails, shoes—gear hard to come by out there—and necessaries like gunpowder, cannon, hemp, chain, tar, lead, all in exchange for rubies and diamonds and gold. Above all, gold. Gold was what you got for everything else.

"There sprang up a regular traffic between Madagascar and New York. One could send mail. If a buccaneer wanted to pay off and go home, he could buy passage on the next New York–bound ship for a hundred pieces of eight, plus food, a small price for a sailor who had made thousands, as Avery's crew did. Avery came out from New York after Thomas Tew, who had sailed home to be toasted as a celebrity in New England. Kidd couldn't stand being left out of it all."

"All right," I said, ready to be included. "I am Kidd."

"You're nothing like him. He was a big brute of a buccaneer captain, readier to bully a rough crew than to handle a teacup. He was no gentleman, your Kidd chap, except for a veneer in society. The days of the gentleman pirates were gone, alas. The thing you do have in common with him is a liking for permissions from the authorities, which is arguably very prudent. Kidd wanted to plug into the age-old formula for the sea marauders: get aristocratic patronage, investment, and some kind of documentation to let him sail off and do things to make all of his investors happy, with lots of loot left over to buy his way out of whatever he'd had to do. That was the system, since time before memory. With a wink and a nudge and a nod." He brooded. "And what's changed, eh?"

"So I sail to the Indian Ocean." I tried to steer us along.

"Not you, Kidd. And the first thing he did was sail to London on a trading voyage, to obtain a real privateering licence, properly signed by the highest authorities, and get a ship to go with it. With the changing times, neither was easy, but Kidd got both; he was the genuine article—a veteran buccaneer captain who knew the game, and had patronage besides. In London, he found further patrons, including King William himself. It was the system. Kidd got his ship, a thirty-four-gun frigate with a turn of speed and a bank of oars for advantage in light airs. It was called *Adventure Galley*. His licence authorised him to capture pirates, including his old shipmates. So, back to New York he sailed, not to start capturing pirates around there, heaven forbid, but to recruit a full crew to go out to the ocean of no rules, and get rich, and make a bigger name."

"And do I?"

The captain cocked an eye a me. "Kidd sails, and fetches Madagascar in January of 1697 after a five-month, nonstop voyage. The usual scurvy is taking its toll. He takes on fresh supplies, rests his crew, gets intelligence, then sails for the Comoros Islands to await the seasonal winds that will carry him to his target—the entrance to the Red Sea. Through those narrows passes some of the world's wealthiest shipping, dhows loaded with prosperous pilgrims returning from Mecca, Arab and Indian merchants with their goods, and other traders. Fat and helpless."

"But his licence was only to take pirates?"

"Pirates and Frenchies. That was his napkin, but this was the ocean of no rules. Awaiting the southwest monsoon, he careens *Adventure Galley,* cleans her bottom. Tropical disease claims thirty of his men, but he recruits others. Remember, the buccaneers had been out there for years. Far from chasing pirates, he needed some to flesh out his crew. As many as he could get. He blew north with the wind at the end of April, passed

Zanzibar and the Horn of Africa, rounding into the Gulf of Aden in late July. There he waited for the annual pilgrim fleet to come out of the Red Sea. He sent raiding parties ashore for water and supplies, killing and alienating locals, as Drake never would have done." The captain's story had been moving slowly, but here it dragged to a halt with one of his long pauses.

"And?"

"He waited, as I said. August came, and the sun blasted down, with temperatures that cooked the brains out of the New Englanders, and the pitch out of the deck seams. Wetting down decks was a primary activity, and the pumps had to be kept going. Also, the long voyage had tired the ship, and she was ever more leaky. Tempers rose with the temperature, and no action." I commented that I was ready for some action myself. He treated me to a languorous nod.

"Think of how Kidd and his crew felt. They'd spent almost a year of hard sailing and deprivation to get to where they were, then waiting, broiling, pumping. It's always amused me that the pirates are seen as lacking patience, when—like fishermen—they were leading exemplars of that particular virtue. You could use a bit yourself." The captain proceeded at a sedate pace.

"The pilgrim fleet did appear, but with three well-armed European ships in a convoy. One of them was a British East Indiaman that fired shots as Kidd approached, foiling his plan. Shooting back at a Company ship would have been hard to explain later. Finally, there was no choice but to sail for the northwest coast of India—yet another long voyage, and to a riskier place."

As *Adventure Galley* sloshed along, crossing the Persian Gulf toward Surat, I learned about Indian politics under the Moghul emperor, and the role of the British East India Company there.

This powerful trading firm was like an arm of the English government, both being controlled by the same interests. They were eager to stay in the Moghul's favour, and buccaneers had begun to jeopardise everything. All the pirates were thought to be English, or English colonials, and when Henry Avery raided the coast where Kidd was headed, he captured an astonishingly rich ship owned by the Moghul himself. Aboard it was lots of his wealth, also friends and family, who were murdered along with most of the other passengers.

"This soured him on Englishmen in general, including the Company, which he suspected of collusion with the pirates. Company officers along the Malabar coast were pitched into jail. Trade and profits were threatened, causing alarm in London on the subject of piracy in the Indian Ocean. Kidd was sailing farther into it with every mile that passed under his leaky ship, with its unhappy crew, out of money and supplies.

"Then came more troubles. The word was out on Kidd; he was a pirate-chaser turned pirate, whatever his credentials, and news of him had preceded *Adventure Galley* wherever she sailed. That was the length of the Malabar coast for the next few months, with no more success than before. Bad to worse. He did cross paths with ships under English colours. Many in his crew wanted to attack, but he would not, making a mood in the fo'c'sle that went to mutinous. It erupted when his gunner, chap named William Moore, publicly squabbled with Kidd, who whacked him with a water bucket. Fractured his skull. Died the next day. Kidd appointed a new gunner, and slept with one eye open."

"If the buccaneers could vote their captains out, why didn't Kidd's crew do that to him?" I wanted to know, commenting that Captain Kidd did not seem very likable.

"No. Poor bloke never had a talent for likability, but he had a hard core of bully boys who stuck by him, and *Adventure Galley* had the highest kind of privateering licence, with the most honourable investors, and she wasn't sailing under the rules of the brotherhood, whatever her intentions. Kidd was master, barring mutiny, with forty shares for himself and his backers. So far, there had not been much to share, but that finally changed. Just after Christmas, at last he took a worthy prize. She was *Quedah Merchant,* a five-hundred-ton dhow, owned by Armenians, with a Moorish crew, and an English captain, under French colours— flown because they were the colours Kidd flew himself. It was his trick. Just about every large merchantman carried passes from every authority—English, French, Portuguese—so, when approached by a warship flying this or that flag, they could fly it, too. All in all, it was a very confusing situation.

"Anyway, Kidd had his prize at last: gold, silver, hundreds of bales of fancy fabrics, gemstones, the lot. He also had an argument for taking it that he reckoned would wash, with a judicious payout or two back home. So home he turned, after snapping up a couple of more small prizes. He sailed first for Saint Mary's Island, *Isle Saint Marie,* Madagascar's main pirate base, where he had to get a lot of things sorted out. One was his ship. When he got there, after a couple of more months, hard pumping at sea, *Adventure Galley* was just about finished. Her hull had to be bound with heavy cordage just to help it stay together.

"But her approach was viewed with some alarm by the pirates of Isle Saint Marie. These were the people that Kidd had a commission to capture, as they knew, and some of them were from the crew who had stolen his ship off Saint Kitts, the same ones he'd pursued to New York. In order to be allowed into the port with-

out a fight, Kidd had to assure these chaps that he was one of
them. Demonstrably, this was true, by his loot and the ships he'd
taken. He'd brought a couple with him.

"So Kidd got the hospitality of Edward Welsh, the New York
factor, who bought and sold slaves and other pirate goods. When
Kidd paid out everybody's shares, Welsh bought their bales of
cloth, their ivory, and everything else they wanted converted into
cash, or rum, or whatever his store had to offer. His buildings
were on high ground behind a stockade—warehouse, slave pens,
cattle. And a tavern, needless to say, the community social centre,
with entertainment of all kinds. A little home away from home,
except it was built of red clay blocks slathered with ochre and
dung. Foul stuff. You had to be careful not to lean against a wall,
because its dry crust would crumble away and get between your
skin and your clothes." He wriggled, running his finger around
his collar as though clearing a paste of dung dust and sweat.

"How would you know that?" I asked.

"Oh, I've been there to be sure. It's where I picked up
Poppins." Here he became quite melancholy. "He was my best
mate; slept with me every night; seldom left my side. We had
some good years together, Poppins and me, until the bloody day
he got torn apart by a pack of wild dogs in Port Said." He raised
his mug and toasted to a point in space: "Here's to you, mate. I'll
never forget you." He wiped moisture from his eyes.

I found this a lot to absorb.

"Poor old darling," he continued, then noticed my face. "He
was a ring-tailed lemur, dear boy, indigenous to Madagascar and
the finest pet a sailor could wish for. Why, Poppins was the best
small-boat top-man I ever had. Didn't need ratlines, ran up the
lacings and trimmed the downhaul to the fore-and-aft tops'l over

the peak taikle in a tack slicker than any light-yard man. I trained him to it. He was a good pickpocket, too," he added with a wink, "without any teaching at all."

"When was that?" I asked. It was the first time he had ever said anything personal about himself.

"Poppins has been gone for a long time. We shouldn't get distracted. Kidd had to spend almost a half-year on Isle Saint Marie, waiting for the next round of seasonal winds. Once they were paid off with their shares, the bulk of his crew went their ways—home, or off to pirate some more. *Adventure Galley* was finished. Kidd had her stripped of guns, gear, and anything of use, then burnt her hull for the iron fastenings. Everything had value out there.

"With the northeast monsoon, he sailed on his biggest prize, the dhow, carrying his treasure. He had just twenty men now, plus some slaves. He re-rounded Africa, picked up the southeasterly trades and made a five-month passage to the Caribbean, where he had to stop for water and supplies. Also, he wanted to fence his bulk cargo, his fancy cloth, and get a smaller, less conspicuous vessel in which to approach New York.

"In the West Indies, he got some disturbing news. Word of his deeds was ahead of him again, and alarms were out about him, with talk of arrest warrants on his ship. But then, he didn't have that ship anymore, and some legal difficulties were to be expected in cases like his. They were always dispelled by success—the right payoffs and some kind of excuse. Kidd had a story he'd been polishing for months, plus plenty of cash to take home to a place that made most of its living from such traffic. He was a prestigious citizen there; a loving family awaited him, the blessings of the elite. The governor was Lord Bellomont, same Whig chap who'd sponsored Kidd back in London, who was heavily invested in the venture, like some other people so powerful as to be able to make troubles go away. As per the system.

"He sailed back to New York but with a careful approach, sounding the waters. The governor was off in Boston, so Kidd had a couple of weeks to greet his wife and daughters, take them for a sail, and hide a lot of his treasure. Most of it got buried in the sands of Gardiner's Island, where Kidd had friends, and that was the famous buried treasure of Captain Kidd. Shovels in the night. How would you like to be Kidd?" he suggested, with a kind of smile I had come to distrust. I shook my head.

"You've saved yourself some very disagreeable experiences," he approved. "The world shifted in the years Kidd had been gone. Eastern outrage over English pirates in general and Kidd in particular was threatening to end the East India Company and all of its good income. Also, all of the European powers were adjusting to real rules as to the governance of colonies, and political relationships with other empires. The simple truth of it is, there came an awareness that trade was more profitable to governments than freebooting, and that's what changed the system at last.

"The awakening world," I quoted a chapter title in my history book.

"I'd say money. Certainly there was an awakening to *that*. It was Kidd's bad luck that it happened on his watch." Grandpa's clock chimed. "Poor old Poppins," he said, lapsing away from his story. He had put away two or three double rums.

"Kidd," I reminded him.

"Kidd got hold of Bellomont, who promised on his word of honour, and in writing, a pardon in advance if Kidd would come to him. So he did, and gave him all the papers he had saved to support his story, including the French documents from his main prizes. Bellomont took them, had Kidd arrested, and threw him in jail. So much for Bellomont's word of honour, eh? Fact is, he and all of Kidd's other backers in London were Whig politicos, and, because of his reputation, their involvement with him was political treasure to their Tory opponents. Either Kidd had to be backed, or abandoned like a sinking ship, which is what they did. He was shipped to London in chains and irons, and put on trial for his life, first for the murder of William Moore with a bucket, second for piracy."

"But Bellomont was the person who sent him out, and there were his big shot backers . . . ?"

"Gone. More than just gone, turned against him: 'What? *Us* send out a pirate? Who sir, we sir? No sir, not us, sir. We just sent him out after Frenchies and pirates; chap went off on his own account. Nothing to do with us.' Kidd's only friends were the merchants of New York, whose opinions weren't worth a brass farthing where he was going. They threw him in Newgate Prison to enjoy a singularly wretched existence—I'll spare us both the details—until the lords of the land got 'round to giving him his show trial, two years after his arrest. The collection of documents to support his case, which he'd given to Bellomont, had vanished. He was given no legal counsel until the morning of his trial. He had no chance for an eyewitness to support his claim that his actions were forced by a mostly mutinous crew, which was largely true, but the prosecution had plenty of rebuttal witnesses against him. Some of his old enemies got to walk away from the whole mess, keeping their loot in exchange for their testimony. A few were the very ones who prodded him into his whole adventure."

"And they hanged him?"

"They did, all with due process. Date of execution set for May 23, 1701, as rightly I recollect, giving Kidd a couple of weeks more in the company of his jailors, and the jail's pastor, who came to him often."

"For his repentance?"

"For his story, or anything else he might say that the pastor could write up in his broadsheets. The tabloids of the time. All the juicy details about notorious criminals. They were the big celebrities. No movie stars then. The parson was the inside reporter who got to write them up. Chap named Paul Lorraine. Made a tidy sum for that, and dragging Kidd to the chapel to pray. People who wanted to see him were charged to get in. So that's what Kidd had to put up with, and fading hope for a pardon. Maybe he could close out the sounds and smells, and the lice, and the painful sights of Newgate, and the weight of his chains. Maybe he focused his mind on memories: the fresh-scrubbed faces of his wee daughters, his wife's laugh, the morning sunlight, coffee and pastry, the call of seabirds.

"When they took him out to hang him, they treated him to a two-hour ride in a horse cart, through the streets of London to Wapping, followed by a mob. Wapping wasn't all that far, but they stretched it out because it was such an enjoyable event. Not to Kidd, o'course, but they stopped here and there and folks handed him drinks, and he drank what was handed him." The captain took a swallow of rum. "Ah, the mob. Their eyes, the fascination . . . it's always the same mob, y'know. Take a look at them," he said, gesturing.

All at once I was looking into the thrilled faces of a mob, but they were people wearing modern clothes, and they were in front of a Hollywood theatre watching movie stars getting out of limousines. There were spotlights. Curiously, the vision was in black and white, and I realised I was seeing my own impressions from a newsreel I'd once watched.

"Do you see?" he asked. I told him what I'd seen. "Quite," he nodded. "Well, here's the same lot, come to see the last of old Kidd, and the cutpurses had good picking. There were two other pirates to swing that day. They made a bad show of it. Cried. One wet his pants. Both were very penitent. Kidd gave a lustier account of himself, getting to say everything out loud that he couldn't in court. It was a fair amount, ending with a warning to seamen to be guided by prudence and caution. Then there was a psalm, and a prayer, and the hangmen prodded him up the ladder."

"Ladder?"

"Aye, there was no neat, quick drop back then. They fitted the noose and turned you off to dance on air and suffer, which is when your friends or family—hopefully somebody—could pull on your legs and make a shorter business of it. Kidd didn't have anybody for that, though there were lots of his old shipmates in town. Fact is, his rope broke. Dropped him on the ground, so they had to get him back up there with a better halter onto him, and one more prayer, and that was his lot. Except they weren't done with him. Ten quid they spent for iron chains and hoops to bind his body, keep it from fallin' apart out on Tilbury Point, where they moved him to serve as a bit of a visual statement for all the mariners sailing in and out of London, showing them what became of pirates."

"Did they ever find his treasure?"

"Almost immediately. Right after they arrested him. Went out to Gardiner's Island in Long Island Sound, dug up the treasure, inventoried the lot, and Bellomont got a nice slice of it for bringing in Kidd, then adjudicating his money." The captain chuckled. "And Kidd thought *he* knew about pirates. As for all that Bellomont sent to England, none of it ever found its way back to the chaps it had been stolen from. In point of fact, it was used to put up a fine public building, which today adjoins the National Maritime Museum. Among other things, that institution has the finest library you or Miss Titherington could ever imagine on pirate history. Very ironic, don't you think?"

"And there couldn't be any of his treasure at Oak Island?" I asked about the local legend that Kidd had buried some there.

"He didn't get to Nova Scotia. His treasure for you is his example." In the captain's view, Kidd's mortal error had been in depending for his authority on other authorities. "In fact, he never was any more than half a pirate. If he'd gone all out on his own account, he'd have had a better chance for a daintier demise. Now we're done with him," he concluded, taking out his tin flute.

"What am I supposed to learn from his example?"

"Not to trust anybody, for starters, except to be who they are, and you'd better be able to trust yourself to see whatever that is. Unless they're your mother. Maybe even then. Tricky business, what?"

anger, and more danger," said Jenny, who had insisted on reading my palm during recess. She had read it before, many times, with changing results, but had recently found a new book on the subject. I'd been complaining that I didn't know where my life was going, beyond the move that Mother and I were going to have to make. I told Jenny the danger had come and gone, and we had lost, and if she wanted to be of some use, she should tell me what to expect next. I didn't believe any of it, but I was glad for her company, and her concern. "Danger," she repeated. "And travel. I see a trip."

"A voyage?"

"Could be." Jenny was more interested in my report on the captain's activities in the cellars. If she'd had her wish, she would have dragged me back down there, but she had to justify every away-from-home visit to her mother, who would have come up pretty sharp if she'd ever learned what Jenny and I were up to in the dark corridors under the inn. Another secret. I had kept an eye on the captain, as promised, but his activities there had not been exciting. The only things he had brought out were some bits from the trash in the cave. He had sorted these into piles. Otherwise, he was even scarcer than usual. He had gone off to Halifax for nearly a week, to have a look at its library, he said. When he came back, he spent long hours in Tom's shop working on *Merry*.

So, April came and went, not taking with it the last pockets of winter snow. Autumn is Nova Scotia's really glorious season; spring is bad to nonexistent. Nova Scotians who can afford to usually move south during March and April. Our own impending move would be no vacation, and it was the main topic after family dinner on the first Sunday in May.

A fortnight earlier, with great reluctance, mother had contacted Moehner Realty & Development Company to accept their long-standing offer for our property, only to find they had retracted their original price. They were now offering a much lower one. Mother had steamed out of their office and advertised the sale on her own, with no agent. Also with no success so far. The Moehners had circulated pumped-up stories about the old property's problems, driving away buyers. Mother summed up our situation to the sombre family table.

"If the place doesn't sell, we've got the money for the June payment, just, and some summer bookings, but the province is going to close us down unless we do the work they want by the end of June. That's the ninety days we're allowed. How can we take the bookings when we don't have a prayer of paying for these?" She held up a stack of contractor's quotes. "So there's that, and then worse if nobody buys it pretty quick, and we default. I'm open to ideas."

"I didn't find any treasure in the cellar," said Robin, who had made good on his promise. He had gone down there, finding the entrance to the cave, and everything else we had discovered. "It's the inn's old garbage dump, it looks like. I think somebody's been into it not too long ago."

"That would be me," came the captain's voice from the foot of the stairs. Having come down unnoticed, he approached our table, carrying something wrapped in a pillowcase. "I couldn't help but hear the last of your conversation. Perhaps it's an opportune moment to show you this." Laying open the wrappings, he produced a very handsome something-or-other with a spout, clearly antique.

"A Georgian coffeepot? Pewter?" asked Aunt Karen.

"Close," he acknowledged, "but what we have here is a Queen Anne period crested coffeepot, sextangular form, with original ebony side handles, and signed Francis Bassett, New York. Circa 1705. Quite a nice piece of pewter, wouldn't you say?"

"You found this locally?" Aunt Karen probed.

"Quite. In your cellar." He turned to Mother. "Per our agreement, Madame, I have investigated down there, and resurrected this junk. It was quite nasty, but I washed it, and it's a very desirable collector's piece, don't you think? I reckon it could fetch five or six hundred dollars in Boston. Maybe more in New York, but I'm not going there. In any case, also per our agreement, you own three quarters' share of this object, and there's lots more. It's not all as choice as this particular piece, but there are lidded flagons, ewers, creamers. There's a warming pan by William Will of Philadelphia, circa 1785; a Charles II charger; tankards with the crest and crown of Holbourge; and all manner of plates and platters. Treasure. There's four crates of it in all. Here's a book I borrowed from the library, which has quite a lot to say." With it and some telephone calls to Boston antique dealers, he had made a rough appraisal and an itemised inventory. "Here's what we've got. It's all down below, and you can take a look at it. *If* it's properly sold, I should imagine it will cover your bills and save the inn. Such is my opinion, and here's my proposal."

Before anybody had a chance to digest what he had already told us, he was presenting a plan that centred on Boston, where he had to be by mid-June on other business. He would sail with his share of the pewter trove and sell it there, and he would sell ours also, if we wanted him to. With luck, the money could be wired home in the nick of time to pay for the inn's repairs.

"Halifax is closer, and time's important," was Mother's reaction.

"Your share's yours to sell when and where you like, but you won't get a dime on the dollar for it this side of Boston, which is where the money is. The timing's a close thing, as you say, but *Merry* will make a faster trip of it if Jim here comes along to stand watches. As crew. If I'm single-handed, I'll be hove-to for days. He can be your representative, keeping watch over your goods. After that, I'm sailing east, and I'll deposit him back here on the way." There was stunned silence all around. "You can tow all of that alongside while you decide whether or not you want to haul it aboard." So saying he withdrew, leaving the coffeepot and the book, along with much to be examined.

The upshot of it was a good deal of confusion. First, there was the providential windfall of his discovery, and the possibility of the inn's survival. Leafing through the library book, Aunt Karen nodded. "He's done his research, and I wouldn't be surprised if his figures are right. I suspect he's also right about Boston being the place to sell it." Here she gave Mother a look. "The question is, do you trust him to do it, and pay you, and return Jim safe and sound? I notice this book is from the reference section of the library, by the way. How did he get it out?"

I piped in, assuring Mother my drinking days were over and that he was a good sailor. School would be finished. Others could fill my duties for the two or three weeks a round-trip to Boston would take in *Merry*.

"Out of the question," Mother shook her head. "He's done some good things; I'll give him that, but trust him with you? Not anymore. What do we actually know about him?" She turned to Robin. "Did you ever check up?"

He had, but with no results. "There are a lot of Charles Johnsons in the system, and it's hard to sort them out. The Home Office in England seems to be having some difficulty in locating his passport number. I'm still waiting to see what they come up with. The Bermudan authorities confirm that his yacht did sail from there when he said he did, and there's no evidence he's smuggling anything. When he got here, he didn't bring anything ashore before he was examined."

"I'll attest he's a real historian," Aunt Karen commented, "though he's as coy as anybody I've ever met when it comes to talking about himself. He's told us nothing."

"I think he had some bad experiences during the war," I put in, "and he doesn't like to look back."

At some point, everybody trooped below, with Aunt Karen being wheeled down the steps by Robin, to view the considerable pewter trove, which had been washed.

"Very impressive," said Mother, "but if it has to go to Boston to fetch what it's worth, I'll carry it there myself, on the train."

"Hmmmm," said Robin, hefting one of the heavy boxes with some effort.

"I don't care how heavy it is," was Mother's response. "It can go in the freight car. I'll deal with it."

"Deal with who?" came a surprise question from Meg.

"I'll have to check into that," said Mother.

"But he's already checked into it," I said. "And . . ."

"Jim, you're not sailing with him, and that's that. Put it out of your mind."

14

Merry Adventure

The yawl *Merry Adventure* put her nose across the eye of a fair, warm breeze. Her sails filled on the opposite tack, and drew; she picked up her skirts and bubbled along in a splendour of new paintwork, under a full flutter of flags. Passing our point, we lost sight of the wharf, and the family, along with Noel Nauss and the other well-wishers who had come to see us off on our adventure. Meg was there, and Jenny, jealous that she wasn't going, too. My last view of them was Mother, waving her blue scarf. *Merry*'s bowsprit aimed to the open sea like a thrown spear, startling a flock of gulls; they rose from the water with a great flapping of wings, then soared into the summer sun, like my heart at that moment.

"Ease the stays'l sheet," the captain growled, "and then coil down halyards and hang 'em off as I showed you. Jump to it."

"Yes, sir." I jumped to it with great eagerness.

"There's no yesses and no sirs here. It's 'Aye, Cap'n.'"

"Aye, Cap'n."

"And when I say jump, I don't mean literally. Take her slow, and she comes easy." Pegging the tiller, he stooped out of the wind to light his pipe. "And when y'r done with that, you can fetch me a rum. Half water. I want to drink a toast to *Merry,* and to all the gods of the seas, and to freedom on the broad plain of the ocean."

I didn't drink with him, but my sentiments were powerfully in the same place, particularly as regarding freedom. It had been hard-won. From the outset, Mother was opposed in a very stubborn way to my being where I now was, but the captain's stock had risen again as my famous binge faded with time, more serious concerns arose, and the pewter find miraculously appeared.

Mother and Robin had made an expedition to Halifax, where they spent an educational afternoon visiting the few antique dealers there. The best offer they got was a tenth of the captain's appraisal, just as he had predicted, and Mother discovered her bargaining limitations. Hoping to induce one dealer into a better offer, she mentioned there were two more boxes of it, and the dealer immediately cut his offer in half. So much for Halifax. As to Boston, there was much family debate over the next fortnight.

Aunt Karen's hunch was that his appraisal was good, but she had character questions she couldn't define. Robin had never been as worried as my mother by the drinking episode, and made the point that in Nova Scotia, sending sons to sea for a summer after grade school was as traditional as letting them have a beer with the crew. Nobody questioned his competency as a sailor. Mother's remaining issues were further smothered by the reality that everything—the inn that we couldn't sell, but couldn't keep— hung on trusting the captain to do what he said he would.

"It's a roll of the dice," as Meg put it, coming in on his side to my surprise. "He's a big actor, and he's very clever, and if he wants to steal your money, and Jim, they'll be gone. But he gave you the money, you could say, and he's already stolen Jim, and what other chance have you got?"

In school, I'd had to turn in my pirates essay ending with Captain Kidd, and the explanation that his case stopped the entire system of state-sponsored piracy. Miss Titherington accepted this, along with the bibliography I handed her. (She made no response to my question as to who had a real democracy earlier than the buccaneers.) She graded the essay A-minus, noting: "Very thoughtful, but you make proper governments seem more piratical than pirates, which is an unacceptable notion. Otherwise well organised, with good bibliog. & exc. spelling."

At my graduation the captain took time from launching *Merry* to show up and sit with the family. I think it was his attendance at that event that turned Mother's mind, at last, because he was invited back to the family table on the Sunday before departure. Aunt Karen had to give him a last grilling. "How do you plan to get good prices on all the pieces, when you're flooding the market with them?"

"Very carefully, Madam, my oath on it." He smiled, and escaped back to *Merry,* and his many preparations to sail. Noel Nauss carried the heavy boxes of pewter and stowed them under the bunk where the captain's chest had been. I moved aboard the next day. Mother had filled a navy surplus seabag with four times more than I could ever wear—a great weight of clothing—plus towels, shoes, boots, Band-Aids, sun lotion, candy bars, and so on. I could hardly lift the bag. Room for it was made on top of some spare sails in the fo'c'sle where my bunk was. It shared space with a small workbench and tools, clusters of tackle blocks, coils of line, and strings of shackles. The whole space smelled of Stockholm tar, and to me it was a headier fragrance than any perfume. I'd had little time to enjoy my new quarters before we were off.

Time was all-important. Mother had taken the summer bookings and used the deposits to hire a plumber, electrician, and carpenter. They were going to start the work in time to satisfy the inspectors, but would soon have to be paid or they would stop, and we then would be in worse debt than ever, truly lost. If we could accomplish what we were setting out to do within two weeks, wiring back the money before then, all would be well.

I hadn't mentioned to Mother one setback, which was Tom's failure to find the parts needed to fix the captain's old diesel engine, but the captain didn't seem concerned. "*Merry*'s weathered an ocean or two without it, and I reckon she can sail the six or seven hundred miles from here to Boston and back."

He thought we would have a slow trip there, against the seasonal southwesterly winds, and had allowed a week for it, giving another week to send the money, and follow with a fast run home. He would stay for only another week or so, pushing off for the Emerald Isle before the hurricane season.

"What's in Ireland?"

"The sweetest uilleann pipes ever to tickle the ears of the gods, for one thing." He smiled. "And for another, I'll confess there's a certain Irish lady with whom I'd like to play a tune or two." I asked her name, but he put his fingers to his lips.

"Shhh," he said. "No names. I've said too much as is. *Merry*'s listening, y'see, and she can get a bit, well, jealous, which we don't want, my oath on it. Her wants are first, so let's start you gettin' to know what she wants from Master Jim. Take care of yourself, Dearie," he said, pegging the tiller. *Merry* nodded on the crest of a small wave, tending herself nicely while I was given my duties. My first job was to work the wobble pump periodically, until her new planks tightened up.

Meanwhile, she leaked plenty, it seemed to me. The pump was situated where the helmsman sat in the cockpit, and all of the lines for sail trimming led there, allowing one person to handle them, watch the compass, steer, and pump when necessary. While I counted strokes, he talked about the headsails (staysail and jib), the gaff mainsail and topsail, and, farthest aft, the little triangular mizzen sail that sheeted to a long bumpkin sticking out from the transom, like a backward-pointing bowsprit. "She's not a true quay punt," he informed me. "She's got the same rig, but she's beamier, and a bit bigger all around, and she's better. Aren't you, darlin'?"

Merry flounced along while I was initiated into the operation of the kerosene (he called it paraffin) galley stove, which had to be pressure-pumped, then heat-primed with alcohol, which he called spirits. "You've got to do it all just right, or you'll get black smoke." The brass lamp that hung over the cabin table worked on the same system. My job was to fill them daily, without spilling kerosene, and also the little gimballed oil lamps, as well as the night navigation lights. The captain was not a believer in electrical lighting or electrical anything aboard *Merry*. "The less to go wrong, the better, eh?" Hence, there were no gadgets, not even a pump-toilet as most yachts had. "Prob'ly they'll legislate against pissing over the side some day, but you can bet that the politicians making the rules have stock in the big chemical factories fouling the sweet waters of the earth."

My immediate concern was noon dinner. Mother had stuffed the galley with food. I learned I was responsible for meals and cleanup, unless the captain took a whim to cook. If he did, I would still have cleanup. Astern, the hills and headlands of the only place I had ever known receded behind us, until they were barely visible as a purplish line on the clear horizon.

"Are you enjoying yourself?" he inquired. I told him it was one of the most perfect days of my life. "That's good," he approved. "Better appreciate it. Wind's going to back sou'westerly, and we're going to lose the lee shelter of the land. How's your boat stomach?" I assured him that I'd been out with Grandfather and Tom many times, and didn't get seasick.

WHUMP! *Merry* took a hard lurch over the wave that had smacked her, did a twist on top of it, and then made a brief but dramatic roller-coaster plunge into its trough, before starting at once to do it again, and then again. True to the captain's prediction, the wind had backed and increased, bothering up a short, nasty head-sea that *Merry* had been smashing into for two long days. I somewhat lost track of time, but I did fulfill all of my duties, and I think I could have gotten through it better but for the smell of kerosene. I didn't get much sympathy.

"You're spillin' that paraffin, and it's stinking up *Merry*, and she says to tell you she doesn't like it." In accordance, the mainmast made a sudden, angry creak as the boat took a lurch. He looked quite comfortable at the helm, given the conditions. His hat brims were tied under his chin to keep the spray off his face, and he was smoking a thin cigar. I cleaned my smelly hands in salt water as best I could, then started to go back below, for whatever sleep I could get. It was my off-watch. It had been four on and four off, with sleep in two-hour snatches, in a universe that was full of sudden and unfair angles, plus noise—waves whumping into the hull six inches from my ear, sloshing sounds, massive creakings from the mainmast, tackle blocks thumping and drumming on the deck, wind gusts across the open hatch, pots and pans clinking and clanking in the galley, and every object below that could move making small sliding sounds and thumps, like our cargo of pewter. Under it all was an irregular groaning in basso that seemed to come from the very fabric of the ship.

"If you're feeling a bit pongy, stay above 'til it passes. Do as I told you: keep a straight spine, chin lifted above the horizon line, and try to eat an apple, or cracker or something." I gave him a baleful look. Aside from being tired and seasick, I was worried, uneasy that *Merry* was not soaking her seams and tightening up, as promised. On the contrary, she was leaking more than ever, and all of her noises seemed ominous. Even with just the mainsail and staysail, both shortened down by reefing, the little vessel seemed overtaxed. Also, visibility was lessening. I mentioned these things.

"I wish I had a bigger ship to offer ye, mate, for your better comfort, but then there'd have to be a crew to deal with to run things, on top of looking after the ship, and I've got my hands full with just you. As to *Merry*, she's laughing. Listen to her." Aloft, the rigging noises came from a whole different orchestra than the band down below. Here, the deadeyes squeaked, the tackles creaked, and all the spars had something to say from time to time, particularly the gaff jaws, rubbing the mast like a string bass with every roll.

"She asks me to tell you she's happy aloft, and she'll let you know if something starts to go wrong. As to her leaking, that's her new planks not yet settled, and we're giving 'em a workout. Us too, after a winter of losing our sea legs, eh? And you're right about the visibility. Wind's backing, and *Merry* might not like that. Let's have a peek at the chart. Where are we?" he asked, sliding one toward me. He pointed to a tick mark. "That's about where we were four hours ago, and . . ." We went into a navigation lesson: courses and speed, current. I was dismayed to find we had spent our two days of punishment making good less than fifty miles, all told.

"Here's where we need the motor," I offered.

"Then you'd know about discomfort, and we'd hardly be helped by it. We've had a fresh twenty-knot wind right in our teeth, and square little seas, just the wrong size for *Merry*. We've sailed four miles for every one made good, and the weather's thickening; I call for a crew vote on whether or not to put in and shelter for a day, or at least until the wind shifts enough to give us a slant for Boston." I couldn't have agreed more. "Right. Now, where shall we go?" And the navigation lesson continued. By popular consent, we would make for Port Roseway, as the captain called it, although the chart didn't call it a port. In any case, it was shelter, and it was a good point of departure from Nova Scotia for crossing the Gulf of Maine. We perhaps could be there by early afternoon.

The weather continued to thicken, and *Merry* continued to plunge and pound, making hard progress toward a green bell buoy that would mark our approach if we could find it in the mist. While it was still a good distance ahead of us, he pressed me into sounding the depth of water. So I brought up the lead line, hooked my arm around the forward shroud, and swung the lead as far forward as I could. The weight splashed and plunged as I let its line run through my fingers, feeling for its tags and for the head to hit bottom. I had never done it in these conditions, or such deep water, and I made a terrific tangle trying to bring it back aboard.

"Have another go," he commanded, and I did, and another after that, looking for changes in the bottom, getting totally soaked in the process.

"Bloody hell!" I said, borrowing his own expletive.

"Shhhh!" he shushed me, putting a finger to his lips.

"Well, *you* say 'bloody hell,' and . . ."

"Shhhh! Listen!" I did listen, and heard the low roar of engines getting louder by the moment. The captain stood up in the cockpit. "Fetch me the foghorn and the flare gun, and look smart about it," he instructed, but before I could extricate myself from the coils of the lead line, a shape appeared in the mist, then defined itself as a massive motor yacht heading right for us at top speed, its Decca radar antenna turning.

"Bloody hell," said the captain, "hang on!"

I got myself inboard just in time; at what seemed like the last moment, the motor yacht's helmsman changed course just enough to pass us close astern. As it flashed by, a party of people on its sheltered afterdeck gawked at us, drinks in hand. At the next moment, the big vessel's bow wave slammed into *Merry*, throwing us nearly onto our side. I clung to the nearest handhold for dear life, cruelly barking my shin. The last view I had of the yacht was the name on its high stern, *Cock Tails*, and its party of people laughing at our little predicament from behind their windows. Then it was gone again into the blowing mist, the sound of its engines receding as the captain brought *Merry* back on course. "Well there you have it," he commented, "the modern world, at your fingertips: radar going, and nobody watching."

I went back to throwing the long lead, which I got right after a while—a good thing, because an hour or two later my soundings told us that we'd passed our marker. "I put us about here." He put his finger on the chart. He had brought it up into the cockpit, where he held it folded on his lap as he steered. "We passed that buoy upwind of it, or we would have heard its bell, meaning we're in here." He indicated an area. I was concerned that our lives might hang on my accuracy with the lead line, in which I suddenly had less confidence. "Never mind. We'll find out soon enough. Make some more soundings."

"What would you do if you were in this situation alone?" I asked, going back to work at the hard, drenching task.

"Dear boy, I wouldn't *be* here if I was alone, if I could help it.

I'd be way out there somewhere," he gestured to the open sea, "and hove to with a sea anchor out, having a snooze and waiting for a nicer wind." Our own wind eased as we sailed in under the lee of Cape Negro, at Nova Scotia's southwest corner, and the waves layed down, making life a great deal more tolerable. A watery sun began to penetrate the mist as an island loomed out of it on our port side.

"Avast sounding," he ordered, wiping his spectacles for a closer look at the chart. "That would be what the admiralty chaps call Grey Island, which I never heard of. We called it Foxy Point, it being attached to the mainland at that time, making a snug little shelter for all kinds of foxes on the prowl." He seemed bemused.

"We?"

"We pirates o'course." He winked. "And I'm here to tell it to you like we lived it." Suddenly he was Long John Silver in the *Treasure Island* movie, doing an imitation that got a whoop out of me. I'd seen the film a number of times, and he must have, too.

"Look at the chart." He was back to business. "By the position of the bar, you can see where the island used to be connected to what's now Fox Bar. We'll anchor in behind there, and give *Merry* a snooze. Use one y'rself, could ye?" I could indeed, but there were several fathoms of iron anchor chain to get up on deck and the heavy anchor to put over the bow on command, as *Merry* luffed up under a sheltering shore with no sign of habitation.

"What you could call a nice, peaceful little place," he mused, waiting for *Merry* to back up and set her hook. I had my face buried in the mainsail, handling it alone, as he stood enjoying the scenery. "Bucolic, I'd say. All it wants is a cow here and there. Let me give you a hand with that furl." When all was done, and the little mizzen was set to keep *Merry*'s nose weather-vaned to the breeze, and we had hung out our wet clothes to dry, I curled up on the foredeck with my head on the furled jib, and the last thing I heard before going to sleep was his tin flute.

The captain let me sleep the afternoon away before nudging me awake with his toe, setting me to lighting up the stove and making supper. Feeling refreshed and dried out, I went back to my duties under his critical eye. He lounged in the cockpit with pipe and rum as I cleaned the dishes in a tub of seawater, thinking about something he'd said during his Long John Silver imitation. Now that my pirate essay was done, I was nagged by having missed the very group of pirates I thought I was going to be writing about in the first place. He nodded.

"Last generation of the brotherhood. Early 1700s. Johnson's lot. Blackbeard, Vane, Rackham, Bonny and Read, Davis, England, Black Bart, Lowther, Low . . . the naughties. Very juicy. Quite right, you've got all the background, but no more essay. Well observed. Did you have a question?"

I was hoping he would continue with his stories, particularly the illusory kind that plucked me into the action. What was it like for the last of the buccaneers? No fairy tales. Aside from his joke about having been here before with pirates, had pirates really been here?

"When have I ever told you a fairy tale? And I've been here before, right enough. And this bay was a wee hidey-hole where the king's big cruisers couldn't patrol. Bartholomew Roberts came in here; so did Bellamy, and that blackguard Ned Low took a big haul right here where we're floating. Back in 1722. July, I think. He surprised thirteen fishing vessels that were doing what we are, and took 'em all. There are too many stories to think about right now, except . . . you said something earlier about

234

Treasure Island, I believe?" I had not, although I had thought about it. "Never mind. Have you read the English poet John Masefield on the subject?" In fact, I'd had to memorise some Masefield; and started to recite it: "I must go down to the sea again . . ."

"Story of my life," he interrupted me, "but that's not the poem; I'm referring to his 'Ballad of John Silver,' which he wrote after he fell in love with Stevenson, who had fallen in love with Johnson's *History of the Pirates,* and borrowed Johnson's buccaneer dialogue, as well as the names of a few of Johnson's actual pirates for *Treasure Island.* So Masefield goes back to Johnson. They all do, in the end." He fetched a book from below, turned to a marked page, cleared his throat, and read:

> *"We were schooner-rigged and rakish,*
> *with a long and lissome hull,*
> *And we flew the pretty colours of the crossbones and the skull;*
> *We'd a big black Jolly Roger flapping grimly at the fore,*
> *And we sailed the Spanish Water in the happy days of yore."*

"Why did they call the black flag with bones a Jolly Roger?" I interrupted.

"Right up through Kidd's time, they used a blood-red flag that meant 'if you fight, no quarter; all-out battle without mercy; massacre.' That was why the buccaneers loved it so. It was a fearful thing when a ship flew that flag; symbol of terror, and terror was the pirate's best friend. A peaceful surrender—better than cannonballs, damage, and difficulties, neh? Froggies called it the *Jolie Rouge,* and out it came as Jolly Roger in English, with the advantage that the Devil was Old Roger. Then, in the later days, it was usually a black flag signifying death, with whatever design suited the vanity of the captain. Lots of skulls and skeletons. Terror. But we digress. Ahem:

> *"We'd a long brass gun amidships, like a well-conducted ship,*
> *We had each a brace of pistols and a cutlass at the hip;*
> *It's a point which tells against us, and a fact to be deplored,*
> *But we chased the goodly merchant-men and laid their ships*
>   *aboard.*

> *"Then the dead men fouled the scuppers and the wounded*
>   *filled the chains,*
> *And the paint-work all was spatter dashed with other peoples*
>   *brains,*
> *She was boarded, she was looted, she was scuttled till she sank.*
> *And the pale survivors left us by the medium of the plank."*

Here he interrupted himself, lowering the book and taking off his spectacles to gesture with them for emphasis: "There's a key and operative word there, which I would underscore, that being 'other,' *other* people's brains. Very important point. He's got the boarding and looting part right, but they didn't do all that much scuttling. If they didn't keep a ship, they generally gave it back to whatever prisoners they couldn't get to join 'em, or burned it. If anybody went overboard, it was likely some officers who had been abusing their crew, making their little last splashes without the ceremony of any plank. Now, let's see . . ." He picked up where he'd left off:

> *"O! then it was (while standing by the taffrail on the poop)*
> *We could hear the drowning folk lament the absent*
>   *chicken-coop;*

"I confess I've never understood how chicken coops got into this otherwise totally comprehensible verse. But he does get back on course, I trust you'll agree:

"Then, having washed the blood away, we'd little else to do
Than to dance a quiet hornpipe as the old salts taught us to.
"O! the fiddle on the fo'c's'le, and the slapping naked soles,
And the genial 'Down the middle, Jake, and curtsey when she
rolls!'
With the silver seas around us and the pale moon over-head,
And the look-out not a-looking and his pipe-bowl glowing red.

"Ah! The pig-tailed, quidding pirates and the pretty pranks
we played,
All have since been put a stop-to by the naughty Board of
Trade;
The schooners and the merry crews are laid away to rest,
A little south the sunset in the Islands of the Blest."

He closed the book with a certain reverence, "An' that's how it was, to be sure, young Jim," he said, back into his Long John Silver imitation. I'd noticed that his everyday voice in fact had changed aboard *Merry,* with much more of his native dialect in it, and it suited the poem.

"What now?" he asked, cupping his hand to his ear. Once more he'd heard something before I did: engines again, this time idling with a low rumble as the same yacht we'd met earlier nosed into view out of the mist, making ready to anchor not too far away.

"Seems we're to have the company of our dear friends of this morning," he commented, wanting me to fetch up his binoculars. *Cock Tails,*" he read the name. "Out of Halifax." The motor yacht's anchor chain rattled out to a festive toot from the ship's horn. *Merry* was downwind and we caught fragments of their louder conversation.

"Now maybe we can persuade our captain to come down and have a drink with us," shrilled a woman's voice, calling up to the bridge. The captain did come down and joined the group, as did a young deckhand in a white uniform. This inspired another toast, and a blast of dance music, and a hundred deck lights all at once, shattering what was left of the twilight. "Their flag has a cocktail glass on it," he observed.

"I'm for runnin' up the Jolly Roger," I said.

"You tell me a story for a change," he suggested, continuing to watch the activity aboard the yacht through his glasses. "I want you to summarise everything about the pirates that I've told you. If I'm going to take you any further into this thing, I want to know you've got it right so far."

I was glad for the chance to show him my grasp of the subject, so I started with cavemen on rafts, then went to Vikings, and through the Middle Ages. I dealt with the introduction of documented pirates and privateers, governments sponsoring piracy, and Sir Francis Drake, the Queen's pirate; Granuaile, Ireland's pirate; then the baronial pirates; and Mainwaring—the pirate who wrote the book on how to stamp out piracy. Then the buccaneers, for whom I had a lot of sympathy even if history didn't, and Morgan. This all took some time, most of which he spent scrutinising the yacht through his glasses. I paused, wondering if he was even listening to me. Across the water, Frank Sinatra was crooning.

"Quite. And what's the thing they all had in common?"

I was good at oral exams, and ready with the answer to his question. I explained that up through Morgan, just about every pirate had the backing of some government or another, with the possible exception of Granuaile, who considered that she was the government, until events proved otherwise.

"Good show. And what changed after Morgan that caught up with Kidd?" I launched into a dissertation on the economic value of peaceable trade between nations, and a tightening of rules and treaties, with lots less tolerance for the loose, old ways of the buccaneers.

"The owner's wife is showing a bit of leg to the captain," he chuckled, glued to the binoculars, "and the rest of 'em are feeling no pain. Tell me about letters of reprisal."

"When somebody took one of your ships, or looted a town, the governor could issue a letter that allowed you to take ships or loot a town from where they came. Getting even." His quiz continued, with my answers ever more interrupted by shrieks of laughter, loud toasts, splashes from bottles tossed overboard, and the occasional sound of a breaking glass. "I can't compete with that," I said after a while. A woman was being pursued noisily around the ship at that moment, and a male guest was having a pee over the stern. I asked the captain what he found so fascinating about a drunken party of ignorant, careless rich people on a fancy yacht.

"Just so," he agreed. "They've been tippling all day; prob'ly went roaring up to Shelburne for a look-see, then came roaring back here where they can finish their party for the night in a more private place, which they are doing. In the final phases, I'd say." On cue, somebody switched off the yacht's deck lights. But for the orange glow from the vessel's saloon, Roseway Bay was abruptly quite dark, with a clearing sky overhead, and haze on the water. "Beddy-bye time," he said, putting aside the optics in favour of his pipe. I told him I'd had a good sleep, and didn't feel particularly tired.

"Nor I. I meant that lot over there. How many of 'em do you

think there are?" I guessed maybe a dozen. "Just so. There's the owner and his wife; he went to bed a half-hour ago in the aft stateroom; his wife's currently in the wheelhouse having a cigarette and a nightcap with the young captain. Then there are seven guests: three couples and a single girl, who's currently dancing with the deckhand, who has taken off his shirt. There is also a steward, who's exhausted but still on his feet, fraternising, serving, and drinking. All very chummy. Crew quarters forward, under the cabin deck. See the portholes? Four double cabins amidships for the guests. Are you following?"

I was, but failed to comprehend his interest. He picked up his binoculars, zeroing in on the yacht again. "There goes Miss Single with Mr. Deckhand, and he has left his uniform jacket over the back of a chair. Couple number four is legless. Couple number two is gone, and I'd say in a half-hour or so—an hour maximum—everybody aboard that ship is going to be dead."

"Dead?"

"To the world. Deep in the arms of Morpheus. Quite gone. Oblivious. Take a tidal wave to wake 'em up. And no deck watch. Very careless of 'em, what with all the jewellery those fine ladies will be taking off and throwing on their dresser-tops, and all the traveling cash those fine gentlemen have in their socks and money belts and wallets. Watches, studs." Here I took his drift at last, and fell in with the joke.

"We'll board 'em! Blunderbuss and cutlass! Arrr, matey." The thought did have a strong appeal. He grunted.

"No weapons necessary. No commotion. Now I'll tell you the plan." This involved getting *Merry*'s dinghy quietly into the water and over to the yacht, which we would board, quickly looting its most convenient valuables, and escaping unnoticed. "The tide turns in our favour before dawn, and we'll ride it and be gone. At sunup, with the westerly I think we'll get, we should be off Cape Negro, and by the time the fog burns off, we should be blowing kisses to Cape Sable. It'll take 'em days trying to figure out which one of their own gang stole everybody's stuff, and by the time they realise none of them did, they won't know where to turn."

"Unless they remember us," I played the game.

"Remember us? They're in no condition to remember anything. They never even noticed *Merry*, except maybe out of the corner of their eye as a local old boat. That's not the problem."

"What is?" This was fascinating.

"Being quiet and thorough but quick, like Drake." My role was to rifle the guest cabins, taking only valuables that were in sight or easy to find, and he told me how to best accomplish that using a masked flashlight. In the saloon, I would put on the white jacket the deckhand had left there, and if anybody did wake up, I would assure them all was well, and was only trying to find a first-aid kit.

"The guests won't know you're not part of the crew." If a cabin door was locked, he knew how to open it; he would loot the owner's cabin, and if by any chance we did encounter anybody capable of standing, he would deal with them. "But we won't," he assured me, taking a swallow of rum. "What do you think?"

I told him that for a joke, his plan sounded pretty realistic, although not as much fun as carrying a cutlass.

"We only go if we both go, so it's your call, mate. What do you say?"

"Are you serious?" It suddenly crossed my mind that it was no game.

"Serious? About a fatter, easier haul than anything Ned Low ever took here? And with a lot less fuss? Nobody even hurt? Call it suing 'em, like, for putting our lives in jeopardy this morning, and for being a bunch of bloody twits besides; likely the stay-at-home profiteers from the war, the folks your father died for. We sue, then we adjudicate, levy our fine, then we divvy up. Rules of the brotherhood—two shares for the captain, one for the crew, which is you."

I sat stunned—I would like to say horrified—except for a thrill that ran up my spine like an electrical current.

"That . . . would for sure be against the law," I whispered.

"Yes indeed," he agreed. "In point of fact, an act of piracy, although a very gentle one, as such things go. In any case, it's one we're going to have to do very soon, if we do it, which is up to you." I tried to think clearly, struggling against an impulse that was welling in me to say 'aye,' when it dawned on me that he was putting me through another of his charades, baiting me with another test. Simultaneously I was overwhelmed by disappointment and relief. Then he struck a match to light his pipe, and I beheld again his eyes as black holes in his face, only for a moment, but just as unnerving as before, and no illusion. I caught my breath. The match went out.

"You have a little think about that, then we'll do whatever suits you," he said, puffing. Over on the yacht, the saloon lights went out, and all the portholes were dark except for one, making a small gold shimmer on the water, among the silvery reflections from the pale moon overhead. The captain's pipe bowl glowed bright red.

15

Reflections during a Short Crossing

A t sunup, Cape Negro was just visible a mile to port, through the morning haze. Swept by the southbound tide, and favoured by a gentle westerly breeze, *Merry* was chuckling along in flat water. She was making good time under every sail she could carry, including her light topsail. Clearing Grey Island, we had tacked south and I climbed the lacings to throw the topsail foot over the peak halyard tackle.

"Poppins did that job in a lot less time," the captain commented when I returned to the deck. He was peeling masking tape off the lens of his flashlight. "Don't you want to get a bit of kip?"

"Kip?"

"Sleep. You didn't get much, and you've got the forenoon watch. That gives you a couple of hours. There's a long crossing ahead of us." I was not tired in the slightest, I told him. "Right. In that case, you'd better have a look at the lashings you put onto the gripes. I know you had to work in the dark, but it's light now, and you should cinch 'em up some." I did it, securing the dinghy on its cradle as tightly as before we had used it.

"That's better," he approved. He was in a very mellow mood, having a rum at six o'clock in the morning, nibbling from an open jar of Mother's solomongundy in the cockpit. *Merry's* tiller was pegged. I looked at her wake, marking the way back to Roseway Bay. It was five miles behind us in the mist, getting farther by the moment. I mused aloud about the pirate Ned Low, who had taken thirteen vessels there. What did *he* get from them?"

"Fish, stores, water, rum—no jewellery, and not much cash." He winked. "But useful supplies. He was on the move. He kept one vessel, took a few people off his captures and made for Newfoundland to pick up some more. A shorthanded buccaneer could always flesh out his crew in Newfoundland, as I've already noted. What's that?" He squinted, looking forward. "Plops of paint on the deck?" It was, a pair of them, glistening in the morning light. "Better clean it up while it's still wet. Use paraffin."

While I was getting the first kerosene of the day on my hands, I urged him to tell me more about Low. Piracy along the coast of Nova Scotia had taken on more than a schoolbook interest for me.

"Low was a bloody rotter, one of the worst sods you can possibly imagine. Liked to cut off ears. Once he caught a ship whose captain threw eleven thousand gold moidores over the side just to keep it from being taken. Very injudicious. Low raved like a fury, swore a thousand oaths, and ordered the captain's lips to be cut off, which he broiled before his face, and afterward murdered him and all the crew, being thirty-two persons. And he did lots of other things you don't want to hear about. Or, if you do, look 'em up in my book."

"Your book?"

"My copy of Johnson's *History of the Most Notorious Pirates*. Haven't I loaned it to you? Remind me to. Low was one of those evil-hearted villains who gave the whole brotherhood a bad name. Low was the English answer to L'Ollonais. D'ye remember L'Ollonais?" He checked the compass heading, then had another nibble of solomongundy. *Merry* bubbled happily along. "Poor Low," he commented. "He was so bad, he had a hard time keeping a crew."

"Poor Low's victims," I said, thinking what it would be like to have one's lips cut off. "Why 'poor Low'? What happened to him?"

"Poor anybody who gets bad teachers. Out we pop, into this strange world, with everything to learn, which we drink up, whatever concoction we're handed by the luck of the draw. Low slid out into a family of criminals in London. First thing he learned after not wetting himself was how to pick a pocket. His older brother taught him. Later got hanged at Tyburn."

"Low?"

"His brother. With teachers like that, what chance did the poor sod have? Could have been a chicken-plucker. Here's to our own better luck with our parents." He took a swallow of rum.

"Who were yours?" I asked him. He smiled.

"A mermaid and a porgy. As to your other question about

Low, last I'm aware of him, he was decorating a gibbet at Martinique, and nobody mourned. Should have happened a lot sooner." He brooded. "It's the Lows and his lot who tickled the horrors of mankind, and got all the press. He wasn't even a member of the brotherhood, but he blackened its name. When the brethren committed kindnesses, they weren't nearly as interesting. Who wants to read about tenderhearted pirates, unless they're that Errol Flynn chap in the flickers."

"Were there any?"

"Oh aye, lots, but if it weren't for Johnson, who'd know about 'em at all? Take Captain Tom White, working the Malabar Coast. Around 1713, he caught a small prize, out of which they took some stores, plus five hundred dollars. There was also a silver mug, and two spoons belonging to a couple of orphans on board, wee passengers, who cried and cried. When White learned they were crying because that was all they had in the world, he made a speech to his men, telling 'em it was cruel to rob the innocent children. So the little ones got back their mugs and spoons, plus a collection among the pirates that netted them another 120 dollars. Then they were sent on their way unharmed, in their undamaged ship. But who wants to read about that? Or the hundreds of ships that the brethren simply gave back? Some of 'em were hardcase ships, needier than the pirates who took 'em, and got provisioned by their captors, then sent on their way with blessings, sailors to sailors. We weren't all Ned Low and L'Ollonais and those types."

"We?"

"You and me, mate. As I've said, there's no such thing as 'the pirates.'" Every one's a different case. Now, you and me, you and I, we wouldn't join up with a psychopath like Low, nor did anybody much who had a choice about it. Some of us sailed with gents like Tom White, who was a flautist."

"And he was hanged?"

"Not Tom. Settled on Madagascar. Married a local girl who had six toes on her left foot, and raised a happy family in one of the prettiest little thatch-roof houses you've ever seen. Got on with all the neighbours. His wife played a native instrument like the flute, and she taught it to him, and they played duets. Kids and pet lemurs all over the place; also parrots, which I can't abide because they make so much bird lime, and gnaw the woodwork, but Tom had 'em everywhere. They couldn't resist earrings. You'd come in and take a seat, get comfortable with a jar of punch, and the next thing you know, here's some bloody great cape parrot flapping down, landing on your shoulder, trying to tear your earring away from your head, which they're capable of doing. Tom had to warn all of his mates who wore earrings."

"What happened to Tom?"

"Captain White to you. He made another cruise or two, then hung up his cutlass, and settled into the bosom of his family. Died of a flux while in their arms, having made arrangements for his children's education. His eldest son became a proper gent. But that's a bit ahead of where we left off."

"Left off?"

"Last night, before we got involved with other things. You made a fair summary of the history I've been teaching you, and now you're properly equipped to meet the chaps you took a fancy to before we met, right?"

"I feel like one of them."

"Then be one. Here's your situation. After Kidd, the good old days are gone. There's still opportunities, because Queen

Anne's War is on, with all the countries fighting each other, as usual, but in 1713 there's the Treaty of Utrecht, and suddenly, for the first time in living memory, you've got the catastrophe of total peace."

"Catastrophe?"

"For the brotherhood, the whole family. You're all out of jobs, some four or five thousand of you, trained professionals with all kinds of properly equipped warships, and no other home or living. You can go back to the indentured slavery you got away from in the first place, or as a hand on a merchant ship, which could be worse than the Royal Navy. On a merchant ship, if you got a black-hearted master with a couple of mates that were like him, they could make your life as bad as anything you can ever imagine. Sailors' rights are unheard of; seamen are exploited without mercy by fat shipowners, who get rich as Croesus in the new peace, and off the sweat and blood of you and your mates. No change there, since caveman times."

Suddenly he sounded like a communist, but, the way he put it, I couldn't help agreeing it did seem like an unfair system that should be changed.

"Changed? What's to change? The way of the world? Mother Nature's own balances? Unfair? Don't overtax your brains with how things should be; you're going to need all the brain power you've got just trying to figure out how things actually are."

"How are they?"

"Well, you can't go back to Port Royal, for starters. In fact, since the earthquake of 1692, there is no more Port Royal, but all the big ports that used to depend on the buccaneers are now closed off to you. You have to use secondary bases. There are still plenty of islands and hidey-holes in the world, but you can't get a forty-gun ship into most of them, so you get smaller ships. You want a vessel with enough speed to get away from the Royal Navy, which you can't outfight, but that can catch the fat merchantmen, which you've got the men and the guns to subdue. You want a fast little sloop that's handy to weather, and can tuck into places like Roseway Bay where the king's frigates can't follow you."

"No more grand, big pirate ships?"

"Some, but by and large they had to keep the sea, getting supplies and gear from the prizes they took. With no proper port open to 'em anymore for refits and repairs. When a ship got too foul or worn out, they'd have to move aboard another one, and repeat the process. Teach had a forty-gun ship that he disposed of in favour of a sloop.

"Teach?"

"Blackbeard. Edward Teach. He was one of the Nassau crowd."

"Nassau?"

"Bahamas. Madagascar was still good, and the Seychelles, and there were still some Caribbean islands, but Nassau was the pirates' paradise. England took it, claimed it, and sent out settlers, but abandoned the place during the war. The Spaniards and the French both raided it so much, it couldn't be defended, and the governor went back to Blighty in 1709. So, after the war, the whole Bahamian archipelago was more or less up for grabs, and the brotherhood grabbed it. Lot's of 'em settled there, having a go at honest professions such as smuggling, hunting, trading, what have you. Some sailed out to the Bay of Compeache, cutting logwood, which makes a valuable dye. Others went diving on the Spanish treasure fleet that was wrecked off the Bahamas in 1715. That was good work for a season, getting up pieces of eight and doubloons, before the Dons came and ran 'em off, and dove on it themselves." He paused to glance at the compass.

"Somewhere down below, I have a Spanish doubloon that Caleb Whitback pulled up out of one of those wrecks, which is the last we ever heard about him. Left a young widow in New York. I looked her up. Had the devil of a time finding her."

"Finding her?"

"In historical records, dear boy. My studies. As to Nassau, the brethren came there in droves, built a little city, out of mostly framed buildings covered with old sails. More watering holes than you can ever imagine. Good harbour tucked in behind Hog Island—lots of fish, turtles, pigs, rum, traders, women, whatever a chap could want. So the brethren fixed up a piece of the old fort, which had been blown up by the Spaniards, big enough to mount an eighteen-pounder on it commanding the approaches. And there they were, with their own establishment off the Caribbean for a little while." I wondered just how much the local settlers liked their new government, but, by the captain's account, these abandoned people welcomed the brotherhood, getting some protection for the first time in a while, as well as financial benefits from a boom in trade, and little forays, mostly against the Spaniards. "Under the rules of the brotherhood, Nassau enjoyed peace, prosperity, and freedom," he added.

Merry's clock rang eight bells, marking the end of his watch. He reached for the chart. "I put us about here," he made a tickmark on the penciled line of our course. "Keep sou'-sou'west. By the end of your watch, we'll be clear of Brazil Rock. Stay alert, and call me if anything happens that *Merry* can't tell me about." He turned to go below, having made no remark during the entire watch concerning the events that were churning in my mind.

"Last night . . ." I started to say.

"There is no last night. What there is, is *Merry*, and this breeze, and those sails, and that compass. Don't hold a course that's too tight, but don't let her wander too far. That's what is. Last night never happened, and tomorrow never comes." He vanished below, leaving me with my restless thoughts, then popped his head out of the hatch a moment later.

"Sail by the luff of your tops'l. Don't let it shiver."

The following days brought winds relentlessly from the direction in which we wanted to go, but they were gentle compared to before. In a small boat, there is a world of difference between a head wind of twenty to twenty-five knots, and one of ten to fifteen knots. It is the difference between hard pumping while hanging on, dead wet, having to haul on lines that are stretched like bowstrings, sailing on your ear—and hardly having to pump at all, being able to live and move in a much more reasonable, graceful way, and cook, and enjoy the splash of summer seas, with hardly a whitecap in sight.

In that way, making daylong tacks across the Gulf of Maine, *Merry* nudged toward Boston. Along with my other responsibilities, I was charged with plotting the broad zigzag of her course, quickly learning more navigation than Grandfather had ever taught me. On this subject, I was commanded to read a book that was so long out of date, I protested.

"It's as good now as it was then," the captain growled. "Read it." And so I did, whenever I wasn't doing something else, so that I had no such thing as spare time on *Merry*. The captain, however-er, had nothing but spare time, after instructing me on how to do everything that he didn't want to, which seemed like everything. It left him little to do except play his pennywhistle, macramé his bottle, and watch all that I was doing so that he could criticise it.

Recent events had led me to expect more pirate stories. When none developed, I asked for one, hoping for another of his yarns of the kind that drew me into them, but all I got was another antique book. This was the long-threatened copy of Johnson's *General History of the Most Notorious Pirates,* which was as hard to read as Esquemeling—harder, by the light of the kerosene lamp over my bunk. It took three days to work my way through the introduction, between other assignments. The only thing that made the captain's crudely printed old book easier to read, once I'd figured out the words, was that it sounded so much like him. It took a very lofty and critical look at the pirates, as well as the governments that had bred them, with the pirates often coming off better.

One evening after doing supper cleanup, I took the book above to where the captain was having his usual lounge in the cockpit. I read an excerpt aloud:

> *"Rome, the Mistress of the World, was no more at first than a refuge for thieves and outlaws; and if the progress of our Pyrates had been equal to their beginning, and had they all united and settled in some of those Islands, they might by this time have been honoured with the name of a commonwealth, and no power in those parts of the world . . ."*

"Could have been able to dispute it with them," he finished the last sentence of the quote. "What's your question?"

"Could they actually have done that? Made their own republic?"

"I do believe we could have done. We had the guns and the best fighters. With Nassau's forts rebuilt, and some more eighteen-pounders in place, and a declared government, and a reign-in on piracy, and our own flag—not black—we could have had a tidy little republic. The first. England would have been annoyed, of course, but most of the Royal Navy had been cashiered by then, retired, and England had lots bigger things to think about. The cost of a fleet to deal with the place she'd abandoned would have been greater than the gain by miles."

"What stopped us?"

"Mostly, just being sailors, too itchy a lot to get cozy in one place. And give up the life? Not bloody likely. Too addictive. Like tobacco," he added, stooping to light his pipe. "So we had to be content with leaving our procedures to the Bahamians, in various ways, and our spawn in America. Do you have any notion as to how many of the founding patriots of the United States were direct blood descendants of the brotherhood? Some genealogist chap wrote notes about that. Quite amazing."

"The brotherhood never wrote down a Declaration of Independence?"

"The brotherhood never wrote down anything at all, if we could bloody well help it, written things being such useful evidence. But we all came to it as individuals, like Captain Bellamy. He had a grasp for rhetoric that was a lot less wordy than the American chap who wrote the 'When in the course of human events' declaration that they've got enshrined somewhere. Hand me that book."

He leafed through Johnson, noting that Bellamy had dived on

the Spanish treasure wrecks with the rest of the Nassau brethren, then sailed off with his sloop on the account, and captured an armed galley named *Whydah*, loaded with rich cargo and pieces of eight. "She was a first-rate catch, and he decided to keep her. Gave her some more guns and raided the Carolina coast. Took several prizes, including a sloop commanded by a chap named Beers. Bellamy did the usual thing, trying to get any recruits who wanted to join up. Here's what he said when Beers turned down his invitation:

> "*. . . Damn ye, you are a sneaking puppy, and so are all those who will submit to be governed by Laws which rich men have made for their own security, for the cowardly whelps have not the courage otherwise to defend what they get by their knavery. But damn ye altogether. Damn them for a pack of crazy rascals, and you, who serve them, for a parcel of hen-hearted numskulls. They villify us, the scoundrels do, when there is only this difference, they rob the poor under the cover of Law, forsooth, and we plunder the rich under the protection of our own courage. Had you not better make one of us, than sneak after the arses of those villians for Employment? Captain Beers told him that his conscience would not allow him to break through the Laws of God and man. 'You are a devilish conscientious rascal, damn ye,' replied Bellamy. 'I am a free prince . . . and this my conscience tells me. But there is no arguing with such snivelling puppies, who allow superiors to kick them about deck at pleasure and pin their faith upon a pimp of a parson, a squab, who neither practises nor believes what he puts upon the chuckle-headed fools he preaches to.*

"There's a declaration of independence if ever I heard one, complete with a full-front assault on all the god-bothering priests. Well, in all wisdom, it is said that the gates of heaven are taken by storm, and I'll drink to that." He did so. *Merry*'s mast creaked with content. "Did you ever hear that old saw about the pirates' assault on heaven? Here's Saint Peter, guarding his golden gates, and what should he see but a whole crew of buccaneers comin' for him, all with cutlasses. He has to think fast. 'A chase! A chase!' he yells, givin' the cry of a lookout who's spotted a prize. 'Where away?' they call; 'over there, Saint Peter points. Off they go, chasing, and heaven is saved."

"Did Captain Beers get his lips cut off?" I wanted to know.

"Nah. Bellamy wasn't Low. Damned few of us were. Beers got set ashore on Block Island, a little lighter in the purse, but safe as a lamb in the arms of Jesus. Bellamy even wanted to give his sloop back to him, but the crew didn't, and they outvoted him."

"What happened to Bellamy?"

"Sailed north on the pirates' round. You worked the Caribbean in the winter, then before the hurricane season can start, around July, you made for New England, Nova Scotia, or Newfoundland, where you could pick a hidey-hole and careen, clean ship, and cruise 'til it was time to go south for the winter. That's what Bellamy was up to. He careened in the Machias River in Maine, where he got an interesting proposal from one of his crew.

"I forget the chap's name, but he was a writer and an actor, and a retired highwayman turned buccaneer. This chap thought Bellamy (and Williams, another pirate sailing in his company) could found their own republic there, and make a go of it, and maybe they could have done, but Bellamy was more amused by this whimsical fellow's talents as a classical playwright. He wrote

255

a full-length drama called *The Royal Pirate,* and then directed a performance on *Whydah*'s quarterdeck, with costumes and music. Big audience."

"A success?" I asked, trying to imagine a company of buccaneers performing their own classical drama.

"Yes and no. It did have an indisputable power. In the play a pirate was brought up for trial, and sentenced to hang, and it was realistic enough to confuse the gunner, who thought it was really happening. The gunner, having taken strong drink, went and got a grenade, which he lit the fuse on, and threw in among the actors, who took a bit of damage when it exploded. One actor lost an arm; another got a broken leg. Anyway, it canceled the performance."

"What happened to the gunner?"

"He was canceled also. And good riddance, I say. Nobody much quibbled with his critique of the play, but it seemed a bit extreme." The Bellamy yarn was interrupted by sunset, meaning I had to light *Merry*'s port and starboard lamps, and the stern light, and the binnacle lamp; down below there was the cabin lamp, trimming all their wicks, and adjusting them so that they burned just perfectly to the captain's eye, which took some doing. When I'd finished, he'd been below, glanced at my navigation, and brought up another coin, which he handed me.

"There's a bit of Bellamy's treasure for you to have a look at. Grab the torch if you want to see it better." In the flashlight's beam, I saw the Spanish cross on an irregular silver piece that was much worn. "It's the sand. It got worn away over the years, laying off Cape Cod. As to how it got there, *Whydah,* with twenty-eight guns, raiding off Newfoundland, attacked a thirty-six-gun French ship, full of soldiers bound for Quebec—an error of judgment that nearly cost all of them their lives. Badly shot up. Three dozen of her crew dead. *Whydah* barely escaped. In this action, the playwright was killed. Bellamy's fortunes had turned, y'see. Soon after, while he was raiding the waters off Cape Cod, he forced a pilot. But the chap . . ."

"Forced a pilot?"

"Conscripted. When the Royal Navy did it, it was called 'pressing'; when the brethren did it, it was called 'forcing.' Both of 'em took people, as they needed 'em. We always needed artists: navigators, coopers, sailmakers, pilots, what have you. So Bellamy forced a pilot out of a small prize. Then, at night in a freshening gale, gave him the job of steering them into shelter, under the hook of the Cape. He had the lead vessel, and it had a careless crew, because while they were all having a jar of punch in the pleasant anticipation of a snug anchorage, their forced pilot runs both their ships aground. The pilot gets himself safe ashore, while Bellamy's vessels take a mortal pounding in the surf, and break up. And that was the end of *Whydah* and her prize."

"And Bellamy?"

"Drowned, 147 of them. All drowned except for seven who managed to swim through the surf. Got arrested by the locals, and sent to Boston for trial. That was in the fall of 1717. Now I'll have my coin back." He stretched out his hand. I put the silver piece in it, telling him I was disappointed that neither he nor it had taken me into any of the action he had described.

"I'll try to make up," he promised. "Meanwhile, there's chests and chests of silver and gold to be found in the sands off Wellfleet, waitin' for somebody to come and take 'em." He put the coin back in his pocket. "But that's another project for another day."

On the morning of our tenth day out, we sighted Cape Ann, which was my first glimpse of the world beyond Nova Scotia. I couldn't wait to get where we were going, now so near. But there was more tacking to do, and trickier navigation as we approached the islands and shoals of inner Massachusetts Bay. The skyline of Boston began to define itself with a wink of sunlight on a golden dome among a prickle of church steeples on a hill. Beyond, to either side, there were chimneys producing a pink and purple haze over everything.

The captain had the binoculars. When he lowered them, a tear rolled down his cheek. He glanced at me. "It's the smog. My eyes aren't used to it. Same in all the old ports, really. And here you have the Paris of New England, Cradle of Revolution." A cluster of racing yachts flashed past. All had yacht club burgees, crews in white, and American ensigns flying, prompting the captain's remarks on America and Americans. In his view, the American phenomenon, as he called it, was entirely predictable from the outset. "You're England," he challenged me, "and you've got this huge chunk of the North American continent that you've pirated from the chaps who lived here; now, what do you do with it?"

"Settle it." I'd learned the history.

"Quite. But with whom? It's a bloody remote wilderness, nothing in it but savages—irritated at having been pirated—and bugs. Bugs that bite, and bugs that sting, and bugs worse than the savages. Read the old journals on the subject of bugs. So, who can you get to settle North America?"

"Adventurers?" I offered.

"Just so. Intelligent lad. Not just adventurers, but the most self-confident, obstreperous, independent, aggressive, impoverished, and dissatisfied people. Then you've got criminals you can deport, and religious outcasts, and you get the miscellany of foreigners and other refugees, and black slaves, plus hundreds and hundreds of pirates, buccaneers, the brotherhood, retired and otherwise. Well," he reached for his tobacco, "there you have a genetic boil with enough steam to blow the lid off the pot for a while in history. I mean, how can you blame the Americans for being who they are, considering they're our own creation?"

As we approached Boston, the captain seemed to be having unaccustomed difficulty in reconciling the chart with his memory of the last time he had been there.

"When was that? I asked.

"I'd have to think back. But over to starboard there's a thundering great aerodrome, where there used to be water, and Noddles Island. And Nix's Mate is gone. That's a little island, or used to be, where some of the brethren were hanged in chains. Just a marker there now. And Bird Island's been renamed. That's where they hung Archer, slathered in tar, in 1724. He lasted a long time out here, but he's long gone now."

"Where are we headed?" I wanted to know. It was getting on toward twilight, and *Merry* was close in.

"How can I say until I see it?" He had the helm, steering us past wharf after wharf, all teeming with commercial traffic.

"Where's a yacht harbour?" I asked, unable to locate one on the chart.

"That'd be our last resort."

And so we nosed into the Charles River, where the masts of a square-rigged ship came into view. According to the captain, it was the United States frigate *Constitution*. She had been launched in 1798, had chased French pirates called Picarroons in the Caribbean as her first assignment, and then gone on to greater things.

"She's the oldest old vessel afloat, very famous, and we should have a look at her," he said, and so we did, with little apparent regard on his part for where we would tie up for the night. Not that I was tired. The sombre muzzles of old cannons peered out at us as we tacked under the ancient warship, its majesty of rigging limned by the dipping sun.

"There's our berth," he said, pointing to a service float laying forward of *Constitution* along her wharf. He gave me a string of instructions as he luffed *Merry* alongside. And so we landed at the Boston Navy Yard in Charlestown, Massachusetts, U.S.A.

"You can't tie up here," yelled a uniformed person, just as we had finished doing it.

"Our engine's down," called the captain, back at him. "Got blown in here! Hailing from Canada!"

"Oh," he said, "I'll have to get the duty officer." And off he went. By the time that person came, we had snugged down *Merry*.

"Can't tie up here," said the duty officer, in whites, with an armband that said SP.

"Means Shore Patrol, Navy Police," the captain whispered. "No choice," he called back to the dock, in a perfectly cultivated

English accent. "Frightfully sorry. Engine's packed in. Come aboard." The duty officer did so, by which time the captain had taken away the coverings to the long-defunct Ailsa Craig motor, and was struggling with it.

"Enough to try the patience of a saint," he said, tapping it with a tool. The long and short of it turned into a conversation regarding the lineage of the duty officer, who was Irish. By the end of their conversation, the captain was talking with an Irish accent, and when the duty officer went away, we were cleared to be where we were as an emergency procedure, pending word from higher authority.

Half an hour or so later a jeep pulled up, and the officer of the day climbed down the ladder to the float, where he was greeted by more engine poundings and expletives by the captain, until being noticed. "Come aboard, dear sir," he said. The officer of the day, a quartermaster, was bemused by us, an old man and a boy against the sea, and even though he could not accept the rum that was offered him, he authorised our being there, pending getting our motor fixed and further examination by other authorities.

These came in two waves. First, there was Naval Intelligence, which was duty-bound to look at any unusual visitation to a U.S. Navy facility, even in a low-security area. Two officers poked around for a minute or two, found nothing suspicious, and left.

"Let's you make some corned beef sandwiches," he told me, and I did, just as a customs officer and an immigration officer showed up.

"Join us?" the captain invited, but they were more interested in asking their routine questions, looking at my birth certificate, stamping his passport, and getting on with their interrupted lives. "Better that they come to us than us having to go to them, no?"

Our last visitors were some off-duty sailors from *Constitution*'s crew, who did not decline the rum they were offered, and there was good will all around. I finally went to sleep in my forward berth to the background rumble of laughter, trucks, airplanes, passing ships, and distant sirens in the night.

16

Boston

H ere's the plan," said the captain, all business. It was early the following morning, Tuesday, and we were up before the Navy Yard, having a wash on deck, then putting on our carefully rolled shore clothes. "First, make a big batch of coffee. Full pot. When the watch shifts, we'll have some more visitors. They'll tell you where to find a telephone so you can ring up y'r mum, and let her know we're still among the living, though a bit behind schedule. When the visitors clear out, I'll toddle over into the city and start business. I'll be gone when you get back. You'll be minding *Merry.*"

My disappointment aside, that is how it worked out. Right after whistles went off in the yard, another jeep pulled up on the wharf with a new duty officer, who'd been told about us, and was just there to view us and say hi. He was soon followed by a lieutenant wearing crisp summer whites and a broad smile as he descended the ladder to the float. *Constitution*'s huge bowsprit projected directly over *Merry*'s little masts. The officer turned out to be her commander, Lieutenant Messier, who was glad to take his morning coffee in our cockpit.

"Captain Charles Johnson, at your service, and this is Jim. Would you take a bit of tinned milk in that? Sugar?" The captain was full of appreciation for our emergency berth. He was going into Boston right away to find the parts he needed to make our repairs. Yes, *Merry Adventure* had just crossed the Gulf of Maine, and before that, the Atlantic. This drew respect, leading into a discussion of the lieutenant's navy career; he had been commissioned from the ranks, "come up through the hawser hole," as he put it. He was from Bristol, Connecticut, which led to a discussion of the place and a clear communion. When the lieutenant left, the coffee pot was empty, *Merry* had permission to stay where she was, and the shore patrol would keep an eye on her. We were invited to use the washrooms and facilities in the old stone barracks building used by *Constitution*'s crew, and I got to use the office telephone for my call to home.

Meg answered, very relieved I was in Boston. Mother was in Halifax with Aunt Karen, who had taken a turn for the worse, and was in the hospital there. The work on the inn was going to stop unless the money that everybody was expecting from us came through by wire in the next four days. Everything depended on us. Meg sounded grim. Unsettled, I walked across the cobblestones of the old part of the Navy Yard, where the public was admitted to "Old Ironsides," a floating museum. There was another old frigate, with no masts, *Constellation;* both gave life to the pictures I'd seen of such ships, and meaning to the stories about them.

"Over here, m'boy," a sailor beckoned, grinning at me. He wore an old-fashioned hat and was at the gangway to *Constitu-*

tion, where he was engaging the day's first trickle of tourists. My immediate impression of him was as a carnival hustler I had once seen, but he got me to come over and join the tour that he was about to conduct. He did a talk that I could tell he had done before, herding everybody from place to place on the ship, past endless rows of huge cannons, surrounded by a cathedral of woodwork under low overheads.

"Name's Mathew," he introduced himself to me in a friendly way, taking me under his wing during his tour. Afterward, he let me climb down into an area low in the ship where tourists weren't allowed. "That's all original ship down there, pal, all old woodwork. Still got cannonballs in her from a long time ago. Can you feel any ghosts?" I didn't, although it was very sombre, and Jenny would have. Mathew was very interested in *Merry,* and I invited him to come down to have a look at her.

This he did when his watch was over. I was glad for his company, being stuck for hours on *Merry* with the whole astonishing landscape of Boston in front of me. I was surrounded by its pulse, feeling entirely left out. I showed my new friend around *Merry,* and felt proud to be the guide. He had a lot of questions that I didn't mind answering, and a few that I did, regarding our business. He got it out of me that we had some antiques for sale. "Well, this is the best place to sell them. What have you got?" he asked, just as I saw the unmistakable figure of the captain, with walking stick, returning at last.

"Hullo, who might you be?" he asked Mathew. "Right, well, thanks for your visit, and now Jim and I have some work to do." Watching him go, I accused the captain of dismissing my friend very abruptly. He gave me a hard eye. "Nobody comes aboard *Merry* unless I'm here to invite 'em. Chat 'em up as long as you want to, so long as they stay dockside. How was your morning?"

I reported Meg's news from home, stressing the urgency about our mission. As the family spokesman, I wanted a report. He nodded, demanded a sandwich, and briefed me while I prepared our lunch. He had selected four antique dealers—one each for our four crates of pewter—whom he had talked to over the telephone. He planned to visit them in quick succession, "so we get the best price, which we won't if word gets around town as to how much antique pewter we're unloading all at once into the market. It's an in-and-out operation. We'll start tomorrow, Wednesday."

"Why not this afternoon?" I fretted, thinking of our deadline, and the clock ticking toward the weekend.

"This afternoon's for examining the terrain. Very important to do that before any engagement."

"Engagement?"

"Just so. When you've squared away the galley, we'll make a start." Our examination of the terrain took the form of a brisk walk across the Charlestown Bridge and into the city, where we followed a map the captain had bought to Charles Street. Three out of four of our prospective buyers had their stores on this street. We visited most of them, looking at price tags on old pewter, which was interesting enough at first, but less so after a couple of hours of it. He didn't enter any of the shops on his select list, although he spent a very long time peering through their windows. Finally, I noticed that he was watching the people within, and said so.

"Just putting a face to the chaps I've been chatting with by telephone. Look at the big florid chap with the red bow tie and braces. Look at him fawning over the lady with the cute little dog, even though he's got a 'No Pets' sign on the door. The old girl's prattling away, isn't going to buy anything, but he's frosting his other customers for her. I reckon she's a Cabot, or a Coolidge, or Crowninshield, or one of the other Boston bunch whose parties Mr. Bow-Tie likes to go to, when he can get invited. I think Mr. Bow-Tie chooses his company very carefully."

"You mean he's a big snob?"

"That looks like the terrain. We'll see him tomorrow morning, when we're a bit better prepared, and have the weather gauge on him. Then we'll look in on Mr. Pipe, who was the scholarly gent we saw reading and smoking the huge pipe, and Madame Lipstick, the lady who had all the potted plants about."

The last shop on our scouting agenda was several blocks distant, taking us on a course that skirted a large park with traffic whizzing around it. "That's Boston Common," he told me as we waited to cross a busy street, "where it is against the law to graze your cow . . . or was when I was last here. Not that I ever had a cow. There's a green light." The fourth of our prospective antique dealers was entirely riveted to a little television set with a loud baseball game, paying no attention at all to his customers. After viewing him, the captain was ready for a sit-down and a pint of beer, which he put away so quickly, I barely had time to finish my soft drink before he was rising from the table, and we were off on our next errand.

"Now we're going to have to spend a dollar or two, getting properly togged out for Mr. Bow-Tie, who's going to pay us a handsome sum for our showiest pieces, right?" This notion cost more dollars than I'd ever seen spent on clothes. For me, they included a pair of sporty white deck shoes, with white socks that came nearly up to my knees, white Bermuda shorts that came nearly down to them, and a fine white shirt that had collars with buttons.

"Well, that's different," I said, looking at myself in a huge mirror that also showed angles of me that I'd never seen. I questioned the sense of spending money on frivolous things. "I look like I'm off a tennis court."

"Or a big fancy yacht. Picture a world-class yacht, one that makes *Cock Tails* look like a dinghy. Steward's mates everywhere. Dozens of crew."

"I'm crew?"

"You are Master James, and it's you and your family that the crew's there to serve." While I was digesting this, the captain tried on khaki slacks until he found some he liked, with deck shoes and a new shirt similar to mine. With our costumes in a shopping bag—which I carried—we trekked back to Charlestown, showed the visitors' passes we'd been issued at the Navy Yard's guard house, and returned to *Merry,* where I settled with a tired sigh.

"Supper time, Mr. Cook," said the captain, instantly calling me back to duty. "And look smart about it, because we've got a lot of work to do before we can turn in."

This included dragging out all four crates with pewter ware and totally rearranging their contents, with pieces set out on every surface of *Merry*'s little cabin, as he re-tallied prices, making a lot of revisions based on our scouting. The night was late by the time each piece was rewrapped in its felt, then repacked in its new carefully chosen box, with revised inventories drawn up.

"Well," I sighed, "this is a lot more work than the pirates had to go through."

"Not quite. Fact of the matter is, we spent most of our lives squabbling over loot disposal. You take a sloop with rum, sugar, and logwood, and then that's what you've got to sell, swap, trade for, take where it'll go for the best price, and knowing who you're dealing with. The biggest day-to-day entertainment was haggling after the divvy, and the divvy itself was the most interesting thing of all, for everybody on the ship. Maybe you get some pearls, but you're short on small cash, so you wrap 'em nicely, maybe put 'em in a sweet little pouch, make a bit of a presentation to the chap who's got more pieces of eight than he knows what to do with. It was the highest art of all, and the most successful of the brotherhood were those who had a nose for it."

I couldn't help a yawn. "Am I supposed to play some kind of role tomorrow?"

"You are. Rehearsal right after breakfast."

How d'you do, sir," I said for the umpteenth time. It was to be my one line, delivered in a very cultured English accent. My director had also coached me in "yes, sir," "no, sir," and "I can't (cahnt) say, sir," my only options if spoken to, except "good-bye, sir," at the end.

"You've got it. You should try to enjoy the drive. How often do you get a chance to roll through Boston in a limousine?" The captain had hired the fancy car the day before, and its uniformed driver, William, who drove up to the dock at midmorning.

William hoisted up Mr. Bow-Tie's box of pewter, putting it in the trunk for us, so we ran no risk of smudging our new clothes. We rolled out of the Navy Yard past Mathew, on duty, gawking at the sight of us, and then through the streets of Boston like movie stars. I said I'd be able to enjoy it more if I wasn't worried about being stilted and wooden in my role.

"Stilted and wooden will serve very nicely," he approved. Then we were there, parking in front of Mr. Bow-Tie's fancy shop, and everything happening very quickly—the captain out, door opened by William as Mr. Bow-Tie came to see who was getting out of a limousine.

"Johnson. Talked to you on the phone. Pewter. William!" He summoned the driver. "Bring the box. Master James, please?" he summoned me. I went to his side, and he introduced me only as Master James.

"How d'you do, sir," I said, saying my line, shooting out my hand to shake his.

"James . . . ?" Mr. Bow-Tie fixed on me with a quizzical look.

"Yes, sir," I said. He wasn't finished with me, but the captain cut him off, speaking in a lowered voice, with no trace of dialect, just the purest upper-class English I'd ever heard spoken.

"I'm given to understand from some mutual friends that you, sir, are not only the chap to bring these," he gestured with his stick toward the box of pewter that William was bringing in, "but that you are a person to be trusted with discretion." Mr. Bow-Tie made an automatic nod. "Quite. Well, we're off our yacht, y'see, and we're here, but we're *not* here. It's a *quiet* visit, with a little shore chore or two to give our young master a bit of a browse without any . . ." he hesitated.

"Public attention?" Mr. Bow-Tie filled in.

"Just so. Good chap."

"Which yacht club?" Mr. Bow-Tie asked, sizing us up, and lowering his own voice. "And if I may ask, what yacht?" The captain became brusque.

"We're guests of your government. The Navy Yard has the private accommodations we need for the short time we're here. Our ship, we call her *Merry* for short, hails from England. Here by way of the Caribbean. And I think that's all that's pertinent in our transaction, which is your buying this lot that we're clearing off the ship. Housecleaning. What do you think?" He unwrapped the top piece, which was the elaborate coffeepot, the collection's prize.

"Oh!" said Mr. Bow-Tie, looking at it with surprise. "Very nice indeed," then, "who did you say sent you to me?"

"I didn't. Let me make it plain," the captain's tone hardened. "Names are not in play. I repeat, we are not here, not for photographers or anybody else except some local friends who have recommended you. I'm given to understand that is something you will understand." He lifted his eyebrows. Mr. Bow-Tie hastened to assure him that he did indeed entirely understand. "Quite. Well, we'll have a bit of a look down the street, while you have a look at the pewter, and," he pulled out a couple of folded pages, opened them and handed them to Mr. Bow-Tie, "here's the inventory—ewers, plates, tankards, all itemised, with notes on signatures, cartouches, stampings, and whatnot, by our curator chap. According to him, whatever evaluation he's come up with is designed to fetch the ship a fair price, leaving you a fair profit, at current values."

He called William from the curb. "Stand by. Expect us back in a quarter-hour." As we strolled away, Mr. Bow-Tie was opening pewter under the watchful eye of William, a large man from South Boston. His one stage-instruction was to say absolutely nothing, standing just inside the shop door. If questioned, he was only to shake his head. He seemed made for his role.

"Let's pop in on Madame Lipstick," the captain suggested when we came to her shop, and he opened its door with a great clangor of little bells. We had nicknamed her for her crimson lips, the first thing about her. They made the rest of her look very soft. The sight of us brought her to her feet, all smiles. There was more or less the same introduction, but here he took what seemed an almost personal interest in the lady, smiling to her, full of compliments on her displays of crystal and glassware, her peach silk wallpaper, her well-groomed, long-haired cat. We were there hardly more than ten minutes, but it was long enough for the captain to make a very favourable impression, plus an afternoon appointment for the following day, with our wares.

William was just where we'd left him, standing mutely with folded arms as Mr. Bow-Tie unwrapped the last of the pieces from his box, looking hurried.

"Well, what do you think?" the captain asked him.

"Very nice indeed," Mr. Bow-Tie nodded cautiously. "I've barely had a chance to look at it, of course, and the price your curator has come up with seems . . ."

"You're talking to the wrong person about that. We're just the deliverers. Look, old boy, we're going to have to toddle off. If you don't want to buy the objects, we'll have 'em sent over to Bertie and tell him he recommended the wrong antique dealer."

"Bertie?"

"I expect he'll find somebody else who wants it, if you disappoint." Mr. Bow-Tie squirmed, with wrinkled brow.

"I . . . I . . . Bertie?"

The captain did not give him any time to sort through his mind, turning at once to William with an irritated flick of his stick toward the array of pieces. "William, would you help this gentleman get this lot rewrapped and packed?

"No!" Mr. Bow-Tie stopped him, showing some alarm. "Of course I'll buy it. Indeed. But, uh . . ."

"Good show!" the captain quashed whatever struggle was left in him. "I believe you've got my signed receipt, for a cash sale."

"Cash?"

"Quite. Don't have time to bumble about with checks, old boy. This way it goes right into petty cash, no fuss. Trivial sum, really. Surely that's not a bother?"

No bother at all. The entire performance came off like a charm. We got our full price, and William got a sizable tip, plus his general enjoyment of an unusual morning for him, as he put it, dropping us back at the Navy Yard.

"Let's have some solomongundy, and sandwiches," the captain charged me. "But first, take off those whites and get yourself into something more galley-friendly." Our afternoon mission called for no costume. By ordinary taxicab we went to Mr. Baseball's store with our least valuable crate, timing ourselves to arrive less than an hour before the beginning of the day's baseball game. Introductions were brief. The captain was all business, helping lay out a lot of plates, mugs, and flagons, which drew the dealer's attention. Piece by piece he looked at it, referencing the captain's inventory list, showing some interest until he was handed the price, which had been marked double what we wanted for it. Mr. Baseball made a face and a dismissive gesture.

"Not interested," he pronounced, turning away. The captain

patiently pointed out virtues of the collection, without success. Only when game-time came, and Mr. Baseball reached to turn on his little television, did there come a breakthrough.

"Very well, have the lot at half price then," the captain said, throwing up his hands in surrender. This was a stunning enough reduction to recapture the dealer's interest, and for the deal to be concluded in time to let him catch the beginning of the game, cash paid.

"Batter up!" came the announcer's voice as we left with our second envelope of money for the day.

This quick triumph left us with the rest of the afternoon, and enough time to visit a few of Boston's historic buildings. We saw the Old State House, where British troops shot Bostonians in what the Americans called the Boston Massacre, for revolutionary purposes. There was also the house that had belonged to Paul Revere, who had warned many Americans that the British were coming. "We Brits had nobody at all to warn us the Americans were coming," he commented.

Our last stop of the day was a bookstore, where we both browsed in our own directions among stacks and shelves of used books, books by the thousands, all tended by a lady who looked like a thinner version of Miss Titherington. "Pirates are right over here." She led me to a small section in a narrow aisle where I found more books on the subject than I could ever have imagined, including a reprint of *A History of the Most Notorious Pirates* by Captain Charles Johnson, and another with exactly the same title and text, authored by Daniel Defoe. I took both of them over to where the captain was looking at a book of girly photographs.

"Which is the author?" I held up the two histories.

"Johnson's the proper author," he pronounced. "His book was attributed to Defoe by a biographer—Harvard chap named Moore—in 1939, bit of a theorist who got everybody believing him because he was such a big professor. I wonder if he actually ever read Johnson. If he had, he'd have known better. Poor sod reckoned that since old Captain Charles Johnson chap couldn't be located as to who he was, it must have been his own beloved Defoe. A better biographer will come along in the next few years who'll demolish him with a raking broadside. If not . . ." he growled, "I'll do it myself." He turned back to his girly pictures. I decided to buy the Johnson book.

The third box of pewter went with us to Mr. Pipe's antique shop the following morning by taxicab, with no costumes or roles. He was a pale and scholarly gentleman, reading, blowing clouds of tobacco smoke that billowed from a huge meerschaum pipe and rose, forming a layered haze that stirred itself on the breeze of our entry. In no time, we unpacked the pieces that had been selected for him—and they were the questionable ones, with features that the captain's references had not shown.

"What does this mean?" he asked, indicating a flower-shaped cartouche on a Georgian teapot.

"Could be Bracegirdle's mark," said the old gentleman, rummaging among his books. And so the morning went, with every piece being carefully examined. Mr. Pipe took the role of teacher, as the captain listened and looked at the books he was shown. It went on for hours. Periodically, I escaped to the outside air of the sidewalk, but the captain stuck with it and, in the end, accepted the old gentleman's revisions to his own pricing, and a favourable deal was done. We did not get quite as much money as we had hoped for, which I asked him about.

"Considering that old darling knows ten times as much as I do about what we brought him, and can't be tricked, and paid cash, I reckon we scraped over that shoal without too much damage. There we had an authority." Our last taxi shuttle dropped us at the shop of Madame Lipstick. "Bring your new book," he had ordered; I did, and was glad of it, as things evolved.

Madame Lipstick was a stretch younger than the captain, but that was no obstacle to their apparent interest in one another. I was offered a comfortable chair, where I sat in the perfumed atmosphere, trying to read about the pirate Bartholomew Roberts, who took over four hundred ships between 1719 and 1721. The captain was all charm and chitchat in the background, and they hadn't even begun to look at the pewter. Bartholomew Roberts was very good at pretending his ship was something it wasn't, in order to board ships he wanted to take, I learned. He had been an honest Welsh sea captain who was captured by pirates, and forced, and took to the life so well as to get his own ship within six weeks. Among his various peculiarities, he drank only tea, didn't allow gambling, and conducted regular prayer services. For battles, he donned a fine red and gold coat, and wore a red plume in his hat.

At some point I was distracted from my reading by the conversation, which had at last turned to pewter. Here was no scholarly discussion; each saucer, creamer, or saltcellar was unwrapped like a wedding present. For Madame Lipstick, the captain had selected all the daintiest things we had to offer. "Ohhh," she squealed, holding up an ornate little goblet with the mark of Thomas Boardman of Hartford.

"Exquisite," he agreed, "and most particularly in your hand, milady."

I found it embarrassing, and had to go out to the sidewalk for some air. It was the first of several outside visits. When the pair finally got into money matters, she had no challenge to his appraisal, except the price was out of her reach. She told him about landlord difficulties she was having, along with inventory problems, speaking eloquently on the trials of a single woman in a man's world. She had known a good man or two. She smiled, and a tear squeezed out of her eye. Sympathetically, he took her hand in his, and dropped our price by 25 percent. This caused her to offer him sherry, and then another one after that. At some point, while standing outside during rush-hour traffic, I turned and looked in at them through the glass, and saw with alarm that he was stroking the inside of her elbow, grinning at her with a kind of helpless look that made me go back in abruptly, setting off the bells over the door. He did not disengage.

"My dear," he said to her, "God's bells are telling me to be a gentler force in your life." He reduced our asking price to half, leading to a quick bargain sealed with a big hug, of which I had no part. According to my rough calculations, after all his discounting, we had gotten our price.

But he was not done with her. After we had been paid, he lavished kisses on her hand in a way that I wanted to turn from, except she was looking at me and tittering, and he was also looking at me, catching my eye with a wink. To my horror, I saw that his hand was working her jewelled ring off her finger with some assistance from his teeth. As I watched, the ring slid off and vanished between his lips.

"My dear." He straightened. "How can I express to you my delight that this fleeting exchange of a few earthly treasures has given me the more divine treasure of your own company." He managed this somehow, and more, without any indication that he had her ring in his mouth. During our good-byes, when she had given him her card with her private telephone number, and while I was still in a stunned condition, I couldn't avoid Madame Lipstick's perfumed embrace. It left us both with the same smell as we made our way down Charles Street, his cane twirling.

"Now," I said to him, "I know for sure you were ready to rob that yacht." By way of response, he took the ring out of his mouth, gave it a wipe, and handed it to me with barely a glance at it.

"Here's your consolation prize," he said. "Have it as a souvenir. It's brass and glass, by the way." Still, I was shocked, which gave him a chuckle. "The treasure's when she realises I've nicked it from her, an' she's had a sweet dance with a demon lover. If I went to see Madame Lipstick again, she'd wear a *real* ring for me." I blushed. He laughed, and whisked us to a fancy restaurant, to celebrate what he called our success at alchemy.

"What's that?" I asked.

"Prawns and Creole sauce," he answered as a waitress put an appetiser in front of me.

"I meant alchemy. What's that?"

"Turning lead to gold," he saluted with his glass.

"How could anybody ever do that?"

"By dancing a good dance. Preferably not on air. In our own case, by exchanging a bunch of lead, with a bit of antimony and copper in it, for this," he patted the money belt in which he was carrying the wads of dollars we'd gotten. "I reckon the family's share will serve your purposes, eh?" I was uneasy that we hadn't gone at once to a Western Union office and wired the inn's money, but he pointed out their safes would be locked for the night. "I'll do it first thing in the morning."

Our celebration supper, as he called it, was much given to his thoughts about the American navy hero John Paul Jones, who was a famed lover, and who had gained more fame by simply repeating the basic tactics of all the pirates. "Surprise, timing, patience, and misdirection," he summarised after a lengthy dessert. "They never fail, whatever your century. I daresay you've seen them all demonstrated during the past couple of days, and in just that order, no?"

After supper we strolled to look at the great city by night, finally turning back toward Charlestown by way of a dark lane that led directly toward the waterfront. The street's only life, and light, came from a saloon with red neon in its windows.

"Hey!" said a gravelly voice as we were passing the place. A piece of shadow detached itself from the greater darkness of an alley, and moved toward us. "Hey, gimme a quarter!" When we paid no attention to the beggar, the man hastened around us, and planted himself right in our path, hand outstretched like a claw. He was a big man, wearing motley clothes. His beg was a demand. "Gimme a quarter," he repeated. When we went around, he again skipped ahead of us, growling like an animal, the same message, now with a threat, moving to block us entirely.

"Yer," said the captain, stopping, "wat be'ee about my 'andsome?" It sounded like a foreign tongue.

"Gimme a quarter."

"Be'ee mazed?"

"Gimme a quarter." Our assailant became more intense, and somebody else came out of the alley.

"You're not asking for enough," said the new voice approaching. "You should get a dollar."

"Gimme a quarter," repeated the quarter man.

"Give him a dollar," said the ominous newcomer. "How about two dollars?"

"Git on," said the captain, "don'ee come the maister wit we."

I'd admired his ploy in using another language, pretending not to understand, but it wasn't working, and every nerve ending I had was telling me that we were in trouble. They were like the Moehner boys, but worse. I hoped he would just pay their tariff, letting the thousands of dollars that he had around his middle stay where they were, and the two of us safe and sound. These villains looked real, and tough enough to make me move close to him. And they had reinforcements.

"What's up?" said yet another voice from the direction of the alley.

"Gimme . . . uh," said the quarter man, who found himself interrupted by a hard, direct jab in his solar plexus by the tip of the captain's walking stick, striking like a snake. The blow was instantly followed by a backstroke that clipped the dollar man somewhere in the area of his ear, as best I could tell. The whole thing happened so quickly, it was hard to see his moves, just two men dropping like stones to the pavement. The quarter man sat in an upright position, making loud, gasping noises; the dollar man writhed, clasping his head and groaning. Before I could make sense of it, the captain whisked me around the corner, and over the bridge to *Merry*.

The following morning, Friday, dawned with a smurry, drizzly sky, so we breakfasted below, and then the captain left, wearing oilskins, leaving me to mind *Merry* for the day. He would wire the inn's money, and tend to his own Boston errands. "Read your books," he said. I wanted to go, too, but had to remain to sign for deliveries he expected. I also had to telephone home again, reporting that the mission was accomplished and the money was on its way, and it was nearly all we had hoped for. That was my first order of business, so off to the headquarters building I went to make my collect call.

This time Mother answered, accepting the charges through a crackle of telephone static. She was much relieved by my report. Her own news was more disturbing. Aunt Karen's condition had worsened further; Robin was by her side in the hospital. She was being as well attended as possible, but was in a lot of pain. Authorities from Halifax had been to the inn, making inquiries about Captain Johnson. The static on the line prevented me from getting any more than a garble, so I said good-bye, hung up, and walked back over the wet cobblestones to *Merry*.

Passing *Constitution*, and approaching the ladder down to the float, I spotted my friend Mathew, who did not at once see me because he was having a conversation with people on a two-tone green sport-fishing boat. As I watched, he was gesturing toward *Merry*. I called to him. He turned, saw me, hastily waved off the boat, and gave me immediate attention. He was off-watch, and suggested we go below on *Merry* and catch up with each other. He had seen us in the limousine, coming and going, and then all the taxicabs. "What have you been up to, pal?" he wanted to know.

I had to explain why I couldn't invite him aboard; I'd gotten in trouble for it before, and that's how it was, but I could offer him a cup of coffee if he didn't mind standing on the dock. He was cheerful about that. He was the only friend of my trip that I had met on my own, and who had taken a kindly interest in my life— enough to stand in wet weather to keep me company. He was glad for me that we had done our business in good order, gotten a fair price, and such. "And I hope you didn't take any checks? Good," he approved when I assured him we had taken only cash. "How much did you get?" I said it was enough to make our trip worthwhile. His concern turned to *Merry,* and her crippled motor. I told him it wasn't yet fixed.

"So you've got no working electrics, or lights . . . or radio?" he asked. I was proud to be able to tell him that we did not need electrical things, which he found impressive.

"So, you're on your own!" he approved, asking what protection we carried.

"Protection?"

"Any guns? You've got antiques, but do you have anything that actually works? Shotgun? Rifle? Anything in case you needed it?" Bothered by his line of questioning, I told him he would have to ask the captain about that. During our conversation, I had been seated in the cockpit, in oilskins, and it seemed a good moment to get in out of the wet. I promised to visit him later.

"How long you guys gonna be around?" he asked. I said I didn't know, maybe when the engine was fixed, and ducked below.

With nothing to do for the first time in a long time, I picked up the book I had bought, leafed to the page where I'd left off with Bartholomew Roberts, then cast it aside. I was tired of pirates in books. He had spoiled that for me. The other choice, his primer of navigation, was no more appealing, so I combed *Merry*'s bookshelves, where almost everything was old. Overhead, the spaces between the beams were packed with rolled charts for the oceans of the world. I could not get interested in any of it. My mind had been given too much to digest, and I skipped lunch.

In the afternoon, the captain's delivery showed up, a sealed box from a Boston printer, which I signed for. I stowed it in the vacancy where the pewter had been, then tried to take a nap. I lay in my bunk with restless mind, listening to the loud ticking of *Merry*'s brass clock, until the captain returned, sliding open the hatch. "Put on your rain gear, follow me, and I'll tell you the bad news." I scampered above, pulling on my oilskins, and learned while walking along the dock that the inn's money had not been wired because of a union strike, with no end of it in sight. It would take days to open a bank account and transfer funds.

"Problem with modern systems is they break down. So we're on our own again, and that means we sail on the next tide for Grey Rocks." He was done with his own Boston business, whatever it was. By his reckoning, the winds we had fought to get here would favour us for the trip back. "It's always a bit of a roll of the dice, but if the weather does what it should, we'll be home in three or four days. What would you do?" I agreed we should go. "Good show. Call your mother and tell her what's happening," he said as he opened the door to the headquarters building, "while I thank the captain for his hospitality to *Merry*." Off I went to borrow the telephone again, but with no answer at the inn. This was odd, because the inn's first rule was that there always be somebody near the telephone. I had done that duty many times.

While waiting to try again, I made my good-byes to Mathew, who was surprised by my departure. "You fixed your motor?" I assured him that experienced sailors didn't need engines. "When do you sail?" I told him on the turn of the tide, wished him farewell, got his address to send him a postcard, and tried to call home again, again with no answer. Nor was there any answer an hour later, when it was time to sail. In order to get the news to Mother that we were leaving, and were bringing her the money in cash, I had to give the message to Mathew, who promised to keep calling until somebody answered the phone. "Good luck!" he waved to me.

The breeze veered westerly, clearing the clouds late in the day. *Merry* nosed away from the dock and into Boston Harbor with a dip of her colours to *Constitution*. "Right there, where she is now," the captain commented, "is where the old ferry dock was, long before the bridge, and that's just exactly where they hanged the seven men they got hold of from Bellamy's crew. Remember Bellamy?" I did, and then turned my eyes toward Boston, framed against the late-day sun, saying a silent good-bye to it. "They also hung 'em on that side," said the captain, following my gaze, "right there under Copp's Hill. Like poor old John Quelch in 1704, and William Fly and a couple of his people, around 1726. So now, instead of a bunch of bodies decorating the harbour, a sailor gets smokestacks, steel cranes, and fuel tanks. And some pretty big buildings starting to grow." He gazed at it in a melancholy kind of way. "Dear old town, what will you ever look like the next time I see you?" Again he brushed a tear.

"It's the smog," he said.

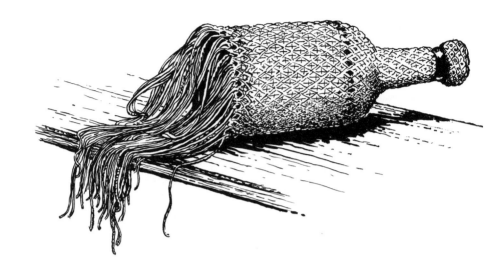

17

Off the Graves

At sunset, the great port sparkled in *Merry*'s slow wake. With barely enough breeze to fill her sails, she ghosted east, skirting the shipping channel through a maze of flashing navigational markers, blinking buoys, and fast-moving lights of water traffic. In this galaxy, our little oil lights with their perfectly trimmed wicks were insignificant. To make *Merry* more visible to the modern world, the captain brought up pieces of a huge radar reflector, a thin metal thing of many facets, and assembled it.

"Quite often it's best to be invisible, but it's very important not to get hit by big ships. This contraption gives a radar signature like an ocean liner, " he said, hoisting it opposite our regular little reflector, which he also left up. The result was that all the vessels around us gave *Merry* a lot of room, which was a good thing, because all night we barely had enough breeze to keep steerageway. "We'll get some wind in the morning," he predicted.

This time he was wrong. Saturday dawned clear and windless. *Merry* was totally becalmed, just clear of Boston's outermost shoal, "The Graves," as it was called gloomily on the chart. There we anchored in order to hold our ground against an adverse tide, and the captain turned in, leaving me on watch.

A perfect summer weekend day for motorboats had brought out every size and kind, all making their wakes in passing. As their waves reached us, *Merry* jumped and rolled constantly. I could see an endless crisscross of wakes constantly approaching in patterns that were as restless as my mind. I thought about my mother, having just been farther from her than any time before in my life, and for longer. I was not particularly accustomed to giving much thought to her, except for how to get around her, but at that moment I saw her as perhaps an even lonelier person than I was, a novel thought. Suitors she had had, but nobody measured up to my dead father. I remembered Mother dancing with Robin after the concert, laughing with him. Then I thought about poor Aunt Karen, and then about Meg. How long would Meg stay at the inn, mopping floors and serving beer?

I was watching a big tour boat sliding past on its way toward Gloucester, when something familiar caught my attention: unmistakably the two-tone green sport-fishing boat with its flying bridge, and new little Decca radar. As I watched, the boat changed course and headed directly toward us, throttling down as it approached. I waved. "Hi! You're Mathew's friends?" I called, as they came within voice range. They were. Mathew had told them he was worried because we had no motor and no wind, and they had been looking for *Merry* to give us a tow, getting us clear of land. Being neighbourly, as he put it. "Yes!" I said.

"No!" said the captain, erupting from below. I quickly explained that these were Mathew's friends.

"Mathew's?" he stepped on deck, peering at them. Their boat nudged closer. There appeared to be three men, one standing on the stern, making a towline ready, a burly fellow in a T-shirt.

"Get your anchor up, and we'll take you out to where there's wind," yelled the helmsman on the bridge. To my surprise, the captain declined what seemed like a heaven-sent opportunity to get out of where we were, and maybe indeed into an offshore wind.

"Mathew says your motor's kaput!" said the helmsman, edging closer. "We're here to help."

"Don't need help." said the captain.

"But you're out here without power? Or any radio?"

The captain thanked them for their concern, but said we'd made our repairs, and could contact the shore if we needed to, and wished them well with their fishing. He gave them a wave good-bye, and they went away. I hated to see them go. "Tell me more about this Mathew," he demanded, and I did. "You told him we're carrying a quantity of cash?" he interrupted, when I came to the part about Mathew's telephone message.

"He is my friend," I defended, adding that Mathew was the only way to get the message to Mother. He chewed his lip. I had a question of my own. "Why didn't you take the tow? And why did you tell them the engine was fixed, and that we had a radio?" He did not immediately answer, watching the green boat roaring away from us. *Lamprey* was the name on its stern.

"There aren't any whys," he finally said, adding, "but there's nose." He put down the glasses. "What if Mathew's friends are pirates?" I started to protest, but the captain quickly made the case that I knew hardly anything about Mathew, and nothing at all about his friends, whereas he knew we had a lot of money, a broken-down motor, no radio, and that we were only an old man and a boy.

"But . . ."

"But nothing. I want you to suppose, just for a moment, that Mathew is not the friend you think he is; that in fact he's a disgrace to his noble ship, and that Mathew's friends on that green boat now know everything you've told him about us, which they seem to. Now suppose you're them, and you want our money. You've been surprised by our abrupt departure, but know we can't get far without wind. It's a clear day; you've got a big power-boat with a Decca, so you come out and shop around 'til you find us. You've got shotguns and pistols. What do you do next?" I pondered his question, but had a hard time accepting his whole premise.

"What do you do?" he insisted.

"Just come out and take us," I supposed. The whole thing seemed like another of his uncomfortable little tests. My half-hearted response inspired him to go forward and have a pee over the side. While doing so, he continued the exercise.

"How? Just pull alongside, guns blazing, in plain view of God, the Coast Guard, and all this holiday traffic? More likely, you'd sniff up to us, very friendly, and offer us a tow offshore, where you could board us after dark with no other vessels around." Finishing his business, he gazed after the green boat. It was far away in the direction of Cape Ann, and getting farther by the moment. On top of the irritations of our bouncy anchorage, and going nowhere, and my restless thoughts, his sinister suggestions did not sit well with me. I mumbled something about pirates, real pirates, having been quashed long ago.

"Quashed? I'd say flourishing. Try the South China Sea, or Indonesia, or the Red Sea, for that matter. Not to mention long stretches of coast around Central and South America. I still allow a ten-mile offing on the north coast of Jamaica, and lots of other places, too. Yachts are such tempting little morsels, so easily taken by surprise. You kill the crew. Sink the boat. No evidence. Just another little sailboat gone missing. Happens all the time, bloodier than ever." He brooded. "It's not like the old days. No more Tom Whites. No mercy anymore, because you can't afford to leave witnesses or evidence."

"And do you really think Mathew's friends are pirates?"

He shrugged. "Not everybody shares your own gentle scruples." This was a direct reference to Roseway Bay, where I had cast my vote not to rob *Cock Tails*. In fact, he had cast my vote for me, as I was chewing my fingernails, trying to make up my mind. ("If you have to think about it so much, the answer's no.") Instead, we had launched the dinghy, and used a quart of red paint writing I AM VERY CARELESS, in two-foot letters all along the yacht's starboard bow, and WATCH OUT FOR ME on the opposite side. Satisfying as that prank had been, it had left me feeling puny, thinking of what else we might have done. The whole thing had left me not wanting to talk about it. Nor did I want to discuss Mathew anymore, so I changed the subject, asking him about the moves he had used to dispose of the men in the alley.

"Thrust and cut. Then there's the parry," he said, "which I didn't need last night." This led to a demonstration on deck, both of us with batten-sticks of cutlass length. "Nine out of ten opponents can be taken out with the first move, because you wait until they start to swing, and they're exposed; if you strike them with a straight thrust, they're goners before anything can start. So much for Mr. Quarter, who can be grateful it was only a walking stick. As to Mr. Dollar, that villain was open to a backhand cut. Think in terms of balance and breath." Demonstrations and practise went on until noon, after which I was allowed to handle his real cutlass, getting used to its live weight. I was surprised to learn there was very little clanging and whanging of swords, as in the movies.

"Can't think—goes too fast. Now, do it again." And so I did, until I worked up a sweat in the still heat of the afternoon. I wanted to take a dip overside after he dismissed the lesson, inviting him to come along.

"There's big fishes down there," he said, adjusting his spectacles on his nose, and taking up his macramé. I returned to find him absorbed in his work. "With another week or two, I'll finish this," he said, tying off one more tiny knot in the mosaic of twines with which he was sheathing the rounded rum bottle. He had been at it forever, and had come to its bottom; scores of strings hung from it like a beard, waiting to be braided into the whole.

"This is the trickiest part," he commented. "Losing the ends, y'see. You've got all these hundreds of little twines, and then you must lose their ends, so there's no hint of one in sight when you're all done." He sighed. "When I can do that perfectly, maybe then I can rest."

"Rest?"

"Retire. Swallow the anchor. No more pottering about on this old world's oceans, doin' whatever a chap has to do to make ends meet to keep his independence, like, so's he can bury his ends. My little strings. Pour me a rum."

"How many years have you been sailing?" I asked, handing it up to him.

"How long can you count?"

"How long do I have to be able to?" This got a flicker of amusement from him.

"Good lad. Well done. Honest answer? I'm like the Flying Dutchman."

"You are saying you are the Flying Dutchman?"

He chuckled. "Call us shipmates. I last hoisted a jar of punch with old Van der Decken off Sumatra, in '95 I think. Not a bad chap. A bit gloomy at times. Can't blame him, really, because when they tell you that you've got to keep sailing forever, well, that's a bloody long time, mate." He took a swallow of rum. "And when they give you the sentence, they don't hand you some magical way to support yourself, either, so there you are, back on your own."

"Who is 'they'?"

"My own thoughts, I think, but what's to be trusted?" He laughed, turning back to weaving his tiny knots. "Don't worry," he added with a wink, "nothing's as it seems."

I watched him at his work, trying again to collect my thoughts regarding him, with no more success than any of the previous times I'd tried. Every time he started to make me believe something about himself, he would dispel it with a wink; on the instant I came to some judgment about him, he did something to shatter it. There was no question that he had blown me out of my personal doldrums, and the inn, too, and had become well regarded in Grey Rocks, and there was all of that. But I knew other sides of him. Aside from being a thief, at least a petty one, he was an actor beyond Meg's most fearsome suspicions—seldom a liar, but a master manipulator of the truth, and of people.

"We gave all those dealers good value, y'know," he said, as though reading my mind. "They'll be a bit put out when they learn how much pewter is suddenly about, but they'll make their dollar on what they got from us, you can trust me on that. Watch out, here comes a big wake." A moment later, the waves from a tour boat slammed into us, making *Merry* bounce and roll.

As to trusting him, I realised that I trusted him because I wanted to trust him, with no more idea than ever as to whom I was trusting. I had come to the notion that he was probably the most dangerous man I had ever known, and for sure the scariest. The risks that attended him didn't begin to touch a dark depth of him that I think I sensed all the time, twice glimpsing it through the fathomless holes where his eyes should have been. I had no idea what that meant, but it was very disturbing.

"What do you want from me?" I heard myself ask him out loud. It was a pure blurt, taking me more by surprise than him. He glanced up with a puzzled smile.

"Why, the pleasure of your company, Jim, what else? We're shipmates." This was so innocent, I was immediately flustered by my own rudeness. He scratched the top of his head, dislodging the flapped bandanna he wore to keep sun off the small bald spot there. "I suppose it would oblige me if you'd read my book, and put to rest whatever questions you've got left about pirates. We never finished with that. I presume you do have a question or two?" I did, first to mind being how a society of freebooters could enforce its own laws. By what judicial system? He commanded me to fetch his copy of Johnson. I did as I was told, mentioning I hadn't finished the chapter on Bartholomew Roberts. "Right," he said, opening the yellowed pages. "Well, old Roberts, for all of his many virtues . . ."

"Virtues? Didn't he take over four hundred ships?"

"Just so, a very considerable virtue in our circles. And he let lots of his captures go, which was kindly. He was a frightfully Christian chap, who wanted a proper, resident clergyman aboard.

He finally took an English ship that had one, and tried everything to persuade the parson to sail with him. When he didn't, Roberts honoured that, gave him money, and let him go on his way.

"In any case, for all of his virtues, Roberts was an absolute sod of a navigator, so he forced the first mate off one of his captures, good navigator named Harry Glasby, and kept him. Hard cheese for Glasby. Being a navigator didn't get you the same option to decline that Roberts gave clergymen. Glasby was a reserved, sober sort, and he had a great disinclination to that life, so he bided his time, then jumped ship while they were at anchor off an island where he thought he might be able to make a good escape. He and two others ran, but they didn't get far. The penalty for desertion was death. So here's what happened when they brought 'em back aboard." The captain found the page he was looking for, adjusted his spectacles, and read:

> "*This was a capital offense, and for which they were ordered to be brought to an immediate trial.*
>
> "*Here was the form of justice kept up, which is as much as can be said of several other courts that have more lawful commissions for what they do. Here was no seeing of council, and bribing of witnesses was a custom not known among them; no packing of juries, no torturing and wresting the sense of the law, for by ends and purposes, no puzzling or perplexing the cause with unintelligible canting terms, and useless distinctions; nor was their sessions burdened with numberless officers, the ministers of rapine and extortion, with ill-boding aspects, enough to fright Astrea from the court.*
>
> "*The place appointed for their trials was the steerage of the ship; in order to which, a large bowl of rum punch*

was made, and placed upon the table, the pipes and tobacco being ready, the judicial proceedings began; the prisoners were brought forth, and articles of indictment against them read; they were arraigned upon a statute of their own making, and the letter of the law being strong against them, and the fact plainly proved, they were about to pronounce sentence, when one of the judges moved that they should first smoke the other pipe; which was accordingly done.

"All the prisoners pleaded for arrest of judgment very movingly, but the court had such an abhorrence of their crime that they could not be prevailed upon to show mercy, till one of the judges, whose name was Valentine Ashplant, stood up, and taking his pipe out of his mouth, said he had something to offer to the court in behalf of one of the prisoners; and spoke to this effect, 'By God, Glasby shall not die; damn me if he shall.' After this learned speech he sat down in his place, and resumed his pipe. This motion was loudly opposed by all the rest of the judges, in equivalent terms, but Ashplant, who was resolute in his opinion, made another pathetical speech in the following manner. 'God damn ye, gentlemen, I am as good a man as the best of you; damn my soul if ever I turned my back to any man in my life, or ever will by God; Glasby is an honest fellow, notwithstanding this misfortune, and I love him, double-damn me if I don't: I hope he'll live and repent of what he has done; but damn me if he must die, I will die along with him.' And thereupon, he pulled out a pair of pistols, and presented them to some of the learned judges upon the bench who, perceiving his argument so well supported,

*thought it reasonable that Glasby should be aquitted;
and so they all came over to his opinion, and allowed it
to be law."*

The captain paused to wet his whistle. "A neat piece of work,
eh? Glasby was a good bloke, right enough, and deserved saving;
the procedure might have been a bit odd, but you could say fair,
for all of that." I asked what had happened to Glasby's two
friends. He finished his reading.

*"But all the mitigation that could be obtained for the
other prisoners, was that they should have the liberty of
choosing any four of the whole company to be their exe-
cutioners. The poor wretches were tied immediately to
the mast, and there shot dead . . ."*

He snapped the book closed, and smiled at me. I said I felt
sorry for the other two prisoners. He shrugged. "Well, the rules
are the rules, wherever you go. Which court would you rather
stand before, Glasby's, or the high court of the land in London
that tried Kidd, with judges in robes and powdered wigs? Remember, they're the sods who kept him in irons for two years,
then gave him a lawyer two hours before his trial, but didn't hand
him back the documents he needed to make his case, or let him
have any witnesses. Then he got to enjoy being displayed like an
animal for a couple of more weeks, 'til they strung him up. At
least Glasby's mates got a fair hearing and a quick end."

Shooting was the favoured form of execution among the
brotherhood, according to my mentor, who considered it more
merciful than any of the methods used by governments. "The

officials hung you slow, or they could draw and quarter you if you had really niggled them, or break your bones on the wheel, or whip you to death, or do any number of other things that produced a lingering that one would rather avoid."

"What happened to Roberts and Glasby?"

"Roberts sailed for the Guinea coast, and his luck held until he took on a Royal Navy ship. There was a hot action; in the middle of it, he took a grapeshot through his neck, which did him in, and old Glasby seizes the chance to lower the colours, and that was that. He surrendered 'em. There was a big trial; most of the company, including Ashplant, got turned off in 1722, but the court let Glasby go free. Here's to Harry," he toasted.

The brotherhood's alternative to a death sentence was marooning, which I knew about, but not in the depth of detail that he presented to me as the windless afternoon wore on. According to his stories, there were various levels of the punishment, all having to do with just putting somebody ashore, usually not in an inhabited place. In the most severe circumstances, it would be somewhere without food, water, supplies, or escape, barring a miracle. At the gentlest, it would be a place with everything needed to sustain life, and the maroon would be allowed to take weapons, tools, even cooking gear.

"That was the case with Alexander Selkirk, most famous maroon in history; as to cooking gear, let's you think about supper." And so he wove macramé while I got the stove going. (He wanted bacon, eggs, beans, and bread, and he wanted the bread carefully toasted, lightly buttered, with a slab of cheese on the side, and a beer.) As I was finishing, he called down to me.

"Avast cooking, and bring me up the Very pistol, and a handful of red cartridges. Look smart." Doing as I was told, I found him gazing seaward. "Your friends are coming back from wherever they've been all afternoon." Indeed, the green fishing boat, *Lamprey*, was approaching again, this time from the east. He loaded his old brass flare gun.

"Why the flares?"

"They're to hand."

"Hey, hi again, how's it going?" called the same man as before. He wore sunglasses and had a big moustache.

"Just about to have supper," said the captain.

"Hey, c'mon, let us tow you outta all this traffic. What are friends for? Can't go back and face Mathew and tell him we didn't help you out. C'mon."

"Very kind of you, but we've a rendezvous here later on, and it wouldn't do to be gone when our friends show up." He thanked them for their concern, assuring them we were quite safe, had lots of flares for any emergency, plus our radio, and would keep an alert lookout all night. With a friendly good-bye wave, he went below, where I followed. They hovered for a few moments, then shot away in the direction they had just come from.

"Who do we have a rendezvous with?" I wanted to know.

"Just whatever people I've planted in their minds," he said, watching their departure through a porthole. "Ah, supper!" He made a plate of the food I'd prepared, and took it above. We ate in silence. It was early evening, and there were not so many wakes as earlier, but my mind was busier than ever. I was ready to concede the peculiar behavior of Mathew's friends.

"They *were* very odd," I said after a while.

"Odd? Not at all. Think back. You're them, and you're out here to get us. We're inconveniently situated right off Boston Harbor, so in the morning you try to seduce us into taking a tow out to someplace more private for your purposes. It doesn't work. You beetle off to Marblehead or somewhere for pinball and beers, and talk it over. Maybe we'll be softer after bouncing around without wind off the Graves all afternoon. So you come back, and we still won't go. What do you do next?" He had me into his game.

"Come back at night. Late. Sneak up without lights, and take us by complete surprise."

"Quite. Well done. Have you ever handled a pistol?" I had, my grandfather's .22 caliber revolver, sinking bottles that floated into the inn's cove behind the dock. "Good. Then I'll issue you this . . ." He lifted the flintlock pistol out of *Merry*'s decorative display of ancient weapons, handing it to me. "And I'll use old Frith." He took down the blunderbuss.

"Frith?"

"After Hezekiah, chap I got it from. It's a bit old, but still effective, as you and Grendel's ghost can testify, eh?" I had learned very well that the captain's innocent display of antique naval weapons comprised a deadly arsenal, hidden in plain view. "But you only get one shot, so you don't use it until your attacker is too close to miss. When you've fired it, you throw it or drop it, and use this," he placed the cutlass on the table. "Remember the straight thrust." In case we were attacked, his own backup weapon would be *Merry*'s spike-tipped boat hook, plus the flare gun. It could be quickly reloaded, unlike the flintlocks, with their powder, balls, wads, ramrods, and priming. Still, I didn't see what chance we would have against three attackers with modern guns.

"Only the surprise of not being surprised. That should fend 'em off, anchored where we are now. Gunfire might bring attention, which they do not want. With luck, we'll not be needing these little darlings," he indicated our weapons. "But here they are; here's how you load 'em." A lesson followed, with gunpow-

299

der from a tea tin with an old label: GUNPOWDER TEA—BY APPOINTMENT TO HER MAJESTY THE QUEEN, and a portrait of Victoria, with a battle going on in the background. On top of the powder, my pistol got a lethal half-inch lead ball.

"The reason that old Alex Selkirk was the most famous maroon of all was because Daniel Defoe got hold of him." Darkness had fallen, but the entire sky to the west glowed orange with the light of Boston, perfectly reflected on water like black glass. Most of the wakes were gone, except for the occasional deep-sea vessel heading through the North Channel. I had the first watch, from eight to midnight. The captain was keeping me company. "*Robinson Crusoe* was Defoe's version of Selkirk—chap on the beach with happy dog, Man Friday, umbrella, all of that, but Defoe missed the meat of it, y'see, because what actually happened with Alex—we called him the governor—was a lot better story." I had triggered this with an offhand comment about feeling marooned by having no wind. "Defoe fancied he knew a bit about the brotherhood, but he never got within smelling distance downwind."

When and if we did get wind, I thought, we were going to be late getting home by at least a couple of days beyond the inn's deadline. He had been wrong with his weather prediction, or we wouldn't have left our snug berth at the Navy Yard. So he was not perfect. What else might he be wrong about?

"Defoe was no sailor, but he didn't need a ship to be a pirate. He was in with the gang behind the South Seas Bubble. Big pyramid scheme to sell worthless shares in a colonial South Seas empire. Lots of poor sods got taken in and wiped out, as is the nature of bubbles. Shook up the whole government. In any case, Defoe's writing was a big part of the pitch. Also, he made buckets of money by pirating Selkirk's story."

As he went on, my immediate concern was the threat of an actual attack on *Merry*. He had made me nervous. I had suggested that we darken the boat, up-anchor, take down the radar reflectors, and drift clear of the Graves on the ebb tide. But the captain had made me light our anchor light, and had kept the reflectors, clearly identifying our presence. Everything was quite normal, except our weapons were within easy reach.

"What do you do?" he interrupted my wandering thoughts. "You're Selkirk. You're twenty-eight years old, a bit of a grouch, hard to get on with, and you've just been dropped off on an entirely uninhabited island about four hundred miles west of the Chilean coast in 33 degrees south latitude. Very temperate climate. Your domain is about a dozen or so miles long, some seven miles wide, the remnant of an ancient volcano, with craggy peaks and cliffs. It has all kinds of springs, lush valleys, turnips, cabbages, pimentos, fruits, lobsters, shellfish, wild goats, cats, the occasional turtle, and other amenities. Much nicer than your native Scotland. That's all to the good, because you might be here forever. Nobody comes to Juan Fernandez except ships like Dampier's, looking for water. But they only come every five or ten years, on average. More likely you'll get Spaniards, looking for the likes of you, meaning worse company than none at all. You're Swiss Family Robinson (another steal from the Selkirk story), but without the family. You've got tools, books, bedding, all of that. What do you do?"

During the next hour or two I learned in considerable detail what Alexander Selkirk did during his four years and four months of solitude, starting with building a hut covered with goat hides, goats being plentiful. From his concealed camp, Selkirk explored the rest of the island, finding a cozy cave that made better living quarters. Also, he learned all the goat paths criss-crossing the island. "The chatter of his own mind was his only companionship, and he was anguished with loneliness; couldn't take his eyes away from the ocean, the wink of a sail that could show up any time, or never. It was all he had to hang on to. Every ambition, dream, loved one, plan, all gone. Unless there came another buccaneer." With that obsession, Selkirk had prepared signal fires to light, interrupting his vigil only for the reading of his Bible, prayer, and killing goats. "But after eight months, tortured all that time from within, he got deliverance."

"A ship?"

"Better. He let go. Freed his brains. Had a good look at them, got tired of the same thoughts over and over again, and got on with life. His gunpowder was running out, and his shoes were wearing out, so he took 'em off and learned to run barefoot well enough to catch wild goats. Got quite good at it. Kept track of how many goats he ate. Made fires by rubbing sticks in dry tinder. Read every book in his little library with a studiousness not given to many scholars, and learned the world around him with a level of attention hardly given to anybody."

I think the captain might have been able to take me over the goat trails of Juan Fernandez with a lot more sense of reality, except for my own distractions, primarily looking out into the night for an enemy. Selkirk had seen ships, and they had turned out to be enemies—Spanish. He had almost been caught, a story within a story. Selkirk's saga spun out like his stockings, which he unraveled for threads to sew a new shirt. After three years, his knife had been resharpened so many times, there was nothing left of it, so he fashioned others from barrel staves. Annoyed by rats, he made friends with feral cats, which did away with the problem. His main injury was a painful tumble down a mountain slope. Digestive problems were cured by a local black pepper that provided good wind. At last he lost the craving for bread and salt that had haunted him beyond all else.

"Then, four and a half years later, when he'd truly settled in, gotten used to his new life, was enjoying it, the fates must have noticed, because—wham!—that's when a couple of British privateer ships show up. The very dream he'd given up on, come true at last. It was Woodes Rogers in the old *Duke*, twenty-eight-guns, sailing with *Duchess*, twenty-six, both of 'em from Cape Horn, bound north. It was 1704, and Queen Anne's War was still on.

"Selkirk was hardly able to speak, at first, having lost practise at it. When he recovered, he made himself immediately valuable, showing his rescuers to the springs and natural supplies of the island, also charming them with a likability that had previously evaded him in his life. With Rogers was William Dampier, who had known Selkirk as a good navigator, so that he was taken aboard *Duke* as sailing master. To the squadron, he was known as "the Governor." Re-adapting to his former world took a while. He got used to the clothes of an officer and gentleman again, but could not wear shoes for some months, going barefoot.

"Rogers's ships were headed north, in Drake's wake, and on

the same business. The Dons could never tend their Pacific coasts. They were as badly defended as ever, with good pillage all the way up to California, where Rogers planned to pluck the plum of all plums, any buccaneer's dream, the Manila galleon. Every November, give or take a week or two, it came down the California coast on the last leg of its voyage from Manila, bound for Acapulco, loaded with loot. Rogers had sailed twenty thousand miles to ambush the grandest prize of all."

The captain paused for a sweeping look around the surrounding waters. I had been keeping a sharp eye out as well, seeing nothing. I asked if they had taken the galleon.

"They did, off Cape Saint Lucas, and then attacked a second one, which was so big and heavy, their six-pound cannonballs wouldn't penetrate, so they got badly shot up."

"Selkirk?"

"Just about everybody except the Governor, who was untouchable. Otherwise there was a heavy butcher's bill. Rogers had a big piece of his jaw shot away, and part of his foot. Then he got a mutiny to deal with, which he did, and sailed the rest of the way 'round the world, and back to Blighty with the richest haul since Sir Francis himself. He inspired your Admiral Anson chap to do the same thing thirty years later. In any case, everybody got rich. The Governor's share came to eight hundred pounds sterling plus a silver plate, which was a tidy little sum then, and he found himself lionised, more famous than Rogers himself. Great literary figures were eager to talk to him, later praising him. And what do you suppose the Governor does next?"

I had no idea.

"He goes back to Scotland, to his father's house in the country. It has a bit of land with a hillside, which he digs into until he's got a cave like the one he lived in on his island, and moves in with the relics he's saved from Juan Fernandez. He's having a bit of problem getting back into the ordinary world, y'see. Quite terrifying. So he becomes a complete recluse."

"For the rest of his life?"

"No. Whatever from his island the Governor wants back, he has to let go all over again. Gets married, which doesn't go well; goes back to sea for a living; gets married again; and dies on a voyage in 1721. Frances gets the house, and . . ."

"Frances?"

"The Governor's widow. She remarried pretty quick, and her new husband filled in Alex's cave, and that was that."

"Poor Selkirk."

"Poor Selkirk? I'd call the Governor the luckiest buccaneer of the whole bloody lot. For only four years and four months invested, he got half of a whole salvation handed to him on a plate; a silver plate at that, plus his eight hundred quid from Rogers's loot."

"What's half a salvation?"

"Twice as good as none, and ten times better than usual. As

for Rogers, this voyage makes his career, and gets him the assign-ment of wiping out the brotherhood in the Caribbean once and for all, which is their final story."

"Does he wipe them out?"

"More or less. Like Mainwaring all over again, but not tonight." The captain stepped up onto the deck, made a pillow of his boat cloak, and stretched out to nap for the rest of the watch. When the cabin clock started to ring eight bells, he was up and alert before the chimes ended. The middle watch, now starting, would be our most likely time of peril, if peril there was to be.

I resolved to keep him company. I was even ready for some more history, but the captain kept his own company, smoking his pipe, sipping coffee. Without the daytime traffic of shipping and airplanes, our anchorage was quiet but for the mournful horn that blew from the light station marking the Graves. A long, low, easy swell rolled in from waves made somewhere far away, and their die-hard remnants slid under *Merry*, until the gentle motion rocked me to sleep.

18

More Dangers

I was awakened by the captain's hand gently shaking me. "What is it?" I was up like a shot, peering around us.

"Nothing to get into a flap about, but take a look with your young eyes and tell me what you see." Under the clear night sky, I saw the same myriad of lights as before. "Look west," he said, and I focused on the brightest horizon, trying to see a light that didn't belong. "Look for the absence of light." Then I saw it, a shadow against the illumination of the city, a boat in silhouette, too dark to identify. "Watch it and tell me what you think."

I watched it for what seemed a long time until I was ready to say that the boat wasn't changing its bearing, but seemed to be blotting out more light, which meant it was getting closer: drifting toward us on the ebb tide, maybe distant some hundred yards. "Right you are. They've positioned themselves up-current of us, killed their motor, lettin' the tide bring 'em down on us. What do you do now, Master James Hawkins, son of noble family?"

The thing I did was find my mind in a knot. I lunged for the flashlights and weapons.

"Say after me . . ." he said, restraining me, "one does not flap."

"Flap?"

"Say it."

"One does not flap."

"Quite. Now, what *do* you do?"

On sober reflection, I proposed we crouch in the cockpit, and when they came alongside, rise up and give them a surprise volley. "If we can get two of them . . ." I started to say.

"The third will murder us with his shotgun, or repeating pistol. If we get really lucky, and manage to wipe 'em out, what then? Coast Guards and police? Blood everywhere? Probably charges, and our money impounded during a long investigation while the inn sinks, and we're in the slam, with poor *Merry* somewhere she doesn't like? Lawyers? A pox on it. We'll want your pistol, my Very pistol, both torches, and the speaking trumpet to hand." I layed them out, learning his own plan. This called for making our move as soon as our attackers drifted within easy hailing distance, which was happening rapidly.

"Now, let us make a joyful noise." He gave the signal; I clicked my pistol onto full cock, pointed it at the sky, pulled the trigger, and blasted a ball into space with a fine explosion. This was immediately followed by the captain firing a parachute flare, illuminating our surroundings in a sharp, red light, including the unmistakable form of *Lamprey*. While the flare drifted lazily down, we both clicked on our flashlights, and the captain bellowed through his trumpet: "Ahoy! I say, *Lamprey*! You're adrift!" As the flare sizzled into the sea, he fired another, trumpeting his alert repeatedly until finally getting a response.

"OK. Thanks," came a shout, followed by the sputter of engines starting. Then the boat roared away into the night. A last call from the captain reminded them to switch on their navigation lights. When it was over, I was taken by the taste of victory, mixed with relief, and admiration for his plan.

"Reload your pistol, and put the weapons back on their display board. We might get other visitors. We've just thrown up two distress signals." Indeed, twenty minutes later, a Coast Guard launch went through the channel, darting a searchlight around, but never closer than a half-mile from us. He did not fire another flare, however, feeling that we would not be attacked again tonight. "Not here. Maybe offshore. Whenever we can get there. Depends on how much time they've got to devote to us, and how much they want us. These sods are weekenders, but they could take us as a challenge. Pirates are quite like fishermen. There's the sporting side of it. Fishermen worked on shares, by the by, just like the brotherhood. You should put your head down again; get a bit of kip before morning watch."

Difficult as it was for me to go to sleep, I must have, because I had a vivid flash of dream in which I was crouching under an open hatch, cutlass in hand, knowing I was about to leap up and use it. Before it got that far, the captain awakened me. He had let me sleep, and it was getting light. A procession of outgoing fishing boats sent their wave patterns over water that looked like blue oil. "Wake me for breakfast," he said, stating his preferences as to menu, then turning in down below. "Keep your eyes open, and call me if you see anything of interest."

I did not, although I could see for miles through the binoculars—every other boat, and all of Cape Ann stretching to the east. Like Selkirk, I was feeling severe frustration. After an hour, I ducked below for my copy of Johnson, reading between sweeps of the horizon, the passages he had assigned. In due course, I started cooking the omelette he had requested, and its aroma brought him out of his bunk. "Ah!" he said, supervising the garnish. I reported that there was no sign of the enemy, and the same frustrating, dead calm. When I started to complain about it, I was interrupted at once.

"You've had a day of no wind, and your mind's all jumbled from it. Think of Selkirk, and bring me a beer." I brought it to him, along with the Selkirk question that he had earlier evaded.

"What is half of a salvation?"

He pondered, nodding, not immediately answering, spearing the last bits of egg from his plate. Finally, he laid it aside, empty.

"Very nice. Has your school taught you about parable, fable, metaphor, allegory, simile, and such? Good. Now, here's your situation." He put his feet up onto the cockpit seat, with the half-smile that meant I was going to have to work for whatever he was about to say.

"At the outset, you want to get away."

"From what?"

He shrugged. "Your world. Whatever it is. It's a rum go, so you get your own ship, boat, whatever vessel, and you cast off its lines and clear out."

"To where?"

"You don't have a clue, but somewhere else, for sure, on your own. So you make a course for somewhere where something might be, not knowing whether there's anything there, or even if there's a there to go to, or anything else at all anywhere. Never mind. Off you go, and then there you are."

"Where?"

"At sea. On the course you've layed. It blows up, and you reef your sails. It falls calm, and you rig out your light-weather canvas, hoping for a whisper of breeze, like where we are now. In short, you get calms and storms, and you sail on. And on and on, to the point of tedium, with nothing on your horizon. You're far too far gone to turn back, but you begin to lose faith in the direction you've chosen. It's hot. Sweat runs down your body. Your rations turn sour, and your water thickens in the cask, so that you have to hold your nose when you drink it, and ignore the wriggly little creatures that are swimming in it. You wonder what in bloody hell made you commit yourself to this insane voyage, and you think about changing course, but to what? To where? In an uncharted ocean, how are you to know if there's anything here at all?"

"Is there?"

"How can you say? You see land, a clear elevation on the horizon, but it turns out to be a mirage, a trick of nature. Very disappointing. You make friends with the little creatures that share your boat with you. You feed the mice, and treasure the company of cockroaches. Did I tell you before about Caleb Whitback's cockroach?" He had not. "Caleb did three years in solitary confinement in a Spanish dungeon. Cockroaches were his only company, so he made particular friends with one. Sarah, he called it, after his wife, reckoning the creature was female, I suppose.

"In any case, he taught Sarah to do incredible tricks—counting bread crumbs, standing up, sitting down, turning in circles, all on command, in some language Caleb had learned with it over time. When the Dons let him go, Caleb's only asset in the world was Sarah, and he reckoned she would be worth a fortune, exhibited in London. His first night back in Blighty, he goes into a pub, orders a pint, takes Sarah out of her special little box, and puts her on the bar, ready to try out the act on the publican when he comes back with the beer that he can't pay for. 'See this?' says Caleb. 'Oh, sorry,' apologises the publican, squashing Sarah with his thumb. 'Beer's on the house.'" He sighed. "But I digress. Where were we?"

"Nowhere?"

"Just so. Poor you. Child of confusion, lost, with heat rash, sunburn, and the squitters. And just when you've resigned yourself to madness or death, you see land, real land. An island. Maybe a continent. Purple at first, in the distance, it's still a long way off, but the sight of it gives you the will to endure, and to work your sails, and navigate your way through reefs to a cool, lush, green land, a place of great beauty, with waterfalls, villages, barking dogs, playing children, flowers, salvation. Half-salvation because the next thing you learn is that you've landed among cannibals." He laughed, not funnily. He seemed unduly dismal, and I told him so, adding the question: "If that's half of a salvation, what's the other half?"

"Learning to like cannibals, I should think." He regarded me, then put down his feet, deliberately straightening into an upright posture in a very theatrical way. His face softened, and his eyes became like the sad eyes of a saint, and when he spoke again, it was in a saintly voice: "More than just liking the cannibals, we must love them, for they are us." He lifted his hands as in prayer, at the same time shifting his body directly between me and the sun, so that he glowed with its halo like a bearded prophet in a stained glass window.

Suddenly he was the most ludicrous thing I had ever seen in my whole life, and laughter took me. It was the kind of laugh that gets hold of you and takes charge and makes your ribs hurt. He laughed too, and when I eventually started to get control, he started to do the same silly thing with his face, and it knocked me down all over again, clutching my sides.

"There's your answer, anyway, my oath on it," he chuckled. "I reckon we should get a bit of breeze by midmorning.

Contrary to the captain's prediction, midmorning came with no more movement of air than before, but more powerboats than ever. Weaving his macramé, he ordered me to tell him about Woodes Rogers, and condense what I had learned from Johnson's *History*. I found this a disappointing turn of events. From my reading, I realised why Rogers marked the end of the brotherhood, and probably of his stories, and he was making me tell it.

It was simple enough. The free society of buccaneers that

took over the Bahamas never formed itself into anything more than a ramshackle collection of bars and bawdy houses at Nassau. Inevitably it became a nuisance. To deal with it, the British government appointed Woodes Rogers. Appointed as the crown's Governor General of the Bahamas, Rogers went with a squadron of Royal Navy ships, plus the royal decree of pardon for pirates, buccaneers, and overstepping privateers, in exchange for their giving up the life, a sweeping amnesty.

"It was their most powerful weapon, the king's pardon," he interjected. "There's a real temptation to take a document that says you won't get hanged for whatever you've done, so long as you don't do it again. Proceed."

I recounted how King George signed the proclamation on September 5, 1717, allowing until the same date in 1718 for its circulation and results. A copy of it was sent out to Nassau, along with word that Rogers was coming. The brethren's response was to capture the ship that brought it, then to call a grand council and send out the word. The captain interrupted again:

"And a grand council it was, Jim. They were all there. The whole family. They came from the Gulf of Mexico, the Caymans, the greater and lesser Antilles. Edward England and John Fife sailed from the Carolinas; LaBouche got the word off Newfoundland, and came in; Teach was there, and Hornigold, Martel, Fife, Burgess, Vane, Calico Jack Rackham (dressed like a peacock, as was his wont), and more, hundreds and hundreds of 'em, not counting wives, girlfriends, and locals; everybody having the biggest chin-chin the brotherhood had seen since Morgan's day. The whole harbour was packed with ships. Black flags everywhere, each with its skull, skeleton, cutlasses, bones, severed heads, or hourglasses with drips of red blood. Such a collection.

I've never seen . . . beg pardon. Carry on with where you were." I proceeded.

Their choice—whether to declare a commonwealth, and fight to defend the island, or to accept the new governor, and take the King's pardon—was decided by Captain Jennings, who was chairing the meeting. Jennings was a commodore among them, and he stopped the argument by declaring that he and some 150 others were going to submit when Rogers arrived. By the time that happened, in July of 1717, the die-hard pirates had sailed away.

"Except for Charley Vane," he growled, "who fired at the first Royal Navy vessel into the harbour, then snuck out under their noses. And there went the notion of any commonwealth." He made a toast to a point in space. "Gone. Why, with a thousand of the brethren (which we had, more or less) and guns commanding the approaches (perfect to defend, by the way) Rogers would never have got ashore. He was a good man, maybe the best, but his only troops were a few dozen old retirees they'd given him for soldiers. Most of his men were sailors, not to be trusted not to just change sides if let ashore, so y'see, they didn't give Rogers a quarter of what he needed to take Nassau, if . . ." He paused, sighing.

"If?"

"There aren't any ifs. None. I keep interrupting, and you're almost at an end, right?"

The buccaneers that remained in the Bahamas took the royal pardon, and Rogers recruited them into a loyal militia. Some ex-pirates were authorised to sail out and capture their unreformed, former friends, which they did. Along with these setbacks, the places where a pirate could safely make port were almost gone, forcing him to live at sea, changing ships as needed, or to put into ever more remote places.

"Like Nova Scotia," he added. "where he could make a shore base." I proceeded. Others sailed for Madagascar, where measures also were being taken against them. They were stripped of their havens. The last pirates of that generation were mostly gone by the time Johnson's *History* was published in 1724.

"Pirates weren't gone," he corrected me. "You mean the brotherhood. Plenty of pirates still around, but no more sense of family, like, y'see."

"So the brotherhood was gone . . ." I started to agree.

"Not gone. Dispersed."

"Well, at some point it was gone."

"Oh?" his eyebrows shot up. "When was that?"

"Whenever the last one died, I suppose."

"I'm here to report that has not yet happened," he beamed, "because here we are, you and me, Jim, and now we can leave the history in our wake. Unless you have any pirates questions?" he added. I did, but before I could organise them, he set me to preparing our Sunday dinner. "While you cook, I'll have a go at piping us up a wind."

I diced some potatoes and onions to fry up with corned beef, and he took up his pennywhistle, playing repetitions of the tunes he had made up during the winter. I lit the stove, and was about halfway through the cooking when I did feel a movement of air, and the steam from the frying pan went whisking through the hatch.

"Wind?" I stuck my head out, feeling a faint but welcome whisper on my cheek. Tiny riffles ran across the water.

"Seems to be. Let me see if I can get us just a bit more of it." He returned to his music, and by the time I had made up our plates there was enough breeze to settle *Merry* on her anchor line.

We made short work of our noon meal, and then I was setting sails, hauling in the anchor and stowing its chain.

"That's pretty good, being able to whistle up wind," I allowed.

"Aye. Cheap trick, really." He smiled. Perfectly set to the light air, *Merry*'s sails drew, just enough to give us way toward home again. I had always thought their brown colour ugly, but at that moment they were lovely to my eye; marred only by the big, unsightly radar reflector. When I suggested its removal, however, he ignored me.

While cleaning up the galley, I had a chance to consider just what questions I did have. None for school, obviously, but things had gone far beyond essays. He had got under my skin with his subject, and in a way that did not feel resolved. I didn't know what resolution I wanted, but the whole pageantry of it had not led me there, and I could not think of how to phrase it. One thing I had for sure expected was at least one more experience of the vivid kind of illusion that I knew he could invoke, but seemed to have abandoned.

When I went back above, I told him I had some confusion, but I thought one more story might tie it all up for me, about somebody from the last years of the era; Blackbeard came to mind. I suggested it would be particularly helpful if he could put me into it again. Perhaps something with cutlass play, so I could practise what he had taught me. This seemed to irritate him.

"Stories, tales, yarns . . . as though that's all I've got to do. Here I am, trying to tie off the ends of my little strings so they'll hold up under divine scrutiny, and here's you, asking me to talk, when you've got your own copy of Johnson, and a good pair of eyes to read the best account of Teach that you'll ever hope to find. I suggest you do that." And so I troubled him no more for the rest of that warm afternoon. Later in the day, the wind backed to the south and increased, letting *Merry* begin to make better speed, with a chuckle in her wake. Dozens of other sails were in sight, until we cleared Cape Ann and began to leave the land behind. From time to time the captain interrupted his work to search in that direction with the binoculars. When my watch came around, it became my job as well, plus some more navigation lessons that lasted until my next round of galley work at suppertime.

An hour before sunset, at the start of the first watch, he decreed a surprising change in course: "Bring her northeast." I protested, pointing out that would take us toward the Bay of Fundy, not in the direction we wanted to go. Furthermore, it meant sailing with the wind right behind us, dead aft, which was not as favourable as our present slant.

"The correct response is 'northeast, aye Cap'n,'" he growled.

"Northeast, aye Cap'n." Baffled about his intention, I made the adjustment to the helm.

"Take a careful look aft." He handed me the binoculars. They took some focusing; I took my time looking at the last of the day's distant boats, seeing no sign of *Lamprey*. "Look some more; range about three miles, maybe a little less, bearing west. Your eyes are better than mine." A minute later I saw what he had, which was a cruiser, bows-on, not in profile, but with just the unmistakable hint of our two-tone green enemy with its Decca gear. There was no question left in my mind that Mathew's friends were indeed our enemies, now stalking us again, but from a good distance, pending nightfall, in the captain's opinion.

"They've taken us on as a project. They're tracking us by radar, thinking we won't see 'em from so far away. I reckon they'll wait until after dark, then home in on us on their little green screen, wait for a space between passing ships, and come up fast this time, before we can fire any flares. They've got to roar up shooting, with no vessels nearby, kill us, get the loot, then stick our corpses below and chop a big hole in *Merry*'s bottom, sinking the evidence. If they're efficient at it, the whole business shouldn't take more than twenty minutes, maybe less; so even if we do get off a flare or two, we'll be in Davy Jones's locker by the time anybody can get here to see where the flares came from."

"Right," said I. Everything was happening very suddenly, my body tensed.

"Take a breath. Take two. We've an hour before dark. What's our own advantage?"

That was little enough, as far as I could see. *Merry* was a slow sailboat, slave to the wind, easy victim to any power craft. We would have two shots, a boat hook, and a cutlass against a probable wall of modern firepower. He agreed, instructing me as to where to rummage for a deflated rubber raft that was there for emergencies, and then to pump it up on the foredeck. After doing that, I held the helm as he improvised a tripod mast to the raft from *Merry*'s small reserve of planks and spars. By sunset he had finished it, plus an improvised yard and a sail.

"What are you doing?" I asked, as darkness closed in, and I could no longer see *Lamprey* in the binoculars. Until it faded into the darkness, its bearing and distance had not changed.

"Making a new us." He ordered me to lower the big radar reflector and, in the last remnant of twilight, he attached the contraption so that it stuck up above everything else on the raft, and then we launched it together. Its sail filled to the wind on the course that we had been holding. To keep the raft guided, he had attached a short dragline to act as a rudder, and it worked very well. Off it sailed at a good clip, skimming. We trimmed *Merry* to a right angle from our previous course, lighting no lights, and taking down our small reflector, making us nearly invisible. "This is where dark sails come in useful," he commented, as *Merry* distanced herself, reaching away from the decoy he had rigged. "Let 'em attack that." By his calculation, it would take our assailants at least an hour or more to find it, by which time we would be long gone in a direction they would have to guess exactly if they were ever to find us again. *Merry* fled into an ocean that widened with every tick of the clock.

B loody hell." The captain was in no good mood, having cast off the same macramé knot three or four times in pursuit of his own perfection, only to find he had to do it yet again. It was late afternoon on Thursday, our fourth day at sea since leaving Boston and *Lamprey* behind us. *Merry* had made good progress, with a fair, quartering wind that only partly eased my ongoing fears about other things. With perfect circumstances, we would fetch Grey Rocks Harbour the following day, a certain four days late for the inn's critical deadline, with unknown consequences. Further, it now seemed unlikely that Mathew had telephoned Mother, meaning she would be some worried; and when we did get home—or soon thereafter—that would be the last I would see of the captain. I had probed the idea of my going with him, but with no success at all. Our final full day together was waning, and I again prodded him for a last tale.

"Bring up the bloody book, and read me the description of bloody Blackbeard," he growled, and I did as I had been told, reading aloud.

> *"Captain Teach assumed the cognomen of Blackbeard from that large quantity of hair which, like a frightful meteor, covered his whole face and frightened America more than any comet that has appeared there a long time. This beard was black, which he suffered to grow of an extravagant length; as to breadth it came up to his eyes. He was accustomed to twist it with ribbons, in small tails, after the manner of our ramilies wigs, and turn them about his ears. In time of action, he wore a sling over his shoulders with three brace of pistols hanging in holsters like banoliers, and stuck lighted matches under his hat, which, appearing on each side of his face, his eyes naturally looking fierce and wild, made him altogether such a figure, that imagination cannot form an idea of a fury, from hell, to look more frightful."*

"Avast reading," he interrupted. "I'd add to that that he was quite a large chap, and was better than anybody at invoking pure terror, as y'can see. If you met him, and he politely asked you if you'd make a gift to him of, say, your watch, you'd give it to him faster than pork fat through a goose."

"Did he cut off anybody's lips?"

He shook his head. "Nor any other little snippings. There's no record he ever hurt any surrendered prisoner; the look of him was usually sufficient to get him whatever he wanted, and if any further persuasion was needed, he had a laugh that was Beelzebub's envy. All jolly good theatre. Worked, too." I asked what was meant by lighted matches. "Slow fuse, for touching off cannon. Chap smelled of singed hair and sulphurous, but it didn't seem to put off the ladies. Bit of a womaniser, in point of fact. In any case, read his story from the beginning. And read it to yourself; I've heard it before. Tell me when you get to the battle at Ocracoke Inlet."

So, silently, I read about the short—less than two-year—piratical career of Edward Teach, an educated man from Bristol who had found his way aboard privateers during Queen Anne's War, until being put out of work by the peace, like so many of the brethren of the coast. Having dived for a while on the Spanish treasure wrecks of the 1715 fleet, he then sailed off on the account—which is to say he turned pirate—in company with his mentor, Captain Hornigold, both in sloops.

When they captured a heavily armed but undermanned French merchantman, Teach was able to change his flag onto a ship that he could reinforce to carry forty guns, renaming it *Queen Anne's Revenge*. After various captures and adventures, and with a small squadron under his command, Teach sailed into the approaches to the port of Charles Town, South Carolina, and blockaded it. He took numbers of vessels there, keeping all their companies prisoner, and holding them hostage until the town gave him the ransom he demanded, which was a chest of specific medicines. Here, I could not help interrupting the captain's work, asking him how such a blockade of a major port was possible.

"Charles Town could hardly defend itself at all, and it would be weeks before the Royal Navy could muster a force to have a go at the terrifying Teach, who so much liked to fight, he fought from exuberance; he once slugged it out with a Royal Navy ship, fought ' em to a standoff with no earthly hope of profit, except the battle itself. He backed up his image, y'see, and made his crew go along with it, because he was worth the lot of them. Used to challenge them to little contests from time to time, like going below decks with burning sulphur pots, then sealing the hatches to see who could stand being there the longest. Teach always won."

"Why just a medicine chest?" It seemed to me he could have exacted a lot bigger tribute.

"He only needed medicines. And to win, of course. With him, everything was winning the game. So there wasn't a scratch on any of his hostages when he sent them ashore, no more than any jewellery." The captain chuckled. I went back to my reading.

From Charles Town, Teach cruised up the North Carolina coast, where he ran his flagship aground as though by navigational error and, while pretending to rescue it, also grounded his second-largest ship. He then sailed away in *Adventure,* the smallest of his sloops, taking all of the loot, plus the forty men he wanted to keep. The rest he left stranded, or destitute, or both, while Teach and his crew paid a visit to the governor of North Carolina, surrendered to the royal proclamation of amnesty for pirates, and got pardons.

After that, Teach was careful to give no offense to local shipping, sailing as far away as Bermuda for his further sport in the eight-gun sloop he had adopted as a kind of private yacht. Returning to the Carolina capes, he cruised, disposing of his loot, trading, socialising ashore with some of the local planters. It was an extended camping and yachting holiday, as far as I could tell, with Blackbeard getting to enjoy his considerable celebrity, and under royal immunity. It did not last. Before long, some of Teach's friends showed up, such as Vane, Rackham, Deal, and Israel Hands, in their own sloops: a family reunion. Teach hosted them all at a camp he had established off Ocracoke Inlet, a pass through the barrier islands south of Cape Hatteras. Two king's cruisers were sent at last to find him there, and there I left off reading, as instructed, with the question, what had become of his royal pardon?

"Governor of Virginia, chap named Spotswood, simply wouldn't honour any Blackbeard pardon signed by his rival governor in Carolina. Politics. In the name of putting a stop to Ocracoke Inlet becoming a pirates' nest, Spotswood could invade his neighbour's state, which he wanted, and get not only Blackbeard and his crew, but their treasure, with no need to shift out of his chair. So, with a stroke of his pen, the Virginia militia marches south, and two sloops sail for Ocrakoke under king's colours, commanded by Lieutenant Maynard of the Royal Navy. He's got fifty-five well-armed men, but no carriage guns; for him, it has to be a boarding action. Teach has only twenty-five men, but eight deck guns."

The captain put down his macramé in order to familiarise me with the tactical situation, as dictated by the surrounding shallows and currents. Teach's close knowledge of these were his greatest advantage, along with his cannon, and he made best use of both. Maynard arrived at the pass late in the day, saw Teach's mast behind the island, and anchored to await a dawn attack, with favourable currents. Teach's preparation for the imminent battle was a late-night drinking party. In early light, with faint breeze, Maynard threaded the pass and steered to within earshot, where Teach hailed, promising no quarter—a fight to the death. A slow-motion, running battle ensued, with Teach working the channels, until his attackers both ran aground; he then turned his cannons on the sloops, giving each one a broadside of grapeshot, with devastating effect.

"Maynard loses twenty men, killed and wounded, and the smaller sloop, with fewer men, loses nine. Now, if you're Lieutenant Maynard chap, what do you do when you get free? You've lost half your men." I suggested a prudent retreat. "No, you keep attacking. Teach also goes aground; you steer for him, but you can't stand any more losses, so you send your crews below decks to shelter from the rain of small arms fire coming at you. A valiant midshipman steers. When your shot-up little sloop finally touches *Adventure,* pirates throw grenades, then board, thinking they've killed you all. Then, on your signal, your men storm up through the hatches in a counterattack that catches the pirates by complete surprise, pistol, pike, and cutlass. They never have a chance to reorganise, and your second sloop arrives. Blackbeard himself wades into the thick of it, roaring, hewing, firing pistols. He takes a pistol ball, then a cutlass hack to the neck, then another stroke or two, but fights on with a devilish strength, until he takes a thrust that finishes him, and he drops dead. Without him, the pirates still standing jump overboard to make a swim for it, but you retrieve 'em, and that's that." He reached for his macramé.

"Wait a minute," I cried, feeling yet again left out of the action. "You mean that's the end of it?"

"More or less. Maynard cut off Teach's head and hung it on his bowsprit. *Adventure*'s crew were tried and hanged, all but Israel Hands, who wasn't even there. Governor Spotswood got the invasion of his rival colony, plus a pile of Blackbeard's loot, and Ocracoke Inlet got the legend of Blackbeard's ghost wandering around looking for his head. But I reckon he more likely came back later as Rasputin, Russian chap with whom he had much in common. Why? Have I left something out?"

"Me," I said, "I thought you were going to put me into it. It's our last chance for that."

"Oh dear," he sighed. "I'd advise against it, actually." He gave me a look, and, in my disappointment, I gave him one back. Resigned, he rummaged in his pocket, and handed me another coin, a gold doubloon this time, with the marks of old Spain, and a 1715 date. "Teach got this out of one of the Spanish wrecks, and held it in his own hands, and now it's in your hands. Just fancy." It was a heavy thing, the heaviest so far, with the unmistakable magic that is peculiar to pure old gold.

"Now, go back to the point where Maynard commands his crew to go below, out of sight; off the deck that's littered with your dead and dying shipmates, while you approach the pirates. Everybody's crouched close, listening to the lead balls slamming into the hull, thinkin' thoughts that make your brains perspire. It's a warm morning, and looking like your last one. Just be there," he ordered, and there I was, as in my recent dream, now living it in a way that was immediately alarming.

The thing was too vivid, starting with an ammonia smell to the sweating bodies around me. The closest thing in front of my face was the meaty arm and shoulder of the man in front of me, glazed with grime, and dotted with a rash. His pigtail was greased. From the man behind me, or thereabouts, came a low humming, the same fragment of tune repeated again and again, with interruptions for hard swallowing. His hand, clutched on a pike handle, rested heavily against my back. At about the time that the first grenade exploded overhead, I decided to withdraw to the real world. Holding that thought, I awaited my immediate return.

It was elusive. Before, I'd always been able to come back to the table by the fire, but I realised I'd better aim instead for *Merry*'s cockpit, so I tried for that, again without results. Another grenade went off.

"OK, I'm ready," I spoke aloud, so the captain would hear me, wherever he was.

"Good on ye, lad, but quieten down," said the man in front of me, shifting his arm to put it around my shoulders and give me a squeeze. Its new position opened his armpit to my face, closely revealing the hot centre of his pimply heat rash.

"Captain!" I called.

"Pipe down, and wait for the order!" came a harsh whisper from the rear of our pack. Three grenades exploded in fast succession. Then the hull ground against another one, as unfriendly voices came from above.

"They're all knocked on the head, except three or four . . . let's jump on board and cut them to pieces!" This was followed by a thumping of feet on deck.

"Captain!" I yelled.

"Right! Go!" came a voice, and every man around me sprang for the ladders, sweeping me with the rush, and I was in it, with everything happening in urgent impressions: churning smoke, pistol blasts, my feet slipping in blood and viscera, falling, dropping my pistol and cutlass, finding them, but who was the enemy? I wanted out of this.

"Captain!" I screamed, unheard by anybody. I was back on my feet, completely confused. I saw one figure that could be nobody but Blackbeard, hewing away. I pointed my pistol at him, pulled the trigger, and the weapon misfired. At the same moment a man with fierce, bright blue eyes appeared right in front of me, raising his cutlass to swing it; before he could strike, I brought my own cutlass forward in the quick lunge that I'd learned, catching him with force. I felt the blade penetrate as his eyes went gentle with surprise, and looked at me in a way that is etched in my memory. At the same time, a warm river of his blood coursed over my hand and ran down my arm. My thrust had found his heart.

When he fell, I could not pull the blade out of him because the grip was too slippery. Something made me look up just in time to see another man throwing a pistol at me; I started to duck, and that is the last I remember of it.

What that lot wants is a sack of ice," said the captain, referring to the egg-sized lump over my ear, "but, you'll have to make do with a cold-water compress." This was a bundled bloody rag soaked in seawater that he told me to hold against my head. "And here's a couple of aspirins." He handed them to me. According to him, I just passed out, falling forward and striking my head on the cockpit seat. He had cleaned up much blood.

"Too much sun, too little salt," was his diagnosis. "Happens all the time. You'll be right as rain for our homecoming. How did you like Blackbeard by the by?" He was looking at me in a bemused way. I was still stunned by whatever had just happened to me, and it took me a minute to catch my breath in the good old world again. I said that from what I had read, and heard, and seen, Blackbeard was like an animal.

"Mmmm. Well, Teach was no L'Ollonais, no brute, more what you might call a determined competitor. But as his prisoner, you were safe as a lamb in the arms of Saint Brendan at sheering time, and Teach could be quite courtly with the ladies. A bit mad, perhaps, but not without a sense of humour," he smiled. "If you'd care to pick up the story where we left off . . . ?"

"No." I was very grateful to be out of it. I had no idea what had just happened to me but I was quite sure that I didn't want it to happen again. My arms were smeared with blood and I had a fierce headache.

"Perhaps he'd be more enjoyable when not in such a gruff mood. Possibly you'd prefer to chat with him as he's writing in his journal?"

"No, thank you."

"Did you know, of all that bloody lot, he was the only one to keep a journal? Nobody else did. I've got some bits of it, more than the one quoted here . . ." He picked up my copy of Johnson, and found a page. "Here's an entry for one day in Teach's career; two days, actually.

> *"Such a day, Rum all out: – Our Company somewhat sober: – A Damned Confusion amongst us! – Rogues a plotting; – great Talk of Separation. – So I looked sharp for a Prize; – such a Day, took one, with a great deal of Liquor on Board, so kept the Company hot, damned hot, then all Things went well again."*

He closed the book. "Now there's a touch of raw poetry . . . but, I must say, you're lookin' a bit peaked again. You should freshen that compress and, when you're feeling a bit recovered, and have a wash, we can discuss the menu for supper. I'm afraid it'll be our last one of the voyage. We're out of solomongundy, but we can peel open a can of herring. While you're below, take a salt tablet. After supper you can clear your area and pack up your seabag. Let's start getting *Merry* ready to come home, eh?"

"Aye, Cap'n."

19

Return and Departure

Friday

The breeze held overnight. I made my good-byes to *Merry* by starlight, explaining to her as best I could why I would be unable to attend her anymore. I was torn again, sad to be going back to my little life, as before the captain had sailed into it, and yet glad to be coming home, especially as the cavalry to the rescue. Mother's worries would be instantly dissolved, I felt. During the morning, dolphins came and played around us, and the captain trimmed his beard, and I washed down the decks. Around midafternoon, the purplish profile of the Nova Scotia coast began to define itself into Grey Rocks Point, with its light-house, and, an hour later, the inn was in sight, aglow, etched in sunlight and shadow, as though lifted there from an old painting.

"We'll go right in. Our engine's down, and it's important to get you home straightaway; there's a foul wind for Baywater, so we'll sod the port-of-entry thing, and let the authorities come to us."

I told him I had no doubt as to his ability to get more use out of an always-defunct engine than it would be worth if it worked, which made his face crinkle into a smile.

"Nothin' against engines, mind; useful in the Torres Strait, or off a lee shore with your rig blown away, or lots of other situa-tions, but the bloody things do stink intolerably." To get the parts he needed, he said he would have to visit the Ailsa Craig Com-pany, which had moved to Sussex, or maybe Kent. "Mail never catches up with me, and I don't send any, so I'll have to show up on their doorstep."

"But you'll write to me?"

"I'll write my letters to you on the wind, Jim, where you can read 'em cleaner than if they're in an envelope with stamps and postmarks, eh?" Here was double disappointment. Not only was he going to be gone, but gone for good, and it felt like a death. My feelings showed. "Dear boy, I'll come and visit you again."

"When? Promise?"

"When I'm younger. My oath on it." Meanwhile, he remind-ed me, he would still be around for a few days, tidying up his affairs in Grey Rocks, making his good-byes. "Before that, we're about to have some hellos."

And so we did, although not as I had expected. When *Merry* sailed past the breakwater, I gave three blasts from the foghorn, but they drew nobody, so that we had to handle our own lines, then snug down everything, wondering where everybody was. As we were finishing with *Merry,* here came Meg hurrying down the steps, a belated welcome at last.

"Yay, Meg!" I called, with a joy that started to dampen; she approached with a kind of quick march, and a face that was short on cheer.

"Dear girl, come aboard," said the captain, offering her his hand for the step. For once, she took it, and the seat he offered, while I gushed about how we had done everything we set out to do, and had the money, and not to be concerned about my bandaged head.

"That's good," she nodded, adding that my being safe would take a weight of worry off Mother. As feared, there had been no message from Mathew, and Mother had finally alerted the Coast Guard. I started to explain about my attempts to telephone, but Meg stopped me.

"Your Aunt Karen's dead," she began her own report. It had happened late last Saturday, sometime while *Merry* was anchored off the Graves. With Mother and Robin at her bedside in the Halifax hospital, Aunt Karen had passed into the next world, making her good-byes to all, including the captain. "She said to tell you she only regrets that she wasn't going to have the chance to ask you some more questions."

Mother and Robin had been constantly back and forth to Halifax together, dealing with all of the things that had to be done. At the moment they were accompanying the body back home to Lucas Lamey's mortuary. The funeral would follow church services on Sunday morning, with an all-afternoon reception at the inn. Mother had taken refuge from her grieving in all the activity involved. She had closed the place, preempting a visit from the inspectors. The work was going on, however; Clyde Hirtle was installing the last of the new plumbing at that very moment, and all of the workmen were still on the job, on faith, and as a gesture of support for the bereaved family.

Meanwhile, the Moehners were applying more pressure than ever, at the very moment when the inn had no income at all. With luck, and the money we had brought, the work would be completed next week, and the downstairs plumbing before that, in time for the funeral reception. Meg had been holding down the fort alone for the past several days, sitting near the telephone, cleaning up after the workmen, and trying to keep Chloe out from under their feet.

"How are you holding?" The captain regarded her.

"I've been better," she conceded, "and if that's rum you're pouring for yourself, I'll have one too, half-water." He hastened to make it for her. All of her rudeness toward the captain was gone. "Then there's you," she regarded him, saying that two men in suits and ties had shown up at the inn looking for Captain Charles Johnson. One was an Englishman, and there was an Immigration officer, who had left his card with instructions that he was to be telephoned if Captain Johnson showed up.

"I couldn't get out of them what they wanted to talk to you about, but here's who might know more." Tom was buzzing toward us in his skiff, then tying up alongside *Merry* and coming aboard. He had condolences for me, and concern for my head, but business with the captain, due to the police question about his papers. The men who had come looking for him had talked to Tom, as harbourmaster.

"What's their interest in you?" Tom asked.

"No clue," said the captain. "Same bleeding paperwork confusion that happens to all the Charles Johnsons, all the time."

"I'm duty-bound," announced Tom, "to notify both the British consulate in Halifax, and some gent at Canadian Immigration, if and when you arrive, and I intend to do that soon, very soon, right after you've poured me one of those." He indicated the captain's mug of rum.

"I'll get it sorted out," said the captain pouring the drink. "I always have to."

"Easy with the water," said Tom. "Anyway, since I won't be able to call them by five o'clock, which is only an hour from now, that means they won't have the message until Monday morning, meaning you can probably expect 'em midweek. Here's to your being back," he toasted, "and to the cannon, which we only need to mount." While we were gone, Tom had finished all the carpentry and fitted the last of the cannon's original ironwork, leaving only a few things to do, which they started to discuss with the zeal of true enthusiasts.

Meg soon left, telling me to telephone Jenny, who had been calling daily for any word about me. I went below, secured the drawstrings on my overpacked seabag, and wrestled it up through he hatch and onto the dock without help. I then carried it across my shoulders up all of the stairs to my room, where I blessedly dumped the thing, vowing never again to let my mother pack it for me.

Mother returned before suppertime, with Robin. Without

Aunt Karen to tend, he had turned to caring for Mother, who seemed steady to me. She was delighted to see us home, concerned about my wound, and carrying a sadness for Aunt Karen.

"Aunt Karen's out of her pain now," she said, putting the subject aside.

During supper, I gave an abbreviated account of our trip, and, after the dishes were cleared, the captain produced the money we had brought home, piles of American dollars, plus a careful accounting of his expenses to be reimbursed off the top.

"Limousine and driver?" asked mother, looking through the account. "Clothing? A rubber raft? A radar reflector? Flares?" This all took some explaining but, in the end, the odd expenses were well justified by the take. The captain seemed very pleased with his own share, remarking that it would cover his year's costs. A little windfall, as he put it. "But you'll be with us for a while?" Mother asked him.

"A while," he nodded.

"Good," said Robin, bringing up the matter of the captain's documentation. "I'm afraid I'm the one who may have caused that, because I ran a routine check on your passport, and when the British consulate eventually got back to us, the Home Office had no record of you on file, and they want to talk to you about it."

The captain made a helpless gesture. "I'm used to it. Happens all the time. The universe is overloaded with Charles Johnsons, and I'm one of 'em, and somebody is always getting confused by there being so bloody many of us. I'll get it sorted out."

Mother went off to bed before long, and when Robin went home, Meg and the captain took their instruments out to the deck where they played music under the summer moon, and into the night.

Saturday

The inn was given to preparations for the reception that would follow Aunt Karen's funeral. Bertha Hirtle arrived before breakfast, and by midmorning most of the Women's Auxiliary were on hand, with cleaning gear to blast away the last traces of sawdust left by Clyde's workmen, and ready to prepare a standing buffet for all the mourners, plus coffee and juices.

In the early afternoon Jenny showed up, catching me between errands. I told her that I had too much to tell her to begin telling it just then, but we could sneak off by ourselves during the reception, if she was coming. She was, but she was more immediately interested in whether I was keeping an eye on the captain's trips to the cellar.

"Where is he right now?" she wanted to know, and when I told her he was working on the cannon carriage in the cellar, she dragged me down there. She had brought her flashlight with her, and was convinced that the captain had found treasure, or at least was still looking for it. Instead, we found him with Tom. They were fitting the last wheel onto the gun carriage, and Noel Nauss was standing by, waiting to lift the barrel onto its beds.

"You're here just in time," said the captain, giving the nod to Noel, who squatted, grasped both ends of the heavy bronze barrel, smiled, rose, and dropped it gently into place. "Perfect fit," the captain pronounced, pleased, "and a lovely thing to behold, is it not?" All agreed. "Now, all we have to do is roll it out onto the parapet, and tomorrow we'll put a charge into it, and send off Aunt Karen with a proper salute. We'll make you the gunner," he told me.

"What can I be?" asked Jenny.

"Gunner's mate," he responded without hesitation. "Mistress

MacGregor. What brings you down to an old cellar on a fine summer Saturday afternoon?" Jenny reminded him that he had promised to tell her the stories of Anne Bonny and Mary Read before he left. "Did I promise you such a thing?" I tried to make cautionary signs to Jenny, warning her away from any more of his stories. Based on my own recent experience, they could be dangerous. "Why are you shaking your head?" he asked me.

"Because I have things to do right now," I improvised.

"Here are some more," said he, handing me a list of supplies he wanted me to get for him from the grocer. Noel would drive me and the load back in his truck. The captain's preparations for his departure were obviously continuing. "Now, let's roll this gun out onto the deck," he said and, with everybody pushing, the cannon rumbled slowly toward the door.

"What about my story?" Jenny persisted.

"Not now," said the captain. "I've weightier matters to deal with, y'see." And so I went off about my errands, and Jenny went home, after urging me to keep an eye on him all the time. I pointed out that she hadn't needed her flashlight, and she noted that the lock was off the iron grate over the stairs to the regions below. There we left it, except I cautioned her not to be too eager for one of his stories. I promised to explain later.

Just before supper, Meg dismissed the latest guitarist from her life. After supper, she took up her fiddle again with the captain, and they practised a song for presentation the next day. I heard Meg laughing.

Sunday

"The Lord giveth, and the Lord taketh away," rang Reverend Corkum's voice, commencing the special service for Aunt Karen, who was properly eulogised. It was well attended with an audience that included a lot more people than ever attended my aunt during her long illness. I sat in the front pew between Mother and Robin. The highlight for everybody was a duet of "Amazing Grace," in which the captain's baritone was like a rumble of low storm cloud, over which Meg's soprano soared into clear skies and sunlight. Some people forgot that they weren't supposed to applaud.

To dispel the gloom at the reception, Meg got out her fiddle, and the captain his pennywhistle, inducing everybody out onto the deck. There Reverend Corkum's salute to Aunt Karen's entry into heaven was my cue to touch off the cannon. It boomed out with a satisfying roar and billows of sulphurous smoke that washed back over the patio, giving all the mourners a whiff of what old battles smelled like. The detonation made Jason Mosher Jr., aged two months, scream and cry and have to be taken away; and Jeff Joudrey's black lab went jet-propelled right through a screen door, making a dog-shaped hole in it; and Beatrice McCurdy spilled whipped cream down her front. I would like to have fired the gun again.

Afterward, Jenny got me away to the cellar, where nobody was, and where the iron door to the nether-regions was plainly locked, and the captain's chest was still where he and I had left it. "He'll be back for that, anyway," she noted. Outside, we strolled to *Merry* as I told Jenny as much as I cared to tell anybody about the Boston trip. She was especially interested in my stumbling description of getting stuck in a real fight, getting knocked out by a pistol, and waking up in *Merry*'s cockpit, where the captain had cleaned up a fair amount of blood. It was even caked under my fingernails.

"From that?" She indicated my head wound, which was sub-

siding. I said I thought so. He had told me scalp wounds bled a
lo. If there was any other answer, I didn't want to think about it. I
didn't want to think about anything having to do with the entire
incident. Not only had it rattled my notions of reality as I had
learned it, but in such a very unpleasant way. I had no desire to
relive any part of it, then or now. I told Jenny all of this as a warning, but it only sparked her interest, and she spent the rest of the
afternoon stalking the captain. This was easy but unrewarding,
because he spent most of it chatting with Meg, between their sets.
I had never seen her so friendly with him. Toward suppertime,
the only people still there were saying good-bye, or helping with
cleanup, everybody making their own suppers from the leftovers.
So did Jenny, who went to the desk to telephone her mother for
permission to stay for a while.

"I'm supposed to be home before dark," she said, returning.
"Where did he go?" The captain had repaired to *Merry,* where
Jenny cornered him alone at last, with me tagging along. Jenny
didn't understand the forces she was fooling with, and I thought
I would try to keep her in the present, if anything strange started
to happen. Also, the entire subject of his relentless teachings was
unresolved in my mind. He had for sure given me a taste and a
half of a different kind of history, but with no conclusion, which it
seemed to want, and this I said to him as we stepped aboard.

"Conclusion? If you've learned anything, it should be about
all the different kinds of conclusions. Make your own bloody conclusions, and then watch how they part company from what is,
unless of course they don't." The captain, who had been drinking
steadily all afternoon, refreshed his mug.

"Anne Bonny . . ." Jenny started.

"Right," the captain cut her off. "This is the last of it, then,
delivered at nine o'clock in the second dogwatch of this fine June

evening just past the solstice, with a gibbous moon rising, and the sun sliding toward the sea. Next thing we'll sight Venus, who was goddess of love and seduction, and highly female. Here's to her," he toasted. "As to you," he regarded Jenny, "it should be easy enough for you to be Anne Bonny; you're the same Celtic stock, same hair colour, build, same fierce and courageous temperament. When she was your age, her father had to disguise her as a boy for a while."

"Why did she have to be disguised as a boy?"

The captain made an impatient gesture. "Long story. You can read that part in my book."

"Your book?"

"You can borrow Jim's. His copy is easier to read. In any case, she gets a taste for acting like a boy, when it serves her purposes. Otherwise, she can be all girl when she wants to. So, now you're living in Ireland in a time when women aren't allowed to go out and do the things that men do, and the only way around it—if those are the kinds of things you want to do—is by masquerading as a man. It's the same situation in South Carolina, where you go with your mother and father, where he buys a plantation. He has high hopes that you will marry well."

"And I do?"

"You marry, but not at all well. You take up with a common sailor, who thinks splicing with you will get him into your father's wealth, but it goes the other way; your father hates him, and you both find yourselves evicted, out on your ear."

"That's probably just what my father would do," Jenny reflected.

"Well, he just did, and you're off with your sailor, who takes you to Nassau, where he hopes to settle you, and get a berth on some kind of ship. You're a burden to him now, and it turns out he's no prize, either. He only wanted your father's money in the first place, and he doesn't begin to appreciate you for who you are, which is probably better than about ten of him. What do you do?"

"I challenge my husband to a duel," pronounced Jenny.

"Not actually. Jack Rackham's in port, a bit of a sport with fancy clothes, and a way with him, and a fast, armed sloop, and a yen for you, so off you sail with him. You have to dress and act like a boy again, but you can do that, and you do, and there you are, off with your pirate lover, sailing the seas, capturing ships, getting a taste of life that few girls of your age ever see."

"How old am I?"

"Early twenties by now, very athletic, first to lead a charge, made for the role of a corsair, except . . ."

"I'm a girl," Jenny interjected, "and with glasses."

"Pregnant, actually, as things evolve."

"By . . . ?"

"What difference? Your cover's blown when your belly starts to get big, so your pirate puts you ashore with some friends in Cuba, and you deliver and nurse your child, pining for the freedom of the seas with your bright lover in his calico clothes. And he comes for you, and off you go with him again, leaving your child in safe hands."

"This happened?" asked Jenny.

"It gets better. You're back at sea, getting a further look at your life, and your lover, and several things about him come to your notice—some mannerisms, hair patches, snortings and fartings, sundry stupidities—and you realise you're worth ten of him, too. What now?"

"Now we duel!"

"Now you notice a certain young fellow who's come aboard

342

after the amnesty, one of the crew, on the account. He's hand-some, has a gentle side to him, and other qualities that take your fancy." Jenny started to interrupt, but he pressed on. "So, getting an intimate moment for it, and feeling a bit frisky, you reveal your gender to him."

"I can hardly imagine . . ."

"You can't, so don't try. The next thing you learn is that the pleasant young chap is doin' the same thing you are, masquerad-ing as a man, isn't a chap at all, and you've just met Mary Read, who's got an even more fantastical past than yours. She's been soldiering with the British army in Flanders. In point of fact, there are quite a number of women who are doing things like that, and Mary's one. Here your paths cross, and you become in-stant friends. Calico Jack is jealous with it, so you have to let him in on Mary's little secret, and peace is restored. Then a young chap is forced from a capture off Jamaica, and he takes Mary Read's fancy, and this time he really is a chap. What do you do?" Jenny was confused.

"Who am I now?"

"If you're Mary, you expose your breasts to the chap, and they are very white. He cannot resist you, but you can and do resist him, pending marriage. Funnily enough, you are, and al-ways have been, chaste. In the meantime, he gets a quarrel with one of the pirates. There's going to be a duel between them. You fear for his life, so you insult the same pirate in order to fight him first, which you do, pistol and cutlass, and kill him on the spot."

"I . . ." Jenny was having a hard time keeping up.

"You are a free agent, and you marry, in conscience, as if it had been done by a minister in church, and you too get pregnant, though you don't know that just yet. You stay on the account, and you're good shipmates."

"Which one am I?" asked Jenny.

"Be both. Either way, it is fall, 1720, and the trade winds blow your sloop from Hispaniola along Jamaica's north coast to Point Negril, where you anchor to enjoy the evening with a jar of punch. You are interrupted by a royally commissioned pirate-hunting sloop sailing into your life, very unwelcome. Your captain ups anchor and you make a run for it, but the intruder catches up; fire is exchanged; the sloop is better armed and better manned, and before you know it, your fancy Calico Jack chap has taken shelter belowdecks with everybody else in the crew except for both of you, Anne and Mary, and one other chap. You fight, but you are overwhelmed and taken prisoner, along with everybody else. You are thrown into irons, and the next thing you know, you're on trial for your life. I've noted the court documents in one of the editions of my book."

"Your book?"

"Jim's got a copy. Mary, your young lover is exonerated as a forced man, but you are sentenced to hang, along with you, Anne, and your lover Calico Jack, and the rest of the hard-core crew. What do you do now?"

"Which am I?" asked Jenny, still confused.

"In either case, you plead that you are pregnant, which you both genuinely are, so they don't hang you. If you're Mary Read, you die of a fever in prison, after childbirth, never seeing your new husband again. If you're Anne Bonny, they let Calico Jack come to your cell for a last good-bye before they hang him. Your pirate lover. It is a poignant moment. What do you have to say to him?"

"I . . . uh, my love?"

"You tell him, and these are your words: 'I'm sorry to see you here, but if you had fought like a man, you needn't be hanged like a dog,' and that's his lot."

"And what's hers?"

"Hers?"

"Mine."

"You don't hang."

"Jennnnny!" came the voice of Jenny's mother, calling from the patio.

"There's y'r mum," said the captain.

"Jennnnny!" came the voice again, very insistent, and Jenny went off, promising to see him before he left. Her footsteps retreated down the dock. It was last twilight.

"There's Venus." The captain pointed to the darkening sky.

"Way back at the beginning," I said, "you told me there was something about the pirates that I should always remember. What was that?"

"I don't remember saying anything about any 'the pirates,' being as how it's too small a word for the collection. That is, there's Drake, Morgan, Kidd, and Calico Jack, the whole lot, plus lots more we haven't talked about. Dear boy, we've hardly scraped the subject. Of no pirates, I mean."

"No pirates?"

"Not as a grouping. No such thing by very definition. Just them as lives in the seams and spaces between the rules . . . in governments, churches, academies, businesses, tennis clubs, and pub society—pirates ready to come out and ransack from the spaces between the spaces, as they properly should."

"Properly?"

"Considering nature. Sparks of life, dancing. Electric opposition of this and that; teeny-weeny particles of energy; flash of opposites and whatnot, balancing; very restless and uncomfortable. If you'll join me in a beer, we'll drink a toast to the brotherhood." I took a bottle from his little cooler.

"To the pirates," I toasted.

"Pirates are a dime a dozen, and mostly villains, but I'll drink to the brotherhood," he said, doing so.

Monday

The offshore fog bank drifted in overnight, "some t'ick," as Clyde Hirtle put it, after backing his pickup truck over a fire hydrant in front of the bank. He had driven Mother there to finish their business. By the time they got back, the paint crew was working on the upstairs hallway and bathrooms, and the inspectors were there with their clipboards. When they were unable to find fault with the work, they signed whatever paper needed their signature, and I went out to the parking lot to take down the "closed" sign.

I was tacking up a replacement that said "Reopening Thursday" under the inn's pink portrait of Admiral Anson with his crooked wig, when a black sedan slid out of the fog and paused by the gate. At the wheel was Roy Moehner, gesturing, talking to another man in the passenger seat. Seeing me, he smiled, made a small wave, and drove away. With him went whatever joy I'd had in hanging our hopeful new sign. His smile seemed to say, "You may have won this round, but we're not done with you yet."

Jenny came by on her bike in the morning, still sniffing after the captain. He had gone to Baywater with Noel Nauss to try to find a replacement for *Merry*'s rubber raft at the army-navy surplus store, and replacement flares. Meg went with them. They returned with a raft, and more supplies in the early afternoon, carrying it all down the dock. When they finished with that, Meg went off to spend hours on the telephone, and Noel lugged the captain's chest back down to *Merry,* where it was stowed again in its original spot. "What do you keep in it?" I asked.

"Oh, bits and pieces, odds and sods." He located the key, pulled off the padlock, and threw open the lid. "Needs a bit of air now and again anyway." There were stacks of papers—mostly papers—with some bound manuscripts, books, and objects hidden in cloth wrappings. A bleached bone stuck out of one.

"That's Luke Willing's thighbone, and it's the last that's left of him. He wanted to be buried on the slopes of Nevis, with a view of Montserrat. I'll plant what I've got of him there next time I get to Gingerland. And here's a fragment of Teach's diary, in his own hand, and the old trial transcripts on a number of chaps. There's a log by Cavendish in there somewhere, some original Anson letters, and Rogers's correspondence with London through May, 1719. Rare stuff. I'll publish it all in my next book."

"When will that be?"

"No clue," he shrugged. "Possibly the passion will take me again as I get younger. Meanwhile, I've got my little macramé, and the occasional delight in passing, such as your good company, Jim. Now, be a good lad and fetch me two balls of number-two marline from town, plus a cake of beeswax and half-a-dozen three-eighths-inch galvanised shackles, and whatever else is on this." He handed me another shopping list, and money, and off I went again. By late afternoon, when Jenny returned, prowling, I had lost track of him, immediately arousing her suspicions.

"The cellar!" she pronounced, bringing out the flashlight she had taken to carrying. I told her she wasn't going to need it, but I went out with her, through fog that made everything drip. The cellar door was closed, and no light burned inside, but Jenny insisted on going in anyway to check the lock on the grating, which did turn out to be again open.

"Aha!" she said, starting below with the flashlight. This time I didn't have one, which made me nervous and left me no choice but to stay on Jenny's heels as she descended to the next level and turned left. Her notion was to explore the corridor that the captain had come out of the previous time we found him there.

"That's where he's working," she said.

"Working?"

"Shhhhh," she shushed me, wanting to find him before he found us, for a change. In order to dim the beam of her light, she held her fingers over the lens as we made our second turn, off the route we had learned, and into the unexplored alleyway. Here was more fallen masonry among pools of tidewater, and a dripping ceiling overhead. We passed doorways to dark chambers at either hand, keeping to the central passage, until it made a fork that we could see by the reflection of our light on wet stonework.

"Now we go left," said Jenny.

"Shhhhh!" This time it was my turn to make a shush. We listened. From the darkness of the right-hand corridor, there was an unmistakable sound, very rhythmic, like a chant from far away. The small hairs around my neck stood up. What strangeness was this? I reached to take the light from Jenny, but she held onto it, picking her way forward, forcing me to follow. The sound became louder, a song, a familiar song, and the captain's voice singing the refrain:

"O solomongundy, solomongundy
Good all week long, Mondy through Sundy
Sailing from Lundy to foggy old Fundy,
How I loves my sweet solomongundy."

Where the passage ahead made a hard turn, directly in our

path, Jenny's light revealed a scattering of stones and a hole in the wall where they had been, before being chiseled out of it. A mallet and cold chisel lay among the debris. Out of the hole came a flashlight beam, picking up both of us. The song dissolved into a rumbling, phlegmatic laugh.

"My little friends. Welcome. I should have known y'd be along." Inside the hole in the wall, the captain sat propped against the face of what must have been the original passage, before being diverted by masonry. His legs were stuck out in front of him, crossed, and he had his rum flask in his hand. The passage beyond vanished into a darkness that outranged Jenny's flashlight.

"You've found another walled-up passage," I noted. "Where does it go?"

"Over there," said he, with a flick of his light into the same darkness that Jenny's had found. We both made our way through the hole he had cut, and Jenny continued onward.

"It just ends," she said, stopping, causing me to run into her. After a short distance, the corridor was completely plugged by a sloping wall of fill.

"Aye," he agreed, taking a swallow from his flask. "It just ends. Like all else, including even me and thee, and the old earth herself some day. Meanwhile, here we are, in a passage to nowhere, with no rainbows or any pots of gold at their ends, what?"

"Where are we?" Jenny wanted to know.

"We're just here," he pointed to his plan of the cellars, bringing us back, "and that's a tunnel that goes off to somewhere we can't get to, because when they modernised the road that's above us into a highway, a bunch of heavy machines came through, cutting out a new roadbed, and sliced right through this wee tunnel.

They probably never even noticed, filling it in. What's there now is maybe eighty feet or so of dirt, rock, and gravel. So there's that."

"Where does the passage lead on the other side?" I asked. "Where does it go?"

"Decent question. Damned decent. I'll drink to the answer."

"We can dig . . ." I started to say.

"My digging permit's expired. Besides, I wouldn't fancy tunneling through that lot, right under the highway. Did you feel that?" His reference was to a deep vibration. "That's a heavy lorry. We're under the end of the parking lot, and fifty feet farther; we'd be under the wheels of every thundering great truck in and out of Grey Rocks, with our little shovels. I'll give you my chart to your cellars, but I'd leave this part of it alone, and not mention it."

"What are you looking for down here?" Jenny asked.

"Mistress MacGregor. What are *you* looking for down here?"

"I asked you first."

He considered. "There's logic and merit in that, and I'll honour your argument, and drink to your good grasp of the legalistic arts." He did so.

"What are you after?" she pressed.

"Dear Jennifer. Jenny. One seeks, knowing not what one might find, the treasure being hidden within the process." He hoisted himself to his feet, shoo'd us back out through the hole in the wall, and followed. I helped him reset the stones he had chiseled out, until it was hard to notice that they had been disturbed.

"What finally happened to Anne Bonny?" Jenny asked, as we made our way out. I wasn't the only one he'd left with questions.

"Why, she retired and vanished."

"Vanished?"

"Poof. Just like that. But, after everything she went through, wouldn't you want to get away for a while? Maybe start being a mother? Close the door on your past?" With a clang, he slammed the iron grating to the subcellar, locking it. "You could say, vanishing's the greatest virtue of all, the very grail itself. No more strings, and all of your ends are gone."

Jenny pedaled off into the fog. Meg was starting a cook-up for a special family supper that she called her treat. She had shopped for it. "Time to cheer up," she said, and the captain and I went off to tidy ourselves, as did Robin, who had been working with the painters all day. Tom came by for a beer, and tipped the captain to be ready for a visit next day, from the same gentlemen who had called for him earlier.

Meg's special supper was memorable from whichever way you looked at it. First, it was indeed cheerful, and I helped pep it up with stories about the antique dealers of Boston. I got some good laughs, particularly with Madame Lipstick, although I did not mention her ring. The captain got even better laughs with his description of me in my white shorts and kneesocks. Under the cheer, the inn was back on its feet, with a fighting chance for survival.

"When will you start the concert schedule again?" Mother asked Meg. The weekly event had brought in many customers, and promised many more.

"On schedule, next week," said Meg, "but I've found you a good replacement to deal with it, because . . ." Here Meg paused for a deep breath. "I'll not be here."

"Are you going somewhere?" Mother asked. Meg began to twist her fingers together. She was indeed going somewhere.

"Ireland, land of my ancestors," she said, "with our friend the captain, here." She nodded to him, as soft to him now as once she was hard. The captain sat looking very relaxed, framed by the fire that I had lit against the cold of the fog outside. Meg took a deep breath, and plunged on. "I don't like long good-byes, so I'll make 'em now. You've saved my life here, and given me the closest thing to a family that I've ever known." She had tender words for each one of us. I could hardly believe what was happening. I had noticed that the captain and Meg had been a lot chummier since our return, but there were obviously bigger forces at work that had evaded me. Mother, too, and Robin, from the looks on their faces.

"I've always been better with a fiddle than a mop, and there's fine music in Ireland, according to him." She indicated the captain. "And he's better in my books now. I'm good on boats, and Chloe's going to have a sandbox, and I've got my passport, so . . ." She ran out of words, and there was a long silence.

"On the subject of passports, there are some gents coming to talk to you about yours," Robin said turning the subject to the captain, who made a languid gesture.

"It'll get sorted out. I've got one or two other things left to do before we sail, so not to worry." It was a relief that their departure did not seem imminent. Meg had made arrangements for her own replacement at the inn, for her work and to keep the concert series going. "I'm a skip-stone that God threw, and I'll sink if I don't keep skipping." Meg didn't much cry, but I made up for it. Overpowered by loss, I felt my eyes fill with tears, and then they came rolling out. His Irish lady was Meg, I realised, and I was losing them both.

"Steady on," growled the captain. "We're not gone yet." He turned to Mother, and produced an envelope with a short manuscript inside. "There's 750 words of good copy about the inn, written so that the Sunday newspapers will like it; get it typed and copied, and send it to every travel editor between here and Florida, with a couple of good photos, and they'll print it. Not enough people know about you." He handed the manuscript to Mother. "I predict, madam, that with you at the helm, and with a bit of help from your friends," he glanced at Robin, "you'll weather your shoals, and give a pleasing retreat to the ghost of the good Admiral Anson, should he ever wander in this direction."

"The things you've done for us . . ." said Mother. "I don't know how to thank you."

"Madam, by drawing us a beer, and one for Jim, here, so we can all drink a toast." With only a moment's hesitation, Mother complied, Meg helping. The captain raised his mug.

"Here's to vanishing," he toasted. Seeing our uncomprehending faces, he amended it: "And to the inn, and yourselves, and music, and fair westerlies, and . . . what have I left out?"

"To the brotherhood," I rallied.

"The brotherhood!" he echoed, and everybody drank, little understanding what they were toasting.

The beer must have gone to my head. I wasn't a drinker anymore, so I went up and to bed, thinking about what questions I had, and what things to say in the few days before the captain sailed off across the Atlantic with Meg. That was different. Some surprise, although it was no surprise that Meg needed more than the inn had to offer her. I was turning the whole thing over in my mind, listening to the foghorn on the end of the breakwater. It made a loud and mournful moan every thirty seconds, perfectly echoing my sad and lonely frame of mind, until at last I went to sleep to it.

Tuesday

"Jim!" Meg's voice came with her hand shaking me awake. "We're sailing, but he wants to give you something, and say goodbye." I sat up, protesting that it was the middle of the night, two o'clock in the morning to be precise, in a dense fog, and she must be kidding.

She was not; then she was away, leaving me to get some clothes on and follow her. On my way down to the dock, I noticed Noel Nauss's truck in the service drive, and Noel himself stood by *Merry,* as I trotted toward them.

"Give us a hand with the spring lines," the captain commanded, casting off sail gaskets. I did it, trying to collect my thoughts, and then there was Meg, giving me a huge hug good-bye.

I had a hundred warnings for her, but all I could get out was "Write!"

"I never write, but I'll blow you kisses."

"So will I," said the captain, imitating her, "kisses from afar."

"Why are you leaving in the middle of the night?" I protested.

"Fair question, and if you are asked that, you can tell 'em that we left on a fair tide, with a perfect weather report, except for this bit of fog, which is no bother. Tell the coppers who are looking for me, that we can't delay, the hurricane season being almost on us, and I'll be sure to check in with the authorities at Nevis, when we get there."

"Nevis?"

"That's where I have to plant what's left of Luke. Must do it. Been putting it off forever. After Ireland. Then, I'll have to touch Blighty to visit the Ailsa Craig people for my poor old engine parts, after which we might pop down to the Canaries, then toodle over to Nevis in the right season. Some year. No need to mention all of that, just say we're bound to the Caribbean. Here's this." He handed me a pennywhistle, like his own, with an antique-looking instruction booklet.

"It'll show you how to play it. If you learn some tunes, we can play a duet when our paths cross again. Now, throw that stern line to Meg." Instantly, he was preoccupied with getting *Merry* under sail, starting with the mizzen; it luffed in the wet breeze. The vessel swung into poised position, nosing the wind; Noel snubbed the bowline, the little ship's last restraint. The captain hoisted the mainsail with Meg handling the peak halyard, getting the same kind of instruction he had given me.

"Well, then, there we are," he said, grinning at me, and there was so much to say, I could say nothing. He told Noel to slip the line he was holding, gave a helm order to Meg, hoisted the jib, and held it backed. *Merry* began to fill away. Meg waved, the captain saluted. Under her sheeted jib, *Merry* began to steal forward and into the fog. In a moment her image was only a ghost, and then it merged with the night entirely.

"Where can I address a letter?" I called.

"The seas," came his return shout, out of the darkness.

20

Afterwards

Merry's quiet departure was unnoticed in the hubbub of Tuesday, "Bloody Tuesday," as it was dubbed by a headline-writer for the *Baywater Beacon* a month or two later, when things really started to heat up. As the citizens of Grey Rocks emerged into the morning mists for their day's business, they were greeted with innumerable copies of a little poster tacked to telephone poles, taped to storefronts, inserted into doorways and mailboxes:

AN OPEN QUESTION!

In the community of Grey Rocks and beyond, a
pattern of questionable incidents and practises has

been well known to most local residents for some years. The following list of ten recent examples comprises only a handful among many. The open question is: Why have the following never come under official scrutiny? Why have no investigations been made? Who is responsible?

There followed the ten promised examples, all well-known incidents that were questionable indeed, all brushed under the rug. The burning of the Moehners' abandoned farmhouse on Boxing Day was mentioned, along with its huge insurance payoff. Roy Moehners' property improvements at public expense was one of the points.

No direct accusation was made, just the recurring question, where were the reports on these matters? The lumping of everything, and condensing it, suggested a whole junk pile of graft, theft, and corruption, mostly in Roy Moehner's lap, by implication. Everybody knew it was there anyway. Nova Scotians are very studied at not having to deal with things that are not seen, which takes a very selective seeing process.

But there wasn't any not seeing what the captain left like a well-fused grenade. He'd kept me out of it, but I knew he had done it. He had learned everything in the barbershop and the post office, and the Sou'wester Beverage Room bar, and he had hung it all out like a load of bad laundry, on a foggy night, with Noel Nauss helping.

The thing was a political bomb, and it didn't take long to get into the newspapers, including the Halifax papers, and even one in Ottawa, which did an editorial about it. A big part of the interest was in who had written and circulated the original broadside. It was signed only "A Citizen." Many names were offered during the rumblings that ensued, but never his. Nor could the printing shop be found that had produced the explosive broadsides. I realised I had signed for their delivery in Boston.

"I would have helped put the posters up," I told Noel Nauss the next time I saw him. He just nodded.

As to Roy Moehner, on that same memorable morning of the posters, the postmistress found a piece of mail, seemingly dropped by accident under the big mailbox in front of the post office. It was a manila envelope addressed to Roy Moehner; somehow it had gotten kicked under the box, stepped on underfoot, and torn in such a way that allowed its contents to be seen by anybody who was curious, as many were. The mauled envelope contained a cheaply printed photo magazine that went so far beyond any notion of decency as to incite immediate indignation among all the ladies at the post office, as well as everybody else who saw it. By the end of the day, quite a number of people had, and the envelope's tear had become enlarged enough that the magazine could be removed, to reveal contents even more outrageous than its cover.

I never saw it, but an amazing number of people did, including a postal inspector who came to see if it fell under the obscenity laws. It definitely did. Roy Moehner vigorously denied any knowledge of the dreadful thing, and there was no way to attach it to him, except by its address. He was of course attached, in many minds (on top of everything else that was falling on him). In the end, Roy Moehner was busy for a long time trying to untangle himself from the wreckage caused by the captain's grenades, much too busy to think about us any more, and the Admiral Anson Inn entered another of its periods of prosperity.

On that same Tuesday, the authorities in suits and ties showed up looking for Captain Charles Johnson. Upon being told that he was on his way to the Caribbean, they visited Tom, who told them the same thing, and their further investigations were frustrated by the general distraction going on around the post office and the town hall. They drove away, leaving their cards again, and that's the last we heard of it.

True to his promise, the captain did not write. Nor did Meg. In the weeks, then the months, following his departure, he and Meg were the subject of endless family conversation and specula-tion. Where in Ireland might they be? We got the atlas out, and there were dozens of ports, too many to start sending letters to, although I did write him a letter, in the middle of a snowstorm, on the anniversary of our cannon caper. He was in my mind all the time. I reported on the successful aftermath of his broadside, and the relief it had brought the inn. His travel story had been pub-lished in enough newspapers to give the old place a real boost. The Saturday night concert series was to be the subject of a radio show. Meg's replacements had worked out fine, although, of course, they weren't Meg.

I was able to report to him that was I learning how better to deal with the Moehner kids, and that I was writing another pirate essay for my first term paper in high school, and that I had fin-ished reading his book. "Your book," that's what I called it. I passed along Jenny's regards, mentioning that she had decided for sure he was both a hypnotist and an avatar. Noel Nauss had become a regular customer at the inn, coming to all the concerts, where he dined, listened to the music, drank a predictable four beers, and waited for the Moehner boys to come back, which they didn't. He seemed to have appointed himself as our protector, unnecessarily, because Robin had quit his job with the police force, and was helping Mother run the inn full time. They had found a depth in their friendship, and had become engaged to be married, which was my biggest news. We were all very happy about it, and come spring we would fire a salute from the cannon for the wedding. We could get black powder from the sporting goods store in Baywater. I had learned a dozen tunes on my pennywhistle.

The letter ended when I ran out of things to talk about, and I stopped on a feeble note, imploring him to write to us and let us know that they had weathered the North Atlantic, and were okay. I sent it to the one place I could think of where he might get it: The Ailsa Craig Company, Ltd., which had moved from Scotland to England. I obtained the address, and posted the letter, marked: "Hold for delivery to Capt. Chas. Johnson, Yacht *Merry Adventure* arrival date unknown. Hold!"

I don't know whether he ever got it, but he did send us something, either he or Meg. Around two years later, we received by mail a package from a tourist hotel in Mahon on the Isle of Minorca, in the Mediterranean Sea. It was professionally wrapped by a commercial photographer, and the only note attached was a caption: "Pirate Party," with the date, the name of the hotel, and the word "Prepaid."

From the picture, it was a pirate party indeed, with a bunch of tourists in a fancy ballroom, dressed up in costumes, mostly feeling no pain. On first look, it passed me by that two of the musicians behind the people in the group photo had a familiar look; but then, there was Meg, dressed in a low bodice, with her red hair exploding around her face; and there was the captain, wearing a paper pirate hat, his lips to his pennywhistle. My eye had gone past him because in the photo he looked appreciably younger than I remembered. But there was no mistake about it. The picture gave us dinner conversation for a long time to come.

Many years went by before I sent him a second letter, which

went with an invitation to my wedding with Jenny. I addressed it c/o Poste Restante, Nevis, BWI, on the off chance that it might get to him if and when he got around to anchoring there, if he hadn't already, to bury the thighbone of his friend. I have no reason to expect that he ever got that letter either.

He *did* let me know that he remembered me, however. Around the time of my twenty-fifth birthday, I received by an international courier service a flat envelope with a customs document listing: "1 souvenir medallion—gift. Value one dollar." The sender was C. Johnson, with a latitude and longitude somewhere off Africa, although the parcel was shipped from Galway. In it was no less than the gold doubloon that Edward Teach had taken out of a Spanish treasure wreck, and which I had held in my hand during my life's most terrifying moment.

Whether or not the valuable old coin itself has any magical power, or whether it was just a real prop for the story that went with it, I cannot say. However, in all the years that have passed since that time, I have not wanted to hold it in my hand and close my eyes. Jenny has tried it, plenty of times, never without making me nervous.

I have wondered about his promise to visit me again. In order to make good on that, he will indeed have to be getting younger, or at least no older. While I was sailing with my son one day, a summer fog bank pounced on us, obscuring the universe, giving me a chance to brush up on my navigation.

"Look!" said James, and I raised my eyes from my chart just in time to see a wraith of an old yacht with dark sails that I took for *Merry*, but when I steered to intercept, it was a different antique boat. If it had been him, I speculated, would he now be younger than me? I can hear the laugh that would have gotten out of him. I hear it often, going about my life.

Nor do I ever miss an opportunity to look seaward, whenever I'm sailing, or walking on a beach, or sitting behind a rain-lashed window, gazing out over a harbour entrance where *Merry Adventure* could appear, foaming on the crest of an incoming wave. The season makes no difference to my vigil. I have been an avid watcher of snow squalls for years, particularly during November, when the first hard northeaster raises a sea that breaks along the bar, churning up golden sand, then surges into the harbour, making all of the boats tug and jerk at their moorings with a great restlessness.

Author's Note

Understandably, the publisher feels obliged to categorise this as a work of fiction, although it does contain certain truths. Most of these will be left to the reader's discernment, but in historical fact there was indeed a Captain Charles Johnson, it should be noted, or at least somebody who used that name. According to the British *Dictionary of National Biography,* the name is "most likely an assumed one." Most of the entry is concerned with several early editions of his famous book.

Johnson's *History of the Pirates* (to use its short title) has seldom, if ever, been out of print since its first edition was produced in 1724. It remains to this day the cornerstone source on the subject. True to the captain's prophecy, recent generations of historians have confirmed its verity, at least in the original edition, in a level of detail that makes it hard to see how the author could have known this information unless he had been there.

There are historical problems with some of the later expanded editions, to which material has been added by subsequent writers, not the work of the original author. That person, whoever he was, does leave a few undeniable impressions. First, he was a sailor, intimately familiar with the technical vocabulary of a sea captain; he was an educated man, a philosopher, a humourist, and a dedicated historian. Many modern historians suspect that the author was indeed an ex-pirate, which would certainly explain much, including his use of a nom de plume.

As to any Johnson/Defoe connection, in 1988 two scholars and biographers, P. N. Furbank and W. R. Owens, mortally challenged John Robert Moore's 1939 theories as to "Captain Charles Johnson" being one of Daniel Defoe's pen names. With publication of their own study, *The Canonisation of Daniel Defoe,* they demolished many of Moore's precepts, including the alleged Defoe-Johnson linkage.

Johnson's actual, historical identity remains a very great mystery.